DESTINY'S END

DESTINY'S END

A NOVEL BY

CAL MUZIKAR

Printed by
BookMasters, Inc.
2541 Ashland Rd.
Mansfield, Ohio 44905
Visit our Website at ww.bookmasters.com

Distributed by AtlasBooks
Visit our Website at www.atlasbooks.com

Printed in the United States of America
First printing: February 2005

ISBN: 0-9765076-0-9

Library of Congress: 2004195503

THIS NOVEL IS DEDICATED TO WOMEN IN CHAINS, WHEREVER THEY MAY BE.

*To go wrong and not alter one's course
can truly be defined as going wrong.*

An old Chinese proverb

PROLOGUE

The main characters in this novel, Jake and Ellen, are from the same generation, although nearly a decade separates them in age. As you begin the story, keep in mind the music and symbols of the sixties and seventies. Doing so will help you gain a better understanding of Jake. Likewise, as you become acquainted with Ellen, you'll soon discover that this shy, sheltered, introverted woman spent the first fifteen years of her life growing up in the Deep South. In contrast to Jake, Ellen didn't experience the era as much as she passed through it.

The social conflicts and symbols of the American cultural landscape of that era deeply affected Jake along with millions of other baby-boomers who, at the time, were desperately trying to find meaning in their lives in the midst of such a tumultuous time. During the same period, there were many young women, who just like Ellen, remained untouched and unaffected despite the maelstrom of the social revolution. They were inherently innocent and believed in the honor and decency of their generation. They trusted more than they questioned.

Take a moment and experience a "flashback" and reflect on the symbols of those years. Remember the peace sign? It was ever present in the media, at campus rallies and protests in the city parks. Its image was everywhere that young people gathered. It was on banners, jeans pockets, and tee shirts. It was drawn on buildings, sprayed on overpasses, and scrawled in magic marker on book bags and three-ring binders. All of it done to protest the war in Vietnam and the threat of nuclear destruction to the planet by the superpowers. And, of all things, it was widely used as a greeting instead of a handshake for likeminded individuals who may not have had anything else in common.

Then there was the image of the clenched fist, the stark symbol of Black Power that was meant to put society on notice that the urban population was united in racial solidarity against injustice and discrimination. Remember the fiercely proud and patriotic "hardhats." The blue-collar working men with the decal of the American flag as their team insignia prominently displayed as a symbol of their unyielding support for the government in its war against communism.

And finally, can you recall the impact of the women's movement? How women across the country raised the consciousness of society regarding gender bias? Do you remember the two-dimensional symbols of the sexes? They were on posters during marches and rallies demanding equality in the workplace, "Equal pay for equal work."

As yet the new millennium hasn't given birth to any symbol equal to the significance that those four had on the boomer generation. At present, the pundits on the cable news tell us we are now in the midst of a culture war. They say it is a struggle for the hearts and minds of American citizens, and that it is a war between the traditionalists and the secular humanists. Interestingly, so far neither side has adopted a sign or symbol to represent them.

Somehow I find it strangely ironic that my generation has taken a long road, with many twists and turns before some of us finally reached our destiny's end. Perhaps a majority of us have indeed become traditionalists much like our parents always wanted it to be. Now we're in control of the establishment. Are we running the show any better?

Fortunately for us, our music can still be heard throughout the land on countless oldies radio stations across the country. Sadly though, the symbols of our youth seem to have faded away. With that last thought, I hope by now I have sufficiently aroused your curiosity to read my story with a slightly different mindset. You may discover someone you've known in one or more of the characters you'll read about.

Cal Muzikar
STORY, WYOMING
CHRISTMAS WEEK, 2004

CHAPTER 1

Jake Carr stood by the office copier staring at the bare maple trees in the courtyard waiting for the job to finish. As the last sheet dropped in the sorter, he stapled the handouts together and placed the packets in a cardboard box along with two dozen pencils. His parenting workshop called "Adolescent Issues-Parental Concerns," was tomorrow night.

A counselor at Middletown High School in Orange County, New York, Jake was a well-seasoned student advocate. He had recently turned forty-nine, and the workshop audience would consist mainly of baby boomers close to his age. The parenting program offered them direction, information and insight regarding the seemingly strange behaviors and attitudes of their kids. Some of the parents were undoubtedly on the verge of "addictive frustration" trying to control their beloved first-borns. For the older fathers and mothers, it was learning to cope with their overindulged youngest child. The program ran for two and a half hours on three consecutive Thursdays. Jake's mission was to prepare them for the ongoing battle that teenagers wage for independence.

As he finished checking the roster, a student appeared at his door.

"Hey Mr. Carr, I'm here and I'm on time."

"Relax Jeff. No small talk...at least not yet. My man, I've got two questions for you to answer. Did you register for the SATs...and how come there's a progress report saying that you're not passing Chemistry?"

"Oh boy, you're getting right to it, aren't ya? All right, I promise I'll tell my mother about the SATs, she'll take care of it for me. As far as that progress report I'm getting', Carr, you have no idea what being lost really means until you're in Blout's sixth period class. That dude lives in space. Without Sherri Albertson, forget it, I'd be screwed, glued, and doomed to failure. The way it looks right now, with some luck I might get by."

Jake wanted to scold him good but appreciated the kid's honesty. "Jeff, why do you always settle? We both know you're lazy and luck doesn't factor into it. How are you going to pass a science course in college? Forget I said that. For the time being, I'll accept your excuse. Blout's like a college professor. He's a lecturer, if you know what I mean. All right, I'll give you that. And, we both know he's not listening to heavy metal on the way home. Then again, the fella went to Colgate; he's a very smart man who knows his stuff. Forget about his personality. You only have to listen to him for five periods a week. Is that too much for you? Why don't you try listening and taking notes? Who knows, it might help."

"Hey Carr, give me a break. I've had some bad luck lately."

"Here we go again about luck. Yeah, I heard about your speeding ticket. That black Mustang of yours may look sharp and I know the babes love it, but it's nothing but trouble. You want me to believe you didn't know about that radar trap on Route 6? I thought everyone knew it's usually set up past the diner behind the billboard sign. Anyway, I'm sorry you got burnt. Don't let it stay in your head…It'll hurt too much."

"Don't worry Mr. Carr. I already put my fist through a wall. Now I guess I have to suck it up. Tell you this much, my ole man's really pissed off at me because now I've got to borrow two hundred from him to pay off that lousy ticket. He also told me that I'd better fix that hole in my room right away or else. Then he said I should put a picture of a jackass over it to remind me of my stupidity. My mother sat still during the whole friggin' meltdown with him. I felt like a piece of crap. She's always trying to keep me out of trouble. Right now things are really tight. She's looking for a part time job and I hear them arguing all the time. Damn that ticket!"

"Jeff, did you ever hear that expression *Shit Happens*? Sorry, but I had to use the "S" word. Truth is…that it happens to all of us. Nobody's immune. Believe me, I know. Think about it. You're out driving, feeling good, listening to your music, thinking about your girl, and bang, a siren. Next thing you see is a cop staring in your face, ready to bag the kill."

Jeff grimaced after hearing the comment and then he pounded a fist against his leg. "You're right. Sometimes I lose it. My mom's as bad as you are at reminding me about that fact."

"Stop whining. The truth is that your mother is the best friend you'll ever have; not because she'll sign you up for the SATs, or forgive you for your foolishness. That's not the reason, it's because whenever she worries about you and tries to get you to think ahead, it's because she really loves you. Know something, you're cared for and you don't even know it. I don't think she beats you over the head with unrealistic demands. Does she? Honestly, you have it better than lots of other kids. Listen to me. Whatever else you do, don't start making excuses for bad choices. Instead consider the consequences before they happen. You got that? How's your job at *The Ice Cream Shoppe*. I haven't gone there once yet."

"Mr. Carr, you'll get an extra scoop if you ever come in and bring that good-looking daughter with you. I noticed her latest picture on your bulletin board. Wow! She's…"

"Stop right there or I'll have to manhandle you. I've got some college stuff I want to discuss. You ready for it?"

"Not today. The bell's gonna ring in a few minutes. I gotta go and hit the john. But I promise to sign up for the SATs. You're really a nag, but the problem is that you're usually right. I'll see what I can do to prepare for the next chapter test with boring Blout. I'll also try to slow down, but I've got a heavy foot."

"Oh really? Well then, you'd better buy lightweight sneakers."

At 3:15; Jake shut down the computer, locked up his office and walked out to the parking lot where his '93 green Ford Aerostar sat in spot #41. Although most of the day had proceeded in typical fashion, he felt emotionally and physically drained. As he warmed up the engine, he decided he needed music and not the blather of talk radio, so he searched for a cassette to accompany him on the forty-minute ride home. He loved rock music with a fervor left over from the seventies and played it loud whenever he was alone. Neither his wife nor his two kids tolerated that particular passion of his. They thought he was hard of hearing. Whenever he could, he would sing along with his favorite groups: Genesis, Sting, The Beatles, David Bowie, the Eagles, U2, and, lately, Dave Mathews. Today he needed some nostalgia, so he played *The Eagles Greatest Hits.*

Jake knew the secret to longevity in a stressful job like counseling was to flush out the day's stress on the way home. There were always unresolved conflicts that had the potential to stick in your head and drag you down. Frequently, when trouble overwhelmed a student close to Jake's heart, it remained in his thoughts long after the workday was over. His agent of release was music and the recollection of his past adventures on the road. He knew the loose ends were always waiting there at the office, waiting for him. And, in reality, they weren't life or death issues.

Many of the most problematic situations were continuing conflicts that in the long run time would resolve. But not because of some miracle Jake had a hand in. Often, he would tell his students in the midst of their tears and fits of rage, *Pray as if everything depended on God but act as if everything depended on you.* It was non-denominational wisdom.

One interview in particular had bothered him off and on for most of the day. He had hoped the music and passing scenery of Orange County were enough to remove it, but after ten minutes of driving it didn't. He was stuck in a mindset of anger and frustration and wanted it gone.

That morning, a junior named Jessica Warren, with whom Jake had a close relationship with, dropped in unexpectedly during her gym period. Lately, she was breaking down with an overload of stress caused

3

by family turmoil colliding with rigorous academic demands.

Jessica was an exceptional young woman, number one in the class of 2000. She was intelligent, good-looking, athletic, creative, and very popular. However, she was also fiercely proud, ambitious, and determined to succeed in spite of any obstacle encountered along the way. She lived with her mom and younger sister. Her two older brothers were away at college. No one at Middletown High knew how stressful her family life was, certainly not the faculty, her soccer coach, or even her closest friends. Jessica maintained a perfect front, but it was all a masquerade. Inside she was breaking apart, suffering from anxiety and chronic fatigue. Jake connected with Jessica because she trusted him.

Throughout their many counseling sessions, Jessica shared a story of ongoing disappointment and heartache. She was deeply hurt from longstanding family issues regarding her father's withdrawal from her. Mr. Warren had divorced Jessica's mother three years earlier, and was openly bitter toward his children because of the financial burden of child support and alimony forced on him. He frequently discouraged Jessica's plans for the future and offered her little financial support in spite of everything she'd accomplished. He had the resources, but the resentment for his ex-wife extended to Jessica for supporting her mother during the bitter divorce proceedings. Jessica's dream was to attend Georgetown and although Jake supported her choice, he knew the odds were unfavorable for her to receive a full scholarship. He hoped another top university would give her complete a complete financial aid package.

Jessica's problems had troubled him on more occasions than he wanted to remember. The overriding reason was that Jake's daughter Annie was the same age and had similar goals. Annie was as hardworking and motivated as Jessica, but with one significant difference. Jake loved Annie unconditionally and was committed to helping her reach her dreams. In contrast, Jessica's father was indifferent, vindictive, and incredibly selfish. Although Jake was the consummate realist, he couldn't accept injustice with regard to any of his students. In Jessica's case, he was powerless to change anything except her attitude about facing hardship and heartbreak. He was totally committed to supporting her any way he could. He was her trusted mentor, a father figure, and above all, someone she could depend on.

As he turned onto County Road 6, he interrupted the music with an emotional outburst of internal fury as he tried to expunge Jessica's problems from his conscious thoughts. "God damn it. Some men are so shallow and selfish. They're cold-hearted bastards with no virtue. Shit, if I had the chance, I'd rip Warren's heart out for the damage he's done to his kids. Even after all this time, I still can't fathom what the desire for revenge does to some men. They disrupt the lives of others with complete disregard for the consequences of their actions. There're fuckin' worms."

Finally, his inner voice of reason took over. *Okay Jake, that's enough! Chill out! The shit will still be there tomorrow and Jessica will somehow get past it. Nothing will be any different. Let it go...*

In many ways he liked the feeling of a workday ending and the sense of satisfaction derived from making a difference in a kid's life. Even on the toughest days when he went home frustrated or angry, he still felt some gratification. Jake knew his counseling job couldn't be measured in any exacting manner. Yet, he set self-imposed high standards because young people like Jeff and Jessica depended on him to guide them.

In addition to the parenting seminar tomorrow night, another concern loomed large on the horizon. The last week in March meant that college acceptances or rejections letters were forthcoming, always around April 1st. As expected, many students would get their first choices, the ones they wanted from the start, while some others would be disappointed and wonder why they got rejected.

Jake had plenty of experience dealing with admission letters. He handled his seniors in a tactful manner, either by giving them a congratulatory salutation and handshake, or by tilting his head down and extending a sympathetic message such as, "I'm sorry it didn't work out for you. Let's look at some alternatives." Perhaps the strength of Jake's reputation was that he was completely honest with his students and their parents. He respected the students that were the givers: the band members, choir kids, members of the academic teams, club kids, and the athletes. His mission was to try and turn around the few who stayed on the outside or who were indifferent to learning. In Jake's opinion, nothing damaged a teenager worse than having a bad attitude, reckless friends, or the bad habit of always cutting corners.

As he approached the center of Walden, his home town, he switched to "red alert" observing the speed limit. For a small town with a population of only 6,000 there were more cops than there were crimes. There were radar traps to snag the daydreamers. One was at the end of County Road 211 and another usually parked in the Fleet Bank lot. The cops were waiting for some unfortunate soul to exceed the thirty-five mile per hour speed limit. This afternoon he saw an additional patrol car sitting on top of the hill on Prospect Avenue, with its radar gun zeroed in on a downhill stretch that changed from a forty to twenty-five mph limit in less than a quarter mile.

He drove up Long Hill Road for a half mile and then turned left into the Highlands development. His home was the yellow center hall colonial, number Ten Treetop Terrace. Once he parked the Aerostar and walked through the garage, he followed the same routine on most work days. First, he picked up the mail and then he'd check in with his kids if they happened to be home. Joshua Daniel, nicknamed J.D., was eighteen years old and a senior at Walden High. His daughter, Annie, was seventeen and an honor student in the junior class.

They were complete opposites and had nothing in common. J.D. was into Ford trucks, dirt bikes, and fixing engines. Annie was an intellectual, involved with school clubs and striving to keep her 4.0 GPA intact. Both of them worked part-time jobs on different days of the week. When they weren't home, Jake would head upstairs and crash for awhile in order to rejuvenate his mind and body. Other than that, he was a low maintenance, middle-aged, male baby boomer.

Jake believed the real pleasures in life were the basics, the little things that kept his world in harmony. He believed that attitude and frame of reference meant everything in dealing with problems. *Make wise the simple* was the core of that philosophy. He was committed to his convictions and considered "karma" as the dominant factor in everything he did, since choice creates consequence and consequence determines fate. Jake also thought that men addicted to power and greed may have the upper hand for the short haul, but they faced the same end as a school custodian or the factory grunt when the grim reaper appeared. In short, he believed if a person failed to appreciate the little things, they'd be in a perpetual state of discontentment and drive people crazy, especially those they claimed to love.

After crashing for half an hour, he glanced over at the clock and knew it was time to start exercising. Like a metro commuter train running on schedule, he did twenty minutes of push-ups, sit-ups, dumbbell lifts, and chin-ups to stay in shape. After that, he would wash up and start preparing supper. He had started doing the meal preparation seven years ago when Sandy, his wife, re-entered the job market after previously being a full-time homemaker and part-time child care provider. Currently, she was teaching food and nutrition courses at a private high school in Monticello, an hour away.

The fish and chips were ready to drop in the hot oil when Sandy walked in at five-thirty. She looked beat as she dropped her school bag on a chair, and then stopped by Missy, their Golden Retriever, to give her a bunch of belly rubs and ear scratches.

Jake looked up from the stove and greeted her. "I must say that for a seven tenths high school teacher you look a hundred and fifty percent beat. Welcome home to your hilltop estate. Bet you're hungry?"

"Hi honey. It's been a long day. I had to stay after to help some kids catch up with their long term projects. Are you making dinner right this minute? I'd really appreciate it if you could wait a while?"

Considering her request and appearance, Jake turned off the burner and told her, "No problem. I've got everything ready to go except the salad. Go ahead and take a break, you'll feel better if you do. I'll kill some time on the deck. Maybe I'll offer up a prayer to the golf gods and ask them to bring spring back to Walden. I want to start playing again."

"Thanks for your consideration. Sadly, it's missing from my students and certainly from my supervisor. Sometimes I get the distinct impression that the kids think I'm there to serve them instead of teach them. What a terrible attitude some of them have. Not all but...but the few who give me a headache. I took this job without knowing much about private school mentality. It was something I didn't factor in. Anyway, that's enough shop talk. I know that's all you hear about. Isn't it? So where are the kids?"

"Tonight, it's just you and me. I know it's hard to believe, but they live separate lives, and I think that's a good thing. We can't be their keepers forever. I know I don't want to be doing that. Amen...Sandy, get out of your school clothes and crash for a while. Oh, just in case you forgot, my parenting workshop is tomorrow night. So, if I act a little stressed over the next twenty-four hours think nothing of it. It comes with the job of having to face a bunch of frustrated parents looking for miracles."

"Thanks for reminding me about your plans. Lately, my world's been a bit unmanageable and it's getting to me."

CHAPTER 2

Ellen Eastman had thirty minutes to herself before her boys came home from school, so she decided to relax out on the deck. Spring was only a week old and it was one of those days in late March when by mid-afternoon the sun would intermittently tease you into thinking it was warmer than it was. Then, whenever a stray cloud showed up and a gust of wind came out of the northeast, you'd hunker down and feel the chill.

Perched upon a plastic lawn chair in faded Levis and a doubleweight corduroy shirt, Ellen took in the panoramic view of the wetland preserve in the rear of the property like it was an expansive wall mural. She relished the moment of solitude and the chance to pause and think. The colors of the dense forest appeared to come off a pallet of brown, black, and white, with varied shades from chocolate chip on textured bark to dull beige on withered vines and deadfalls. It was a landscape of old growth hardwood trees blanketed by a dense covering of scattered leaves displaced from their place of origin.

Ellen possessed an artist's eye. She loved to experience nature up close and began to draw before she mastered the alphabet. Since childhood, she loved the coming of spring, when emerging buds on maple trees and the newborn growth on rhododendron seemed to magically appear overnight. Whenever she was unable to sketch by hand, she would memorize the image for another time. During the past year she'd painted a couple of nature scenes: a log cabin on an alpine lake with a snow-covered mountain range against a radiant azure sky and a stand of coastal redwoods, reverential in the morning mist of the Pacific. But her personal favorite was a painting of a wolf staring out from a stand of aspens.

Art was much more than a hobby for her. It was a personal passion, an act of self-indulgence that allowed her to express her imagination without restriction or criticism. It was a physical and mental distraction that took her away from the all-encompassing world of home and family life. Another means of escape came from reading romantic fiction. Her favorite novels were about heroic figures, handsome young warriors who used strength, cunning, and courage to rescue a desirable and deserving woman. Her bookcase was filled with an eclectic bunch of paperbacks covering topics like astrology, angels, art history, and even Tarot reading. There were also several books about pioneer women.

Much of Ellen's identity was well-hidden, protected beneath her reserved manner and introverted personality. She'd kept it there since early childhood to avoid conflict with others. Growing up in the Deep South, in a strict home with two younger sisters taught her the best way to stay of out trouble was to practice avoidance and be respectful at all times.

After a few minutes in quiet reflection, her inner voice spoke. *The season's changing, but I'm not. I'm forty years old and I'm standing still. I haven't accomplished much since moving from Atlanta. My God, that was eight months ago. The only positive thing is that Guy isn't here. I thought by now I'd have some sense of direction. I've tried to put away a hundred a month by cutting back on household expenses, but that's practically nothing. At this moment I should be looking for a job. That's the key to my freedom. I know I should be moving ahead, making something happen rather than waiting, waiting for some unusual circumstance to change the course of my life. That's never worked before and I know it won't work now. I feel trapped and what's worse, it's my own fault."*

Since returning to Middletown where she attended high school in the mid-seventies, she'd grown to like her new lifestyle, with its occasional moments of peace intermingled with the challenges of parenting. Her husband, Guy, had stayed in Atlanta where he was a highly successful investment consultant.

After she first made her proposal to move, Guy told her empathically, "You can do it if you think it'll help the boys, but realistically, I have to stay here and serve my clients. I think when the time is right I'll expand my business to the metropolitan area. Right now I'm not prepared to do that." So far, the arrangement seemed to be working, leaving Ellen able to experience the joy of having personal freedom for the first time in her marriage. However, over the course of the past winter her older son was using his father's absence to take advantage of her.

Danny was a freshman at Middletown High and causing her problems with his behavior at home, coupled with an indifferent attitude about school, and a poor choice of friends. Almost daily, he was becoming more and more confrontational and continuously challenged Ellen's authority. The fact that he was over six foot tall only made matters worse. And there was no way of physically controlling him anymore. Foolishly, she had believed she could handle him without Guy being there, and that was a serious error of judgment on her part.

Joey, her younger son, was in fifth grade, was cooperative at home and a conscientious student at school. He made friends easily and listened to his mother regarding homework, chores, and curfews. Joey was still on the fringe of innocence; a child who liked Disney movies, video games, and playing outside. Like his mother he was shy, artistic, kind-hearted, soft-spoken, and hated family conflict.

Operating the house efficiently and taking responsibility for the children's education were Ellen's daily challenges. Regardless of his absence, Guy held her accountable for staying within a fixed budget and monitoring the children's academic progress. Their behavior at home was in her domain. That was the agreement, since it was her idea to move to Middletown. To Guy it was all black and white, Ellen was the full-time caretaker and he was the full-time breadwinner. She'd made the choice and with it, Guy was relieved of the burden of parenting while he was away working in Atlanta.

Middletown was a small suburban town in Orange County. It had a population of twenty-thousand with a "Blue Ribbon" school system, excellent recreational facilities, and bucolic surroundings. She sold Guy on the idea of moving north because Danny was struggling in one of Atlanta's mediocre junior highs, and she didn't expect the city high school would change things for him.

Privately, Ellen saw the move as an opportunity to exit from a loveless marriage that demanded everything from her and a minimum from him. She needed the year to prepare for an eventual separation. Unknowingly, Guy accepted the arrangement because it permitted him to continue his personal affairs without Ellen's knowledge. Ironically, it never crossed his mind she might have an ulterior motive.

At forty, Ellen viewed herself as intellectually competent but physically inadequate. That assessment was based on years of Guy's ridicule for her extra weight and her lack of a sexual appetite. In truth, with a little cosmetic attention and exercise, Ellen could be quite attractive. Although, she had a bachelor's degree in business from Georgia State, her husband considered her an intellectual lightweight. Whenever she voiced her opinion about parenting, politics, education, or the American scene, he made her feel inadequate by his condescending remarks. Similar to her habit of avoidance as a child, she became subservient and accommodating, constantly trying to appease him rather than confront him in order to keep the peace.

Ellen had lived mostly an isolated existence during her twenty year marriage and nothing changed in that respect by moving back to Middletown. She had no immediate family in the area. Her parents were long-since divorced. She had one married sister living in Oregon and one in Alabama. The only other woman she knew was Lucy Capone, the mother of one of Joey's friends, but their connection only involved car pooling and school-related issues. Ellen had become a social recluse by choice, due in part to Guy's indifference for socializing with neighbors.

It was during an ill-fated vacation in the White Mountains of New Hampshire in the summer of 1998 that finally proved to her there was no reason to continue the marriage. She had hoped for the opposite result, figuring the vacation might be a springboard that would remedy a deteriorating relationship with Guy. However, throughout the week, regardless of her unceasing efforts to create a memorable vacation, Guy turned sour. He was critical and uncooperative. He blamed her for rainy days at Franconia Notch, crowded restaurants, and having to wait in line at major tourist attractions. Even the absence of air-conditioning at the old fashioned motel stirred his ire. Within a few days, it became obvious that Guy found the whole nature experience to be tedious and bothersome. It would have been tolerable if he had kept his thoughts to himself but, day by day, he infected the boys with his negativity.

The result was that by the end of the week the three of them turned on her. Guy crushed her spirit with his disparaging remarks and constant teasing about the so-called "nature experience" that she had promised would be fun-filled and exciting. He had no compunction about his rude behavior in front of the boys. The incessant criticism made her feel inadequate, incompetent, and worst of all, totally unappreciated. During the drive home, although maintaining her dignity, she realized that her utter contempt for Guy had finally taken over. She didn't hold the boys totally responsible, although she began to realize they were now modeling their father's worst habits.

After they returned, Ellen continued to be an unselfish caregiver, whether Guy appreciated her efforts or not. She knew it was the right thing to do in spite of whatever she felt. That was her character, and up until the debacle occurred in New Hampshire, she had foolishly clung to the belief that she could change Guy by placating him and being a conscientious mother and dutiful wife. Her plan failed, and thus the move to Middletown presented a window of opportunity to eventually leave him.

❧

In another ten minutes the school bus would arrive. Ellen went back inside to make some oatmeal raisin cookies. As she turned to open the fridge she noticed a postcard behind a seashell magnet. Then she remembered why it was there. She was advised to attend a high school parenting workshop by Danny's counselor. Ellen grudgingly took the advice and signed up, hoping to learn some strategies to lessen the stress of single parenting. She had put the postcard on the fridge as a reminder.

Grabbing the card, she read the back. Sure enough it was tomorrow night at the high school. The notice was hand written and signed by a

Middletown counselor named Jake Carr. Ellen started to question if this workshop would be worthwhile. Then suddenly, she thought it would be an excuse to get away for a few hours, and that fact alone would be worth the effort. In addition, she could tell Guy she was "doing something" about the deteriorating situation with Danny. As she tossed the postcard in the garbage she murmured, "Umm, I might as well go and make the most of it. God, I hate leaving the boys alone."

As she was ready to begin baking, she heard the creaky groan of the school bus brakes. After placing the first batch into the oven, she walked to the front door to greet the boys.

"Hey, you two look hungry. I made some cookies and they're almost done. Are you ready for a treat?"

Danny walked right past her without saying a word. But Joey smiled brightly, sniffed the air, and gave a perky reply to her invitation.

"Hi, Mom, you bet I'll have some cookies. I love 'em when they're right out of the oven with cold milk. But after I eat I got to go and meet my friends at Memorial Field for our first pick-up game. Don't worry. I'll do my homework right after dinner. Mom, I swear, today took forever. I think the best part of the day was having art, gym, and lunch. Probably cause I can talk during those periods."

After giving Joey a snack she did some laundry and made the boys a meatloaf for dinner. It was one of their favorites.

While having dinner, Ellen told the boys she would be attending the parenting workshop tomorrow and asked them to cooperate so she wouldn't have to worry.

"Tomorrow night I'm going to a parent workshop at the high school. It starts around seven. I should be home by ten. Can I count on you two to cooperate?"

Joey nodded in agreement, but Danny had to have his say.

"As long as Joey listens to me, everything will be ok! Sometimes he forgets that when you're out, I'm the one in charge. Why are you going? The whole thing's probably a waste of time."

Unlike her ill-tempered husband, Ellen made it a point to give the boys a sincere reply whenever they asked a question. It wasn't her style to "snap" at them with ridicule like Guy frequently did, especially with Danny. She learned to always consider the source. Exercising restraint, she explained, "Danny, I'm going because I want to get a better understanding of your world. Maybe I've missed something. I'm not too old to learn. I know things are a lot different now."

"What does that mean? You're crazy! You'll never know about my world? You grew up down south and…and you were a hick."

Danny's gruff response only reinforced her decision to attend. Still unwilling to sink to his level she said, "Supposedly, the counselor who's giving the program knows a lot about teenagers and I need to learn some of that stuff. Daniel, ever since we moved here you've been difficult to live with. You don't want to listen and I hate arguing about everything. I want things to get better for us. That's why I'm going and why I want you to behave while I'm gone. Do you understand?"

"Mom, I don't care if you go or not. It's your life. Just go!"

By 11 p.m., the boys were asleep and the house was quiet. Ellen laid in bed dressed in a long yellow cotton nightgown with a glass of wine on the nightstand and a new romantic adventure novel to read. Just as she finished the first chapter, the phone rang. Startled, she cringed and instantly shifted to the defense mechanism she used for dealing with Guy's typical cross-examination of her parenting and housekeeping abilities. Sucking in some air, she tossed the novel aside and picked up the phone.

Responding to his late night calls was the equivalent of filing an accident report with an indifferent insurance claims agent or testifying for a county prosecutor. All Guy wanted were the facts and who was to blame for the trouble. Typically it went like this, *what happened, when and how did it occur, and who was responsible*? Those were the essentials of his nightly conversations.

"Hello Ellen. I'm sorry for calling so late, but you know the routine. I was out with a prospective client. In fact, she could be a big investor, interested in the blue chips like IBM and Pepsi...might have a hundred K to invest. I've got to impress with my knowledge, entertain her a little and pick up the check. It looks promising though. Anyway, what's happening up there? Are the boys in bed?"

"Yes, they are. The house is in order and the bills are paid."

"Well that's reassuring to hear. Anything else I need to know? Did you get those back tires for the van? Make sure you check for the best price. Call for a couple of estimates. You paid the American Express, right? Any snow left up there? Last month when I got home no one had shoveled off the back deck. You can't forget something like that. It's no-good. That wood's not pressure-treated. Are you listening to me?"

At first she let it go without commenting, then she thought better of it and told him, "When the sun came out today it seemed that spring was finally here and I felt..."

He interrupted her in mid-sentence. "Ok Ellen, I got the point. The deck's clear because the sun came out. That's just fine. Did the boys get their homework done? Did you check it? Whenever you forget to do that it causes big problems. You know what I mean! I'm depending on you."

"As far as I know their homework was complete."

"Is Danny failing history? Have you talked to his teacher this week?"

"Guy, do you really expect her to call me once a week?"

"You're damn right I do. Besides, what do you have to do all day? You'd better call that teacher tomorrow. I want to know what's going on. If Danny needs more help; she should be available for him. That's her job! Don't you agree with me?"

By this time, Ellen only wanted to be finished with the conversation. Guy was bullying her again, giving her orders, and second guessing her. After not hearing an answer from her, he continued his interrogation.

"How's Joey doing? Did you sign him up for baseball? Where are the signups? You'd better call the recreation department tomorrow."

Irritated by his constant badgering, she firmed up and tried to give some back. "I really don't know what his plans are."

"Well, I know for a fact that he wants to play baseball. Maybe I should talk to him now."

"No! He's asleep. Try calling him tomorrow at a reasonable hour."

After her terse reply, Guy's voice noticeably changed. He started questioning her. "Did you take that overpriced light fixture back to the store...remember, I told you it had a scratch on the brass cover? Come on, I'm depending on you to make sure we don't get ripped off. Take it back tomorrow! When did you get the oil changed last? God, I hope you're paying the bills on time, you'd better be. I don't want any late charges."

"You know I am. Why are you asking me the same things over and over? You're being redundant...Have you been drinking? I could ask you how you're spending your time and money too, couldn't I?"

Guy wasn't about to let her get away with the challenge and told her so, "As long as I'm paying the bills, I'll be the one who asks how my money is being spent up there. You bitch! You act like I'm demanding so much from you. God damn it, just take care of the house and the kids. Is that too much to ask a housewife these days? You got a lot of nerve trying to start a fight with me at this time of night."

After another minute of belittling her, his temper resided and he began another one-sided cross-examination about mundane things. The call finally came to an abrupt end with Guy finishing in classic style.

"I'm tired. I've got an early breakfast meeting. I'll call you tomorrow night."

As usual, no matter what Ellen said, from his perspective something was always wrong, wasn't done the way he wanted it, or wasn't completed on time. During his conversations, he never asked how she was feeling or anything concerning her well-being. That was typical of his nightly calls. He never suggested she treat herself to new clothes or take a trip to one of the art museums in New York City. Consequently, she usually gave him the silent treatment whenever he began repeating himself for the third time. Her icy indifference always got under his skin and took him to a higher level of agitation. Then exasperated and boiling over with anger, he'd clamor, *"Well Ellen, what do you have to say for yourself?   What're you going to do about that problem, and when are you going to do it!"*

Ellen never deceived herself into thinking he was passing time watching TV or reading the *Wall Street Journal* at home after work. She believed that's why his check-up calls came at such unpredictable hours. His past indiscretions, at least the ones he admitted to, led her to suspect that he was probably cheating on her. But considering her plan to eventually leave him, she had long since given up caring.

After checking on the boys, Ellen began chapter two of her novel. Over the years, whether on the living room couch or anywhere else where she could find some privacy, she found that reading was the best diversion. Like so many women of her generation, she read in order to exit from reality, and visit places where there was romance, adventure, and always the conquest of good over evil.

She identified with the fictional characters in the romantic adventure stories she read and joined them vicariously in their pursuit of happiness.   In her imagination, she traveled to faraway places of breathtaking beauty that served as a backdrop for the struggles of young lovers. Lovers drawn together by fate and pursuing their dream in spite of wicked warlords plotting to destroy them.

After finishing another glass of wine and two more chapters, she blew out the scented candle on the nightstand, turned off the lamp, and drifted off to sleep with visions of her latest fictional hero riding on horseback beside her, leading her to freedom.

CHAPTER 3

At 5:15 a.m. the alarm screamed out like a warning buzz for viral contamination escaping into the atmosphere. Sandy stirred a little when Jake hit the shut-off. He rolled over and whispered, "Sorry honey, but it's time to get up...another workday."

"Just give me a few more minutes...then I'll get in the shower."

Jake pushed the covers back, stood up and stretched without turning on a light, and went downstairs to make coffee. Missy barely raised her head in recognition of her master. After making the coffee, he stretched side to side for a minute and then did a set of ninety pushups on the rug in the family room. Now fully awake, he opened the fridge to figure out what to take for lunch. Rather than take another deli sandwich, he made a peanut butter on the spot, taking no more than two minutes. Finally, he peered out the sliding door opposite the kitchen table to check out the stars that were still in the western sky and get a sense of the weather.

In less than ten minutes, the coffee was ready, lunch was made, Missy fed, and he'd done his exercises. That was Jake's morning routine.

When he returned upstairs to take his turn in the steam-filled bathroom, his wife was blow drying her hair. Sandy's early morning speed depended on the amount of rest she got the night before. Morning conversation was limited. Jake often joked about their a.m. rituals, saying that it would be an entertaining video to watch in their old age. He claimed that it would be an intimate peek at two middle-aged boomers as they transformed their wake-up appearance to a professional look in thirty minutes flat.

After a quick shower and shave, Jake dressed in the typical attire of a suburban high school counselor, well almost. He never wore a suit or sport jacket unless it was absolutely necessary. Instead, he chose a variation of fashion combinations: a white, yellow, or blue short sleeve dress shirt, a matching tie, and a pair of charcoal gray, black or light tan slacks. Complimenting his outfit were black or brown Florsheim dress shoes. Nothing he wore was very expensive or flashy; he was satisfied with a basic unpretentious look of a public school employee.

Jake was solidly built, six feet tall and one hundred eight-five pounds. He took great pride in being physically fit and looked ten years younger than his age. His stomach was flat and his arms were muscular from using weights every other day. It seemed that years of hiking trails and walking golf courses had turned his genetic time clock back. In addition, he stuck to his daily routine of taking Missy on a two mile walk every night after supper. He had medium brown hair with the same color eyes and a fair complexion.

Sandy told him repeatedly that he was quite handsome whenever she could get him out of his old Levi's and black pocket tee shirt. But Jake was stubborn about dressing up. He hated attending affairs where he had to play the role and dress the part. He had no choice at work, but any other time belonged to him, and he wore whatever he liked. Over the years Sandy had to confiscate threadbare flannels, ripped jeans, and stained tee shirts to avoid embarrassment. Generally, she had to buy him dress clothes and any garment that would be considered stylish like Ralph Lauren or Bill Blass.

Sandy was ready to leave when Jake came downstairs. Her drive to Monticello was longer than his, so she left fifteen minutes earlier. She'd just finished her coffee and was putting on her wool navy winter coat when he stopped her at the door.

"Do you think you could get home a little early? Remember, the workshop? I won't have time to make dinner. Sandy, be careful driving through town cause the radar cops were out in full force yesterday. There's not much fog outside, but it's still pitch dark. Take your time. Have a good day."

"All right, I'll be home by five. Don't worry about the kids and don't worry about dinner. We'll be fine. You concern yourself with prepping for the workshop. See you tonight. I gotta go! Bye honey."

After his second cup of coffee he went upstairs to wake his daughter. Slowly, he opened the door and stood smiling as he noticed that she was still in deep sleep with the comforter covering her head. That she was capable of sleeping through the morning noise was a marvel to him. He walked over and lightly touched her.

"Daddy, I know it's you. Not yet, it's too early."

"Sorry babe, but it's time to get up. Want me to pick you up after school?"

"Not today. Jen has the car. You're sweet. I'll get up in a minute."

"I'm going out tonight so I won't see you at all. I love you. Have a good day!"

He kissed her on the cheek and left. Then he entered his son's room. The overhead fan was humming and the room was cool. The boy was sound asleep and completely covered up by his comforter. Jake turned the fan off and called out, "Hey buddy, you can come out of hibernation. I just woke your sister. She'll be in the shower in a minute. Tell me. How's the term paper coming along? Isn't it due Friday? If that's so, make sure you finish it tonight. I won't be home and I don't want any last minute problems that involve your paper. Just get it done. Are you with me?"

"Dad, chill out will ya...I'm sleeping. I got it under control. Now close the door."

"J.D., make sure you get to school on time and get the paper done. Have a good day. See ya later!"

Jake left the fifteen year-old center hall colonial every morning around 6:15, habitually taking a final glance at his home when he turned left out of the long asphalt driveway. It never ceased to amaze him that he lived in such an upscale neighborhood considering his humble background. The "Carr Estate," as he jokingly referred to it, was a palace to him. Even after several years, he still wasn't used to living there. Privately, he poked fun at the symbols of the American middle class dream: the oversized home with a two car garage, the family van, the John Deere tractors, cable TV, designer mailboxes surrounded by flowers, and cedar mulch under every bush. The irony of it was that Jake, a baby boomer of the post Woodstock Generation, had pursued a perfect version of that American dream.

They moved to Walden in 1990 when he changed counseling positions and accepted a job at Middletown High. In making the move, they left behind close friends and a small ranch house on a gravel road in Blairstown, New Jersey. It was their first home and it was filled with ten years of fond memories; memories of raising a young family in a secluded area in the northwestern part of the state. But Jake knew he had left behind much more than a tree house and a tire swing. He was content there.

Unwisely, Jake unilaterally gave Sandy her choice in picking a new home. She wanted something bigger and better than the little brick ranch bordering the Kittatinny Mountains. Much to his dismay, nothing matched her expectations or his wallet in the area. Only the Treetop Terrace home in Walden met her expectation. Although Walden was a small rural town, it had two upscale developments and their attorney friend had told them, "It's a steal for less than 200K, and you'll never lose a dollar of investment buying there." The new home was affordable and much closer to Jake's new job. In the end, he found it amusing that the address happened to be number ten and reluctantly accepted her choice.

There were no sidewalks in the Treetop development. Belgian block lined the curbs and there were maple trees planted every hundred feet on both sides of the road. The electrical wires and cables were buried and all the homes were attractive, well-maintained, and landscaped. The vinyl sided yellow center-hall colonial with blue shutters was situated on an acre and a quarter with a gently slopping yard that bordered wetlands. Three islands of birch trees adorned the front while mature white pines and a couple of blue spruce blocked the view of the houses on each side. An immense back deck provided a place to relax and the low rolling hills in the distance made for an exceptional view.

While Sandy loved it, Jake never found the comfort zone he had at the little ranch in Blairstown. Nor did he ever get used to the thirty thousand dollars worth of new furnishings that Sandy bought with the excess profit from the sale of the first home.

Traveling County Route 6 was an easy commute to Middletown. This morning, as usual, Jake picked the music to match his mood. As he warmed up the van, he glanced inside the cassette box in the console that separated the seats. Most mornings Jake picked his music by chance. He'd place twelve different cassettes in that console every couple of weeks and would go through them one at a time. Today it was Neil Young who came along for the ride.

Thirty-seven minutes later he pulled into spot forty-one in the faculty parking area. None of the school buses had arrived and the hallways were empty. Jake usually arrived before the other members of the staff. He walked into his office, turned on the light, put his lunch bag in a file cabinet, and went down the hall to check in with Bob Washburn, the Guidance Director. This morning, Bob appeared puzzled leaning back in his leather chair and staring at the computer screen when Jake appeared at the doorway.

"Hey Bob! Thank God the Yankees are opening up next week., I miss 'em. It's funny. Since they've won the World Series for the past couple of years everybody's a fan. Pretty soon I'll be down in my basement watching the games. Believe me, it can't come soon enough. You know what I mean?"

"Yeah, I do. I'm about ready for the season to begin, but I'm not nearly ready to sort out this god-damned master schedule. I got in forty minutes ago and I'm still trying to get it straight! Again, the PE sections are too crowded. Boy are those teachers gonna bitch about this. So is everything ok for tonight? Are you ready to give those parents a reality check? Do the custodians know you need them to setup the library? You better let them know whatever seating arrangements you want. Another thing, I heard from Mrs. Long. She informs me you won't make a math teacher change for her son. That wasn't what she wanted to hear You told her she had to have a conference? Good for you. I'm glad you're not bending the rules because she's giving you the same shit she gave your colleague when that boy was in his caseload."

Jake answered Washburn with a dose of enthusiasm. "I'm looking forward to the workshop! I like seeing parents let their guard down. And yes, everything is in order. As for Mrs. Long, she's a pain. She's always putting the blame on the teachers. Shit, she's the one who should be coming to the seminar. You know Bob, this group of thirty-three parents is the largest I've ever had. I don't know why. Last year, only twenty-four signed up."

Pausing for a moment, he stepped in front of Bob like a veteran ball player voicing his optimism before pitching in a playoff game.

"I'll give it my best effort and hope they think it's worth it. Other than that, I've learned over the years that every one of these seminars is a different experience, for them and for me. I think it's because they come for all sorts of reasons and have different expectations. The mix of parents creates the energy and interest level. Especially, how much they're willing to put into it. Well enough said. I'm going to start my day. Don't let that master schedule hold you hostage all morning. I'll see ya later."

One of the major tenets of counseling is to "expect the unexpected." Jake considered crisis situations to be like a game of chess. He resolved conflicts through a series of well thought out moves and by all accounts, from his peers and members of the school community, he was an outstanding problem solver, respected by his students and parents.

Jake turned his computer on and checked the email messages. Lately, there was no way to hide from parents or teachers. Not in the era of emails and communication technology. Parents could send you a plea for assistance or request information anytime. So could the staff. If Mrs. Smith had a family meltdown with her sixteen-year-old daughter, she could send a SOS at 11 p.m. and be able to get a night's sleep because she "did something." He would get the message at 7 a.m. the next day.

There was only one voice message left on his answering machine.

"Mr. Carr, this is Fred Murray's mother. Could you please see him today? His father was readmitted to Sloan-Kettering. I'm terribly distressed and I don't know how Freddy will handle it."

Thirty minutes later Fred Murray, a junior, member of the band and an honor roll student, sat across from Jake. When Jake asked how things were going at home he answered. "I can't believe it but my dad's sick again. He's back in the hospital for the fifth time and my mom's worried sick. It's gotten to a point of mass confusion for me. I don't know what to think about it anymore. Whenever I ask her about his prognosis…you know, like what's gonna happen to him… she treats me like I was a child. What's her problem? It's not right. What do you think?"

"Freddy, you're a child until you're able to sit alone with your father and have the guts to ask him about his illness. It's gotta be done face to face without an audience. Your dad knows his medical situation. Maybe he thinks you can't handle it because your mother told him so. I don't know. Freddy, please listen to me. Tell him you're ready to hear the truth and that you can handle it. If you must, ask him to put himself in your position and vice versa. It's crucial that you let him know you're taking care of things at home and he shouldn't worry. I'm not telling you what to do. I only want you to think about what I've said and consider it. Trust me on this. Your father will take notice of your maturity and your courage. He'll tell you the truth and the truth is what you deserve to hear. Whatever you do, don't blame your mom. With all that's happened, she's not herself and neither is your father. You show them the person you are."

CHAPTER 4

Ellen woke up feeling unsettled and anxious. The book she read last night, though entertaining, didn't distract her enough and neither did the second glass of wine. She had drifted in and out of deep sleep most of the night. Still tired, she tossed aside the covers, put on a bathrobe, used the bathroom, and went downstairs to make coffee.

Surprisingly, the first cup snapped her out of her lethargy, and she began making lunch for Joey while listening to the *Today* show. Danny usually skipped breakfast and bought an early school lunch, so she put two dollars on the counter for him. In spite of a new day and another chance to think through her options, her mind focused on the task at hand. It was getting late and Danny wasn't up yet. From the bottom of the staircase she called to him, dragging out the words for emphasis.

"Danny...Daniel Eastman, get out of bed this minute. Joey is already downstairs ready for breakfast. I'm not driving you to school, not this morning. Do you hear me! P-L-E-A-S-E get up and get ready for school."

After a few of moments waiting for an answer, she went up to his room and stood over him. She was feeling frustrated and ready to jerk the covers off. Raising her voice for effect, she scolded him. "Why do I have to go through this? You're in high school. Can't you get up yourself?"

Instantly, he flipped off the covers and made a terse comment. "Because that's what you're supposed to do. You act like it's a big deal to wake me up. And don't compare me to Joey. I don't want to hear about him. If he gets up first, its cause the baby goes to bed before ten o'clock."

Reluctantly, Danny got up and walked slowly to the bathroom down the hallway. Ellen gazed around the room after he left, shook her head at the disarray, picked up his dirty clothes off the floor, and then returned to the kitchen. Joey had just finished eating a bowl of cereal and was in the dining room stuffing textbooks into his backpack. She casually glanced at the calendar on the kitchen wall and realized that Guy might be coming home on Friday and she wasn't looking forward to his visit.

Last night, he was more overbearing than usual and was highly critical of her. She thought his rebukes were knee-jerk reactions to whatever honest explanations she gave to him. He had no patience with her and all through their marriage she had let him have his way.

Tragically over time, her self-esteem had diminished more and more, yet she still surrendered to his bullying. She felt it was the price a mother had to pay for peace in the home. Guy had always demanded absolute control over her and the boys and so she let him have it rather than fight.

For the past couple of years Guy's financial consulting business had been doing well and was expanding through referrals and advertising. Recently he hired a part-time assistant to allow him more time with prospective clients. His financial success only added to his cockiness and propensity to act like a "big shot" around her and the boys.

Guy's job as a financial planner was to advise clients and make investments for them. With an MBA degree from prestigious Emory University prominently displayed on the paneled wall behind his walnut desk, he felt supremely confident about his future. He was in charge and that's the way he wanted it. Just like at home, whenever it came to a business venture that soured, it was the client's fault. Fortunately, the economy was still in a bull market and his clients were making money.

After being employed with a prestigious financial firm in Atlanta during the past decade, Guy preferred working alone rather than on a team. He knew he would be much better off being his own boss. Oddly enough, with Ellen's encouragement along with some borrowed money, he was able to setup his own business, *Eastman Financial Consultants*. It was located on the outskirts of the city in a brand new office complex, called East Point Towers, not far from the airport.

In truth, Guy went along with the move back to Middletown for selfish reasons. Of course, he masked it by agreeing with Ellen that it was for the kid's benefit, but there was no question that he'd had enough of home and family life. He thought Ellen was a less than desirable wife and mother, but kept up the appearance of being a model husband whenever he was in the public eye. Clearly, he was unsure of any long term future with Ellen. Nevertheless, for the time being, he was more than satisfied with the current arrangement.

In truth, Ellen had sold Guy on the idea of moving with the knowledge that it might save her in the process. She wanted the time and separation to figure out what direction to take in her life. Nothing with Guy had turned out the way she thought it would. Her married life was unfulfilled, and if not for her commitment to motherhood, who was she?

With the boys gone, Ellen put the breakfast dishes in the sink, Danny's laundry in the washer, and went upstairs to take a shower. After disrobing, she paused before the full mirror as the steam from the shower started to mist the glass. Then she took a discerning look at her body and mustered up the courage to step on the scale. It read 142. Disgusted, she stepped off to let the digital scale reset and tried one more time hoping to knock off a pound in the process.

"How can this be? A hundred forty-two...I haven't lost a single pound since last month. I'm stuck! I'm stuck and I'm angry!"

She had never started the exercise program she'd promised to do after the move. And, like so many other women fighting middle-aged weight problems, her resolve and self-discipline fell short whenever motherhood called. Her legs were her nemesis; they were athletic looking like those of a varsity swimmer. No matter what she did, they never seemed to get any thinner. That's why she preferred to wear jeans most of the time and not shorts. Her stomach wasn't firm and flat, it was soft and loose. She referred to it as her "crinkle" and hated it. Fortunately, her breasts were still shapely and firm. Modest by nature and feeling awkward standing naked on the scale, nonetheless she was unable to hold back her frustration and screamed at the mirror as if it was there to listen.

"Yuk...Look at me. This wasn't supposed to happen. I'm ten pounds overweight. I'm fat and I can't stand looking this way anymore. It's all in my belly. I hate my legs. I hate the way I look. I can't stand it!"

In a fit of anger, she bent over and shoved the scale back in the closet causing it to flip over. Then she opened the shower curtain, stood under the stream of hot water, and started to cry.

The truth was that even with the extra weight Ellen was a very attractive woman. She was five-four with a medium build. Her eyes were magnetic blue with an enchanting look whenever she smiled. Her complexion was flawless and matched a perfect set of teeth. Her shiny auburn hair looked natural and hung down over her shoulders. Contrary to Guy's disparaging remarks, her figure was reasonably proportioned to her height. Ellen never thought she was pretty because no one ever told her, but lately she didn't seem to care and that's what bothered her the most.

Even before Danny was born, Guy was never complimentary about her appearance. Regardless of what she wore or how she trimmed down, he was in the habit of being critical of her looks. If he was watching TV or shopping, and a beautiful woman came into view he'd comment, "She looks great! Why can't you look that good?" His off-hand comments weren't innocent teases. They were offensive and sarcastic. However, being so insecure, she was defenseless against his rude behavior. He knew he had the edge and used it whenever he felt the urge.

After putting on her underwear, she looked in the mirror again. Something inside her snapped and on impulse, she suddenly dropped to the floor, put her feet under the bed for support, and began doing body crunches until she reached fifty. Sprawled out on the rug and out of breath, she felt the adrenaline start to take over. Then she stood up and began doing some stretches she remembered from an old Jane Fonda exercise tape. After that, she forced herself to do ten push-ups, several torso twists, and followed that by doing jumping jacks till she started sweating profusely. The workout had been done is less than fifteen minutes and much to her satisfaction, she knew that the curse of complacency was finally broken. She had reached her limit.

Rather than quit at that point, she put on sweat pants, grabbed a hooded sweatshirt out of the closet, and decided to take her first two-mile walk since last fall. She opened the front door, took in a couple of deep breaths, and then took off at a quick clip down Westgate Drive. As she passed what she thought was the first mile, she stopped at a corner, raised her arms, clinched her fists, and cheered. "This is a new beginning. I can do it...I know I can!"

CHAPTER 5

Jake sat at his desk in the living room with a glass of iced tea reviewing notes for his opening presentation. It was 5:30 and he had an hour left to get his act together before returning to the high school. He skipped the family dinner because Sandy planned to order a pizza to have with the kids. Twenty minutes ago, Jake had gobbled down a couple of tuna sandwiches.

Sandy entered the living room and saw Jake in deep thought. "Are you finally prepared? Would you like a cup of coffee before you go?"

Jake was so focused on the task at hand he didn't hear her. So she repeated the offer. "Jake, can I make you a cup of coffee?"

"Sorry Sandy, I'm getting my thoughts together. I guess you know how hyper I get about this kind of stuff. I've got a big group to handle and I'd like to win them over... you know, right out of the box. Thanks for the offer but I don't want anything."

Sandy had wanted to spend some time with Jake before he left. She had serious concerns about the state of their relationship. Lately, it seemed harder and harder to find the time to talk. Her new job at a private high school in an upper-crust area of Orange County was becoming extremely stressful. Every workday she spent an hour driving to Monticello and another returning. She'd maneuvered through bad weather all winter on Interstate 84 to be there on time. And, as if that wasn't bad enough, her department supervisor was a major factor in contributing to her stress. She was gone from 6:15 a.m. to 4:30 p.m. on any given school day. Although she appreciated Jake's help, especially his skills as a financial planner, homemaker, and caretaker of the family, she often wondered how she fit into his life, and vice versa.

Often, she'd come home exhausted and felt constricted by a family schedule that was difficult to be in sync with, and which presented few opportunities for any personal time with her husband. None of that seemed to bother Jake. He always served dinner close to 6 p.m., and then they watched the national news, followed by kitchen cleanup. If she had the energy she'd join him on his nightly walk with Missy around the development. But by mid-week all she wanted was to get her school work finished by nine o'clock and be in bed by ten.

"Jake, what time do you think you'll be home tonight? I'll wait up!" Sandy inquired, as Jake held a small cardboard box filled with materials and stood by the back door ready to leave.

"I'll probably be home around eleven but don't wait up for me. You need your rest. Maybe they'll be something decent on TV. Listen, I'm sorry we didn't have any time together. I had to get ready. Give the kids my regards. Thank God tomorrow's Friday. I miss my hiking. Bye hon."

He leaned over and gave Sandy a farewell kiss and left.

Later, around nine o'clock, when her school work was completed Sandy passed up TV and opened the sliding door to the deck to get some fresh air. Wearing her ski jacket, she stood against the cool evening and wondered why Jake had become so detached. She thought, *Was it that long ago when Jake would've asked me to wait up for him? Maybe share a late night drink or better yet, make love to me?* She felt more discouraged than she could remember in a long time. Yet, she had no clear idea how to change the stagnant state of her marriage. Admittedly, she was consumed by her new teaching position and she knew the ten hours a day devoted to the job was a very high price to pay for resurrecting her career.

Suddenly Missy appeared at the sliding door and barked a request to join her. Missy was Sandy's companion when no one else was around. However, in the Carr household whoever paid attention to Missy or offered her a handout was her best friend. If there's such a quality as unconditional love in the canine kingdom, then Missy possessed it for anyone who fed her. She was a gentle and loving animal and everyone in the house thought Missy was theirs.

Missy plopped down next to Sandy and without making a single sound, used her snout to persuade Sandy to pay attention to her. The brighter stars were just appearing on the eastern horizon. The night was clear and brisk. Sandy thought that spring might have arrived, but a winter chill was still hanging around. Thankfully, the lawn work and gardening would start very soon and she loved spending time outside, trimming bushes, planting new bushes, and adding more flower bulbs in the front yard.

After petting Missy for a minute, Sandy shifted her attention away from the dog and thought about the future. J.D. was waiting for acceptance to a small college in Vermont and Annie was a year from graduation. Sandy worried what her life would be like without them.

৩৵৶

The turning point in their married life was the death of Sandy's parents within six months of each other in late 1991. First her father, Bernard, died of liver cancer at the age of eighty. During his illness, Sandy had spent many weeks in Florida when he was critically ill, and Estelle, her mother, desperately needed Sandy's presence. Shortly after her husband of fifty-three years passed away, "Essie" seemed to wither both in body and spirit living alone. She moved to a respectable nursing home in Palm Beach and she died peacefully in her sleep exactly six months after her husband. She was eight-one.

Unfortunately, Sandy wasn't present when they passed away. Both times she was in Middletown taking care of her young children. Her absence, especially from her mother's bedside, only magnified her grief. Their deaths, so close together, left an enormous void in her life.

In spite of their longevity and the quality of life they enjoyed, Sandy truly had depended on them for emotional support, a Jewish family connection, and above all else, her mother's love. Those were intimacies Jake didn't appreciate or understand.

Soon after that the marriage changed in subtle ways beginning in the fall of '92. Sandy felt that Jake was pulling away and they began to argue for the first time. Sandy persisted in accusing Jake of "emotional abandonment" and blamed him for the marital stress. Likewise, Jake was convinced that Sandy was guilty of the crime of indulgence for continuing the grief process for so long. Both of them were full of righteous indignation. Soon their relationship was running on empty and neither of them seemed to know how to change the direction. During the period of their emotional stalemate Jake began remodeling the basement and over a period of two years spent countless hours away from her working on the project. The marriage grew more stagnant and stayed that way. They got along for the most part and masked their problems in front of the kids, but the passion, love, and genuine appreciation for each other they once had completely disappeared.

As if things weren't deteriorating fast enough, in the late fall of '96 both of them were hit with the worst calamity they had ever faced. It was more frightening than Sandy's two breast surgeries to remove benign lumps in '88, and it was far more anxiety ridden than Jake's cancer operation to remove a malignant melanoma on his shoulder. In both those medical cases, the doctor's prognosis was positive. However, Annie's illness was self-imposed. It came out of nowhere and almost destroyed her health.

When Annie left middle school, she was an energetic and enthusiastic fourteen-year old full of anticipation about entering high school. That summer was one of the happiest times of her life as she spent day after day with a couple of close friends. She went shopping at the mall with her mom and hiked weekends with her dad. The family spent many afternoons at the community pool. Then as freshmen year began, the trouble started.

That winter was pure hell for the Carrs. During many of the family counseling sessions with a specialist in the field, it became evident that the illness was lying in wait for the brutal reality of their daughter trying to cope with the pressure of achieving academic and social success. The problem was that a sweet and conscientious freshman couldn't fit into the "click" driven teen culture at Walden High. Neither Jake nor Sandy had any indication that the new learning environment would be that stressful for their daughter. It was too late when they learned that Walden High School was a place where the strong survived and the shy and unsophisticated remained outside the social mainstream.

Whenever Sandy and Jake questioned her about school activities or the lack of a social life, Annie insisted that things were fine and she was putting grades ahead of everything. With no reason to mistrust their daughter, they accepted her explanation. By Thanksgiving, it became clear that something was amiss. On that holiday Annie exhibited behaviors which alarmed the guests at the dinner table by refusing to eat anything served. Her attitude and behavior caused Sandy's cousins considerable discomfort and foreshadowed the meltdown that occurred a week later.

The truth was discovered accidentally when Sandy caught a view of Annie while she was getting dressed one morning in early December. Her loss of weight was startling. Sandy demanded an explanation from Annie, but there was no rational explanation offered. That same evening, Sandy told Jake about the crisis and then collapsed on the couch in a state of anguish. When Jake went upstairs to confront Annie, he got a reaction he didn't anticipate. With unyielding defiance she yelled at Jake, "All my life I've been the perfect child and tried to make you proud of me. Where did it get me...nowhere! I'm in control now!!! It's my life! You can't make me eat if I don't want to. So do what you must. I don't give a damn anymore. You're not in charge! I am! Leave me alone!!!"

Jake held his ground in spite of her hurtful remark. He waited a moment and replied, "Why are you acting like this? I'm not your enemy. Suppose you tell me who is!"

He'd thought he could catch her off-guard and hear something revealing about her attitude.

"Dad, you still don't get it! Nothing at Walden High was what I expected, nothing at all. I'm stuck there and I hate every minute. It's not the teachers! They're not the problem. It's the kids. They're shallow and phony, they're backstabbers and gossipers, they're nothing but pretenders, and it's more than I can handle. My own friends have turned out like everyone else, including Jenn, who I thought would be loyal to me. Look Dad, I'm not going to argue with you. Do what you must! I don't care. And you tell that asshole brother of mine to leave me alone. You want me to feel bad because I upset Mom. You want me to say I'm sorry, for what? She's been Miss Perfect her whole friggin' life. I'm not her!"

Jake knew arguing with her was counterproductive. Instead, he merely affirmed what she told him.

"Annie cool down, I only came in to see how you're doing. Thanks for giving me your take on the problem. I'm sorry, but I can't tell you what's gonna happen next because it's not my decision. It's yours. You know you need professional help to sort this out. So we'll let the dust settle tonight. **You** have to consider what to do about **your** illness. It's impacting **your** health. In the meantime, at least please be considerate of your mother's feelings. She's very upset and doesn't understand how or why you're doing this. Your mother thought she was a lot closer to you and that if there was a problem you would ask for help. Honestly, her feelings are hurt, hurt bad."

"What do her feelings have to do with me? I'm the one stuck in that shitty high school, not her. And stop trying to fool me. Stop pretending that this family is normal. The truth is that she's stuck...stuck with you and that rotten brother of mine. You think I don't know? Please Dad, leave me alone."

Jake left his daughter thunderstruck and unable to cope with what Annie said. He sat alone in the basement, sorrowful and emotionally crippled. Annie's anger whether justified or not was enlightening, but it crushed him to hear it. Over and over, he questioned how this could have happened and he was ashamed for not being more aware of her unhappiness. The rest of the evening he wrestled with two questions. *Was he demanding too much and was his deteriorating relationship with Sandy that obvious to Annie?*

Whatever responsibility Sandy had in Annie's illness wasn't clear to him. However, one thing was certain. Over the past year he'd overheard Sandy making too many suggestions to Annie about diet and fashion, but hadn't interfered. All he could hope for was that during her future counseling sessions Annie would explain in detail to the therapist what went wrong, relieving the emotional pain she was suffering. For her part, Sandy desperately wanted Annie back to her former self.

Initially, Jake spared Sandy any major connection to the illness explaining, "Sandy, I honestly believe that the problem was caused by factors within Annie's need for meeting self imposed high levels of academic, physical and social achievement. I think she's had an addiction to perfection early on and that could've set the stage for the illness to occur. Perhaps we both unknowingly contributed to the problem by being demanding and loving at the same time. I'm not sure because our memories only record what we want them to remember. Eating disorders are complex illnesses that defy logic and Sandy, you need to know there's no reason to believe it could have been your fault. Better to believe that Annie was somehow brainwashed by the media and was vulnerable to her own demands for perfection. Somehow she unwillingly set a course for self-destruction."

As the visits began to Plaza Health Care for bi-weekly check-ups it became apparent the worse might happen. As the months passed, Annie's physician was running out of patience. Finally on a Tuesday afternoon in early April of '97, the doctor walked out of the examination room and regretfully announced that if Annie dropped any more weight and dipped below seventy-five pounds, she would require immediate treatment at a Philadelphia clinic.

Later that same evening Sandy listened in total disbelief as Jake spoke to his older brother Skip. From behind the bedroom door she heard Jake's choked-up anguished voice say, **"I don't know what to do,"** over and over, in a manner so foreign that it frightened her. Because Jake always knew what to do to help others, especially teenagers, now it was Jake who was bursting with heartache, unable to hold back his pain any longer. She'd never seen him in such an emotional state. But what made it worse was that she now knew they were unable to comfort one another.

The idea of losing their daughter to the ravages of the eating disorder produced such overwhelming grief in each of them that they couldn't cope as a couple. There was no denying it. Truly, it was a defining experience of immeasurable sorrow for Sandy. She believed Jake's breakdown during the call to his brother meant he had lost faith in her as a confidant.

Miraculously, the very next evening Jake came up with an idea that he thought had promise. Oddly enough, it didn't originate from any outside source, office colleague, or professional journal, in spite of all the research he'd done over the past few months. It came from Jake's own problem-solving ability.

Jake's idea was to provide a "diversion" by getting Annie away from home for a week to travel somewhere, away from everything. He thought the journey might break the compulsive behaviors that were destroying her health. Like most of the personal insights that surfaced in Jake's mind this one was born on his nightly two-mile walk around the Treetop development. With his companion at his side tugging at the lead, tears filled up in his eyes, and Jake considered his own way of coping with emotional pain. He believed that Mother Nature in some strange way blew away the uncertainties of life's ongoing struggles, and gave him insight to see clarity where once there was confusion. He figured the trip might be the catalyst for turning Annie around. Sandy and Annie had spring break at the same time, so Jake suggested the idea of a road trip and Annie went along with the idea.

Mother and daughter left on a Monday morning in mid April of 1997. Jake let them do all the planning. Fortunately, a teacher friend of Sandy's offered the use of a condo on Sullivan's Island, South Carolina. On the Sunday night before they left, Jake only made a couple of suggestions to his wife. The first was not to beg Annie to eat, although in the beginning of the disorder that's what they had constantly done. The second suggestion was to be as lazy as hell, because it was necessary for Annie to rest up and maybe put on some weight by watching the waves, walking the beach looking for shells and reading. Finally, Jake told Sandy not to leave Annie alone if she could help it. It was up to Sandy to focus all her efforts and all her love on helping Annie break the stranglehold of the disorder.

For his part, Jake could only go to work and keep himself busy around the house. The crusade was being fought five hundred miles from home. The initial report came late Wednesday night with a phone call from Sandy. She began to notice that the snacks left out on the kitchen table were vanishing a little at a time. Sandy sounded cautiously optimistic but completely exhausted. When he didn't hear from her again he thought that to be a positive sign.

They returned very late on Saturday night. Jake woke up when he heard Missy barking and went downstairs. When he saw his wife and daughter he only nodded to Sandy but held Annie in his arms and told her, "I missed my little girl. You look so much better and I'm so glad your back." Then Jake took her bag upstairs beckoning her to come along.

Jake's disregard for Sandy was a stunning blow that defied explanation. Reluctantly, she let it pass. Besides, Annie had witnessed enough arguing between her father and mother in the past months. She thought it would undo all the positive improvements to Annie's health if she yelled at Jake for neglecting her. Instead, Sandy decided to take a shower and deal with it another time. However, she knew without a doubt that his behavior only reinforced her worst fears. She was losing him.

The trip proved to be a dramatic turnaround for Annie's health. With an undeclared truce in the house and J.D.'s cooperation, Annie gained weight. At the next check-up she weighed seventy-seven pounds. The pediatrician recommended continuing family therapy. Slowly,

Annie's health improved, although it would take another year for her to get back to her normal weight.

❧∽❧

The phone rang, diverting Sandy from her reflective mood. She wanted to relax and really wasn't in the mood for conversation, so she let it ring until the caller left a message. "Sandy, are you there?" It was her longtime close friend Rachel. Sandy raced to pick up the phone before the next word came out.

"Hi Rachel, I was out on the deck."

"So how are things with you? How are the kids? What's Jake up to?"

"How odd that you called, I was just wondering how my life will be when Annie leaves for college."

"I remember when David left for Syracuse. Things really didn't change that much. As you know he was always in his room listening to sports or involved with the Internet. And it's not like we used to sit in the kitchen and talk every evening. But I know what you mean. Who know what the future will bring."

Then their conversation took a predictable course, like so many others. As usual, Sandy never revealed anything that would endanger the image of her family life or her marriage. As much as Sandy desperately needed to confide in Rachel, her pride and dignity wouldn't allow it.

❧∽❧

In a eulogy eloquently delivered at her mother's funeral service in 1992, in the presence of family and friends, the final few sentences Sandy uttered that morning were the most revealing to her husband.

"My mother was a lady above everything else. She had the dignity of the British royal family, but always the caring soul of a Jewish mother. She loved her family more than life itself. She enjoyed the opera, ballet, theater, and beautiful things, but most of all she delighted in the company of my father. She loved him for 53 years. He was a doting husband and caring father. I'll miss her every day of my life, and nothing or no one could ever replace my love for her."

Without knowing it at the time, Sandy was in many ways describing herself, but the only person who realized the significance of her eulogy was her husband. Although not close to his in-laws, he finally recognized the indelible mark they left on their daughter, both emotionally and culturally. Perhaps, until that funeral service occurred, he had refused to see the dominant influence her parents had on her and now he understood that it was a force far greater than his ever was.

33

CHAPTER 6

Jake pulled into the same spot he occupied only a few hours earlier and made his way to the front entrance of the school. As he hurried down the main corridor leading to the library, he shouted a greeting to Hector, the night custodian, to get his attention.

Hector, dressed in a navy blue uniform with his sleeves rolled up, put down his dusting mop and approached Jake. They had known each other for many years. With a wide grin covered by an impressive dark mustache, he shook Jake's hand firmly and then spoke slowly, using his hands for emphasis.

"Mr. Carr. I have not seen you since the Christmas concert. You look the same to me. You look good and I eat too much. The good Lord knows...food is a passion for me. I love to eat. My wife Maria, she takes very good care of me and the children. Ok, down to business, my clipboard tells me you're using the library till ten o'clock. That is close to the end of my shift. Will you be finished by then...Yes?"

"Hector, stop worrying so much. It's good to see you. How's life treating you?"

"Most of the time life is good. You know, I'm trying to pay the bills, keep the truck running, make Maria happy. Sometimes it's tough. Everything cost too much. Ayee...my kids, they always ask for more. I don't remember asking for much as a child. How are things with you?"

Jake put down his cardboard box and put a hand on the man's shoulder and said. "Hector Martinez, I am no different than you are. I also try to make my family happy. I worry about my kids, pay the bills, and try to stay ahead. You have my word, the program we'll be over on time. Did you set up the tables in the library so the people can sit when they enter? Did you, my good friend?"

"Come on, Mr. Carr, you know me too well. I would never disappoint you...No way."

"Very good Hector. Are the restrooms by the cafeteria open?"

"Everything is ready. You know Hector, I always come through."

"Mochas gracias amigo! You're a very good man. You do your work with pride. You're a gentleman, a good father, and a good husband. As always, I am most...most grateful for your assistance."

No sooner had Jake finished his conversation with the night custodian when he noticed a group of women slowly walking toward him. Instantly, he raced down the hallway, shoved a plastic doorstop under the entrance door to the library, and turned on all the lights. Then he surveyed the room and nodded in appreciation for Hector's effort.

Jake was dressed casually: tan chino pants, brown leather Timberland shoes, and a black knit golf shirt opened at the collar. He looked more like a tourist ready to take a carnival cruise to the islands than a counselor about to deliver a seminar about parenting. He thought wearing anything formal would give a false impression of who he was and he didn't need to impress anybody in that manner.

He welcomed each parent individually as they entered the library over the next ten minutes. "Hi, I'm Jake Carr, a counselor here at Middletown High. I'm glad you could make it tonight. Please find a table, take a seat, and settle in. We'll be starting shortly."

At 7:15 Jake walked to the front of the room and faced the audience who were now seated in groups of five or six around tables and talking among themselves. He stood relaxed and looking confident, while leaning on the edge of an old oak desk and making frequent glances at the wall clock until another few minutes went by. Then he began the evening with one of his patented "ice-breakers," a short opening monologue meant to loosen up the crowd before starting his formal introductory remarks.

"Welcome to "Adolescent Issues and Parental Concerns." First, let me ask you a few things. So gang…how was your dinner tonight? I ate early without the family and had a couple of tuna sandwiches with my dog keeping me company. Anyway, tell me was everyone seated at your dinner table tonight? Did you have a relaxed family gathering, taking turns sharing experiences…you know, passing the mashed potatoes and finding out who had a good day and stuff like that. It went like that…right? And obviously the kids cleaned up while you and your spouse had coffee and dessert. Yeah, then the kids began doing their homework without any threats. Oh… and just before you left, they stopped everything and kissed you goodbye. And, naturally they told you not to worry; they'd be fine. Is that how it went?"

His comments usually brought varying degrees of laughter, head turning, or an unsolicited comment like, "Are you kidding? What dinner, I came home, gobbled a sandwich, and left." and "What gathering, my daughter wasn't home yet. She was still at softball practice." As the group quieted down, a woman opened the entrance door of the library with a loud squeak and quickly walked to a rear table

"Seriously, welcome parents! My name is Jake Carr. I'm in the understanding business and it's a humbling business at best. I'm a POA just like you are. I'm a weary parent of two adolescents, a senior boy and a junior girl. I've survived so far, and yes, you heard right I did use the word, survive. Tonight I'd like to share some of my collected wisdom about adolescents and help you understand their world."

Over the next ninety minutes, Jake presented the first part of his program. His words were spoken with conviction, confidence, and clarity. His concepts and ideas made sense and were often humorous. He made fun of his own frailties and inconsistencies as a parent and he let them know he was one of them. In a matter of minutes the audience was his because he connected with them. He was energetic and entertaining; his body language, gestures, and eye contact commanded their attention.

Equally important was his ability to walk around the room, pause every so often, gaze directly at a surprised parent, and say, "Are you getting this? Are you sure you don't want to argue with me?"

The program worked because Jake would introduce a particular topic, then explained the concept. The first handout was informative and enlightening to novice parents. It was called "The Normal Characteristics of 13-to-15 year-old Teenagers." He discussed things clearly, not using the psycho-babble of child psychologists. He told them "Communication Addiction" was exactly what the term implied. It meant constantly being on the phone, in the chat room, or needing the company of friends. Afterwards, he'd take any questions regarding the theme.

He loved reading his own material because he knew it was written in a style that parents could appreciate without being overwhelmed by psychological or statistical terminology. It didn't matter if Jake discussed "The Magnetic Force of Peer Pressure" or "Why is Independence the Goal of Adolescence?" He explained everything from site-based experience. He always made it clear that he was, in fact, describing the culture at Middletown. His insight and perspective came from thousands of interviews and countless intervention strategies used with parents and kids over the years.

Jake's basic premise was that most parents reacted to their 14 or 15 year-olds without enough knowledge to understand the dynamics of adolescence. In short, they didn't think before they reacted. It was simple. To stay ahead in the parenting game one had to be thoughtful and strategic. Working parents lacked the energy to keep up with the battle for independence their kids were waging on a daily basis. Therefore, over and over, Jake reminded his audience that if they could learn the basics of adolescent development, it would improve their communication with their kids and with their spouses. He pleaded with them to let go of their preconceived notions based on their own experience twenty or thirty years ago. Moreover, he told them that if they made a conscious effort to stop trying to control everything concerning their kids, and began to use their influence, then relationships would be less strained and problematic.

"Stop preaching night after night and begin using some common sense. Most of all, lead by example because your kids will call you on your inconsistencies. Do yourself a favor and write down this parenting commandment: Don't sweat the small stuff and most of it is small."

Jake's other words of wisdom that seemed to hit hard were these: "You must stop threatening to punish and promising to reward! That strategy won't ever work as a long-term fix in any parent-child conflict, yet, so many of us are stuck in that pattern of control."

That one statement always generated an immediate response because not only was it controversial, but for some people it sounded contradictory. Jake believed many parents, especially fathers, were stuck in that short-sighted strategy of control. He knew the power of a statement like that but also the truth. It was supposed to make parents think, and possibly critique their pattern of disciplinary communication.

At 8:45 Jake told the parents to take a ten minute break and then return to begin the group process part of the workshop. As the parents filed out of the room Jake listened to what comments they made as they passed him. He also took a closer look at each one of them.

Jake thought close observation would tell him how they were holding up. Ninety minutes was a long time to sit still. There were only a minimum of questions asked during the first session, but that was to be expected. It was the primary reason the second part of the program was a group activity where the participants could share personal experiences regarding the theme materials in an intimate environment. He liked sitting in on the small group discussions, listening and observing the interaction. If he saw the group degenerate into a bull session, he'd stop them in a heartbeat and get them back on track. He gave each group a specific problem to discuss and encouraged them to share whatever they wanted, whether it was from personal experience or their personal opinion.

There were thirty-three individuals in the entire group, which meant that when they broke into pairs for the first exercise Jake would have to participate to even out the numbers. The first activity was an "icebreaker" interview using a specific set of questions that permitted parents to meet someone they didn't know. Married couples and friends couldn't be paired. Jake assigned odd and even numbers to the group and called out the paired numbers, again encouraging people not to end up with someone they knew.

When the group returned for the second half of the workshop it took a few minutes to get the group activity started, but it had to work that way in order to be of any benefit. One person was left without a partner. She was standing alone, staring out the library window. Everyone else had taken seats opposite each other in different locations around the library. Jake waited for the woman to turn around. When she did, he realized that she was the late entry. He motioned for her to join him, like a father would coax a toddler down a slide.

At first glance the woman looked to be in her mid to late thirties, but certainly was one the youngest women in the group. She wore black corduroy jeans that fit well and a long sleeve denim blouse. As she came closer he noticed a clear crystal elongated pendant that hung from a silver chain around her neck. Her outfit, although casual, was secondary to her attractive facial features and long auburn hair.

When she was a few feet away, their eyes met. Jake broke first; he gave her a sheepish grin and thought, *Damn, she's pretty.* Ellen's eyes were absolutely magnetic, a bright shade of blue that radiated out and took him by surprise. She seemed bashful and barely managed to give him a slight grin as if this kind of close encounter was embarrassing. Jake hadn't planned for this to occur. The numbers made it happen. Nevertheless, the opportunity to meet the woman intrigued him, and from the start he was determined to charm her. Finally she introduced herself.

"Hello Mr. Carr. I'm Ellen Eastman. Sorry I walked in late. My son Danny is a freshman. I guess I'm supposed to be interviewed by you. Do you think instead of standing we could sit down?"

Indeed, they were the only two people who were still standing. All the others were engaged in their interviews. Jake nodded in agreement, and they sat down to begin the opening exercise.

The noise level was beginning to rise around the room as partners started responding to the interview questions. There were eight questions and the answers were to be written on a form. When the first individual completed the interview, the process was reversed. Once all the interviews were completed, the parents were assigned to a round table that seated four. Then each interviewer would introduce his or her partner to the other members of the small group by reading the answers they'd written down. Jake instinctively knew that Ellen would be nervous about sharing personal information with him, so he thought he'd give her a moment to relax. Sitting opposite her, he leaned close with his elbow on the arm of the desk chair and his fist under his chin. Then he began.

"Are you ready now? Here we go? Tell me about your family?"

Ellen breathed a sigh of relief, thinking she could handle the activity.

"I have two sons. They're 14 and 11."

"Well, are you married or doing the single-parent balancing act? You know, work and kids?"

"Oh no, I'm...I'm married."

"Are both of you working full time?"

"At this time my husband works while I take care of the boys and run the house."

"That's interesting! Mrs. Eastman, you're one of a dying breed, a stay-at-home mom. Good for you. How long have you lived in Middletown?"

"About 8 months, but I've lived here before. It was when I was in high school."

"How interesting! You sat in this same library and giggled with your friends pretending to study."

Ellen smiled a little and nodded in agreement. Then Jake continued. "This one's easy. Tell me, when and where was your last family vacation?"

Ellen thought that she'd really like to tell Jake about the New Hampshire debacle, but thought better of it and took the safe route. "I took the boys to the Shawnee Ski area during President's Weekend for the day. It didn't work out. My younger son picked up a sore throat by lunchtime and I had to spend the rest of the day keeping him company instead of skiing. Bad luck, I guess."

Jake shrugged his shoulders and thought of J.D. and some of his dirt bike calamities.

"I've been to that area dozens of times but not to ski. I've gone there to hike the Appalachian Trail on the opposite side of the river. I love the Delaware Water Gap. I'm sorry. Now I'm the one off the subject. I'm supposed to be asking you the questions."

"Mr. Carr, you really got excited when I mentioned Shawnee. How come?"

"That's just the way I am when it comes to the places I've been to and that I liked."

The easy questions were over. Jake paused momentarily, pretending to be looking at his notes. Then he sat up, crossed his arms over his chest and looked pensive. "So tell me. What part of parenting is the most demanding for you and takes all your energy?"

Ellen paused and took some extra time to consider. Should she really tell the truth? "Motherhood demands lots of energy and all my patience. Not so much with my younger son, but with Danny. It seems from the moment I wake him and whenever he's at home, it's so difficult for him to cooperate. Especially at homework time and when I ask him to help with the chores. I guess I'm not that different than anyone else here. God, I wish my son would learn to listen and stop doing whatever he feels like, when he feels like. I find myself trying to be tough and I'm not, not at all. I think lately all I do is plead with him to behave. It's embarrassing to admit that. Honestly, sometimes I want to strangle him. If I tell his father about it all I ever hear is criticism. Some weekends Danny stays out past his curfew. His father's not the one waiting up for him. I am. I'm sorry for complaining."

"Ellen, you're frustrated. Believe me, you're not alone. That's why you came to the workshop."

Jake knew Ellen was going through a tough time but he had to finish the interview. "What's your major weakness in parenting? Do you think you have one?"

Ellen realized she wasn't prepared for this kind of interview and it was becoming more intense than she expected. She thought to herself, *this man is probing me in a way no one has ever done before, not even my husband who doesn't give a damn about my struggles with Danny.*

"Ellen, be honest. Not for me but for you. You need to hear your own words."

She looked down and with uncertainty in her voice she responded to his question. "The plain truth is that I have no support. I've done this parenting thing alone from the start. Only a year ago, Danny wasn't as troublesome. But tonight I learned that his time for independence has come. Does that mean most fourteen year old boys are going to take advantage of their mothers?"

"That's a good question. Ellen, I hate to break the news. It goes something like this. If you're standing in the way of what they want, or they think you can be out-maneuvered or out-smarted, then the answer is yes. It's not really a weakness. It's a battle of wills. Anything else you want to tell me?"

"My husband works in Atlanta. That's where his financial consulting business is located. He comes back for a weekend every month, but he expects me to handle everything related to the boys. Sorry for dumping on you. I'll answer your question now. I think my weakness is that my son takes advantage of me and I suppose I let him. He's been spoiled most of his life. Now I can't force him to do what he should. My weakness is that I don't know how to handle him and it's creating problems at home."

When she was finished she looked up with a blank expression on her face, not of embarrassment or sorrow, just the look of a woman who was unsure of herself and worried.

Jake gently touched her shoulder as a gesture of kindness and said,

"It's all right Ellen, I'll just write down that you could use more support from your husband."

She seemed relieved, so Jake quickly jumped to the seventh question. "Ellen, what's your major strength in parenting? Do you have a sense of humor? Can you bounce back from disappointment?"

Without the slightest change of facial expression, she shifted in her seat and said. "I think I'm kind, unselfish, and forgiving. Probably too much for my own good, but that's the way I've always been. I get manipulated easily. Lately I've become more aware of it and it bothers me."

It was clear to Jake that this woman needed to be there, maybe more than she would ever admit. He decided right then that he would try to talk privately with her if the opportunity presented itself. The last question came none too soon. Ellen's hands were getting moist and her mouth was very dry.

"This is it…the last one. What's your favorite family activity?"

The question was ludicrous because she couldn't recall the four of them doing any activity without conflict or controversy. Again, she took the safe way out. "Eating, my family has no trouble going out for dinner. I suppose that's our favorite family activity."

"Ellen, you did fine. Really! Now I'm going to ask someone to introduce you to the others at your table. I've got to go and check on some things. Listen, I enjoyed meeting you and hope some time in the future we can continue this discussion. Believe me, like I said, you're not alone in your struggles. Lots of women are going through the same thing. I hope you get a chance to meet someone here. Good luck!"

After leaving Ellen, Jake went from table to table and listened to the introductions. It appeared the questions regarding parenting strengths and weaknesses took everyone by surprise. Several parents shared varying degrees of frustration and talked about trying to establish some peace with their kids. Several others felt alone in their struggles, and like Ellen, weren't supported by their spouses.

The workshop moved to the next phase of group activity called, "The Way We Were." This was an opportunity for each person to describe in their own words what their adolescence was like when they were 14 or 15. Regardless of sex or age of the individual, this was always an entertaining and enlightening activity. Jake listened to the wide variety of responses. Many were alike but a few were brutally honest, like the woman who explained the horror of living with an alcoholic mother and a father who was condemned by genetics to being short. He told his group he was nicknamed "stump" while in elementary school. The name stuck through college and up till the present. He hated the label and now his own son used it to get him angry. Jake saw the beginning of some group bonding as statements of support and encouragement were heard from those in the group who experienced similar ridicule or emotional trauma.

The last activity of the evening concerned how peer pressure was impacting on family life. Again and again, the stories reflected the deepest worries that parents held secret about drug use and promiscuous behavior. However, with Jake's encouragement they brought their concerns out in the open, unashamed and confident they weren't alone. Jake let it ride. He dropped into the discussions at each table and shared his insights and experiences, but only if it was solicited by someone in the small group.

Finally, with only fifteen minutes remaining, he gave them nine questions to consider on a worksheet called "Major Areas of Concern about Peer Pressure." They could begin the exercise now or do it at home.

Jake demonstrated a level of common sense and wisdom that surprised even the most case hardened skeptics in his audience. He clarified issues and gave the warning signs that parents should look for, or they might find themselves in serious jeopardy of losing their children to outside influences that would derail their children from success.

This last group discussion of the evening set off a volley of anxiety and although it was nearly ten o'clock, Jake let the parents vent.

"How can I keep my kid from smoking pot or trying cocaine when the availability for it seems to be everywhere? Tell us, how does that poison get into Middletown? I trust my daughter, but I don't really know much about her friends. Why doesn't she tell me more about them? Why does my son withdraw all the time? Why does he want to be alone?"

Those questions raised more questions, and one of the more outspoken parents in the audience declared with sense of deep conviction. "Tonight I've decided to demand that my daughter bring her new friends to spend time at our home. Then I can make up my own mind about her choice of friends. I won't compromise, not at all about this anymore. My husband has to support me on this issue!"

As the evening drew to a close, Jake saw that there were leaders and followers in every group. There were some baby boomers raised in strictest homes and they continued that tradition with their own. There were alumni from the Woodstock generation who were still unsure of how to use their parental authority. And of course, a few lost souls who were guided by the stars and had a "live and let live" attitude about rules, regardless of the consequences. Some were secular humanists and spiritually guided individuals whose faith in the Judaic-Christian ethic was the keystone in their philosophy. They were all present in the library that night and Jake heard testimony in one way or another from all of them.

Jake called the group to order at 9:55 for a closing comment.

"I know I've given you plenty to think about in the coming week. Do yourself a favor. Write down your observations about your interaction with the kids. Try to do it each night before you go to bed. Resist commenting on every disturbing statement you heard. Remember, the language of adolescence is impulsive and always exaggerated for maximum impact. I hear it everyday. Finally, review the materials I've given you and never forget this statement. **You're running out of control**. You must learn to use your influence. See you next week and once again, thanks for giving up your evening."

The group gave Jake a round of applause as he bowed like a rock star after finishing a concert. Then the group slowly exited the library. As Ellen passed by Jake, their eyes met and he smiled and nodded to her. It made her feel connected if only for a moment.

❧

The house was dark except for a floodlight spreading its yellow beam on the driveway. Quietly, Jake walked through the garage and opened the kitchen door. Missy was spread out in her usual place and didn't even bother to move. Opening the liquor cabinet, he poured four shots of Gordon's Vodka into a large tumbler, dropped in lots of ice, and capped it off with orange juice. It was his favorite drink. When he sat down at the kitchen counter he saw a note left there.

Dear Jake,
I hope your workshop was a success. Everything went fine tonight.
Please get J.D. to straighten out his room and bring down his dirty
laundry. He won't listen to me, and I am tired of begging.
Love, Sandy

❧

Some twenty-two miles away, around the same time, Ellen Eastman was going through her nightly ritual. Instead of her usual glass of merlot and a new novel called, "Dragonfly in Amber" by Diana Gabaldon, she filled half a tumbler with Wild Turkey Bourbon and ice. After taking ten minutes to relax, she looked over the workshop notes. She began the mental exercise of jumping from one person to another trying to remember something about each person and what they shared during the group session.

Ellen was confused about her parenting much more than ever

before. One commitment she was determined to make was to continue attending the seminar and possibly find another woman to build a friendship. She realized that living in isolation was one thing, but not having another woman to share some of the burden was foolish.

She liked Jake Carr. Initially, it was his physical appearance, but after a while she realized he was a compassionate, understanding, and patient man. His engaging personality intrigued her and there was something about him that let her imagination takeover. She thought he was like a character from one of her adventure novels, he was strong, wise, and heroic, a man who could change the course of a woman's life. As peculiar as it seemed, the workshop had been informative and exciting, she found herself anticipating the next encounter with Jake as much as she did listening to her fellow group members discuss their families.

Ellen had listened attentively whenever Jake shared any personal information with his audience. A few times he alluded to his road travels and outdoor experiences, always with enthusiasm and spontaneity. Most of the women present had only heard their husbands refer to professional sports with such excitement. She connected with Jake because she loved Mother Nature the same way he did, but expressed it silently in her paintings.

When Guy had called up to inquire about Ellen's whereabouts, Danny forgot to tell him that she had gone to the workshop. Much later, when he called back to inquire where she was, Ellen mentioned very little about the evening explaining, "There was a teen parenting program and I thought it might be helpful. Danny has given me so much trouble lately. I've run out of answers and you're no help."

"Why would you say that to me? I'm working my ass off so you don't have to work. Stop complaining! Why do I always have to remind you of that fact? It was your idea to move, remember? Did you go alone or with someone?"

"Guy, I don't know anyone in the neighborhood. I went alone."

Satisfied with the explanation about her absence, he continued on with the usual inquisition. Was she staying within the budget, doing house maintenance, paying the bills on time, and supervising the boy's homework? Guy ended the one-sided conversation with the perfunctory phrase, "I love you," but Ellen disregarded it as a meaningless gesture that lacked sincerity and she didn't answer him back.

After the call, Ellen renewed her solemn promise that she would continue exercising, eating less, and trying even harder to understand her adolescent son. Ellen finally had come to realize that she was stuck in a rut of self-pity, unable to step outside of family problems and see herself as an individual. The failure of her marriage and the ongoing battles with her son had diminished her capacity to act on her own behalf. Now she was more determined than ever to alter that situation. She thought that having something unexpected happen, like attending the workshop added impetus to change the direction of her life. She felt enthusiastic and hopeful. It was a welcomed change for someone who was devalued, suffocated, and imprisoned by an overbearing and ill-manner husband.

For the past year Guy had refused to believe her warnings about the boy. All too often his response to her concerns was, "What's the big deal. He's acting like most kids his age. I was no different than he is. He'll come around. Just make sure you handle the school stuff." As usual, Guy discounted any bad news that he didn't want to deal with. If anything, lately he was more self-centered, arrogant, and consumed with his material well-being than at any other time.

After the first workshop it became evident to Ellen that regardless of the love and personal sacrifices she was willing to make on her family's behalf, it meant nothing to Guy. He was busy living his other life in Atlanta. Even so, she believed Danny was worth the effort because she loved him in spite of his adolescent shortcomings.

CHAPTER 7

Spring finally poked its sleepy head out on the first Saturday in April. The day looked bright and promising, possibly reaching the mid-fifties by early afternoon. With escape in mind, Jake knocked off the house chores without a glitch. Much to his satisfaction, everyone was out of the house, which made the job move along faster, because he could play his music. Only the low-pitched hums of the clothes dryer, along with Neil Young singing oldies were heard as he stopped vacuuming to survey the family room. Suddenly a thought occurred as he was about to put the vacuum away. *Damn it. I forgot to order a film for tonight. There's no way I wanna go out to a movie.*

He grabbed the weekly video magazine off his desk to check what had recently come out in the past week and then dialed the number of the local outlet. A young female answered.

"Walden Video, how may I help you?"

"Good morning young lady. Can I reserve *The General's Daughter* or how about *Zorro?*"

"Sir, could you hold for a second...Let me see.....No problem, mister. We have both of them in."

"Terrific! I'll take *Zorro*. My ID is 678. When can I pick it up?"

"Like I said, we have it. I'll put it aside. Get here before nine, ok?"

"Sorry kid. My mind is a thousand miles away. Thanks."

With the film ordered and the house in order there was one final chore, the supposedly simple task of folding clothes from the dryer. Jake considered what he'd already accomplished that morning and chuckled to himself, and said sarcastically to Missy, "You know my loyal friend, for an educated man, I can do housekeeping like I was the owner of a bed and breakfast in Bennington, Vermont."

❧❦

Earlier that morning, at fifteen minute intervals, the other family members left the house; J.D. to work at a local liquor store, Annie to Marshall's department store driven by her brother, and Sandy to spend the day shopping with a recently widowed old friend. Jake relished the thought of having some time alone; completing the chores was something he willingly did to give Sandy the day off.

Jake routinely cleaned the kitchen, family room, and three bathrooms. He changed the sheets, emptied the garbage, washed the floors, dusted furniture, did his own laundry, vacuumed the stairs, and did the master bedroom like a whirlwind super-maid in some dumb TV commercial. To him, it was a form of exercise. He'd been doing the house chores since he got married almost twenty years ago.

Very few chores bugged him, except for two. He absolutely hated raking leaves or pulling weeds because it brought him back to his days of servitude working as a landscaper on weekends during college. The other was the unmanly act of standing on a footstool and gently cleaning bulbs and polishing the chandeliers in the formal dining room and the center hallway like he was a southern plantation slave. What gnawed at him was the sense that Sandy took him for granted, in spite of all he did to make her life easier. That perceived lack of gratitude, more so over the past six years, developed into a deep feeling of resentment. The reason was that she never seemed satisfied with things. Something else always needed to be done tomorrow, next week, or next month. In short, Sandy couldn't take life a day at a time.

The kids' contribution to the home was an incessant source of conflict. Jake knew their order of priorities would never be in sync with Sandy's, and therein was the problem. Most times when Jake did their chores it was for the sake of peace. His assessment was that if both children were working, it wasn't worth waging a battle with them every day. If Jake did the kids' bathroom, Sandy would complain bitterly to him about doing the job. Given an inordinate amount of disorder, she'd automatically preach a "when I was your age" sermon. Jake was quite the opposite and simply taught his kids to "live and let live." His bias, right or wrong, was centered on the fact that they were in the final years of high school and close to leaving home. Jake knew their life consisted of: school, work, play, sleep, and friendship.

J.D.'s major interest involved engines and rebuilding vehicles. He turned half the garage into an automotive service bay; complete with tools and, of course, too many junk parts. He was always in need of close monitoring to keep him out of trouble at home or at school. He was selfish with his time, but he managed to cut the grass in the summer and shovel snow after a blizzard. To his son's credit, J.D. fixed the family vehicles free of charge and Jake was eternally grateful for the money he saved.

Currently, J.D.'s primary interest was restoring busted dirt bikes to resell them and caring for his newly constructed monster truck, a 1992 Ford Ranger. He didn't care much about dating or seeking popularity with mainstream kids. He never hung around school for clubs or athletics. At eighteen, he was very much a free spirit and his father didn't foresee any period of enlightenment in the coming months that would change his son's attitude. Much like Jake, J.D. was a staunch individualist who could tune out unsolicited commentary.

Jake understood J.D.'s obsession with technology as the natural outcome of his childhood years when he spent countless hours mesmerized with any toy that whirred, was wound up, or sped away. The boy was clever. His Tonka fleet of construction vehicles had to be any color other than standard yellow. Consequently, he spray painted each of them into every conceivable color to satisfy his imagination. At the age of nine, he shifted to remote-controlled race cars and customized them to his liking. He was the kind of kid who threw away the *Lego* diagrams and redesigned *The Castle* and *Police Station* his own way. When he was ten years old, he was fully capable of using the John Deere tractor to cut the lawn.

Now, even though eighteen years old, on impulse, the boy would still pull out his old chrome BMX bike to jump curbs, do wheelies, and show off for his buddies. Jake thought his son was born with "golden hands" and had a special gift for making things work. J.D. was a persistent problem solver for any mechanism that refused to obey his command "to start," whether it was a weed whacker, minibike, chainsaw, or power lawnmower that someone discarded in the development. Jake appreciated J.D.'s talent and how it enhanced his son's self-esteem and praised him for his abilities even if he made a mess.

Annie was entirely different. She was, first and foremost, a thinker. From preschool on, she loved learning like a purebred racehorse loves to run. She was focused on her goals like a surgical laser, accomplishing her objective in spite of whatever difficulties she faced, social or academic. She was extremely conscientious and willing to make sacrifices in order to maintain her 4.0 grade point average. Popularity with her peers decreased in importance after her closest friends abandoned her when she was sick. And, like her brother, she lived another life outside of Walden High School by dating guys from other towns and establishing relationships with the kids she worked with. Many of them were part time Orange County Community College kids paying for their tuition or auto insurance. She learned the workplace was the great equalizer, where everybody was on the same pay scale.

When Annie gained membership to the National Honor Society and became the editor of the school's literary magazine, her life became a whirlwind of activities. Therefore, Jake generally wouldn't ask Annie for help with house chore other than keeping her room in order. That dispensation, granted unilaterally by Jake, caused strife and rancorous debate between them, particularly during holidays when the house had to exceed "broom clean" standards, or there would be hell to pay.

Sandy set the standards in terms of cleanliness, and Jake's job was to accommodate her wishes. She frequently reminded him that she was raised in an immaculate home where neatness and order were the top priorities. When she was growing up, a dirty dish left on the kitchen counter, a coat hung on a chair, or two days of dust on the credenza were simply unacceptable. Social commitments were secondary to house cleaning when Sandy was growing up. Consequently, Sandy's house standards, although not as strict as her mother's, were nevertheless essential for her peace of mind. If by midweek, she felt the place was getting messy, Jake would get the message and he'd pass it on to the kids.

᳞᳜

After bringing the laundry basket upstairs, Jake separated the clothes. He put his own socks, jeans, and tee shirts in his dresser but left J.D.'s on top of the last pile he'd put there in midweek. Now his son's stack of tee shirts was teetering over a foot high. The socks he assembled into pairs and put them in the dresser drawer so they'd stay together. Then Jake began his final inspection tour, checking one room at a time till he reached the basement. When he felt things were squared away, then he'd leave.

At noon he had a grilled cheese sandwich and some chocolate chip cookies. Afterwards, he filled his canteen with lemonade and made for the door. Just then, he heard the mail truck and thought maybe his income tax refund had finally arrived. Just before reaching the mailbox, another thought crossed his mind. *There might be a letter from Vermont Technical College.*

Convincing his son to attend college was a battle of wills between father and son. J.D. never liked school and getting J.D. through high school was a challenge, especially with his ADHD disability. Worst of all, he wasn't a reader, and Jake knew there was no way around a deficiency like that. Jake literally forced J.D. to go through the application process. Additionally, Jake knew that Sandy would never accept any excuse for their son ending his education with a high school diploma and Jake believed she was right. However, her method of persuasion was constant nagging or threats to toss him out.

Remarkably, even with his academic indifference and disability, J.D. had an adequate admissions profile for acceptance to a technical college. Eventually, Jake wore his resistance down, not with threats but by using his influence until his son finally gave in, because Jake only asked for a single semester tryout. That was the deal. Jake explained to Sandy that their son's ambivalence about college had more to do with a lack of social self-confidence than an ability to master automotive technology.

The letter from Vermont Tech was there and, although it was addressed to his son, Jake couldn't resist opening it. His eyes

49

immediately directed to the key sentence. *We are pleased to inform you of your acceptance to Vermont Technical College's next freshman class. Congratulations!*

The news was thrilling. Jake sighed deeply as if an enormous weight was lifted off his mind. Strangely, for a brief moment, he felt a deep sense of love for his son and it came as a shock. Loving him as a little child was easy. But, loving him during the turbulent years of his adolescence was altogether different. There were countless times he cursed his son for the pain he caused his sister and mother.

Now, it was as if the past five years were expunged from the record. Maybe it was the fact that he'd be leaving in a few months or maybe it was knowledge that disciplining the boy had been a constant battle and it was finally nearing an end. Either way, the emotional jolt was overpowering, and Jake felt it both in his head and his heart. Miraculously, after so much heartache and bitterness, he realized the truth. He'd do anything for his son in spite of everything the boy had put him through. How or why it took a letter of acceptance to reveal so much about his inner feelings didn't matter.

Holding the letter in his hand he sat on the curb and remembered taking J.D. for a visitation to the small college in Randolph, Vermont, about fifty miles from Burlington. He'd arranged special placement testing procedures to accommodate his son's ADHD disability and spoke at length with the admissions director to enhance his son's chances. He also wrote an impassioned letter to the dean explaining his son's disability and the obstacles that the boy had to overcome throughout his years in public schools. He included a resume of J.D.'s work experience with small engine repair; beginning with a job at a hardware store where he learned to service John Deere lawn tractors, to being a part-time service technician at the local dirt bike shop. Jake wanted his son to have an edge.

Jake felt enormous pride for his son's accomplishment. He knew Sandy would be greatly relieved. Without hesitation, he grabbed his hiking gear, locked up the house, and drove to the liquor store in the center of Walden where J.D. worked on weekends.

After a five-minute drive, Jake parked the van, walked to the front of the store, and peered in the huge front window covered with sale advertising. He saw J.D. standing behind the counter waiting on a customer. Jake tried to contain his excitement. As soon as the customer left, Jake bolted inside, clapped his hands and made the announcement. "Congratulations! You've been accepted to Vermont Tech. You did it! I'm at a loss for words. Can you imagine that? Joshua Daniel Carr, I'm so proud of you!"

His son was taken by surprise and embarrassed by his father's excessive exuberance. At first he said nothing. He just shook his head and muttered, "Dad, you act like I got into Harvard. Relax, what do ya want to do, let the whole town know?"

The owner, Big Bob as he was called, walked toward them and chimed in, "What's up Mr. Carr? You're not taking him with you... are you? I need him today we got lots of stock to put up."

"Bob, J.D.'s going to college!!! I just got the news. I'm so damn proud of him."

J.D. released the handshake, looked away from his father, and said bluntly to his boss, "My dad, he's making such a big deal over this. I'm happy. Ok, I'm happy."

Big Bob, who lived down the road from the Carrs, knew all about J.D.'s dirtbike exploits and the trouble he caused his parents, Bob was curious. "What's with you? I don't remember you telling me any of this college stuff. Does this means you're gonna leave my store? Huh? Sorry, I can't let you do that. Tell you what. If you stay, I'll give you a fifty cent raise. Do you accept my offer?"

Then the owner broke out into a big belly laugh and put his arm around the boy's shoulder. Jake took it all in without making a single comment, knowing it was all a ruse. When Big Bob left, he leaned over the counter, squeezed his son's arm and quietly told him, "Maybe someday you'll understand...understand how I feel. For so many years I've been congratulating other kids about getting into college. Now I can feel the satisfaction of knowing that my son is making his way in the world. I really don't expect you to grasp the meaning of all this and that's fine. You made me proud and that feeling belongs to me."

"Dad, I'm still a kid, this is stuff you understand and I don't."

"That's cool. All right, I better let you get back to your job. Anyway, I'm going hiking. It's a memorable day and it'll be filled with all kinds of memories for me. I'll see you later. One more thing, your mother's going to be so happy, happy for the first time in a very long time. Please let her enjoy the news. I left the college letter on her pillow. Believe me; you have no idea what this will mean to her. And you know what? Whenever James or your other buddies ask about your plans, you'll have an answer to give them. And better yet, if someone asks me, I'll have an answer for them! Have a good day. See ya!"

Jake's mood was euphoric as he left Walden and drove toward Interstate 87. As he turned south onto the highway, he inserted a cassette and started to sing along with the "Genesis" tape, *Invisible Touch*. Originally he planned to go to Highland Lakes State Park, but now considering his mood, he headed south to the Delaware Water Gap.

It was an hour away, and it would be nearly deserted at this time of the year. As happy as he was with the college news, he was ready to begin another season of hiking. The afternoon trek would enable him to reflect on his life. Plus, nothing quite matched the thrill of seeing some hawks soaring on the thermals over the meandering Delaware River.

An hour later Jake parked the van in a hiker's lot at Worthington State Forest, he brought along his favorite walking stick, locked up the van, and left for the trailhead. Dressed in faded Levi jeans, a black tee shirt, green Gore-Tex wind breaker, and well-worn Dunham hiking boots, he looked like he belonged right where he was.

He'd been hiking the Gap trails for the past twenty-plus years. But it was only a small part of his total hiking territory; Jake had been all over the country since finishing graduate school in '75. He'd traveled from ocean to ocean, from border to border, through most National Parks, and especially the Rocky Mountains from northern Montana to Taos, New Mexico. There was nothing in Jake's experience that even approached his longing for being in the forest near the mountains.

ॐ

His love of road travel and experiencing natural wonders began in the fall of his twenty-sixth year. Jake had a life-altering experience that changed him, especially his philosophy of life. It came completely unexpected and was not at all like the other milestones one looks forward to in life. Events you could anticipate, like graduating from college, finding a job, getting married, or witnessing the birth of a child. Maybe it happened because he was ready to change and desperately wanted to separate from his cynical outlook on life and the caldron of anger inside of him.

Jake had volunteered to attend an outdoor educational training session. His school was sponsoring the program with the intention of bringing junior high students to the forest for a weekend nature experience. By chance, he met an instructor named Tom Costello. Tom was an Outdoor Education Trainer who took small groups of teachers through a series of problem-solving and trust exercises to prepare them to be facilitators for their own school programs involved with environmental education.

Prior to that training session at Stokes State Forest in New Jersey, all of Jake's weekends were spent with his teaching friend and partner, Lou Guarino. Together they did home improvement jobs. Lou had recently purchased a home and Jake had to pay off college loans, along with financial commitments such as car payments, insurance, apartment rent, and all the other costs that came along after leaving college and beginning a career. He needed the part-time work to augment his beginning teacher's salary.

Costello exhibited a balance and inner peace that belied explanation. He was soft-spoken, patient and thoughtful, but very manly with a tough physical exterior. Yet, he was kind-hearted in his approach to dealing with the novices. Tom's demeanor intrigued Jake. Tom could communicate and act with authenticity and authority at the same time.

Whether he was demonstrating a physical exercise like moving the group up and through a spider's nest exercise, which demanded the utmost cooperation and problem-solving ability of the group, or giving feedback after witnessing the group mishandle a blindfolded trust fall, Tom demonstrated qualities that Jake admired. Tom had a quiet confidence to go with a commanding physical presence and a sense of calm and optimism that Jake picked up right from the start. Jake had to admit that he was sorely missing those attributes.

Before meeting Tom, Jake rarely was envious of any other men, with the exception of a few college professors, professional athletes, and some frat brothers who graduated without having any debt. He believed envy was a weak excuse for not accepting the consequences of the choices he freely made. At the time he met Tom, Jake's head was confused about family, love, politics, religion, friendship, and self-worth, none of which came with a guarantee because he had a college degree.

After a day and a half at the training facility, the first opportunity for some private time with Tom came while the training group was taking a break. They'd been engaged in a night exercise that involved hiking the Appalachian Trail blindfolded, trusting the lead person to guide the next one in line over rocks, each person passing on verbal directions. Only the rising stars that surrounded a dull yellow moon were out on that night.

Tom told the group to relax and take an extended break to discuss the exercise. Jake noticed that Tom sat apart from everyone on a flat boulder looking up at the evening sky. He approached him and spoke in a sincere, but casual manner. "Sorry...sorry to bother you, I know we're supposed to be discussing the exercise. But umm...I'd really like to talk with you. Got a few minutes? It's important."

"No problem. Anyway, I can tell the group's getting tired. The training's almost over and I'm feeling pretty mellow right now. Tomorrow the bus comes at noon to take you back. Park your ass on this ancient boulder and I'll give you my fullest attention."

"Thanks Tom. I don't know whether it's this place or what, but I love it out here! I'm finally alone and in the mood to think clearly. I'm not sure, but I need to get some clutter out of my congested head. I know this probably sounds strange and maybe there's no rational reason for this, at least none that I can understand. But somehow I know you're the right person and I feel like I'm ready to dump. This weekend has given me a chance to stop and reflect, reflect deeply on my life. I can't even remember the last time I shut down. Shutting down is as hard as hell for me. Do you know what I mean?"

"Hey Jake, believe me, I know what you mean. Hardly anything makes sense to me any more. The war in Vietnam sure didn't, Ford pardoning that asshole Nixon didn't. Christ, waiting in line for gas, seeing chemical pollution killing the Delaware, and above all that shit, the number of screwed up kids I teach everyday. Yeah, I think I know where you're coming from. I've been there. Go ahead. You got something you need to let out?"

Over the next few minutes, in short bursts like firing a semi-automatic rifle, Jake told Tom some personal history, so he could at least seem credible to Tom. He spoke about his working-class upbringing with candor, exposing old wounds.

"Six kids in my family...I was the fourth, the third son and I learned early on to take care of myself. I loved the woods...loved the county park. My dad was a real man by any standards and struggled to make ends meet. He just recently retired...no pension. Unfucking real!!! Anyway, I was the first in my family to go away to college, poor people's college, but even that was by pure dumb luck. I never figured to be educated beyond high school. I had to borrow a shitload of money to make it all work. I've got too much debt! I was always a tough guy. I can't make any excuse for being that way. I guess I've always had a hard edge. I'm stubborn. I wouldn't ask for advice and that hurt me!"

Jake continued to fill in the blanks as if he was on a job interview. He gave enough information for Tom to ascertain that he was adrift and lonely. However, Jake refused to give him a complete picture of his inner turmoil and made no mention of past romantic heartbreaks.

Up until that night, Jake had been struggling against the odds for as long as he could remember. He was case-hardened by economic hardship and from the emotional scars leftover from his childhood and demons that still hadn't been exorcised. He was severely critical of himself and hated making mistakes in judgment. Since graduating from college the last few of years were a blur of drudgery. He was teaching, going to grad school, hammering nails on weekends, and getting wasted on Saturday nights. Day after day, he felt he was disconnected and running on empty.

Like many of his generation, he couldn't break free from the madness of the times and believe, like his father, in the pursuit of the American Dream. On one hand, he wanted to make it into the suburban middle class and on the other, he abhorred the idea of the aluminum sided split-level with the rose bushes in the front, the two kids playing on the jungle gym, and the Ford Country Squire wagon taking the family to Disneyworld. And yet, there were times when all he aspired was to reach that goal.

Although he was spared being drafted with a high lottery number, the cynical period of post-war Vietnam poisoned him and many others of the boomer generation. He was an angry young man, handicapped by the knowledge that he'd made a couple of huge mistakes in his past, misguided and misdirected errors that no one could have altered, because he wouldn't reach out for advice. His mistakes involved an ongoing disassociation from his family and a decision to work in Newark that was made more as an act of rebellion than as a career choice. To compound his troubles, he made some financial blunders involving car loans and repaying college debt. Finally, he had broken the hearts of several young ladies who had visions of walking down the church aisle with him.

Jake lacked self-acceptance and, to a large degree, self-love. He couldn't find any peace inside himself. It wasn't because he smoked pot occasionally or got drunk on Saturday nights or that he took sexual advantage of unsuspecting women who liked his looks and his style. Social behaviors like that were common among his contemporaries. Even though he put himself through college and received a master's degree in counseling, he was as unsettled about his future as he had been during senior year of high school. In short, he was another young idealist whose dreams faded with the times.

At twenty-six, he was fiercely private, independent, intelligent, and physically formidable. Yet, he was emotionally detached, living alone in a loft apartment in downtown Elizabeth, New Jersey, across the street from the Penn Central railroad tracks. He was disciplined enough to start paying off his debts and smart enough to stay away from cocaine. His problem was that he was always searching for the same answers as everyone else in his generation, a belief that his life mattered.

"Jake, you got balls. I admire your honesty." Tom said and then continued, "It's a rare commodity these days. So you're ready for a change, huh? My family, they were also working class people like yours. My father had the same quiet courage and unselfishness. Those men had guts and like you said, they weren't looking to change the world like we were. That's what our generation claims it's gonna do. What horseshit! How they gonna do it? I'm glad to hear how much you respected your father. You mentioned he recently got the death sentence…cancer, huh?

That's bad news. God damn, you're right, those guys got by with so little. I know what you mean about settling. Yeah, I admit, there's not much choice when you grow up in a big family. You mentioned you went to 'Poor People's College.' I like your description. I did the same thing. No family resource...I went to East Stroudsburg on loans and worked in a warehouse. I was a PE major. But enough of me...there's something you want to know. What is it?"

Jake slipped off the massive granite rock and turned away from Tom as if he didn't know what he should say next. Then, digging deep, he summed up his thoughts. "Tom, this is weird, but I really need to ask you a personal question? I gave you a piece. Can I?"

"It all depends... but go ahead, it's cool. What would you like to know?"

With that said, Jake wanted to be absolutely clear, so he gave it his best shot. "I've been listening, really listening to you and I've been watching you since we first arrived at camp. One thing's certain. Tom, you speak and act like you understand so much about life and you're not more than five years older than I am. You seem to have your shit together. You're at some peaceful place and you're not afraid of being who you are. You're not mad. You're calm. I'm fuckin' full of turmoil. I've got no peace. I'm lost. Not because I'm lazy or a follower. I've never been like that.

"I've watched you interact with a couple of teachers who act like assholes and somehow you were patient and even kept a sense of humor. I've seen you sit quietly during lunch and listen to some fat math teacher whine about poor toilet facilities and the lack of enough hot water. Then there's that opinionated bitch of a history teacher talking at the dinner table about the piss poor state of affairs in this country acting like she knows who's to blame. Fuck her. I don't know how you do it. But you look comfortable out here doing what you're doing. It's like...like you've got nothing to prove. It's not that you don't care about your fellow man because I can tell you do or you wouldn't be teaching. I don't know what I'm specifically asking for, except that man to man I admire you. I just want to find out how it happened? Did you take some EST training in California? Just kidding! How did you get to such a good place in your head because I don't think it came from tripping on LSD or Hashish? I probably sound like a simpleton, but what happened to you that made it work? I can't believe I'm asking, but I really wanna know."

At first, Tom said nothing to Jake; instead he looked up at the night sky and pointed with his hand. Jake took the queue and looked to where Tom directed his attention.

"Pretty amazing, isn't it? On a pitch-black night like this, up on a ridge and away from everything, if you want, you can view the wonders of the universe with a child's sense of awe and the knowledge that millions of stars were there long before man. And there they are, whenever we choose to look at them. Isn't it remarkable when you think about how all this works without a single human in control of any part of it? Whether you believe that the Almighty had a hand in it doesn't really matter.

"My secret is that I've learned over the past few years to distance myself from the assholes, people driven by greed and the need for power and self-gratification. I know we live in a materialistic society. It's a fucking disease. I won't join them, but I'm not gonna convert them either. They all want too much. Way too much! That's where you can get lost. I suppose for some individuals that's fine. They believe in the house in the burbs, having two cars, three TV's...you know the status thing. They've bought into it completely. I know I'm not like that. I'd rather take advantage of what nature has to offer. It's not anything other than that. It's all right here and it's free. It's about values.

"I have a wife who's a great companion and my closest friend. But, and I mean but, we're as different as the colors of the rainbow, however, we're similar in our values and man, is that important! I have two little boys that I play with whenever I can. I also have bills up the ass and all the responsibilities that go with the choices I made. They were conscious, well-thought out choices. Listen, the point is to never let outside influences poison you or define you! And don't let them deceive you into playing their game. You sure as hell ain't a follower. That's where you're different than everyone else up here. Accept it. You probably already know it and yet, somehow I think you feel like that's your source of grief. Shit, you're different. So am I. Anyway, this is what I think is wrong with you. Jake, what you're missing is...is self-acceptance. You're tougher than I am, but it's not enough. Find a way to get along with yourself.

"I've learned to break away when I need to and experience nature whenever I can, sometimes with my family but most times alone. I suppose it renews my spirit. Anyway, don't believe this awareness came easily to me. No fucking way. I've smoked weed and listened to Clapton and Morrison. Strange but, just like you, about six years ago, I was dissatisfied with stuff, unsettled, and disappointed with all the political lies and bullshit. A colleague at work, another PE teacher, took me out for a weekend. It was fucking great! That was a revival. I began hiking in the mountains and forests on the east coast. I didn't make it to the Rockies. I will some day, but I hiked everywhere and slept under the stars and danced by the campfire. I found peace out here, and I took it back with me. After a year or so, I learned to free my thoughts from most of the modern day insanity we have to put up with.

"Listen, my young unsettled friend. Take it for what it's worth. Get yourself a knapsack and canteen, find a walking stick, and free your mind from all the bullshit that's in it. I've watched you. You're a natural. Escape to the outdoors. Honestly, I think all you need to do is get that head of yours reprogrammed. Begin the journey and you'll come to understand that it will all make perfect sense."

ରେ୶ର

As improbable and unexpected as it was, the conversation with Tom Costello that night on an Appalachian Trail ridge dramatically altered the course of Jake's life. He was convinced that if Tom could find inner peace by experiencing nature, then he would check it out. What followed was a change in lifestyle that began with day hikes in local areas, and culminated with Jake's first cross country road trip. First he went to New Hampshire on the east coast and climbed to the summit of Mount Washington on July 4th. Then, he drove across country to the giant Redwoods of the Pacific Coast of Northern California and Yosemite Valley. The transformation was nearly complete by the start of school in 1976. Jake was different, a changed man. He was introspective, less judgmental, more private than ever, and comfortable with his new persona. He finally found some contentment.

Along with the change of recreational pursuits, there came a renewal of energy and the search for a philosophy, one that turned him inward and beyond the basic survival mode he had been stuck in everyday of his life. After the first trip, he accepted the fact that his detached emotions and hollow feeling evolved from a built-in disconnect from people that provided security from hurt. It was all about hurt. He never disclosed his inner demons, the foolishness of unmet expectations and the resultant disappointments, but accepted the fact that they were real and part of who he was. He found that by taking to the mountains, hiking the trails and listening, he got closer to self enlightenment.

Jake needed a different perspective beyond being brainwashed with capitalism, pop-psychology, mass media, theology, or liberal politics. Slowly, his values shifted away from the culture of the American middle class which was once his ultimate goal. His fervent desire was to break free from his stagnant mindset and seek an identity that was in sync with the person he wanted to become, a man who could be at peace with himself and function in the work place without selling out his soul.

Jake turned his attention to an exploration of eastern philosophy and Taoist principles to alter his frame of reference. He stopped working the part-time job in home improvements and instead lived a more frugal existence. Time mattered to him more than ever. Free time was an opportunity to expand his self-knowledge. He began taking a karate class twice a week to further establish credibility to those who might question his dedication to change. He worked out hard at the dojo and exercised daily in his apartment. He took long walks on frigid nights, not to clear his head but to test his will power. He searched for insight along the beaches of the Jersey Shore like a child looks for starfish and shells. As much as he could he hiked the Appalachian Trail. He read best sellers: *Centennial, Roots, and Shogun.* He lived vicariously inside the main character "Blackthorne" from Clavell's blockbuster novel. He read the classic western paperbacks of Louis L'amour and the journals of Lewis and Clark. He also read *Bury My Heart at Wounded Knee* and found an interest in the Native American experience.

By the end of 1976, the bi-centennial year, he had succeeded and changed into a person he accepted and liked. The new model Jake Carr was nothing like the child, adolescent, or college student. He didn't wake up every morning worrying about money, or finding someone to share his bed with. He learned the basic Taoist principle: "If happiness is in your destiny, you need not be in a hurry."

After a year of dynamic change, Jake made a pledge to himself that he would never curse the choice he made. And, regardless of what may happen, he wouldn't look back and embrace the unfulfilled expectations that had troubled him in his former life. He also let go of his anger that once had been the demon in his head.

Jake believed his renewal became a reality because he was willing to search for a new way to think about life, thus separating from the post-Vietnam social cynicism and widespread materialism that was polluting society. His chance meeting with Tom Costello in the fall of 1975 and the conversation on the Appalachian Trail proved to be the catalyst for change. Indeed, as the Tao teaches, "When the student is ready, the teacher appears." In his case, Costello happened to be the teacher. The wisdom of the Tao taught him more about himself in a period of nine months of reading and reflecting than his entire graduate coursework in counseling. He accepted the mystery of nature and the profound simplicity and beauty that was within the forest and the mountains. At a point in his life when he should have been satisfied with his progress and looking ahead to a career of helping kids as a counselor, he was sufficiently aware of his changing attitude that he decided against making the move.

In Jake's point of view, the Masters degree in counseling did not qualify him for the job and regardless of the opportunities available, he would wait. He truly believed in the Taoist wisdom that said, *Understanding comes with the realization of the true self, and realization of the true self comes to those who have gained understanding.* He continued his personal journey toward self-knowledge and discovered he was able to make good choices because he finally stopped looking for acceptance and approval from outside sources. He became consumed by his desire to explore the natural world around him. A Taoist proverb which affixed its meaning to him was, *He who knows others is wise, but he who knows himself is enlightened.* Enlightenment took time and it took patience. But it also had to be faced without fear of the consequences of change.

Herman Hesse's masterpiece *Siddhartha* had a powerful impact on his thinking. Although it took place out of the western cultural experience, Jake loved the story and the wisdom it offered. Like the main character, he wanted to learn how *"to think, fast, and wait."* Lastly, Jake came to understand and accept the principle of karma as a determining factor in one's fate.

❧

After hiking to Sunfish Pond, Jake returned to the trailhead by late afternoon. The elation he felt from of his son's college acceptance and his remembrance of the road he traveled half a lifetime ago, gave him a feeling of both joy and sorrow; joy for his son's accomplishment and sorrow for having compromised in order to pursue the American Dream.

His life was in a state of dynamic change. J.D. would be leaving for college and Annie was on her way out in another year. Time was passing by and once again he felt confused and ambivalent about the future. Many years ago Tom Costello had pointed the way for him. Now Jake understood that he'd have to find the path alone.

CHAPTER 8

Annie's SAT results came exactly a week after J.D.'s acceptance to Vermont Tech. Jake was flabbergasted to put it mildly. His daughter scored an incredible 700 in verbal, along with a respectable 570 in math. Being closely involved with advising high school students regarding appropriate college choices, Jake knew Annie's SATs, along with her 4.0 G.P.A. and top ten-percent class ranking, would qualify her for admission to some very prestigious schools. However, it also meant that paying the tuition costs for both kids at the same time was going to be a financial challenge.

Over the next four years, Jake would have to manage the home budget plus pay his children's college costs. He knew it would take financial discipline, but that was Jake's forte. When it came to managing money, he was like a company comptroller at long-range planning. During the past fifteen years, he'd put away whatever extra money he had in series EE government savings bonds. The kid's college fund was a combination of gifts, yearly income tax refunds and Sandy's contributions. At present, the cash value was $70K but still not enough to cover the private colleges that Annie would be interested in attending.

When Jake picked Annie up after work that night, he showered her with praise even before she got her seat belt buckled. Handing over the SAT score card, he declared, "Your eyes aren't deceiving you. That score reads 1270. Honestly, I've got to confess that I didn't expect it. Forgive me. You certainly kicked butt on that test. Guess I should've had more faith in you. Sorry. Can you give me a hug?"

Annie turned, hesitated for second, and then leaned over and surrendered to his request.

"After I opened that letter at the curb…well, I just stood there frozen. I tried to think of what it must have meant to you. Then I went into overload. I wasn't a counselor handling the news. I was a father."

If Annie was surprised with what she heard she didn't let on and acted like the whole thing was no big deal, similar to her brother's at the liquor store when Jake delivered the his good news.

"Ok Dad, you got your hug. Now let's go."

As Jake drove out of the store parking lot Annie asked him with a tinge of sarcasm, "Dad, what did you think? That I'd do less on the SATs…Huh? Didn't I follow your advice and take all those honor courses? Didn't I study every night? That much effort should've worked!"

"You're right, Annie. You really are. It's just that only a week ago your brother gets into Vermont Tech and now this terrific news. Now you've got braggin rights at your lunch table."

Annie didn't like the last comment so she poked him hard in the ribs and spoke in a serious tone. "Truthfully, Dad, I'm way past that competition crap. I'm sure you remember when it almost destroyed my health a couple of years ago, trying to keep up with ...whatever. I suppose you might think that way because of the way things are at Middletown High. It's not the same for me. I'm glad the testing is over. I can tell you're happy. Does Mom know the results?"

"Hell yeah! She's so proud of you that she already called Rachel to brag. Guess she couldn't help herself. When I left to go hiking she was still on the phone talking. Annie, this victory is yours. Savor the moment. I hope you're happy. You've always been my star. Have any plans for tonight?"

"Nothing really very exciting; a group of us are going over to Jenn's to play *Trivial Pursuit*. Jeff finally bought the new edition, and it's a lot of fun."

"Who's Jeff? Can I take you over to Jenn's? You need a ride?"

"Dad, you're silly. My new boyfriend's name is Jeff Mahoney, and he'll be picking me up later. Don't scare him with your powerful hand shake. Dad, I think you sometimes forget I'm not your little girl anymore, but thanks anyway."

With the Carr children receiving their news within the space of one week, Jake dared to think his home life might take a turn for the better; at least that's what he thought as he began an afternoon hike at Highland Lakes State Park. Since receiving Annie's score, Jake felt more confident about his children's future than ever before. He still had the college financing to figure out, but there was a distinct possibility that Sandy might be teaching full-time in the coming school year. That would mean a raise in her paycheck instead of the seven-tenth's sum she was now getting. And that would mean more money to invest in the savings bonds. Even so, Jake's vision for the future was unsettled.

The truth was that ever since his daughter's illness in 1996, and even prior to that, his relationship with Sandy had started deteriorating right after her parents died during the spring and winter of 1992. As Sandy's grief caused her to flounder in the role as wife and mother, Jake gradually withdrew and they stopped discussing the everyday things that make a marriage succeed. Gradually, they let go of the routines that had been permanent fixtures in their relationship since the beginning; foregoing personal interaction and spontaneous intimacy. Playful inferences that led to passion filled lovemaking became more and more infrequent. Both of them were guilty of physical and emotional negligence, and they knew it. Just as Sandy's parents succumbed to cancer and heart disease, their relationship was slowly expiring.

Primarily, Jake's perspective on her parent's death came partly from his Taoist sensitivities and his pragmatic approach to life. He reasoned that given their passing came after such a long life, Sandy's period of grief shouldn't have extended for so long. Foolishly, Jake gave Sandy his viewpoint on the first anniversary of her father's death. It only made things much worse. If Sandy had dismissed his eastern philosophical notion of mortality with silence, then that would have been tolerable. But the damn holding back unresolved issues collapsed at the Florida cemetery. When they were away from the kids, Sandy delivered a blistering indictment that hurt him deeply. As they walked away from the gravesite she stopped him in his tracks and scolded him with the full force of her pent up anger at his insensitivity regarding her grief.

"They weren't your parents! You didn't love them. You were never raised properly! Don't you think I know that? I've always known it! What do you know about the grief I've felt since my mom died? I miss them terribly. Don't you dare lecture me like I was one of your students thinking you can make it all better with your rationale explanations? You haven't done a thing for me since they died...you don't know how to help. That's what's wrong with you. And there's something else. Ever since your father died, I've never seen you mourn a single day. You talk about him, but it's always something funny that happened when you were a kid. And your mother...we'll let the facts speak for themselves. You mail her a check every month and take us to visit twice a year. But when you're at her apartment, you rarely ever talk to her. That leaves me with the job. I know you don't care about your relationship with her. Damn you Jake! Don't you see? I've come to realize that we're different, totally different in many ways. You'll never understand because you've never experienced the love and kindness my mother gave me. Never!"

Sandy's words burned right through Jake's soul but he didn't argue with her because all the statements she made were all true, except one. He thought about his father every day. It was a living memory, not about his dying but about his living. After her diatribe at the cemetery, Sandy didn't speak to him for the next couple of days. It was during the long drive back on Interstate 95, while everyone was asleep, that Jake knew things would never be the same.

Everything he knew about Sandy's parents had come first hand during dozens of visits to Florida. Indeed, they had lived the "good life," secure and comfortable on the sixth floor of a condo in a luxurious highrise in South Palm Beach. They enjoyed reasonably good health and loved the weather, the condo social life with its card games and socials. Money wasn't a problem for them; Sandy's dad had put away plenty by working as a freelance tax accountant in addition to his regular job as a state tax auditor. He invested in municipal bonds that paid tax free income every month in addition to a retirement check.

They were in their early eighties when they died, and to Jake's way of thinking they were very fortunate to have lived so well for so long. Not that they didn't deserve the fruits of their labor, but in Jake's opinion they had more than a fair share of good fortune. In contrast to Jake, Sandy considered their deaths being so close together a terrible tragedy. After a while, she came to believe Jake was indifferent to her grief and she was angry at him for not caring. Sadly, the seeds of discontent were sowed in '92 and, although she didn't bring it up again, she never forgave him.

Then, by the winter of '93, the force of teen parenting hit Sandy before she was emotionally equipped to handle the stress. The irony of it was that Jake had repeatedly warned her it was coming. The worst calamity came on the first day of summer vacation. J.D. broke his leg in a dirt bike crash along the old railroad tracks that ran through a quarry on the outskirts of East Walden. By J.D.'s own admission, it was a reckless act, and it put the family vacation plans into turmoil.

That event marked the beginning of the toughest years in parenting for both of them, but more so for Sandy. J.D. was in a leg cast for six weeks, and gave everyone constant grief with his whining about being immobile and not able to do any of the activities he had planned. J.D. was marooned, stuck in the family room watching the tube and playing video games.

Jake tried to explain to Sandy that this was the beginning of the greatest challenge in their marriage. He warned her, based on his knowledge of adolescents, that they would be subjected to enormous stress, primarily because of J.D.'s impulsive behaviors, along with the high standards Annie demanded from herself. With or without Sandy's help, Jake thought he could keep things under control. He was mistaken; it was too much for one parent to handle and they separated their parenting responsibilities.

To keep busy and distracted from family stress, Jake began an exhaustive and expensive construction project. He was going to finish the basement and began using every spare moment and extra dollar to build a set of rooms that would occupy almost one thousand square feet of empty space. Jake made no pretense to disguise his intentions. He wanted a place for them to secure some peace. Sandy would get a third of the open space for her sewing table and exercise machine. He would take a corner for a recliner, TV, and end table; a sanctuary away from the wild bunch. Finally, J.D. would have his own workshop area with extensive shelf space and a workbench. Annie loved the privacy of her bedroom so she didn't figure into the floor plan. Sandy thought the project was a terrific idea without realizing how much time it would take to complete.

As it happened, Jake spent all of his extra time working on the project, except for interruptions on weekends for golf and hiking. The remodeling furthered the distance between them. He and Sandy lived like strangers. It was as if the "Law of Unintended Consequences" took over. If the kids noticed the marital problems of their parents, neither of them mentioned it to their parents. They were emerging from early adolescence and were consumed with meeting their own needs.

However, Jake was determined to complete the project before his son entered high school, and once he started there was no stopping him. True to his word, the carpet was installed in September of '95. Thereafter, Jake didn't spend much time upstairs. His exclusive domain was the basement apartment. The fact that he separated from his family for extended periods bothered him in the beginning, but he soon realized it was essential for his mental health. He still did all the chores, made meals, maintained the home, paid the bills, and shared family time at the dinner table. But when the kids started to argue or when Sandy "lost it," he knew the escape route was under the main floor.

During that first year, Sandy would visit Jake while he was watching sports events or following the Clinton fiasco on cable news. Just like a Special Forces soldier on a recon mission, she would report the situation on the upstairs battlefield and wait for Jake, the commander, to act on her intelligence data and make recommendations. When she'd visit, Jake would stop what he was doing, listen to her, and do whatever she asked. The situation, though strained at times, was generally acceptable to each of them for the better part of two years. In actuality, they simply got used to it. Their date night was still Saturday, same as always. Then they went out for dinner, rented a movie or went to the local cinema.

On Sunday mornings, after doing the food shopping, Jake usually took Sandy for a walk at a local park before leaving to meet up with his buddy, Kevin, for an afternoon of golf. Outwardly, they still appeared connected. The routines were there, but the fire was slowly dying out. The spontaneity and enjoyment of their earlier years was greatly diminished. In the aftermath of Annie's illness there was little emotional reserve left to rescue the marriage. Their careers became their excuse for failure to connect and share their unmet needs. Sandy tried in her own way to regenerate the marriage, but admittedly she was ill-equipped to communicate effectively in such stressful condition.

However, on the last family road trip to the Rockies in the summer of 1997, a trip specifically planned for the purpose of restoring Annie's health, both Sandy and Jake were unable to rejuvenate their relationship. During the three week camping vacation, they thought they managed to camouflage their problem, but the kids began to realize something was wrong. The romantic love and adventurous spirit they had once enjoyed dwindled down into a mere companionship of two middle-aged parents staying together for the purpose of raising their teenage children. They tried to keep the marriage afloat and agreed it was a noble thing to do, but the past five years had taken the heart out of Jake and the patience out of Sandy. Now, in the spring of 1999, their kids would soon be leaving for college. Would they have enough faith left to continue the marriage?

About an hour into the hike, Jake paused for a short break to get a view of the surrounding hills. It was quiet. He closed his eyes for a moment and let his mind escape to faraway places that had special meaning to him. It was nothing unusual for him to do; he did it on his walks with Missy, in the basement watching baseball, and sometimes in his last waking moments before falling asleep. Frequently, while out on the trail, he'd daydream about hiking through various mountain ranges, creek-side camping sites in far away places, and the awesome grandeur of the Big Horns and Tetons in Wyoming and the Salmon River Wilderness in Central Idaho. But today, long-standing, unresolved conflicts leaked into his head. Lately, Jake didn't know what he was feeling for Sandy anymore. Six years ago his love for her had been unconditional, passionate, and unselfish. Now he was just going through the motions.

Jake wasn't indifferent to her needs. Quite the contrary, he was well aware of her fragile emotional state, but he was beginning to believe his commitment was based on responsibility and not on love. It was about doing the right thing like his father would have done. For the time being, he understood his place was to remain where he was and deal with it. Throughout his years as a counselor, he was well aware of husbands and wives who were doing the same thing, living in denial and coping with it. They were doing the best for the family, sacrificing their own needs. Why should his life be any different?

By the end of the hike he resolved to maintain the outward appearance of a stable marriage and treat Sandy with kindness.

Moreover, he would enjoy the small pleasures whenever they came along. For some inexplicable reason during the drive back to Walden, Jake's thoughts drifted back to his childhood. He wasn't hung-up or obsessed with his past because dwelling on it was contradictory to his Eastern philosophy. And, as Tom Costello had advised him, he had let go of his anger to be free.

❧

Jake grew up in a working-class family near Elizabeth, New Jersey. There wasn't much to go around during his childhood years, not materially nor emotionally. Jake was one of six kids and was twelve when the last one arrived. Somehow he learned early on how to look out for himself and see to his own needs. Many years later, he learned from his brothers that they thought he was born with a low maintenance gene; at least that's how it appeared to them during childhood.

On the outside, he was resourceful, out-going, independent, and tough. Within, he was gifted with a keen sense of self-awareness and the ability to observe and reflect on things beyond the scope of other kids. He was self-reliant and tried to face his fears with courage to maintain the appearance of self-confidence. He knew he was different because he was tenacious in every possible way, consistently holding on to his determination to act like a man at all times.

Jake wasn't that unusual from the other kids in the neighborhood. He loved walking in the county park, tossing rocks across lake, pelting tree trunks with crab apples and spying on couples necking on blankets in the meadow. He loved climbing the ramparts of the old stadium and standing on the highest bleacher, pretending to lay claim to his domain. He spent countless hours at the local playground, pitching baseball cards closest to the wall with an opponent, playing stickball till dark, sitting perched on the top of the monkey bars taking in the flow of traffic and waving to truckers, hanging out on the fire escape occasionally and spitting at selected targets on the ground below. He loved sharing tall tales with his pals about where he planned to live when he left home.

He also led treasure expeditions to construction sites, auto junkyards, and the Penn Central railroad station in search of discarded or forgotten deposit bottles or anything else that had cash value. Being able to take four or five bottles to the local candy store and cash them in for a dime meant he could savor a delicacy like Drake's chocolate cupcakes or quench his thirst on a frozen mug of Hine's Rootbeer. Every so often, if he located a large cache of nickel deposit soda bottles and cashed them in for more than a quarter, he'd hide the spare nickels in the corner of his bunk and go to sleep that night knowing there'd be another treat for tomorrow. Nothing pleased him more than that.

From the start of attending a Catholic elementary school, he took pride in his own individuality and resourcefulness. As a student in crowded classes of over sixty or more for the first six grades of his education, Jake somehow managed to learn the basics, in spite of his mind continuously wandering to other places while waiting for the 3 o'clock dismissal. He got his B's in most subjects to keep out of trouble at home. Learning wasn't fun and the old nuns didn't make it any different. The day was filled with never ending commands. "Read the chapter and answer the questions in the back of your copybook. Do the spelling words ten times each and use the Palmer writing method. We're collecting for the Bishop's relief fund Friday. Remember to bring in your donation. No talking. No running. Not now."

Whether Jake knew what he was doing in class didn't matter, because he wouldn't give the nuns the satisfaction of knowing he was lost or didn't understand. He'd find out the answer from a classmate or sweet talk the smartest girl in the class. The nuns always had their favorites who were usually the shy girls who feared them or the goofy kid with the extra cash who always donated to one of the charities.

Jake thought the nuns were nothing but overseers, partly from his two older brothers but also because personal experience made him aware that every kid was under their total domination. Neither the kids nor their parents rebelled against the way things were done, probably because they went through the same regimen. It seemed to Jake that nobody ever checked up on the quality of the nuns teaching skills or the fairness of their arbitrary decisions regarding discipline. Strict obedience was the order of the day.

Jake understood that the school kingdom was theirs. When you entered through the big gray double doors you knew your life was under a strict set of rules and their total control. Young Jake tried to make it through each day without a detention or a thrashing. That was his definition of a good day. Nevertheless, Jake made every effort to try and beat them once in a while. He thought putting something over on a nun was like counting coupe for an Indian brave against the enemy. Consequently, he got his share of corporal punishment for talking in class, fooling around in the lunchroom, passing notes, drawing tanks and machine guns, and for not paying attention during prayers. But most of all for trying to be brave when they wanted him to break. If the other kid got slapped and started to cry, he'd hold fast and let them have their way with him. Taking another slap was a heroic deed in Jake's mind.

It wasn't until he reached eighth grade that he finally caught a break with Sister Genevieve. For whatever reason, she liked him and he responded in kind. For once in his life, he was given the feeling of acceptance and even notoriety by the sister. She sat him up near the front desk and sent him on countless errands around the school. She gave him spelling papers to mark and even left him in charge of maintaining discipline a couple of times. At the end of the year, she presented him with an Honor Roll Certificate, and Jake left that parochial prison feeling as though at least one nun respected him.

Young Jake was daring and adventurous, constantly encouraging other kids to follow him on his exploits to "dangerous" places where there were woods to explore. He loved to read stories about heroic figures like Davy Crockett, Daniel Boone, Jim Bridger, and Wyatt Earp. He particularly admired fictional characters like Robin Hood, Tarzan, and Lancelot, and of course the famous explorers, Lewis and Clark. He was fascinated by stories of the Crusades and the Vikings. Charging the enemy with a garbage can lid as a shield and a broomstick as a spear, Jake slew many an imaginary villain to save the king, win the hand of the princess, and gain admiration of the townspeople.

He watched westerns and World War II movies sitting inside a cardboard box with his eyes riveted to the seventeen-inch black and white Sylvania TV on the porch. And, just like every other kid in America, he dreamed of becoming a Mousekateer and living in California. He watched the *Mickey Mouse Club* like it was a religious revival meeting and shared many hours of laughter with his brothers watching *The Three Stooges, Abbott and Costello, the Eastside Kids,* and *Laurel and Hardy.*

Jake's brother Joe was two years older, his constant TV companion and attic bunkmate. Joe wasn't much of a playmate for Jake and they never became close. They'd continually fight over the few privileges they had, like who could stay up late, sit by the window in the old fifty six Chevy on rides to visit the relatives, or pick out the Saturday morning TV shows. During their childhood they had dozens of battles over who was right, who was smarter, stronger, braver, or who could handle disappointment. Honor was always at stake and withstanding their father's corporal punishment without crying was an act of courage. Jake tried never to give Joe the satisfaction of seeing him "flinch" from a punch and he never allowed Joe to boss him around simply because he was older.

Jake rarely had friends over to play or have lunch at his house. In truth, there wasn't much to do there, either in the small yard or up in the attic where he shared a small room with his two older brothers. The Carr boys were short on toys of any kind other than a worn-out Monopoly game or a deck of cards. And without question, there certainly wasn't any extra food of the variety that he'd be proud enough to serve his buddies. He lived on peanut butter and jelly. If a friend invited him over for lunch and it was sliced baloney or liverwurst on *Wonder Bread* it was like eating a gourmet meal. When the relatives had a BBQ and served hamburgers, it was a rare treat. Luckily for Jake, most of his friends had mothers who liked the disheveled kid, so he was frequently fed at their table. When he was in their home, Jake was well-behaved, courteous, and grateful for their generosity. But later on when he walked home, it usually reinforced his feelings of being a have-not and he hated the fact that other kids lived better than he did.

Playing in creeks, wrestling with his buddies, climbing oak trees, building forts and pretending to escape from Indians or Japs were the things he loved to do. Playing war meant fierce battles with pea shooters and hand-to-hand combat with rubber knives. He was eight years old when little league started and sports became a reality. He gave it his best effort, but he had to teach himself how to catch by watching other kids play with their fathers. After a while, he was just as good as everyone else but no better, and he didn't like it one bit. Playing ball was something every kid did at that time, and no matter how many prayers Jake said to hit a game-winning home run, it never happened. Both his older brothers suffered the same fate and didn't get to feel like heroes either.

Jake wasn't close to his mother. Florence was of Scottish and German heritage, and that's not the best combination for a mother of a large family. She was poverty stricken during her childhood and never received a high school education. She was married at twenty-one and a homemaker from that day forward. Florence wasn't outwardly emotional nor did she demonstrate any affection to the three older boys, but she loved Jake's little sister Kathy, who the boys called "Katrina."

There were no hugs or kisses before the boys went to bed or if they banged their heads or fell and got bruised. Florence didn't do homework or read stories on the couch. She held back any outward demonstration of affection, except for her husband when he got home from work. And Florence was certainly not like one of those TV moms of the fifties, the ones who came into their kid's room and said, "Let me tuck you in." or "Do you need any help?" Even so, Jake didn't know any better. He respected her and loved her in his innocence, the way a dutiful child was supposed to do in a big Catholic family. As far as Jake knew he wasn't treated any better or worse than his older brothers.

Jake's mother was invisible to him throughout most of his childhood. She did the house cleaning, ironed shirts, watched afternoon soaps, and put dinner on the table every night at 5:30. If the boys were on time, they ate. If their adventures or companions kept them from being there, not only did they catch hell or a slap from the ole man, but if they were lucky they ate peanut butter for the second time in a row.

Sometimes Jake would take the punishment for being late if he knew he'd be "forced" to eat fried beef liver, barley soup, or creamed salmon and peas on white toast. He dreaded those meals and gagged on the taste of them. He sat many evenings at the table not able to get the meal down. Of course, that wasn't one of his civil rights and eventually he had to force the food in bit by little bit whenever his father ran out of patience and opened his belt buckle. Then Jake usually got the message and had to surrender his iron will. He'd dump ketchup on whatever he was eating and tried to swallow it without puking. Later, he'd secretly chow down two more PB&J sandwiches.

Typically, Jake preferred not to be home if he could help it. After school he'd change his clothes and bolt out. When he returned at the dinner curfew he'd wash up, eat with the family, clean off the table, do his homework and then watch TV. All evening television choices were his parents whenever they entered the porch. If they were busy doing other things, then countless skirmishes took place among the brothers over television rights and seating arrangements. The porch was the only place the boys were allowed to hang out other that the attic. The Carr living room was strictly off-limits, saved for relatives.

Number three son, as Jake always referred to himself, tried to stay out of trouble as much as possible. He did his chores and gave his parents little grief. Besides, there were no arguments with his parents. They weren't allowed. Jake was a kid among a bunch of kids. All cash handouts were in the exclusive domain of his father. He was the one who granted allowances on Saturday and decided if your sneakers were sufficiently worn to warrant four dollars for a new pair of high top black Keds.

Joe Carr ruled the clan in every way. If the children ever talked back or refused to do something, it meant possible "death." Not from Mom, who didn't dole out punishment, but from the "Lord of the Carrs." He'd find out about the bad behavior at 5:35, and when you caused unnecessary trouble, your punishment came after dinner when he finished his coffee. His wide belt delivered the pain. Fortunately, when it was over after five or six lashes, it was over. Whenever Jake had his turn he'd try to hold back the tears but usually failed. Afterwards, he'd crash in his attic bunk, pull the covers over his head, and resolve to stay out of trouble tomorrow. His brothers always left him alone.

Jake learned the best way to avoid getting the belt was to stay out of the house as much as possible, and above all, never talk back to Florence or she'd tell on you. So from the age of eight, he was likely to be outside most of the time, regardless of the season. Even when he was sick with a stomach ache or a cold, he took great pride in handling the pain and discomfort alone. His mother separated from him.

By the second grade, Jake came to understand that a connection with his father was the better choice. There was no gray area with him. He was black and white in his habits and beliefs. You always knew where you stood with him. Jake didn't have to be loving and sweet around him because giving his father obedience and respect was more important. To his credit, his father never held a grudge or made fun of him. He wasn't a teaser. And, he never knocked young Jake so far down that he couldn't get up. Nor did he drown Jake by preaching Christian values. To Jake, he was the sole provider of security and stability. He paid the bills and brought home the groceries. And when he had an extra dollar, he'd take the kids in and treat them to an ice cream cone without any reason for doing it.

During his childhood, it was obvious to Jake that his mother favored Kathy. Strangely, that was fine with him because he loved his little sister. Katrina was the crown jewel of the Carrs. She was smart, cute, obedient, huggable, and made her parents proud. Jake's older sister Barbara, the first born, was ten years past his age and out of the house and on her own before Jake ever got to know her.

Florence Carr was a deeply religious woman who observed the Roman Catholic faith. Therefore, the family had to obey religious traditions and rules. If she heard you swear, it meant soap in your mouth later that night. Jake figured that was how the church must have taught her to cleanse a child's sins. If you talked back, that was against one of the commandments and you had to be punished. Hence, the Carr kids were enrolled in a local Parochial school, discounting the fact that Harrison Public School was a block away with class sizes of thirty instead of sixty.

In spite of economic hardship, the Carrs got by. The kids survived because they didn't have a choice and didn't know any better, figuring that was the way most people lived. Little Jake accepted the situation without giving it much thought until he got older. Then he began to witness that some of his friends were way better off. That only made things worse, because then Jake started to wonder why.

Only Jake's older brother Skip, who was five years older, had the courage to ask for more; whether it was money for sporty clothes or an extra dollar to hang out with his buddies. Jake was ten years old when Skip entered public high school, and saw firsthand the battles that took place between his father and older brother. America was neurotic about the Soviet threat and Skip's generation gave its attention to Elvis, James

Dean, and customized cars. Skip wanted to embody the culture of the time. That's why he got more of the belt than Joe and Jake ever got. The church thought Elvis was evil. But Skip believed Mr. Presley was the man to emulate.

Joseph Carr managed to feed and put clothes on his kids but couldn't afford much more. That being the case, when Jake turned eleven and learned his mother was having another child it made no sense to him. Privately, he resented it deeply because he knew it meant there'd be even less to go around. Consequently, he pulled away from his mother and got closer to his little sister. He wanted to spoil Katrina because he figured she would be surrendering her place of honor with the birth of the baby.

Florence's unexpected pregnancy at the age of forty-two was a shock to the boys and even to the relatives. It brought Jake closer to his father than ever before. He began spending extra time with him knowing his status would shrink with the impending addition of another child. Joe Carr was larger than life to Jake, not because he was a WW II hero, educated, played baseball, or had any kind success. It was because Jake knew in his heart that his father was a decent and honorable man who kept his word. He never made promises he couldn't keep or ever bragged about himself or his kids. Nor was he a complainer who blamed others for his misfortunes. He was the consummate blue-collar working man.

To his credit, Joe Carr had a great sense of humor and was a superb story teller. On countless evenings, and always at the urging of little Jake, he would tell of his adventures traveling across the country with his buddy during the worst of the depression, mentioning various mountains, deserts, and noteworthy landmarks of the west. He'd take out an old metal cigar box full of black and white photos and talk about each one of them like they happened yesterday.

Jake and his brothers never forgot that whatever their father said was the law. Joe Carr had a temper that was not to be taken lightly and wouldn't permit his children to challenge his authority. He was the source of all pride for young Jake regardless of his dictatorial manner.

A good example of that duality was when Jake was six years old and practically cut his index finger off while using a kitchen knife to make a bow and arrow. Florence didn't know what to do, so when Joe Carr got home from work he had to take Jake to the emergency room with a blood soaked towel wrapped around the hand of his little son. An emergency room intern sewed it back on, saving the finger, but it took an hour. Joe Carr did his duty as a father but didn't have supper until 7. Riding back from Elizabeth General Hospital, Jake shed tears of shame in the car, not because of the pain in his finger but because he had caused his father trouble.

In the final analysis, the three brothers never asked for much affection from their parents. They knew their family wasn't like *Father Knows Best* and they had no expectation anything would change with the birth of the last child. Unselfishly, the three of them were content knowing that Katrina and the new baby would probably have a better life than they did. As their childhood passed by, not much of anything remained for the older boys to pursue with regard to an emotional connection to their parents. Instead, they each had girlfriends to focus their attention and energies on.

❧❧

Jake thought about his father frequently during that afternoon on the trail. He realized he still respected his father more than anyone he'd ever met. He remembered a man who never complained about anything except the welfare system, Republicans, the New York Giants, and not having a pension for security. That's why during the hike, Jake resolved to get through the bad times with Sandy. After all, why should he think he's got it tough compared to the sacrifices his father made providing for six children? He had a well paying professional job, a comfortable home, and no significant debt. His father had lived from paycheck to paycheck, budgeting every dollar. All of Joseph Carr's money was made with sweat in a non-union sheet metal factory for thirty-seven years.

His father was a quiet, uneducated, working man, physically worn out from backbreaking labor using grinders and polishers to spruce up all kinds of containers and machinery made of stainless steel in a small factory in Newark. He was the father of six children, with minimal financial resources, in reality only enough to cover half that number of kids. In Jake's opinion his dad was the epitome of character and virtue.

Jake instinctively knew that his dad demonstrated love everyday by going to that low paying factory job for thirty-seven years straight. And although Jake felt disappointed that the ultimate affirmation statement was never said directly to him, he accepted the simple fact that it just wasn't in the man to say it. When Jake was older, in his mid twenties, he finally came to accept his father and didn't need to forgive his dad for any sin of omission or anything else, actually respecting his father, probably more than any other of his sons. It happened that way because Jake believed his father was a good man, an honest man, who lived with the humility and moderation of a working man.

Tragically, Joe Carr died of industrial related liver cancer in late March of '79. The bad news came only two months after retiring at sixty-five. He lived another five years on a social security check of $440 per month. His longstanding dream of a decent retirement, relaxing on the front porch reading the Star-Ledger every morning with his coffee, and watching sports and variety shows on his new color TV was never to be.

Jake visited him often during those final years. They'd sit on the porch together and Jake would use his interviewing skills to get his dad to talk about his life. Joe Carr managed to survive five years after the diagnosis, with continually deteriorating health, considerable pain, and the awful embarrassment of needing a nurse. The disease stretched his retirement budget to the limit. He fought the cancer and cursed it privately with the certain knowledge that he would eventually lose the fight. And yet, Jake never heard him complain that his life was stolen from him.

All he ever wanted in retirement was to watch *All in the Family*, the *Giants* and *Yanks*, and eat Florence's Hungarian cooking.

Jake never believed it was in God's plan to "take" his father as the priest had said. His Toaist ways taught him that was nonsense, while his mother and two sisters fervently believed the opposite was true. They believed God "called" Joseph to his holy house because of their rock solid faith in Christianity, trusting that all the answers were in the interpretations of the Vatican. Jake never bought into any of it. In contrast, he believed that the gates of heaven were open to all good people who tried to make the world a better place by doing acts of loving kindness. Hence, Jake believed that God had nothing to do with his dad's bad karma getting cancer caused by lead and copper dust that slowly poisoned Joe's body. In medical terms, he was another victim of industrial pollution; just like a coal miner, asbestos worker, or any other blue collar factory employee whose body was exposed to cancerous substances all those years before OSHA and never knew it.

Joe Carr died peacefully in his own bed with Florence beside him. Jake wasn't there in the end, and no one questioned him about his whereabouts. In truth, he couldn't deal with the tragedy in front of his brothers and sisters. After he heard the news, he mourned in his own way by taking to the forest to remember the man he had loved and respected without ever hearing a single *I love you Jake* from his father's mouth.

A couple of days later, four adult sons carried the oak casket containing their father into a Catholic church in Brick, New Jersey. They sat in the front pew and heard a priest offer the family comfort by preaching, "Joseph is in heaven, and that is worth everything in the end. His suffering brought him to eternal peace with the creator."

After his father was laid to rest, Jake swore that he'd never wallow in self-pity or let the demons of depression take over his life. Truly, he knew he was his father's son and would try to be as noble as his father was. Probably without ever knowing it, his father had passed down the quality of inner strength, love for the road, and self-reliance. Joe Carr had shown by example that men must take full responsibility for the choices they make. It was a belief that was forged into Jake's consciousness early on and would remain there for the rest of his life.

It had turned out to be a soul-searching afternoon for Jake. For some reason, the recent success of his children brought him back to remembering his boyhood and the memory of his father's legacy.

CHAPTER 9

The third and final parenting workshop was tonight. During the previous week, Ellen had read and reread Jake's handouts searching for answers about Danny's rebellious behavior. She had enjoyed the presentations because Jake delivered them in an informative and entertaining manner. She also looked forward to the group exchanges because after hearing the personal stories of other women she felt less blame regardless of what Guy had told her. Moreover, he didn't believe her whenever she tried to explain Danny's problems during the nightly phone calls or monthly visits.

Unlike many other parents who remembered their own lack of communication with their parents, rebellion against authority, and reckless behavior, it was difficult for Ellen to identify with because her high school years were under the direct control of parents who demanded and received obedience. Looking back, Ellen realized that by the age of fifteen, she was still very submissive to them. She also remembered how guilt ridden she felt whenever she displeased them or did anything wrong.

In retrospect, she knew she never participated in any activity which would get her in trouble or cause her parents to think she was a "bad" girl. She didn't drink her first can of beer until junior year on a ski trip to Colorado. She never tried marijuana and remained a virgin until her senior year. She was a terrific student and was inducted into the National Honor Society. Nevertheless, she had listened attentively during Jake's workshop and tried to relate to Danny's world.

At 7:15 Jake began his final presentation to the group. Unlike the previous nights, he didn't make any effort to entertain as he began.

"I really appreciate the commitment that each of you has made in coming here for the third straight Thursday evening. God knows we've all got other things we could be doing. Tonight I'm going to give you some insights into your parenting with the sincere desire of helping you to break some incorrect attitudes that may be impacting your family. I'm going to the heart of the problem; try to hang in there even if it's uncomfortable. Take notes. Ask questions. And please be honest with yourselves."

Over the next hour, Jake laid bare the core problems occurring within the Eastman family and others in the audience. His tone was serious and the delivery was rapid fire. In the beginning, a few general issues were reviewed from the previous nights, and then it became a soul-searching experience. Like everyone else, Ellen listened intently as some topics hit her harder than others.

Jake discussed "Why families are in conflict with their kids," "Parental Power–Its Use and Misuse," and finally "Marital Stress in Adolescent Parenting." There was a sense of urgency in everything he shared with the parents, along with a depth of conviction that sounded like a prayer for world peace at a college demonstration. Ellen felt fortunate to witness his performance, surmising that Jake's counseling and personal experiences had to be dictating the nature of his commitment.

At her table, Ellen sensed there was a collective feeling of discomfort among the group whenever Jake ventured into the areas of parental expectations and marital stress created during adolescent parenting. He asked parents to explore their motivations.

"All of you listen to me. I'll give you a moment to reflect on each thing I say. In fact, I'll tell you what… if any of you want to stop me right on the spot, go ahead. But please think. I'm going to admit something to all of you. I'm no different in my struggles as a father and husband. So please put aside your notions that I'm any more equipped than you are. Both my kids went through one hell of a time during the past few years. I want you to be aware of who you are and what makes you the type of parent you are. Ok…try these questions: What do you expect from your kids and why? Are the expectations reasonable or not? Is your child capable of achieving them? Stop and think about some of these examples. They might illustrate what I'm trying to teaching you."

Jake strolled around the tables while he spoke, staring at every face.

"Is it fair to demand speed and agility from a kid who doesn't possess the physical attributes to run fast or jump over hurdles? Do you demand high achievement in algebra or geometry when a student clearly has demonstrated through standardized testing and poor performance that math concepts and abstract thinking are fundamentally a struggle? Do you tell them if they only tried harder, they'd succeed?

"Do you think just because you could master the piano, trumpet, or violin it is fair to assume your daughter or son should be as talented as you were? What about ballet or art? Do you really think that because you loved to read and write original short stories that your kids will follow the same path? What makes you think it's axiomatic? Do you think popularity will come by forcing them to join student government, join the newspaper, help on the yearbook, or by waving a flag for the color guard?

"Oh, one more thing. For all you psych 101 grads, do you side with the nature or nurture advocates? Please jump in any time with your disposition regarding that ongoing conundrum. I know…you gave your kids everything you didn't have because you thought it was giving them an advantage. Isn't that right? I confess. I did the same. And just like you, I thought that they'd be so grateful. But sometimes it doesn't turn out right?"

Jake knew he was stirring the coals on a blazing fire of self-doubt. The more he went on, the more Ellen became aware of her son's academic and personal shortcomings. It all made sense. Jake had said that some parents didn't allow for any difference in their offspring. She realized that Guy brought up unmet expectations all the time, scolding her, instead of reprimanding the boys and disciplining them. Guy's answer to everything was to offer a bribe. Now she knew it was a major mistake. Danny was spoiled and Guy blamed her for his laziness instead of holding him responsible. She remembered what Guy had told her the other night. "The boys have to do better in school. **Why aren't you seeing to it? I give them everything. They should be getting A's like I did when I was in school. Ellen, you're failing them!"**

As Jake continued, she began thinking, *Maybe it's not all Danny's fault? I don't know for sure anymore. Is it that he can't or that he won't change? Is it possible that his poor grades are part of a learning problem? No matter how many times I ask, he'll never admit it. Maybe because he knows his dad's a smart man and he thinks he should be too. They've been battling over homework and grades, ever since elementary school. Danny acts like he doesn't care and won't do anything to change, even with threats. That can't be right. Jake told us that kids never start out wanting to be failures. So why doesn't my son care about his future?* She wasn't sure about her conclusions, but she was definitely going to learn more about ability testing. Maybe the boy had a disability.

Jake continued giving more examples. Chastising all those athletic dads and gymnastic moms who expected their kids to play team sports and thrive on competition. He talked about "traditionalists" who were raised to be obedient, honest, truthful, and respectful of authority and demanded the same behavior from their kids, and wouldn't tolerate any deviation. Again and again, the same message came across, often with his voice literally commanding them to evaluate their motivation with regard to setting attainable goals and having some tolerance for differences, essentially to rethink parenting.

He suggested that they try to understand the following: "Just remember this particular piece of the puzzle. If your expectations are a continuing source of conflict with your child, it's probably because your demand may be unrealistic, restrictive, or totally biased. Everyone in this room has similar hopes and dreams for their children and the desire to see their children be more successful than they are. We want our kids to be intelligent and to turn out to be fully-functional, well adjusted individuals who contribute to society, people who are givers...not takers. We expect this outcome because we need to believe that we're giving them our best...plenty of wisdom along with the correct guidance and support. We must believe that we know best! That we are superior role-models of virtue and responsibility."

Then he sounded like an evangelical preacher telling his audience, "It's a complete mystery to me how parents with cynical attitudes because of their memories of a toxic childhood can't leave their crap in the attic, stored away and out of sight. I can't tolerate parents with prejudicial viewpoints, and who for whatever reason, simply lack compassion. Do you really believe these kids are stepping into a great society of justice, opportunity, and promise? I don't know. You all should learn to use common sense and exhibit patience and strategic thinking skills. How can you honestly expect kids to turn out to be fully functional adolescents if you're not a fully-functional adult? I've come to believe that some parents need to go on a retreat or something of that nature to do a complete self-examination or self-exorcism. Ask yourself this. Do you generally demonstrate optimism, friendliness, cooperative behavior, intellectual curiosity, integrity, and responsibility to your family? Just think about this for a moment. Is your love and support for your child conditional?

"I want each of you to consider these things over the next few days. See if you ought to rethink your expectations. Maybe there's room for adjustment. Maybe you need a major overhaul. If you have the guts and the courage, sit down with your spouse and find out how close or how far apart you are with regard to what's fair to demand, not only from the kids but from each other. Honestly, it's the best advice I can give you. It's gonna hurt and you might get stuck in the blame game. For God's sake, don't go there.

"Remember, you're losing control a little at a time. Now...right now, it's finally time to influence your children with thoughtful discussions and a willingness to accept your child as a unique individual, not a copy of what you desire. Remember, each of us determines our own destiny. We're responsible for what we become, not our parents. If your folks messed up in some way, eventually you've got to put it behind you. Listen, try to forgive foolishness. It's an ingrained trait of youth. And remember this. If you only give love, it's not enough. You mustn't abdicate the responsibility to teach your kids to make good decisions and learn from the pain of their mistakes.

"Finally, you have to accept that the goal of adolescence is independence. As Kahil Gibran wrote, '*Let your children be as arrows and you the bow.*' You fought for your independence, and so will your kids! Accept that conflict with parental authority is part of the normal development of teenagers. Expect to argue about values, clothes, music, choosing friends, or the definition of doing what's right. You're standing on firm ground, but only if you are modeling the behavior you expect. Now, let's take a break."

When Jake finished there was dead silence. Then he made an unexpected announcement. "One moment please. For those individuals who are willing to participate in a three-hour group session to gain a deeper insight into the motivations behind their parenting methods, eight of you may join me next week. Give me your name and phone number if you're interested. Please return promptly in ten minutes."

When he finished, Ellen heard the woman sitting opposite of her declare, "I can't imagine what it would be like to be in a small group with him, but I'm not afraid to try." Then she turned to Ellen and said, "Ellen, you seemed to be into tonight's presentation. What do you think?"

Caught by surprise, Ellen nevertheless replied candidly, "I would never underestimate this man in any endeavor he puts his efforts into. I'm so impressed with his knowledge, but more so with his candor. He's...he's different. He's believable. In any case, he's not what I thought a school counselor would be like, at least not from my experience as a student. It's a very intriguing proposal. I might do it."

Spurned on by Ellen's appraisal, the woman got up and made her way toward Jake, apparently getting a jump on the others in order to sign up for the group. Ellen knew without the slightest doubt it was important for her to take a chance and also join.

She quickly got up and stood behind three other people. When they finished, she moved directly in front of Jake and made her request. "Jake, I'd like to join your group. I'm in a confused state of mind. Is there still room?"

Pausing, with his hands crossed on his chest, he replied, "Of course there's room for you. You're the fourth person to volunteer. Another thing, most of us are confused when it comes to figuring out our kids...me included. I wish you could witness some of the maneuvering I have to do to keep the peace."

"That's great. I've enjoyed this experience so much. I'll be here next Thursday...Thanks!"

He offered his hand in gratitude for the compliment saying, "You'll be getting a call from me next week. I appreciated the comment."

Ellen walked out the door leading to the corridor. Near the water fountain two women who sat at her group table asked her to go for a drink after the program. It was a gracious invitation and a chance to possibly make a new friend. Yet, right at that moment she wasn't sure if she should leave the boys unsupervised that long on a school night. She thought if she accepted the invitation, and stayed out past 11, it would be pushing her luck. Also, the probability that Guy might call prevented her from taking the chance. He would have a fit, and she figured it wasn't worth the aggravation.

"I'm sorry but my boys are home alone, and I must get back after the seminar ends. I'll take you up on the invitation next week, that is if either of you are going to be there."

"I'll be there for sure," said Linda, a tall blond woman in her forties. So Ellen made plans to have a drink with her the following week.

The final topic of the seminar was about marital stress during adolescent parenting. As a rule, Jake knew most people didn't want to share much about that issue in public.

As Jake began his talk, Ellen considered the current situation with Danny. She wondered why the boys were continually bribed by their father as the mechanism to get them to cooperate. It didn't matter if it was doing a simple chore or a major project around the house. Guy thought it was the way to get them to obey. Ellen shuddered with disappointment knowing that she had gone along with her husband's philosophy. Ellen now realized there were mistakes in her parenting as well as in Guy's which contributed to Dan's negative attitude and defiant behavior.

In the past few months Danny had demonstrated a total lack of self-control whenever Guy was away. If Ellen wasn't present, anything could happen. Occasionally, she could reason with him to get his assignments done on time or abide by his weekend curfew time. But that was the exception and not the rule. Usually, she took the heat to avoid the unpredictable tempers of her husband and Danny whenever they engaged in a verbal battle of wills. Frequently it became physical whenever her son challenged Guy's authority. Then Guy would "snap" and Ellen would try to keep them from hurting each other.

Tonight, she realized that from the start of Danny's preschool, there was never a unified effort in raising him. They approached parenting from completely different perspectives. There was no collaboration in the task. Hence, they were never partners. Guy issued expectations for Ellen as much as for Danny. Nothing she ever said or did convinced her husband to trust her mothering instincts. He was pompous, domineering, and always righteous. It was always his way or no way. Now, after spending nine hours listening to Jake and the other parent, she arrived at one conclusion. Changes had to be made in the coming month or things would get much worse for her. Guy had to start supporting and respecting her.

In the final half hour of the program Jake told them to rate their marriage stress level in ten specific areas of potential conflict. The activity had to be done privately and Jake explained each issue in detail. Each person evaluated their level of stress: normative, frequent, or extreme. This was Ellen's assessment:

> *Conflicting parental expectations-EXTREME*
> *Unfair distribution of adolescent monitoring-EXTREME*
> *Unclear disciplinary philosophy-FREQUENT*
> *Inability to admit mistakes to each other-EXTREME*
> *Taking sides with kids and against each other-EXTREME*
> *Having unrealistic expectations of power-EXTREME*
> *Inability to discriminate major from minor incidents-FREQUENT*
> *Failure in being honest and sincere-EXTREME*
> *Telling the truth for better or worse-FREQUENT*
> *Withdrawal from parental role?-Guy's not there enough for me rate him. EXTREME*

After Ellen completed the self-knowledge checklist, the truth hit her hard. Her marriage was seriously flawed. What made it worse was the fact that for so many years she had deceived herself into thinking the children had to always come first. Sadly, she remembered a warning given to her by an office colleague several years ago. Danny was in pre-school at the time and Ellen had worked part time at an office. Occasionally during a lunch break she'd vent her frustrations about Guy's behavior. The other women's message was simple. "If you have serious doubts about this man, under no conditions have another child. Plan your escape. Don't be foolish and make it worse for yourself down the road. With two young children you'll be financially dependent and breaking free will be twice as hard."

The workshop ended at 10:15 pm. It was an exhausting evening for many of the participants. Everyone appeared to be in a somber mood. As they walked out, Jake stood by the doorway and wished them well. When Ellen came up to say goodbye, Jake took her hand and whispered, "I sincerely hope this was worthwhile for you. You've got a lot to think about. Believe me, you're not alone. Try never to lose sight of that. I'm glad you came. I guess I'll see you next week. Good night and good luck."

Later that night, nestled in a corner of the couch with a glass of wine and the company of a single lit candle, Ellen recognized that at the age of forty, she was lost and afraid. She felt a deep sense of regret for the years she had wasted, and knew more than ever before that she was guilty of personal neglect and self-deception. Truly, if not for the boys her life would be meaningless. Beyond being a mother, what else was she other than Guy's wife. Although she tried to read her latest romantic adventure novel she wasn't able suppress the heartache and disappointment that overwhelmed her. Tears of self-pity rolled down her cheeks and she was smothered in shame for making the choices she did over the past two decades.

CHAPTER 10

Jake slumped in his recliner as the game went into the top of the ninth with the Yankees ahead by a run. Armed with his remote to escape commercials between innings, Jake intermittently watched the Yankees and cable news. Adjacent to his LazyBoy was an end table piled high with an assortment of maps, AAA tour books, a couple of magazines, and a notebook. A couch was diagonally across from the twenty-seven inch TV, but Jake preferred using the recliner.

"That damn bullpen better keep the lead. I hate Boston. If they score off Rivera, then all the other diehard fans that are staying up late are assholes just like me. Shit it's almost eleven-thirty. Tomorrow I'm gonna pay for staying up so late."

Jake had been surveying his travel plans throughout the game. Absolutely nothing buoyed his spirits more than planning for his summer road trip. With every pitch distracting him for a brief second, his attention was like the intermittent movement of wiper blades. One moment his eyes were on the batter, the next moment their attention shifted to a location on a state map or tour guide.

With the long-awaited season of sunny days arriving in a couple of months, Jake would be leaving home for three weeks of road travel. The arrangement was mediated through a marriage counselor in the aftermath of Annie's battle with her eating disorder. It was a compromise between Jake and Sandy at a time when their relationship was faltering. A veteran female social worker who specialized in marriage therapy asked the identical question to each of them at the end of their fourth session.

"What do you want from your spouse?"

Luckily for Jake, Sandy had volunteered to answer first. "I want my husband to listen...listen to me and share his thoughts. I expect his support raising the children. I don't think that's unreasonable."

When the counselor looked at Jake to see if he would agree, he answered with a single nod of his head and one word. He said, "Ok." Then she put the same question to Jake and he answered, "I **need** some time on the road. I need to escape the stress of my job and responsibilities I have at home. In return, I'll make sure everything runs smoothly for the other forty-nine weeks, but I must have time off."

What happened next was a shock to Jake. The marriage counselor jumped right in and said to Sandy, "That seems fair to me." It was a stroke of good fortune for Jake. There wasn't much that Sandy could say in opposition, since she had picked the therapist. Consequently, that was how Jake took his first road trip back in 1998. At the time, things were so stressed that Sandy accepted the proposal. She wanted to keep the marriage afloat, in spite of the raising torrent of discontent that existed between her and Jake.

"Rivera, for Pete's sake, come on, strike that lousy Johnny Damon out...P-L-E-A-S-E!!!" With his next pitch, Rivera got Damon to fly out to center and the Yanks won the game. Jake shut the TV off and made his way upstairs. On some weeknights, he couldn't stay up till the end of a game and he'd have to turn in while Sandy might still be awake. He felt guilty about this avoidance behavior, but her sense of timing for crucial discussions was terrible. Jake preferred to have serious talks on their walks or whenever they were away from the house and kids. In contrast, Sandy generally waited until she was in a state of rage over something and then she would let it all out regardless of the time or place.

As he entered the kitchen, Jake saw Missy stretched out in her corner spot on an old rug. The stove light was the only illumination in the room. The house was quiet at this time of night. Rather than go to bed, Jake made his way to his oak desk in a corner of the living room and opened the bottom drawer. That's where he stored last year's road pictures. He didn't want an album of these memories stuck in a bookcase. In his mind, these shots were personal memories. They were reminders of the road.

Five or six years ago, pictures were routinely enjoyed because the Carr family adventure photos captured the happy times they had spent together. They were reviewed at the kitchen table for entertainment and reminiscing, and they covered every summer from 1984 until 1992. The kids loved to comment on them. But Sandy, for whatever reason, had ceased to use her artistic ability in creating new albums. The 1993 family trip pictures were stored in bunches with all the rest, including the summer 1997, which was their last family trip to Wyoming in the summer following Annie's recovery.

All those shots were in their original envelopes with elastic bands securing them. There were five separate picture stacks, each about six inches thick, all without a single notation. Jake had long since given up asking Sandy when the latest travel album would take its appropriate place in the cherry bookcase that housed the pictorial archives of the Carr family, along with the rest of the family memorabilia.

It seemed that every photograph of the past seven years, whether birthdays, holidays, family gathering, or any notable event were in storage. There were hundreds and hundreds of forgotten memories of people, places, and moments. Now they were relegated to a storage place under the lid of a mahogany end table.

Sitting at his desk with a bottle of Molson, Jake thoughtfully reviewed each picture of last year's trip with clear recollection, a shot in the late afternoon at Lake McConaughy in western Nebraska. Another of a young boy perched atop a huge boulder, the rock's profile resembling a dog's head. That one was taken at Rocky Mountain National Park at a place called the "Alluvial Fan." There were three shots of the sunset over the mountains near Estes Park, Colorado bursting with colors of powder blue and crimson orange, rising over the backdrop of black silhouetted peaks.

Jake loved looking at his road pictures and reserved the ritual for those special times when he needed to reconnect with his "other" world. The shots were not only reminders of the places he loved, but of the inner peace he felt being there. So he searched for one picture in particular. It was a shot taken in the Cloud Peak Wilderness Area of the Big Horn Mountains in north central Wyoming, of his name carved on the trunk of a majestic fir tree that had been shattered and scarred by lightning. The tree was on a trail ridge deep in the wilderness area. On seeing it for the first time, he was thunderstruck how that tree refused to die in spite of its severe wound and left his name.

After that experience, Jake came to accept his undeniable need to escape to the mountains in order to rejuvenate his spirit. Perhaps he wasn't ready to acknowledge that need until the moment when he saw that single tree with its charcoal black blemish, standing alone against the blue skyline on that rocky ridge. It was a visceral experience, symbolic of his life. With that awakening, he patiently carved his name, **J-A-K-E**. When he inspected his handiwork, he made a solemn pledge that he'd revisit the place again because he identified with the scarred tree that stood alone and survived in the wilderness.

He put the pictures back in the drawer, turned off the desk lamp, and quietly went upstairs. Sandy was asleep and breathing deeply. He didn't disturb her. His last waking thought was his campsite next to a roaring stream in the Big Horns, at a place called Sitting Bull. With a little more than two months remaining before his next adventure, he felt content. Tomorrow morning he had to be Jake the counselor and the family man and not Jake the pilgrim on a vision quest.

CHAPTER 11

"Hello Mrs. Mulford, this is Jake Carr from Middletown High School. Could you please tell Charles our meeting's tonight at seven. Thanks so much."

Jake's day was busy with regular interviews, student progress reports to review, and next year's master schedule that his supervisor wanted finalized. As if that wasn't enough, his thoughts were cluttered with the agenda for the group session. From past experience, Jake reminded the participants so everyone would show up. The people he called seemed enthusiastic and ready for the experience. When a spouse or someone else answered the phone, Jake merely passed on the information in a business-like manner. Ellen Eastman's number was next on his list.

"Good Morning! May I please speak with Ellen?"

"This is Ellen."

"Hi! This is Jake Carr from the Middletown High parenting workshop. Remember me? I'm the fella who interviewed you a while back. I'm calling to remind you about tonight."

Ellen needed no reminder. The problem was she didn't feel well. "How could I forget? A note is on the fridge and I've been using your handouts lately for daily reinforcement. I'm not sure about coming tonight. I'm not feeling well."

"Can't you take some medication? The group's all set and I really want you to participate. I know we haven't had much of an opportunity to talk since that first interview. But I enjoyed the exchange."

Ellen paused; she was surprised by his comment. "Mr. Carr....."

"Call me Jake. I hear Mr. Carr all day long around here."

"Well Jake, I'm sort of shy."

"I didn't get that impression from my interview."

"That's because you made it easy for me. I'm a good listener. The fact is...I really don't know what I could offer the others. I'm pretty shy. Maybe the group stuff won't work for me."

Jake wouldn't let her off so easily and said, "Ellen, I can assure you with utmost confidence that the experience will be worthwhile. You can trust me on that. Maybe you'll discover part of your hidden self. You know, the one that's been overshadowed by your parenting responsibilities. Then again, you might start a friendship with another member. You'll also have a chance to hear about life on the other side of the fence from people who have kept everything a secret for the sake of appearances. That's what Middletown has become. Besides, I remember you telling me you just returned. Who knows what you may learn spending an extended session in close proximity to parents struggling along just like you. Ms. Eastman, you know, you're really making me beg. Try and come. I can't ask for more than that."

Ellen was taken by his sincerity. It sounded like he really wanted her to be there, and in spite of her ailments, she felt it was impossible to refuse him. "Jake, I appreciate what you're saying. All right, you've convinced me."

"Ellen, that's great! Now try chicken soup and get some rest! See you tonight."

Ellen felt terrible; she knew it was her allergies. Encouraged by Jake's extra effort to convince her to come, she went from considering skipping the event to searching for the right medicine to dry up her nose and diminish her pounding headache. She decided to take Benadryl right away and crash for a couple of hours so she'd feel good enough to make it through the rest of the day. As sick as she felt, Jake's personal plea had an incredible impact on her willpower and she made the choice. She would attend.

That same evening, Jake sat down with Sandy for an early dinner without the kids. J.D.'s whereabouts were unknown, but an empty spot in the garage suggested he was riding his four-wheeler. Annie went directly to work after school and wouldn't get home until after nine. Sandy was going to pick her up.

They'd just finished eating when Sandy asked, "What's the group of parents like?

"A couple of years ago when I used to finish a workshop I handed out a rating sheet. Now I don't bother with that anymore. Based on the participation of this current bunch of parents and some of the comments they've made to me, I believe they like the program. You got to understand that there's more that goes on in their heads than ever comes out of their mouths. I mean it's not like someone is gonna admit they've screwed up and can't clean it up. Anyway, I really haven't paid to anyone in particular."

Sandy left it at that and turned Jake's attention to another topic. "Last night Annie told me that J.D. expressed no interest whatsoever in going to his senior prom or even project graduation. That makes no sense at all. Why doesn't he want to go? Do you know why? I want you to talk to him about it. Annie told me the bid must be purchased by May 8th. I really think he should go. I went! My parents went all out for me. Well…don't you agree with me?"

Jake hated having conversations like this one. He didn't disagree with anything his wife had said. She had a point. The boy should go, but as usual her timing was off. If J.D. was at the dinner table, then it would have been the appropriate time and place to discuss his reason for not wanting to go. Of course, that made sense to Jake so he shrugged his shoulders at her suggestion. But then she pressed on.

"Well Jake, what do you think? Are you going to talk to him?"

"All right, all right! I was just thinking about what you said. Now don't misunderstand me. Maybe you looked forward to your senior prom, like shopping for the perfect dress, spending the afternoon at the hair salon, your father taking pictures. I agree. It must have been...I'll use a word from the past...cool. And your right, celebrating your graduation from high school was also a big deal. Hey, maybe you got checks from relatives or went to a graduation BBQ in your honor. But that was the way you were thirty years ago. Our son isn't like that and frankly, neither was I. He's not your typical senior. Honestly, he's never been a kid who liked school functions, much less school-sponsored social events. I don't think he went to a single dance. So asking some girl to go with him plus renting a tuxedo and all that other razzle-dazzle that goes along with the prom...I guess it's just gonna be a hard sell. Anyway, that's my opinion."

Sandy, believing she knew best, shot right back. "Annie thinks she can get him a date, even on such short notice. Think how wonderful the evening would be for him."

Jake abruptly replied, "Oh boy, I don't believe this. Why can't you let the kids work things out for themselves? Stuff like this...believe me, we really should stay out of it."

"What about project graduation? I'll bet his friends are going!"

Jake didn't want to continue. It was going nowhere. Nevertheless, he gave in. "Ok, but this is it. I'll talk to him about project graduation, but not the prom. That's sticking my nose too far into his personal choices. You wanna talk with him that's fine with me. You satisfied?"

Sandy was. She had made her point and won half the battle. "Jake, can't you understand? I'm his mother and I don't want him to feel left out. That's all. He's been on the outside for the last four years. I want him to have memories...good memories like I have."

He didn't answer. He got up, thanked her for cleaning up and went to the bedroom to change clothes.

Jake knew no one in the universe could change J.D.'s mind once he'd made a decision about most things. J.D. wasn't a groupie. He had two good buddies, James and Matt. Sure, J.D. knew most of his senior classmates and had successfully established his own identity, given the fact that his Ford Ranger "monster truck" was well known to everyone at the school. J.D. was a motor cross racer and daredevil rider who wore garments to let the world know it. Most Friday nights he'd be with his two comrades. They'd bullshit, smoke cigarettes in the garage or rent an action movie. When he wasn't working at the liquor store he spent his time fixing vehicles. That was J.D.'s world.

Satisfied with his appearance, he went downstairs to say goodbye to Sandy and travel back to Middletown High School. After Sandy received a kiss, she asked Jake, "When will you be home? Should I wait up for you?"

Jake thought for a second and told her, "I figure around 10:30, but it's hard to say because usually somebody wants a final word on the way out. You know, they say something like, I didn't want to share this in front of the others but. That's happened at every seminar. Trust me. I don't need to be reminded that the alarm goes off at 5:15. You get your rest! Try to turn in by ten. Good bye."

He gave her another kiss on her cheek and left. He cursed bitterly as he had to carefully move around assorted greasy junk in the garage. "God damn that J.D. He's turning this garage into a friggin nightmare! This place resembles a toxic dump site!"

Opening up the van door, Jake fed an "Eagles" tape into the cassette slot and took off to make it to Middletown High on time. While the sounds of *Hotel California* played on, he sang along moving his head like he was sitting at a college mixer instead of preparing to facilitate a serious group encounter.

☜⊷☞

This was not an activity for the indecisive or weak at heart. When Jake asked a group member to reach inside and identify the strengths and weakness of their parenting, the demons from their past, or their greatest fears, he knew he was asking a lot. But he knew what he was doing. He had learned from personal experience and he believed anyone who knows a dime's worth of practical knowledge about the helping professions will tell you that some counselors have "it" and some are mere psycho-mechanics. Jake thought credentials meant nothing. You had to have intuitive skills, patience, and the courage to successfully lead a group. He also knew that counseling was not an exact science. Allowing a person, whether sixteen or forty-six, to feel safe enough to think out loud, and then listen to what others think about them is as challenging to a counselor as a multi-national corporate tax audit is to an IRS accountant. Lots of information is there but usually hidden under the weight of the load.

Jake was very much in tune with the self-discovery process. He believed self-awareness was crucial to self-knowledge and changing a mindset was the greatest challenge any person would ever face. The process only worked if someone helped to direct the search. Therefore, he was ready, willing, and capable of giving eight people the benefit of his extensive experience in dealing with the perils of parenting teens.

Above all, he wanted the parents to gain some insight that would be beneficial to them and to their families. Hopefully, the eight individuals would listen to each other during the next three hours and try to laser in on their own parenting weaknesses or individual blind spots. He also hoped that they'd wake up the next day with a resolve to adopt a better attitude and make the necessary behavioral adjustments. How much they'd be willing to share with the group would depend on what they chose to reveal. Would they have the courage needed to admit that they were going wrong?

Jake had lots of examples to give them, like the father with a red-hot temper who could scorch his son's spirit with complete immunity if he felt the boy disrespected him. The task for Jake would be trying to persuade a man like that to reflect on why he's so dictatorial and hostile and teach him to understand the consequences of his aggressive nature.

Was this challenging work? Always, but if a counselor had a fair measure of patience and could look beyond the natural defense mechanisms of his group, then he could facilitate change. He could teach mothers and fathers to re-evaluate their mindset and alter their course.

Jake had lived through several confrontations with his own son. Many were fueled by Sandy's insistence that he immediately "Do something." Usually whenever he lost it with J.D., he deeply regretted it later. It seemed always unnecessary when in hindsight he reviewed the battle. Of all the instances that Jake was commanded to "Do something," the first one occurred when he son was only three, and it foretold how future parenting with regard to disciplinary matters would go.

It was Halloween. J.D. was playing alone with his Tonka trucks in the finished basement playroom while Sandy was watching Annie upstairs doing the laundry. The three-year-old was left alone for no more than ten minutes. For whatever reason, little J.D. was inspired, probably by a *Curious George* story, to empty an entire gallon of liquid clothes detergent on the tile floor and then proceed to slide around in the suds, break-dancing and having the time of his life.

When Sandy returned, she had a fit. The cleanup was an immense job and took hours to complete. That was Jake's first experience with Sandy's way of turning discipline over to him and the first time he heard her scream, "Jake, do something!" On that day, justice was handed down to appease Mommy. Little J.D. was forced to surrender his Halloween trick or treat privilege. Jake couldn't persuade Sandy that mimicking *Curious George* might be the reason for his actions. She wanted J.D. punished.

Fortunately, during the past few years Jake developed a fail-safe mechanism, sort of like a trigger delay. Upon hearing about the latest incident he wouldn't take action until the appropriate time and not when Sandy demanded. He tried to be patient and "Stand Down" instead of making things worse. Waiting allowed him to be thoughtful. And being thoughtful was the essential ingredient of successful influence with children.

CHAPTER 12

Jake arrived at Middletown High before seven and attached a white cardboard sign to the front door. In dark blue felt marker it read "Workshop in Room 201." Then he proceeded to the classroom to prepare. The classroom was stuffy and uncomfortably warm. Cursing loudly, he opened every window half way and moved nine desks to form a circle. Surveying the scene and satisfied everything was set up correctly, he grabbed a piece of yellow chalk and printed the group rules in large letters on the chalkboard.

To gain the most from this group work please follow these rules:
1. *Only use the phrases, "I think," "I believe," "I feel."*
2. *Everything you share with the group should stay in this room.*
3. *Don't generalize - personalize.*
4. *Say what you mean, mean what you say, and say it to someone's face.*
5. *Within each of us there's a story waiting to be told. It's your call.*

With everything in place, Jake went to his office to pick up some notes, the roster of participants, and a quart of water he'd left in the office fridge. He used the restroom and then took a final check of his appearance. Staring at the face in the mirror, he breathed deeply three times and exclaimed. "Just do your best, your absolute best."

Jake was on his way to the classroom when two women turned into the corridor and walked towards him. They gave him a warm greeting before asking the inevitable question that always came up before group. Then, of course, they answered it themselves.

"Mr. Carr, to be honest with you, I'm a little nervous about this group thing and so is my friend. You're not going to force anything out of me…like something revealing. I know you wouldn't. I trust you. But, I've been taking your advice and keeping notes on my interactions with my family during this past week. Like you said, I did discover a few things from doing that exercise, some were pretty bad. The worst was that I'm really not the patient and considerate person I thought I was. Now I know it. I'm always yelling too much. Funny, I'm even a little anxious now. You know what? I'll guess I'll be ok."

Jake took her hand and reassured her that she was going to be fine. "Listen Beth, you're here because you're committed to making a change. That's the way it should be and nothing is going to be forced out of you. If you threw a dish at your son or kicked the sofa in the heat of battle...that's for you to share, if, and I mean if, you need to let it out. Believe me; we all share our humanity and frailty in the passion of our parenting. You're gonna be fine. In fact, we all are."

Within another five minutes everyone else arrived, and Jake reassured each person that it would be a worthwhile evening. When he saw Ellen he couldn't hold back his pleasure and bowed slightly like he was a commoner meeting a member of the royal family. Then he said in a teasing fashion, "I am so honored by your presence, Mrs. Eastman, and the fact that you've conquered an ailment to come."

Ellen wasn't embarrassed as much as she was amused, and she gave it right back to Jake. "Why Mr. Carr, if you hadn't personally called and asked... I wouldn't have come."

The other members of the group chuckled and then they waited for the action to commence. No one commented about the statements written on the chalkboard, so Jake did. "You're all here! Thank you so much for keeping your word. I'll bet you thought about this off and on for the past couple of days. That's pretty normal. So is having a feeling of apprehension about what we're gonna be doing. Everything will work out fine if you follow the rules on the board. So there they are, and there they'll stay. Are we clear? I don't expect you to know how to do what we're about to do. Trust me and you'll have a positive learning experience."

Ellen happened to end up sitting next to Jake. She wore bluejeans, a black turtleneck top, and navy blue blazer. The medication and rest had worked and the boys actually encouraged her to go, albeit she wasn't sure if her attention span was a hundred percent. Nevertheless, she was going to listen and learn how others were coping with life. She realized she'd be vulnerable if she opened up and gave an accurate picture of her present situation. Nevertheless, Ellen was ready for it.

"Life is difficult.' That's what's written on the first page of Scott Peck's book, *The Road Less Traveled*. Anyone wanna disagree? But is it more difficult in teen parenting? What do you think?"

And so the session began. First they gave their opinions on the statement and then they took turns in revealing what had changed regarding their kids after six hours of seminar training and three sessions of group process. The "icebreaker" exercise worked without them even knowing what was happening and they opened up without much urging. Jake directed the proceeding and then sat back and took it all in. He noticed that Ellen and a fellow named Charles seemed distant and uncomfortable, even though other people shared variations of communication problems that were going on in their families.

"For the first time in memory, I really made an effort to stop giving orders all the time. Like Jake told us, you can get addicted to that type of speech and I was. You know what I mean. I'm always threatening my kids. Maybe it's because I was raised like that. In fact, it was my mother who did it the most. I hated her for her arbitrary decisions concerning me. Now I realize, more than ever, I don't want to be that way. Recently I mentioned this to my closest friend. To my utter dismay, she said, 'What's the big deal? It's the nature of motherhood in this day and age.' I know in my heart she's dead wrong. This past week I noticed that everything got done without my continual barking. It was a refreshing change."

Jake appreciated her comment and was gratified when another woman agreed with her assessment, claiming that she also was brought up in a similar fashion. There were three men sitting in silence. Jake had no alternative but to pick one out in fairness to the women.

"Harry, I seem to remember you telling the group a couple of weeks ago that you were a control freak. Have you made any adjustment in the past couple of weeks, or are you still stuck?"

Startled by Jake's invitation to testify, Harry wouldn't respond to Jake's question. No one said a word. They waited, knowing full well that Harry would cave in to Jake's demand. "Harry, you've accepted the rules, isn't that right? Tell me, you gonna play fair or just sit there?"

Harry took the bait and gave it a shot, stumbling out of the gate. "I confess. I mean I'll admit. Ok...Ok...I can do this. Now I understand why my son doesn't talk to me or want to be in the same room with me. I suppose I'm a pain in the ass and not much fun to be around. Some days we've stopped talking altogether. We don't do anything except eat dinner together, but that's because he has no choice in the matter. My wife thinks it's because I can be obsessive and compulsive. Does that make any sense? Here's the truth. My god damn job has taken over my life. I hate admitting it. I've got to be a super efficient manager at the office and because I'm that way people who work under me probably can't stand me. I mean what the hell are they going to say? But with my family...for Pete's sake, I can't believe it. I'm an asshole for being the same way, trying to get the house and kids to function like my department. What's worse is that I'm keeping a running score on my son's ability to handle his life. Imagine that? Now I realize that's not fair. He's only fifteen. Frankly, I don't see how this got so out of control. I'm scared about what's going to happen next."

Jake believed that Harry was giving it his all and piped in, "Slow down Harry, just slow down. You're doing fine. Take a breath."

Then Harry continued. "Because of this workshop I've learned to appreciate the fact that my son's timetable doesn't always fit mine.

When he procrastinates with his school work or his chores it drives me nuts and makes me yell at him all the time. I scream the same stupid threats. And then when I back him up too far...he tells me to my face 'Take it easy ole man before you drop dead.' Or worse, he tells me to give him a break and stop being such a tight ass. Well... it's all too much for me to handle. I mean...Like I can't fire him; he's not an employee. I get so goddamned frustrated I could punch holes in the wall, just like he does when he's pissed off at me. I want things to go my way, tasks completed on time and done right the first time. I want the house to run smoothly....Only now do I realize this isn't what's good for my marriage or my relationship with the boy. Christ, it's hard to change!

"Jake, I was angry when you said a well-balanced family needs to be democratic and flexible, and allow for individual differences. Then you said it was critical for all of us to encourage independence, or we'd all end up with twenty-five year old kids still living at home. I hate to admit it, but you struck a nerve. I've got to start loosening up. Maybe most chemical engineers are like me, but now I finally realize that I must change or else in the end...I'll lose my son and maybe worse."

"That was a very insightful statement and it took guts for you to say it. Don't turn back now. You're doing the hardest thing in the universe; you're changing your mind."

Several people gave Harry words of encouragement and there were some tears. The group was now set in motion. The momentum was there and Jake kept it going. "I'm passing out your first activity sheet. There are several questions for you to answer. You may find them to be quite unusual, but, if answered honestly, they'll be very revealing. It won't be an easy thing for some of you to do. Set aside your pride; it's your opportunity to share a piece of yourself."

Ellen sat a seat away from Jake. She wasn't sure if she was ready for this. She felt like a complete stranger, not knowing much about the other seven individuals seated around her. But Harry's comments were sincere, and from that moment on she realized that none of the others knew much about one another, and it was just as well. She focused her attention on the activity sheet. At first glance it didn't seem too threatening, but a few of the questions made her feel uneasy. Even so, she answered them all but not to the fullest extent possible. To do so would have exposed her far more than she'd be comfortable with.

Jake gave the group members about five minutes each to make their introductory statements. Ellen listened carefully as each person went through the process. Some people took the task seriously and made no attempt to censure their comments. Others, for whatever personal reason, took a casual approach. Jake designed the activity to set the tone for the rest of the evening and to connect the group. As he listened to each person, he made a mental note of something significant each revealed. He also observed their body language and if they appeared to be "cheating" by giving censored responses.

In situations like this, Jake knew some people would choose to be humorous as a means to shelter their insecurity and keep others from knowing they were anxious or vulnerable. Conversely, some others adopted an analytical approach and would follow up a response with a statement of rationale. There were answers that came out sarcastically, judgmentally, or cynically because they were defensive in the context of the question. Jake's ability to screen the answer and decipher the true meaning was like a laser guided missile. Were they honest about themselves? Were their introductory comments to the group a candid description, or a deception to leave them undisturbed?

When Ellen's turn came, she was prepared to answer the activity sheet in a manner that would be interpreted as completely open, but safe. Surprisingly, she was pretty calm.

1. "Tonight, please call me: Ellen."

2. "These words best describe me: I think I'm kind-hearted, honest, very private, and generous. I hate to argue with anyone. I've always been that way as long as I can remember. I was raised in the south and my mother was very strict. I was always a cooperative and obedient child. I went to Catholic school. I guess I'm not much different today. I hate to yell or be yelled at."

3. "Physically, I think I look: This is hard question for me. I think I look ok for a woman who just turned forty. I'm not satisfied though and lately I've been trying to remedy the situation."

4. "This question, about what I do in work world: I'm a housewife. I used to work in an office and once I owned a small retail business. It was a card store and gift shop. It was successful, but I had to give it up. My husband was able to convince me that the boys needed me. I guess that's how it goes."

5. "My idea of a perfect day: What an interesting question! All right here goes, having no problems with my kids or arguments with my husband. That's a perfect day for me. I love being alone once in a while and especially being able to paint whenever I have the urge."

6. "My greatest act of independence happened last year: It was moving back to Middletown where I went to high school. It was something I executed without any help. Somehow I convinced my husband to agree to the move. I've enjoyed the peace and I'm finding myself in the process."

7. "My best friend and I share: Unfortunately, only occasional

phone calls. That's all. She lives in the Chicago area now. We went to high school right here in this building. She was pretty and popular. Her name was Marlene. She married an engineer, a nice guy, though very intellectual. They have two terrific daughters and unlike me, her plan for happiness worked out fine. She predicted it would."

8. "If I ever run away, where would I go? It would to the mountains, someplace out west that's quiet, away from people and where my time belonged to me. I'd have a cabin and live a simple life in natural surroundings. I wouldn't mind being alone. I'd walk the trails every day and I'd paint and read."

9. "My attitude about the world is: Or rather was, positive. A very long time ago, I was hopeful about my future. Like some of you mentioned…when I didn't know any better I made some very bad decisions and paid the price. Cause of being here, now I know I'm not the only one who screwed up like that."

10. "Before I die, if I could know one truth, what would it be? This is a great question! I used to think about stuff like this all the time especially when I was young. I haven't changed my mind. I'd like to know if angels are watching over me. The idea appeals to me."

It took less than five minutes for Ellen to give her answers. When she finished she felt relieved. However, for whatever reason, there wasn't a single follow-up question given to her.

"Ellen thanks for sharing a piece of yourself with us. I would also like to have a cabin beneath the mountains and have my angel introduce herself to me. Let's hear from someone else, how about you Jim?"

As Jim began, Ellen suddenly realized that she wanted to say a lot more, but it was too late. She thought she succeeded in coming off as "average" but perhaps more so than she desired. Other people were more trusting and gave a clearer picture of their lives. Many said they were scared, or confused about coping with middle age and parenting their teenagers. She felt ashamed for not giving more to the group.

Ellen couldn't have anticipated what was about to happen. Jake tossed out his first group question. It caught them by complete surprise. "Answer this. Can you still play? Play by yourself, with your children, your friends, or your spouse? Can you honestly admit you like spending free time with them? Are you running on empty or burned out from responsibilities at work or at home or in both places?"

The dialogue took off at such a fast pace that Jake had to slow down the group several times to allow for feedback. Everyone wanted to comment on what the word "play" meant in the context that Jake used it. Some people were drowning in the problems of their family and didn't even realize they were stalled in misery. It was a hard thing to admit that they were spent or "lost" in transition.

After a while Jake introduced another thought provoking question. "How do you relax? How do you find peace during turmoil? Where is there calm in a storm?"

The group really got into it with more and more personal opinion and disclosure. There were no more generalities, only specifics. The group was operating at a peak performance level.

"How well do you learn from mistakes? What is your way of dealing with mid-life? Are you resourceful or needy most of the time? Have you met the expectations you had for yourself? What's your biggest challenge? How are you coping with it? Do you have the incentive to change your destiny?"

After an hour of dialogue all the remaining defenses were knocked down for everyone except Ellen. She was under a self-imposed safety net while others willingly shared disappointments, feelings of loneliness, unresolved conflicts, personal flaws, childhood tragedies and broken promises. Like Jake had written on the board, everyone had a story waiting to be told and sharing it with a sympathetic audience was an opportunity to purge out sorrow. Ellen sat in silence as if it was all happening on a stage right in front of her, but she chose not to participate.

It wasn't as if anything she heard was extraordinary. She knew it was a group of middle-aged baby boomers that Jake had given an opportunity to respond to unusual questions, questions that no one had ever asked them. The sincerity of the members of the group was evident in their testimony.

"I can't remember the last time I played with my kids. My life is driven by meeting the demands of schedules made by others. I'm always going and going like that Everyready bunny with the stupid grin on its face. I hate that friggin commercial. I'm trying to get everything done. I'm feeling squeezed. If I could relax, then I could play."

"Everyone talks about mid-life with jokes about losing hair, nodding out at movies, aches and pains, bulging stomachs, no more romance and having a full plate of stress for dinner every goddamned night. Frankly, I'm scared. I've lost control of my life. My job has become my life. I hate it. There's nothing left for me. I feel older than I am."

"If I could learn from my mistakes I wouldn't be sitting here. I feel like all I do is screw-up the relationship with my daughter. I want us to get along and stop fighting. Now I know the truth. I wasn't allowed much independence when I was a kid. My parents were always frightened of me and boys. It was the sex scare thing. It drove me nuts. I was so good. I didn't even make out till I was a senior and lied about my experience to my best friend. Now I'm battling with my daughter. I hate it. I'm exactly like my mother was, scared to trust my daughter on her choice of friends, clothes, music, the works. I've failed to listen. I'm an all-star screamer and world class dope for not learning from my mistakes. I'm a stubborn woman and it's hurting me probably more than her. I'm hung up on fear. I believe everything I hear from other parents about...about sex.

"When the kids were young I was as resourceful as any young mother could be. I got the best daycare available, sent my daughter to dancing school, soccer camp, Sunday school...the works. I did the homework thing, the PTA fundraisers and all the Girl Scout projects with her. I made my life second. Now peer pressure is creeping into her life and taking it over. It's influencing her in ways I couldn't have imagined. I feel lost and frustrated. My husband has withdrawn from both of us. He claims he's got to provide for our well-being and that's his job. His ignorance and indifference have shortened my patience.

"He forgets, she's only fifteen and in need of a united effort to guide her through high school. For God's sake, I've found letters and e-mails all sexually related. Are they real or the same exaggerations that I made up when I was her age? They tell her to jump on board and get sexually active before she misses her chance. I'm scared to death. I'm as needy as a lost child myself. What's happening to her? What's happening to me? Oh my God! I'm crying in front of you because I remember my little girl. The one I used to watch play with her dollhouse and finger paints. She's gone. Now she wears make-up, has hair with blond streaks, and she has a bad attitude... accusing me of being too old to understand. I'm only thirty-seven. Is that old? I'm needy because I feel alone."

Jake stopped the discussion after he felt everyone had an opportunity to play. Purposely, he paused for a minute. Then he looked directly into the eyes of each person sitting in the circle before him until they acknowledged his attention. Not a single sound was heard. It was a poignant moment and not a theatrical stunt because he had reached out to them in a profound display of acceptance and affirmation.

"I am going to give you two more thoughts to consider. Some of you shouldn't respond tonight. You may be better off answering them in the privacy of your home. But that's your choice. I believe these are the key questions. The ones we're all afraid to answer. First, do you feel satisfied with what you've accomplished so far in your life? And second, looking back in your life, what could you have done differently? Were you too innocent for your own good? Think about it. Now take a ten-minute break. Let go of your tension. Get a drink, use the restroom, go outside, or make someone laugh. I'll see in ten."

Ellen found herself standing next to Linda at the vending machines during the break. Based on first impressions, Ellen thought she had nothing in common with the woman. Nevertheless, she accepted Linda's invitation to step outside in the courtyard.

"There's a lot going on and I think it's helping me see myself as a person, as well as a mother. I'm a single-mom; I bust my butt trying to make sales in the real estate business. It's a cut-throat world that's turned me into a cynic. My daughter is the most important person in my life. I occasionally date, but men mean nothing to me except some diversion from work and parenting. Most of them think having a dinner date eventually leads to the bedroom. Do you have any idea what these men are like? Most of them are divorced, short on cash, and they all look like hell but they still need their egos stroked and their sexual fantasies fulfilled. Ellen, if I stood them in front of you, as pretty as you are…shit, you wouldn't give them a second look. You know…I hate to say it but most men are assholes. We just put up with them because…because that's the way it is.

"My daughter Amanda's in eighth grade and I'm so unsure of myself in this single-parenting role. That's why I signed up for this workshop. Jake is something. I mean who the hell is he? I have to admit it… he's my idea of a real man. What the hell is he doing working as a counselor at a Podunk high school? I thought he was pretty good lecturing the big group and giving us tons of information, but tonight I realize he's amazing at this group stuff. It's much more than I expected when I volunteered. It's helping me understand myself in ways I'd never considered. I've learned some things. You know that expectation stuff. Attitude and expectation, I've got to figure that out.

"Jake's right about one thing, when it comes to teenagers; it's all about breaking away. But tonight, I also understand I've got to pay attention to my own needs in order to be an effective parent and fully functional person. He's not only making me remember my teenage years, but also my life in the here and now. Honestly, I never expected this much depth. I'm sorry, I'm rambling. I couldn't help myself."

Linda was the complete opposite of Ellen. She was open with her feelings and fears. Ellen was uneasy about what to say to her. Should she share something about Guy, herself, the boys, or her opinion of Jake Carr? Characteristically, she chose to stay away from herself but considering her latest thoughts about leaving her husband she needed answers.

"Linda, is it tough going it alone? I mean how difficult is it? How long have you been doing it? Is your ex-husband still part of your life? Does he pay you what he's supposed to? Is he intrusive and..."

"Ellen, ten years ago I left a man I didn't love, not because he cheated on me, stole my money, or robbed me of my individuality. I'd never let that happen. No way! I've always had plenty of self-confidence and self-respect. Ellen, the real truth was that when I looked down the road, after Amanda was gone, I absolutely knew it wasn't going to work. We didn't enjoy the same things. Jake asked the right questions tonight. Believe me, my former was a decent man with a good paying job but I didn't really like him. That was it. It's not at all complicated. Boy, did I realize that tonight!

"I haven't found the right man. Then again, at forty-five, I know there's no perfect mate. I don't even know where to look for one. Do you? Maybe I wouldn't know what to do if I came across him? How would I connect with him? That's a lot to consider, isn't it? Right now...I'm in neutral. I have no clue how to reach out to a man. But I am independent and I enjoy being me. After three moves and three jobs, I'm settled in Middletown now, I'm selling real estate. I'm ok financially. Luckily, my ex-husband never stopped supporting his daughter and for that I'm grateful. I know I'll survive and I'm glad I have Amanda, but where's the love? Where's the passion? Oh my God, you must think I've lost it."

Ellen didn't answer her but gave Linda a hug. They finished their diet cokes and returned to the classroom. On the way back Linda stopped Ellen and shared one last thought. "In answer to Jake's questions, I guess I'm satisfied with what I've done with my life, but I certainly should have finished college and postponed getting married. I was way too young. There are a few other things too, but they're pretty deep and I'll think about them later. Thanks for listening to me."

When everyone was back Jake told them what to expect next. "In this final ninety minutes I want to revisit some workshop issues with you. But first, please take another look at the rules on the board. Ask yourself if you've been participating fairly, and if you have given some thought to the last statement written up there. Within each of us there's a story waiting to be told. Don't miss your chance. Remember, no one in the group will make you do it. It's your call."

With that said, Jake returned to a similar group dynamic used in the first session. This time, most of the participants spoke with an even greater depth of feeling and honesty. It was the best example of group dynamics working effectively. The dialogue was high-spirited and candid. There were those who felt change was impossible or impractical at the current time, and those who believed that change was their only course of action. Ellen never took a turn because she was afraid.

The closing of the seminar proved to be the most enlightening moment of the evening. Jake left them with these parting words. "This is the end of your voyage. I'm proud of you. Remember this. I sincerely believe that the only way an individual will have a change of mind or a change of heart is when they're confronted with the truth. Then, and only then, you'll have to decide if the pain is so severe and immobilizing that it will make you change. That's right…when the pain is unbearable, that's when change happens. Listen, I've lived by this proverb since my mid-twenties. Think about it for a while. Never forget it. Take it home."

Then he went over to the blackboard and wrote the following. *To go wrong and not alter one's course can truly be defined as going wrong.* When he finished writing he stared at each person for a moment and then said, "I want you to know that the entire thrust of this group process experience was to get each of you to look within yourself and decide if a change is appropriate. It doesn't get any more fundamental than that. Thank you for coming and taking the voyage of self-discovery. You have plenty to think about in the days ahead and that's a good thing. Don't be frightened. Write your thoughts down about what changes you want to make in order to improve your life as a parent and a person. Don't be afraid to share them with someone you trust. If you'd like to write a note to me, do it. Good night."

It was near 11 p.m. when the group filed out. Jake was exhausted. Every person came up to him and expressed their appreciation for his masterful handling of the group. Some actually hugged him. Not Ellen. She stood alone with her thoughts. Jake noticed her. He came up from behind and touched her arm to get her attention. "Remember Ellen, I also want to be in that cabin beneath the mountain. In fact, I'm heading there this summer."

Taken by his words, Ellen replied. "I guess your family isn't too happy with that choice."

"They accept it…it's kind of a trade-off. I make sure the house runs smoothly all year and in return I take a three-week road adventure out west. You see, I'm not much different than you are with regard to loving mother-nature and needing some personal space. I'd like to spend every afternoon on the trail and every evening on the front porch watching the sunsets. Do you get my meaning? I gotta go now. Hey, good luck!"

Ellen caught up with Linda walking out to the parking lot. They heard Charles talking to Harry saying, "Hope we can get together for coffee or a drink next week." Other group members wouldn't let go of the evening and were engrossed in animated conversations near their cars.

It was a moonless night, dark and still, without any sound except the faint murmur of conversation between people, who only hours ago, began the session with introductory statements about themselves. Linda couldn't let go of the evening either. "Ellen, let's go for a drink. Come on, I'm not ready to stroll into the house and resume being a single parent, not just yet. I want to talk. What do you say?"

Ellen wanted to be alone. "Linda, I'm sorry to disappoint you again. Please, please forgive me. Give me your phone number and we'll make a date. I promise. I…I just can't do it tonight. I hope you'll understand."

Linda gave Ellen a farewell hug and told her. "I do understand. There's a lot going on in my head, maybe too much. So long."

❀❀❀

The house was quiet when Ellen entered the kitchen. She stopped at the foot of the stairs and listened. Thankfully, the boys had turned in. Tired and feeling a little sick, she opened a bottle of merlot and filled a tumbler instead of her usual wineglass. Then she went to her bedroom to wind down. Sure enough, the light was blinking on the answering machine. "Not this time," she whispered to herself. After she finished half a glass, she undressed and decided to take a long hot shower.

She stepped under the spray, closed her eyes, and began to slowly massage her neck muscles, then her temples. Her mind wandered and wandered. There were many thoughts and feelings that entered her consciousness during the group, but she wasn't prepared to share them. They had to remain buried. Yet all through the evening, things began to reveal themselves with such clarity.

One particular sentence stood apart from everything else she heard. Over and over, she repeated it to herself. "I'm not much different from you." At first, she didn't appreciate what it meant, but now Ellen thought she understood. Jake had given her a small piece of himself; the man, not the counselor.

CHAPTER 13

It was Wednesday, a little past noon and time for Jake's lunch break. With a can of Pepsi and a three-layer turkey sandwich to devour, he had twenty minutes to withdraw from his duties. So far the feedback he received from the workshop was encouraging, and soon he could expect a check for $550 for his services. Summer was fast approaching, and with it the expectation of a break from the stress of counseling and the regimen of home life. The college application season ended a month ago, the master schedule was finished, and Jake's long anticipated sojourn to the Rockies was two months away.

J.D. was graduating high school and would be leaving for college in late August. Annie was involved with school activities and a new relationship with a part-time college student and shoe salesman named Jeff. She already had a summer job lined up at a local restaurant that would give her experience as a waitress. And, Annie had just passed her driving test, now had a permit, and was excited about the prospect of using her mom's Geo Prizm. Meanwhile, Sandy was worn out from teaching two new curriculums, but impressing the principal enough to expand her schedule to full time next year.

Generally, mail delivered to the guidance office arrived around noon every day. Loretta, one of the two secretaries, usually stopped whatever she was doing to sort it out and drop it in each of the counselor's box before going to lunch. Occasionally, she would personally deliver a letter if it looked like something important, from the Department of Family Services, county probation department, or the admissions office of a university and was stamped, "Urgent, open immediately." She appeared at the doorway of Jake's office to deliver a personal letter.

"I see you're at the computer and eating a deli sandwich. Tell me, are you ever going to sit in that faculty room with the staff? I guess not this year. Well I have another letter for you. It's probably from somebody in your workshop. Do you want it left in your mailbox or placed in your hand?"

"You just love to tease me... don't you? And you're right. I'm looking at the scenery from Yellowstone. But, I'll stop right this moment, because maybe there's a gift certificate in that letter. Ah...wouldn't it be nice if a fifty dollar bill or a twenty dollar voucher from Busby's liquor store came along with that letter? Then you could report me to the authorities for taking bribes. You'd get a reward and I'd get an official reprimand. Just give it to me and I'll read it later. How's your grandson? Didn't you mention to Carol about him having a bad case of poison ivy? How in the hell did he get it so soon?"

Loretta turned and gazed up the ceiling in disdain before answering. "Carol's gonna give me one of her patented grief looks if I don't get back. She wants to leave for lunch. Anyway, I'll tell you about Anthony's predicament when she's gone."

Jake finished his sandwich while looking at shots of the thermal pools around Old Faithful. Then he sat back in his chair and took a three minute voyage back to the place. The last time he was there was with his family in the summer of '97. Laughing a little, he recalled five hundred people or more from all over the planet expecting to see a spectacular display of nature's power as they stood behind a secure log fence and readied their cameras for the action. Of course they were somewhat dismayed by a mere sixty-foot-high burst of steam and hot water for only fifty seconds. Then another hour would pass before the next group saw a repeat of the same show.

After leaving the website, he picked up the letter Loretta had given him and noticed there wasn't a return address on envelope. That made him curious about the contents, so he opened the seal and unfolded a single sheet of yellow stationary.

Dear Jake,

You told us that everyone has a story waiting to be shared. I know I didn't participate much in the group. I think I was scared to talk about myself in front of strangers, but I wanted you to know part of my story. I was adopted when I was two weeks old. I located my birth mother a few years ago in Dallas, Texas, but nothing really came of it. She was friendly but guarded. I guess I was the same way with her. I never found out who my real father was and she really couldn't tell me too much about him. I didn't hold it against her. When I was a small child, my father used to call me his sweet adopted angel and told me that I came from heaven. I'm not sure what that means at this point in my life. I believed him and yet he walked out on my mother when I was nineteen. I haven't seen him since! I've always wondered why I was given up for adoption and thought there must have been something wrong with me when I was born.

Here is another missing part. I got married when I was twenty. Pretty stupid move! It happened quickly and I wasn't pregnant. I was naive. Things didn't turnout too good for me because of that decision. Luckily, I was able finish college in Georgia.

All of my life I've loved nature. I love the springtime. I also love animals, especially horses and German Shepherds and I love to paint. I returned to Middletown because I wanted my boys to get a better education than they were getting in Atlanta. That's what I told my husband.

You're a complete mystery to some of the people at the seminar. I can understand that. You're not the typical counselor. In fact, you're not a typical man! What mattered to me was that I believed the things you said. You're confident and I'm not.

Thanks for the workshop and for getting me into the group experience. I learned some things about myself, even if I didn't show it. It's given me a lot to think about lately. I hope some day soon we can talk again. You were terrific!
Sincerely,
Ellen Eastman

Jake read the letter and then read it again. At first he tried to remember all he could about Ellen, like the statements she made and the questions she answered. Did she say something that remained in his memory? Did she impress him with her participation? One specific thing he did recall was that she was attractive, but what else stuck in his mind? Strangely, he couldn't remember anything, other than she was somewhat shy and made a very revealing statement in answering her last introductory question declaring with conviction, "If I could run away it would be to a log cabin beneath a mountain." Then after another few seconds he remembered. *She wanted to escape to a place where she'd have the freedom to do whatever she wanted. She's not much different than me. That letter sure must have been difficult for her to write. She sounded so sincere. I'm gonna have to think on this for a while before I get back to her.*

Shortly thereafter a student appeared at the door and held up her pass. It was time to get busy.

Jake signaled the student to enter. Her mother had called the day before to request that he to speak with her daughter. In counseling jargon, it was known as a referral. Only in this case, the sixteen-year-old sophomore honor student had no idea why she was there.

"Have a seat Sharon; I'm sorry if you were waiting long. I just finished lunch."

Sharon suffered a fall during competition cheerleading practice, and her wrist was in a cast. It couldn't have happened at a worse time. Regional competitions were in progress, and she was forced to cheer for her teammates instead of competing alongside of them. The accident was a result of not having the fall broken by a spotter. Regretfully, she had severely broken her hand in two places. It was a painful injury. Now she was depressed and full of anger from the heartbreaking disappointment. In the past week she had totally withdrawn from her family. Sharon's mom knew her daughter liked Jake, and maybe he could help her get past the setback. In such referral cases Jake told parents that he'd check things out and reminded them to "let it be" and wait for a call back from him.

"Sharon, I've seen you quite a few times with a senior boy I don't know. What's his name?"

That was the "icebreaker" and Jake used that strategy to ease students into difficult counseling sessions. Personal small talk meant everything to kids. Sharon then gave Jake the inside story of her relationship. After a few minutes he took her in another direction.

"Anything lined up for the summer? Are you ready to join the rest of us in work world? You're sixteen and everyone needs pocket money when they're that age."

Sharon laid out her plans, two weeks of vacation at the family cottage on Cape Cod, a week at cheerleading camp, and a commitment from her neighbor to watch two young children who were in need of a babysitter for the rest of her summer.

"Not only are you an academic superstar with that 3.75 G.P.A., but I'm so impressed with your ability to plan ahead. It's a terrific asset to have!"

She appeared relaxed, so Jake seized the opportunity to probe. "So what happened to that hand? What gives?"

She sighed heavily and looked down at the injured hand. Jake leaned back in his chair and waited. Over the next five minutes, she explained how as a competition cheerleader she believed nothing bad would ever happen to her because she was in perfect shape and experienced on the stunts. Then she stopped suddenly, fighting back the tears.

"Mr. Carr, nobody broke my fall? Maybe you don't understand. I depended on a spotter being there to catch me. It's crazy. It didn't have to happen. Then, I'm lying there, crying in pain...crying. Why didn't they recognize it was serious instead of sitting me on the bleachers with an icepack? I'm angry! Tell me, how come my coaches have nothing to say about it? They see me every day at practice, cheering on the other kids. Where was their compassion for me? Why did they act like that? Only my teammates came through with support and they're not the adults. Why?"

Jake made no attempt to give her an explanation. It wouldn't have changed a thing. How could he explain what happened? He wasn't there and didn't know all the facts. Instead, he held out his hand and said, "Sharon, I'm so sorry. I'm so very sorry. It's tough…real tough dealing with an injury that takes you away from an activity you've come to depend on for exercise and enjoyment. I feel that way about hiking. You love that image of yourself as a cheerleader, don't you? And I can understand why you would. It's a super activity, and very few kids are up to that level of dedication and athletic ability. Very few kids work at it the way you do."

Jake had hit the bulls-eye, and he knew it.

"Mr. Carr, why doesn't my family understand what you just said? They think everything is about A's on my report card. They seem to forget that I've put my heart and soul into being a comp cheerleader. It means everything to me. Damn them, they don't get it!"

Jake waited for a few moments and replied. "Did your older sister cheer? Did your mom? Maybe they can't make the connection to the injury because it never happened to them. Maybe they never pushed themselves the way you've done. I don't know. The cheerleading identity is what separates you from them. Your level of intensity is different. It's not something they may be able to relate to because you've never shared… sounds corny, but maybe you never told your mom or dad how much the cheerleading meant. You follow what I'm saying?"

Sharon sat up in the chair and squeezed her tissue into a ball. She then replied, "I've kept it to myself because that's the way I want it. My life is upside down and topsey turvey. I feel like a cripple and the other kids don't know what to say to me."

Jake respected her feelings and thought he'd be the same way. He pushed on. "Listen kid, you know better than anyone in the place that this injury took you out of your daily routine. And, as if that's not bad enough, I think a person experiences grief when they suffer a loss of identity as you did. There's grief whenever the loss is something that was meaningful to us. The loss of a friendship is one of the worst things you can experience. However, in your case I believe losing your place on the Regional Competition Team is suffering a loss in an activity that has great meaning for you. It's the same as if a starting shortstop on the Varsity baseball team broke his ankle before the final championship game of the season. You know you can never go back in time again.

Sharon please believe me…it's normal to feel anger, guilt, sorrow, and also plenty of fear. Fear that something like this could happen again. The answer to finding some peace lies in being able to accept the things you cannot change. But that's everyone's toughest challenge in life, yours and mine. Are you getting this?"

"I think I get your message. I guess I've got to think about what you've told me and I will…that's for sure. I thought my friends and family would get me out of this…this misery. I'm the only who can do it."

"Sharon, before you go. Did you listen? Did you hear how clear your thinking is? I'll grant you this. It's a very sad experience to have people you love fall short of your expectations. It's very much the human condition. But never doubt for a moment…not for a split second, how much your mom and dad love you. It's true they can't fully appreciate what you're going through, but consider all the times they drove you to practice and picked you up afterwards. Am I right? What about all the times they adjusted their schedules to meet yours? Believe me it's hard for them to see you withdraw from your family. Listen, you've got to get to class in a few minutes. Wash your face before you go. You can use our restroom down the hall."

She got up and gave Jake a slight smile of relief, shook his hand, and then turned to leave.

"Remember Sharon, I'm always here for you but please try to understand that your parents are awfully worried. It's the truth. Maybe you ought to let them in. Good luck with the recovery."

"Hey Billy, how's it going? How are they treating you over at the Stop and Shop? Seems to me you've been there over a year. Are you their future manager? Man, that's a lot of time at one place!"

"Are you kidding Mr. Carr? It'll be two years at the end of June. Remember, I started right after 10th grade. Sure as hell I was going to summer school, but you managed to get me a break with that English teacher. What was her name? Whatever… she bent the rules and gave me an extra day to hand in that essay. I slipped by with a passing grade. Then after that crap was over, you told me it was time to start saving for a car and…and I did…Well for a truck…that's what happened, and now I'm driving a '92 Chevy Blazer. Not bad. Huh?"

Jake laughed at the kid's sense of good fortune and prodded him on. "Billy boy that sounds like something I would say. Anyhow, that's all well and good, but its history. I sent for you because time is running out of your high school hourglass. You know, like grains of sand passing through a plastic egg timer. Ever see one? Have you considered doing the county college application I gave you a month ago? You can always change your mind later, but its time to get going."

Jake noticed Billy cringe with his last comment and knew he struck a nerve.

"What's with you, Mr. Carr? Why is that so important? Most of the time I don't even like coming here, and you know it! Even with my co-op schedule letting me leave at noon, jeez, I barely got through this year. I'm sick of this place. I'm sick of the rules and the constant busting by the V.P.'s for stupid stuff...like wearing a Bud Light tee shirt. What's my G.P.A.? It's like 2.1, and I wasn't even close to a 1,000 on the SATs. Why should I fool myself? If I didn't take the past four years seriously, what makes you think I'll be any different sitting in a college classroom listening to a lecture on Shakespeare?"

As was his style, Jake waited without answering. Then Billy continued his retort.

"My parents are not in a position to help me. I told you that before...not even with the fifteen hundred I'd need for registering full time at county. The cost would create a problem for them. And...and I don't have it. In fact, I owe my mother a hundred."

"Billy, are you trying to convince me or trying to convince yourself? I appreciate your point of view about the costs involved with tuition and books. Honestly, I'm not trying to force you to do anything; that never works with eighteen year olds. I simply want you to go through the process of investigation. In other words, just check it out. Please fill out an application. Pick up a twenty-five dollar money order. I'll mail it for you. Then the process will begin and you're in the game. You visit the college, discuss program choices with one of my counselor colleagues, and find out about possible financial aid. I know it sounds complicated, but it isn't. You just have to take the first step."

Jake made it seem so simple that Billy's resistance was breaking down. So he threw all sorts of negatives into the dialogue over the next five minutes. Finally, at the right time with a well-orchestrated technique, Jake delivered a knockout punch that Billy wasn't prepared for.

"You know Billy; you deserve a chance to find out about this college thing as much as anyone else in your senior class. I know you're sick of hearing all the non-stop chatter from your classmates about where there're going to college. Honestly, you deserve an opportunity to see for yourself if the community college is right for you. It'll be a place for you to grow intellectually and as a person. Trust me! Trust your instincts. Take a chance. Then you'll never have to look back with regret. Regret is awfully painful. So you think about it. Try this for me.

Listen to the Stop & Shop workers during break time. Listen to what they say about their lives. Then consider if you want the same for yourself or something different. I'm not accepting your final decision until you give it a few days consideration."

After the senior left, Jake thought to himself, *He should give it a shot, one semester to see if it works. I got J.D. into Vermont Tech. Why can't Billy have the same advantage? I'll call his father.*

Just before shutting down for the day, he took it out Ellen's letter, leaned back in his chair, and read it again. Nothing in the letter was urgent, and yet he knew he'd be writing back a thoughtful response in the next day or two.

CHAPTER 14

It was Friday afternoon, and Guy was due to arrive around six at Newark International on Delta Flight 702. From the time the boys left for school, Ellen spent the morning working continuously to get the house in order. After a short break for lunch, she put on rubber gloves and did the three bathrooms. After dumping the dirty water, she noticed it was 2 p.m. and one last chore remained. It was washing and waxing the kitchen floor. When that was completed, she went through a mental checklist to be sure that nothing was missed in preparation for Guy's return. Finally, she thought her husband would be eating on the flight so she didn't plan to make dinner.

By three o'clock, she was physically exhausted and looked no different than a minimum wage cleaning lady. Even so, she was satisfied the house would pass inspection, and from past experience that was crucial if there was going to be any peace. Guy acted like a drill sergeant at boot camp if something was amiss. She hated going through the critique but grudgingly accepted it as a trade-off for her freedom.

The boys would be coming home shortly. After undressing, Ellen stepped on the scale and screamed a loud cheer, "Yes! Yes, it's happening, 137 pounds. I did it. The weight's finally coming off!" Then she took a ten-minute shower thoroughly enjoying the pleasure of having made progress with her weight. She recently purchased some classy underwear from Macy's for just such an occasion. When she put on the mint colored bra and panties and faced the mirror she felt some joy and exclaimed, "Today I feel good...better than I have for a long time. I'm starting to look better and I even feel better. No matter what happens when Guy comes home I'm not going to let anything drag me down."

Ellen put on jeans and a gray long sleeve cotton shirt, laced up her walking sneakers, and went downstairs. Then she opened a can of diet Coke and waited for the school bus to arrive. She recalled that since returning to Middletown, she'd been through this insane housekeeping routine about half a dozen times.

Finishing the drink, she couldn't help but think; *Getting ready for his return is driving me crazy. When he's not around, I keep a clean house with or without the boys help. I'm sick of it!*

When Guy called every evening, it was a certainty that he'd want to know how she spent the day. As if he were keeping a timesheet, he'd ask; Did she meet anyone? What jobs did she do around the house? And, of course, how the boys were doing in school? Ellen made it a point not to give him any bad news because it would result in him losing his temper over the phone.

The parenting seminar had laid bare many parenting mistakes and marital problems that she once felt were better off left alone. As a result of attending, Ellen promised herself that in the coming week she would focus all her attention on re-examining her relationship with Guy. After reading Jake's material about marital stress issues involved in teen parenting she had started taking notes. In truth, she'd rather he never came back to Middletown, but the boys needed their father's presence even if she didn't. Then again, it was hard to imagine anything positive occurring between Danny and his father. They'd battled over chores, curfews, clothes, and of course music.

Fortunately for Ellen, when Joey came home he accepted her invitation to go with her to pick up Guy. Right after he had a snack they left for Newark International Airport. Danny didn't come home on the bus so Ellen assumed he was with his friends. The last thing she told him that morning was "There's pizza in the freezer, but please make sure you clean up afterwards and be home by your midnight curfew."

Danny had acknowledged her instructions in typical fashion. "Mom, chill out; no problem."

On the way to the airport Joey talked about the excitement he felt with the prospect of a carefree summer and going to Middletown Middle School in the fall. On the drive to the airport he asked Ellen, "Mom, do we have any plans for the summer?"

"Joey, believe me, it's not my decision to make. Your father doesn't like the kind of places I enjoy visiting. Think back to our last trip. Remember, New Hampshire, the White Mountains…how miserable he was. Anyway, don't worry about it. Save this discussion for another day? Ok?"

"Jeez Mom, I forgot about last summer. All right, I won't bring it up with Dad. I promise."

At eleven years of age, Joey was in the last stage of childhood. He was polite, agreeable, and helpful around the house. Unlike his older brother, who was confrontational and sullen by nature, Joey tried to make his father proud of him by being respectful and compliant. Danny's negative attitude was confusing to Joey. He genuinely liked his older brother and thought his dad frequently picked fights for no good reason but knew better than risk angering his dad by voicing any opposition. All he wanted was for his dad to like him and think he was a good kid.

Joey loved his father but had witnessed too many incidents of shouting, threatening, and brawling between Danny and his dad to feel secure. Those bad memories influenced Joey to work harder at trying to be the perfect son. He feared his father's temper and was wise enough to retreat to his room or escape to the neighborhood playground whenever he saw evidence of trouble brewing on the horizon. Worse than his dad's confrontations with Danny were the numerous times Joey heard his father's demeaning criticism of his mother. Those incidents were more painful than watching his brother's battles. He coped with them by hiding in his room. Joey's temperament mirrored Ellen's; he was mild-mannered and preferred peace over confrontation at his own expense.

After circling the parking area for ten minutes, they finally pulled into a spot not far from the exit doors. It was almost six when Ellen locked the van and with a quick trot they made their way to Terminal C to locate an arrival monitor in the lobby. When she finally found one, the news wasn't good. Delta flight 702 was delayed and the expected arrival time was 7:20. There was nothing for them to do other than browse the gift shops and wait, so Ellen made a suggestion to her son. "Joey, you'll be starving if we don't get some dinner. We've got another hour of waiting before the plane arrives. I don't think we'll get home till nine. Let's find a place to eat."

Five minutes later they found a Deli Restaurant. Ellen decided it would be a wise to have a garden salad and skip the dinner menu. They sat in a booth and she watched Joey gobble down a turkey club, while she considered what she intended to do over the next week. Right then she decided to chronicle each day's family interaction, listing all the activities, arguments, discussions, and more importantly, the level of respect her husband demonstrated towards her privately and in front of the boys. Guy would be on trial without his knowledge and Ellen was going to pay close attention to his behavior for the purpose of putting hard evidence on paper.

Whether she had an objective mindset about the test period wasn't clear. What mattered more was the fact that by putting something down in writing, there could be no way of hiding the truth. Ultimately, it was up to her husband to show her if he still valued her as a marriage partner. After two decades of trying to keep the relationship working, Ellen had enough of being second guessed on everything she ever did. Moreover, she was unselfish, faithful, and even accepting of Guy's shortcomings. She even forgave his numerous infidelities, believing it was the price to pay for keeping the family intact.

After several months as a single parent and as a result of the workshop experience, Ellen finally had gained the insight she needed to begin coping with her fears. Her self-confidence was still shaky, but after a complete shutdown for years it was finally beginning to grow. The seminar had given her a jump start.

"Mom...Hurry up and finish your iced tea. I'll throw out this garbage. Don't you think it's time we get to the gate? Dad will be coming in soon. Come on, let's go!"

"Sorry...my mind was wondering. Did you have enough to eat?"

"Mom, you're not listening. Just pay the check and let's meet Dad."

They started for the waiting area outside the arrival gate and found a spot among the large crowd already standing there. At 7:30, Guy saw his wife and son from a distance. He didn't wave or acknowledge them. At first glance, Ellen thought he looked a bit heavier than usual wearing a tight black sport shirt and dark blue slacks. As he got closer Ellen noticed there wasn't a smile on his face. The delayed arrival, along with having to sit next to a chatterbox of a sales executive, had gotten him agitated and turned his mood ugly. Making things even worse, Flight 702 wasn't a dinner flight, the meager snack of chips and a soft drink was inadequate to suit his needs.

"Hey Dad, I'm glad you're home. Mom and I have been waiting over an hour."

"They didn't serve us anything. Imagine that? I'm hungry, why don't we find a place and eat?"

"Dad, we already ate before you arrived. It was because the plane was late. Sorry."

Guy shook his head in disbelief and mumbled a curse under his breath. Then he barked, "Ellen, couldn't you have waited for me? Didn't you check the status of the flight? What am I supposed to do? Huh? Settle for McDonalds?"

Ellen and Joey knew better than to answer him. She also knew that this wasn't a good beginning.

"Never mind...You didn't know it wasn't a dinner flight. Forget it. I'll wait till we get home. Now let's get out of here. I've got a headache from sitting next to some jackass from Manhattan trying to impress me with his sales knowledge about data systems. The damn flight was torture. The fella wouldn't take a hint even though I made it obvious I couldn't care less about his products. All I want is the peace and quiet of my own living room and a cold beer. Joey, lead me to the parking area, will you."

Ellen walked behind her husband and son as they headed to the terminal parking lot, thinking this was so typical of him when things didn't go his way. It was a long ride back to Middletown and she was glad Joey was there to provide some distraction. Just before they got to the van, Guy suggested. "I think I'll drive back. It'll relax me. Give me the keys?"

Without any resistance she handed them over and then said to Joey, "'Why don't you sit up front with your father? I'll sit in the back."

"Thanks a lot Mom. I can't wait to tell Dad about the stuff I'm doing."

Joey opened the sliding door for his mother and she sat in the back, quite content to pass the time with her own thoughts and hoping her son would entertain Guy. Much of the time during the ride back she alternately listened to the conversation upfront or daydreamed about being somewhere else. A few times Guy spoke directly to her inquiring about Danny, but she wouldn't give him much information. He also asked if the spring landscaping was done and if the mower was working properly. Finally nearing Middletown, he turned at a light and asked Ellen, "Well, what are you going to make me for dinner?"

"At this moment, I'm not sure what's available. I'll make something easy. Something you won't have to wait for too long. Is that all right with you?"

"Whatever. Just get it ready quickly."

Joey had stayed on the safe track with his father during most of the drive, except for one instance when his dad asked about his progress in school. Skillfully, somewhat like his mother would do, he left out anything negative or that would be upsetting to his father. As they neared the last stretch of the ride Guy asked his son, "Well Joey, how do you like living up here? Is it better than East Point?"

"Oh yeah, with the woods and lakes and the kids in the neighborhood...you know Dad, I like it a lot here. I was bored back in Atlanta. There's plenty of stuff to do here."

"I'm glad to hear it. I wonder if your brother feels like you do."

"I don't know Dad. He's got his own life and I've got mine. That's the way Danny wants it to be."

It was after nine when they arrived at the house on Westgate Drive. Ellen had hoped Danny would be there when they pulled into the driveway, but it was Friday night. She knew when he didn't come home after school that he'd be out hanging with his buddies either uptown or at the playground complex.

No sooner did Guy open the front door when the first thing he noticed was a couple of plates and glasses on the kitchen counter, along with some empty soda cans and napkins scattered in close proximity. Apparently Danny had a couple of friends over for pizza. Ellen always kept a few "Tombstone" pizza pies in the freezer for the boys and wasn't surprised with the mess left behind. She probably should have left a note in addition to her parting words to Danny before he left that morning. Now the fuse was lit and there was no way of putting it out. Guy wasn't happy and he let her know it.

"For Christ's sake, how can you let me come home to this mess? With the time you have, can't you keep this place in order? You know I want to walk into a clean house. This is absolutely ridiculous. I thought by now you would've taught your son some responsibility. Where the hell is Danny? Didn't he know I was coming home?"

Ellen tried to defuse the situation by giving her husband an explanation telling him, "I'm sure he wasn't thinking about you or anything else when he left the dishes. It's all right. I'll take care of it."

After apologizing on behalf of her son's thoughtlessness, Ellen commenced a ten-minute clean up that returned the kitchen to its prior condition. When Guy returned and sat at the counter she made an effort to restore some peace. "Guy, can I make you a tuna sandwich or a cheese omelet?"

"I'll take the tuna sandwich and I'd really like a cold beer."

His request could only be met halfway, and Ellen once again tried to handle it. "I'm sorry Guy. I forgot to put any beer in the fridge. I'm a wine drinker and truthfully, it didn't occur to me. How about some ice tea or a coke? Is that all right?"

It was useless and Ellen knew it, the late flight, no dinner, the kitchen mess left by Danny, and now warm beer. How could this happen? Then she thought, *What's the big deal? Why should it matter?*

Guy's mood turned sullen with Ellen's offer. "I don't believe this. Don't you ever think of me? Why don't you ever plan ahead? You're free all day. Jesus, I expect more consideration. How come whenever I call you're always telling you have everything under control? I don't see that at all."

Over the next few minutes Ellen remained quiet to avoid any trouble. She made Guy tuna salad the way he liked it, served it on toast, and then went upstairs to read. It was past ten o'clock when she returned to clean off the counter. At that time her worries mounted. *Would Danny come home by his curfew time and would her husband request something else that she didn't have?*

Accepting the fact she had no control over Danny's arrival, she had one other troubling concern. She dreaded facing the prospect that he would want to have sex with her. Given the tense mood he was in, there was no way of knowing. With Guy, it never was about making love in any sense of the word; it was about performing a sexual act. That was all it ever meant to him, and for Ellen it had always been that way. There was no romance or passion between them during the brief time they engaged in any sexual activity. He didn't even kiss her, and she felt lucky if she could get it over with quickly. Guy's only concession was that the room could be dark, and because it was he was generally satisfied quickly.

Everything concerning that part of their relationship was mechanical and predictable. As far back as Ellen could remember, it was always that way. When she was just twenty and recently married, her lack of sexual interest angered Guy to no end. He constantly criticized her lack of performance, and he wasn't teasing when he let her know it. Throughout their marriage Ellen had felt uncomfortable about his sexual behavior in the bedroom. Guy could be reasonably kind and take her without comment, or he could be demanding and inconsiderate of her personal preferences. Ironically, although Ellen had been slightly overweight, he was never in great physical shape either. He was flabby, yet in his mind he thought otherwise and told her repeatedly that she was lucky that he was still interested in her. He used her as a sexual partner for reasons of biological urgency more than any expression of love.

Years ago she tricked him into thinking the lack of light was more romantic. In reality, it was the complete opposite because the ruse made an extremely uncomfortable task tolerable. During the sex her mind wandered to faraway places and characters from her romantic novels. In her mind, Guy was never with her. The same mindset held true for him because he found her so unappealing. Over the years, her interest in sexual activities had diminished to a level inconsistent with her age. During that time, and especially after Joey's birth, she gave up on being physically fit and saw her weight climb to an all-time high of 160 pounds. Consciously or not, Ellen wanted to be less desirable, concluding it was the only way to extract some payment for Guy's extramarital affairs over the years.

After leaving the kitchen Ellen followed her usual routine of checking on Joey who was getting ready for bed and pouring herself a glass of wine. To pass the time she decided to do a load of laundry, hoping she'd avoid Guy.

It was 11 o'clock and she was taking the towels out of the dryer when Guy appeared at the doorway. He looked bedraggled and needed a shave, as he stood slouched over wearing a pair of old pajama bottoms and an undershirt. She immediately turned away from him and continued the chore. Then he asked her, "Danny's supposed to be back at midnight. Could you finish what you're doing and meet me upstairs? I want to mess around." Then he abruptly walked away without giving Ellen a chance to answer him.

What he requested wasn't unexpected; nevertheless a feeling of uneasiness permeated her whole being. For whatever reason, she told herself that this time would be different. She would give in and do what he asked for the sake of peace, but she instinctively knew this would mark the end of her submissiveness to him. Like an unexpected cloudburst descending out of a clear summer sky, the revelation was startling to her. Not loving this man was the undeniable truth. Ashamed as she was for allowing herself to be used all these years, Ellen knew it was coming to an end. At forty years of age and after twenty years of an unfulfilling relationship, she knew she would finally break the chains that had bound her like a slave girl to a master. She thought. *I've had enough. This is the end.*

Gathering up as much courage as she could muster, she walked to the stairway that led upstairs to the second floor. As she approached the door she heard the bathroom shower and decided to take another look at her notes from the workshop. They were hidden under some tablecloths in the bureau.

Pulling out the notes from the group session, she came across the set of questions that had brought her to this change of mind and read them over again. **Are you resourceful or needy? Looking back on your life, what could you have done differently? What overwhelming regret have you been unable to let go? How well do you learn from mistakes? Where do you want to be ten years from now?**

Tears welled up in her eyes when she looked at the answers she had written in response to those definitive questions. She read the answers and her inner voice proclaimed. *I've let myself become needy and dependent. None of this would've happened if I hadn't been so afraid and alone after my parents divorced. When my father left my mother he also left me. Believing Guy was ever capable of loving me and accepting me as an equal was a mistake. It was a stupid choice made by an innocent college kid. He controlled me from the start and took advantage of my insecurity. Over the years I've let him brainwash me into believing he knew what was best for the family and what was best for me. I've lived a lie and I've wasted too many years believing in miracles. He's never allowed me to be me. To him, I've always been a possession. My God, I could've done so many things differently. I finally admit that I'm filled with regret and, what's worse, I haven't learned from my mistakes until now. I swear I won't be with him next year. I owe it to myself and the boys. Someday, I hope to be in that cabin out west. I won't settle for less.*

Why it was finally so clear to her was inexplicable. But from the moment she met Guy at the terminal, to seeing him standing in the laundry room asking for sex, it all became clear. She was certain that without the group experience, it would have taken much longer for her to realize that the inevitable resolution to her personal stagnation was to get out of the relationship.

Carefully, she placed the notes back in the bureau and then went to the sink in the hallway bathroom to wash away the dried tears on her cheeks.

Guy was waiting in bed when she entered the bedroom. The nightstand light was on. He looked up from the *Time* magazine he was reading and commanded, "Come on Ellen; let's get to it. I'm tired!"

His routine was all too familiar and usually happened on his first night back.

"Give me another few minutes. I have to use the bathroom."

"Could you hurry up? I've been waiting. Come on!"

Her heart was racing, not from the anticipation of having sex but from the realization that she absolutely hated what she was about to do. She breathed deeply several times as she took off her long sleeved shirt, sneakers, and finally the jeans. Then she brushed her teeth and combed out the knots in her hair. Taking a final look at the mirror, from the depths of her soul she silently declared, *Close your eyes, Ellen. Close your eyes and be strong. Think of anyone else, someone from another time and place. Think of him. Close your eyes and take hold of that warrior in your thoughts. You're not with Guy tonight. Remember that. He might have his satisfaction, but he can't control your thoughts. Make this sacrifice one last time for the sake of the boys and for peace.*

She approached the bed wearing the mint green bra and matching panties she had put on that morning, got under the covers, and turned off the light. Immediately, he began to undress her as if she were a department store mannequin. Not a sound could be heard, except for Guy's heavy breathing as he pulled down the straps of her bra to reveal her breasts. Lying still on her back, under the bed sheet with her eyes closed, she reacted to the first touch in a robotic manner as if a button had produced the movement. She placed an arm on his shoulder and then turned her head away from his gaze. She had no desire to look at what he was doing. After fondling her breasts for a few moments, he moved his hand across her stomach and pulled down her panties with a single tug as if he was taking off his socks.

That first minute seemed like an eternity to Ellen and she made no effort to excite him. She merely waited for the intercourse to proceed. Then Guy murmured in her ear. "You know, I missed you. It's been a long time."

She said nothing in response to his comment. As he shifted his body on top of hers, she made no attempt to react to the movement and offered no assistance when he made his initial penetration. Awkwardly, he pushed her legs apart and began the intercourse with intensity. She continued to remain unresponsive; oblivious, as if in a hypnotic state yet it made no difference to him for he'd always been a selfish lover. His concentration was on reaching a climax, and he continued his up and down motion for a few seconds longer. Breathing heavily, he stopped a minute to rest, and then he continued again while rubbing her breasts. It was Guy's typical brutish style of lovemaking. He made no effort to hold up his body weight and, as difficult as it was, Ellen kept her composure without making a sound during the next few minutes. She retreated into her inner world, her imaginary hideout where Guy disappeared from her consciousness.

Finally, with a last trust of energy and a shudder from his lower body, it was over. He rolled off of Ellen immediately and laid there breathing deeply as if exhausted. In the next minute, Ellen was out of the bed and in the bathroom. Stepping into the shower stall, she turned the faucet and let the steamy hot water rinse away the entire episode. The longer she stood under the spray, the cleaner she felt. She washed her body in the places where Guy had violated her with scented coconut soap in a slow, circular motion, over and over until she felt purified from having been with him. Tonight, she wouldn't allow herself to feel ashamed. She'd been held hostage for the last time.

After fifteen minutes, she stepped out of the shower and patted herself tenderly with a bath towel. Then she doused baby powder all over, from her neck down to her toes as if it would further remove any remaining contamination. Slipping on clean underwear and a well-worn blue flannel nightgown, she shut the lights off and opened the bathroom door halfway to peek in the room and see if her husband had fallen asleep. She heard the even sound of his breathing and was satisfied he was out for the night.

It was now almost midnight. Joey's room was at the end of the hallway, and she wanted to check in on him before going downstairs. Stepping inside the dark room, he was sprawled out on top of his bed, still in the same shorts and tee shirt he wore to the airport. The eleven-year-old was the picture of boyhood innocence. Smiling, she tenderly covered him with a lightweight blanket, whispered "I love you," and then left his room.

Ellen had waited up countless times for Danny, tonight was nothing unusual. Pouring a full tumbler of merlot, she curled up on the couch with her book and began the next part of Sue Harrison's paperback, *My Sister the Moon.* After finishing a chapter, Danny came in through the garage door.

"Mom, I'm not that late. Only a half-hour, so don't give me one of your lectures. I'm going to bed. Don't wake me early."

Ellen got up off the couch so she could speak face to face. She blocked his path and told him, "Danny, your dad's home. Good thing he's sleeping or you'd get one of his lectures. Do you understand what I'm saying? So please... keep the music off. Ok? Just go to bed. I'll let you sleep till eleven, but no later. I love you...Good night sweetheart."

"Good thing you reminded me about him. Mom, you're pretty good at that."

With everyone finally settled for the evening, Ellen went back to the couch. She reached over, took the glass of wine, and drank it straight down. Alone, her thoughts turned inward.

Unlike other times when Guy sought and received sexual gratification, tonight was a turning point. Almost without exception, prior to this night, Ellen usually felt nothing but contempt and a deep sense of humiliation for the way he used her. She had tolerated his disgraceful behavior for too long. Sadly, from the beginning of her marriage, she'd observed his "dark side" thousands of times. Incredibly, he always made sure no one outside the family ever witnessed his acts of unkindness.

However, tonight her feeling of humiliation was finally gone. In the future, no matter what threats or intimidation came from Guy, she would stop submitting to him. If she had to have sex again, she'd only use it as a method of taking advantage of him. Guy would be divorced from her emotions, disconnected in every possible way. She would never again permit him to make her feel shameful, inadequate, or guilty. Tonight, as if the holy rite of exorcism had taken place, she was sure she had the motivation, resourcefulness, and courage to take back control of her life.

Sooner or later she was going leave him. There was no turning back. Sadly, there was no one to help with an escape plan. She knew that a difficult road was ahead. It would take all the determination and fortitude she had to make it work. But the alternative was unacceptable. With all her heart she vowed to make the break and take the boys with her.

To prove the point, she went to the hallway closet and found a spare comforter, placed it on the couch, and covered up for the night. This first act of independence marked the beginning of her journey. She thought of a wise saying after finishing the last sip of wine, *"A journey of a thousand miles starts with one small step."* She couldn't recall where she had read it, but for some strange reason it had always stayed in her head. Tonight was that first step, and tomorrow she'd take another.

Ellen turned off the light and waited for sleep. Her last wakeful thought was of the log cabin beneath the mountain, the place she described to the group.

CHAPTER 15

A small white gift box rested in the center of a green desk pad surrounded by memos and files. There was a gold ribbon wrapped around it with a card under the bow. Curious, Jake examined the container with a shake, a smell, and a weight check and then slipped off the ribbon to examine the contents. How it got there was a mystery because it wasn't there yesterday afternoon.

Placing the card aside, he took off the lid and a half-dozen pieces of *Godiva* chocolates stared up at him. The candy was exhibited like a set of expensive white pearl earrings or a precious antique cameo. He read the advertising blurb about the history of the chocolate company and chuckled. Then he picked up the card, it read, *Thanks so much for the workshop. It helped me find my way. Ellen Eastman.*

He made no effort to hide his delight at receiving the unusual gift. He laughed out loud and decided he was definitely going to have a good day. It was too early to eat one, so he placed the box in his center desk drawer and took a closer look at the card. Grinning, he observed that Ellen's printing was adolescent in style and commented, "This is weird. What a fantastic gift! How the hell did she deliver it?"

Jake searched his desk trying to locate the letter he received a week ago. While doing so he cursed himself for forgetting to answer it sooner. The letter was in his center desk drawer stuck under a copy of the new master schedule. After reading it again, a couple of impressions left their mark. There was a tone of resignation and an understated message of loneliness. Yet it still was mostly about her past, and an incomplete picture of what was going on in her life at the present time.

Jake's instincts told him to reply right there and then. However, after checking his schedule there wasn't an opening until third period, so he decided he'd write something then and put it in the morning mail pickup.

After interviewing several students, it was time for a break. Jake put a mug of water in the microwave and zapped it for a minute-and-a-half. Then he stirred in Carnation hot chocolate mix. Nearby the ultimate office treat, an Entemenn's deluxe crumb cake, stared him. Somehow he fought off the temptation and walked away. The secretaries teased him about his self-control, Loretta reminding him, "Hey Mr. Carr, what about those chocolates you received. You're not eating them?"

He let Loretta's tease go without comment and turned his attention to writing a letter.

Dear Ellen,

I was deeply touched by your personal revelations. No doubt it was extremely hard for you to explain your past in a few hundred words. You know, I've always believed that adopted kids pass along fifty percent of their failure to the people who took them in and the other fifty percent to their biological parents. Does that make any sense?

The sensitivity and depth of your parenting commitment is obvious to me. I can tell you're trying to figure out what's ahead in your life. Believe me, I can relate to that. My own kids are heading off to college this year and next. Then what? Lately it's been on my mind quite a lot.

I gathered from the group experience that the decisions regarding Danny are yours and that you're held responsible because your husband is away. I suppose he manages work world and expects you to manage home world. I understand your situation. It's a tough job, especially with a troublesome fifteen year old. I know you're trying to be his lifeguard and keep him from drowning in failure. I do the same thing everyday for a living. It's quite an uphill climb!

You mentioned your son is being difficult at home and with his studies. I'm positive Mrs. Fannen is doing her best to assist you and give him the proper guidance. She's an extremely competent counselor. Stay on top of things! There's only four weeks left till summer. Hooray!

If I can be of any service or help you in any way, please call me. Don't hesitate. I mean it!

> *Very Sincerely,*
> *Jake Carr*

CHAPTER 16

Ellen passed the night on the couch and woke up at the usual time. She folded the comforter, fluffed up the pillows, and made it look like she hadn't even slept there. Then she made coffee and used the downstairs bathroom to wash up. She figured if Guy asked why she hadn't slept with him, she wouldn't make anything of it, other than admitting she fell asleep reading after waiting up for Danny.

While drinking her first cup of coffee Ellen considered her plan. For the rest of the weekend she'd purposely stay out of Guy's way and remind the boys to do the same. The weekend weather was perfect and she was sure they'd be gone most of the day. On her part, she had no intention of discussing anything of a personal nature with Guy and more or less would continue observing his behavior towards her.

Later that morning she made Guy a cheese omelet and while she was doing the dishes listened to him complain about the stock market's bearish behavior and how it was costing him commission fees. When he left the table, Ellen felt relieved that she could now do her chores without his interference. However, that reprise was short-lived when she heard some loud screaming coming from the basement.

Apparently, the boys had gotten into an argument over using the "Playstation." Danny wrestled Joey to the basement floor and was sitting on his chest, holding him down. That act of bullying brought out a loud string of every curse word known to the eleven-year-old, which in turn brought Guy down from his upstairs easy chair, where he had been reading the Saturday *New York Times,* and into the middle of the foray. Standing over them he shouted, "What the hell is going on down here? Danny, get off your brother now, damn it!"

Danny looked up at his father and with adolescent audacity bellowed, "The little shit is pissing me off with his nagging. 'It's my turn. It's my turn.' I'm using the Playstation and Joey's bugging me."

With indifference to his dad's presence, Danny continued his domination. Guy gave it one more shot, restraining himself from entering the arena, which was something he told himself he'd avoid. However, he knew his authority was at stake and wouldn't give up.

"God damn it Danny, leave him alone right this minute and get upstairs. I'm not telling you again. You hear me? Don't make me lose it!"

As belligerent as ever, Danny refused to bend to his father's threat and yelled right back, "You have no right telling me what to do. You didn't see what happened, so back off and I'll let Joey go."

Guy's temper was at the boiling point. He was angry beyond words and pushed to the limit of his patience. Seconds before he was about to begin a physical confrontation with his son, Ellen stepped between them. With an icy stare, she pointed a finger at Danny and commanded him to get off his brother. "Danny, stop it! Stop this fighting over that dumb gadget. Don't you understand what you're doing to us? Your father just got home last night. Is this the kind of welcome you give him? I won't allow it!"

Ellen had no intention of permitting her son to set off Guy and make things worse.

"Okay Mom. I'm out of here. Joey's nothing but a friggin' baby."

Guy made no attempt to hide his aggravation, even though his wife had resolved the situation. He found it impossible to step away. He wanted the last word. Standing face to face with his son and shaking his fist, he said, "You better learn to listen to me or you can pass the rest of the weekend in your room. You hear me? Now get the hell out of here, and clean that messy room you live in."

With that said, Guy turned away and left the house twenty minutes later. Ellen didn't inquire where he was going, and he didn't tell her. And so the first full day of Guy's return to Middletown began with turmoil. Little did he know how often Ellen had to deal with similar confrontations.

During the following week Ellen avoided Guy in the same way she always did, spending time gardening and doing the routine housekeeping chores. He didn't seem to care if she was around and acted indifferently towards her. Ellen exercised in the privacy of her bedroom and took long walks around the neighborhood every evening. She also took great pains to keep the boys separated and out of his way.

Guy brought home enough work to occupy part of each day. He visited his parents twice, once alone and the other time with Joey. Ellen enjoyed the respite whenever he was out of the house and managed to keep her journal up to date. Danny continued to stay out whenever possible, or he escaped to the basement. Joey was now involved with Little League activities, and his father accompanied him to games.

Guy didn't demand another sexual encounter after the night he returned. Mother Nature had delivered an excuse if he had wanted more. Ellen got her period the very next day.

One important decision was made during the visit. He decided, because of financial considerations, that the family would spend the summer in Florida. Guy's parents offered to let the family use their winter home, and he accepted the proposal without consulting Ellen. He told her to make arrangements for lawn service and prepare to close up the Middletown house at the end of the school year. Both the boys had friends in their grandparent's neighborhood in Hollywood, Florida, and went along with the plan. Ellen showed no enthusiasm for the free timeshare but saw no reason to register a protest. Guy did what he wanted and this was his idea. He claimed that he would take the shuttle from Atlanta to Fort Lauderdale on weekends and spend the first two weeks of July with the family.

Ellen was on her way out for groceries when she noticed the mail truck pass by. She picked up the small stack of letters, and placed it beside her as she got in the van. When she reached the first traffic light nothing in particular was on her mind. She was listening to the news on the radio. Then she glanced over to the bundle and noticed the return address of Middletown High on one piece. Lifting up the letter, she immediately saw it was addressed specifically to her and not the usual address label that always read "To the Parents of Daniel Eastman."

Curiosity overcame her, and she pulled into a liquor store parking lot to read it. Instantly, the name on the bottom registered. Drawing it to her chest, as if a prayer were answered, she closed her eyes and made a wish the way a child does before extinguishing birthday candles on a party cake. Slowly she read the single sheet, pausing from time to time to reflect on the contents.

At first Jake's comment about being adopted and his "fifty-percent theory" made her laugh because it brought back memories of her mother excusing certain undesirable personality traits Ellen exhibited as a child. Then she read the final line and then read it again. *"If I can be of any service to you, or help in any way, please call. Don't hesitate."* He also added, *"I mean it!"* She thought, *Why would he say that?*

The letter was signed, Jake Carr. Staring at his signature, she found herself reflecting back to the hallway of Middletown High when the group was leaving. He had come up behind her and touched her arm. Then he mentioned his approval of her choice of a place to escape; the cabin under the mountain. He told her that he shared the same thought. She saw him clearly in her mind, and remembered his smiling face and handsome looks. She admired his willingness to be open, direct, and honest with her about things he truly believed in. She recalled the effect the program had on her. It had changed her.

But there was something else about her daydream image of Jake Carr; she realized she felt an intense physical attraction to him. It was a powerful force that completely captured her primal instincts. Sitting in the van, she held on to the romantic image. It was an erotic sensation that had been dormant during her married life. For her to have the feeling she was experiencing was extraordinary. It had never happened before and literally took her by surprise.

In truth, she had sent him the chocolates as a gesture of appreciation and not as a solicitation for an encounter. That wasn't who she was or who she had ever been. When she asked Hector to open the guidance office to leave a gift for Jake, the man spoke kindly about the counselor, "I know Mr. Carr a very long time. He is a very good man and cares about his students. He always talks to me and asks me about my family. Believe me, he will like the candies."

Presently, she found herself hopelessly mesmerized and taken prisoner by a vision. She imagined them standing together in the forest, surrounded in filtered sunlight created by a noon sun passing its rays through the openings of a massive oak tree. He was holding her against his chest and kissing her passionately.

Ellen also remembered the impact he had on her after that first interview. That encounter resulted in her having a greater awareness of her physical self. At that time she felt insecure in his presence. Yet based only on that five-minute encounter, she was sufficiently motivated to begin exercising on a regular basis and was more conscious of her fitness and weight than ever before.

Parked outside the liquor store, Ellen considered what her next move should be. *Should I follow up and write him back. No...that's dumb. But he left the door open for me to enter. He wrote, "If I could be of any service"...that's an understatement. Guy's leaving tomorrow, and then I'll be free to do what I want. Maybe I should drop by the guidance office and see what happens.*

By the time Ellen returned from grocery shopping she had made up her mind. She was going to stop by the high school next Tuesday at the end of the day. She'd go to the guidance office and ask where her son's locker was located and tell the secretary that she had to take Danny for a dental checkup. That would sound believable. Then, if luck was with her, she'd stop by Jake's office.

The week ended without any more problems and Joey accompanied her when she took Guy back to the terminal. There was no need to park because it was a departure flight. The hour ride to Newark International was uneventful. Ellen drove in silence, Joey listened to his Walkman, and Guy read the *Wall Street Journal*.

As they pulled up to the curb, Ellen knew a lot had happened since she came to this airport nine days ago: Guy's anger that first evening for not being better prepared for his visit, the sexual encounter, the meltdown with Danny, the vacation plans, and of course, the letter from

Jake Carr.

When Guy announced that he'd call later Ellen didn't even hear him. It was Joey who jumped out and gave his father a farewell hug. Ellen didn't make the effort of parting graciously. She had no desire to give him that courtesy. With the port authority cop gesturing to move the van, she merely said, "I'd better go. That transit cop is staring at us. Good luck with your clients. Goodbye."

"I'll probably call you later. Joey, be a good boy."

Guy picked up his suitcase and walked through the revolving door of the terminal, never once looking back to see Joey waving to him.

All the broken promises of the past twenty years seemed to penetrate her thoughts on the drive back to Middletown. What angered her more than anything else was the knowledge that his affairs probably went on unabated throughout their entire marriage. She actually believed some of his lame excuses when he insisted the other women meant nothing to him. She'd been duped repeatedly, but was she to blame for enabling his behavior? In her own recollection of time and events, she was, by disregarding the warning signs that were obvious.

When Ellen told the workshop group on that final Thursday session that her greatest act of independence was moving back to Middletown, no one there could have understood the significance of that statement. She returned solely for the purpose of gaining enough self-confidence to break free and start a new life for her and the boys.

"Mom, we're almost home. Can you make some meatballs and spaghetti tonight?" Joey asked as they pulled onto Main Street a mile from home.

CHAPTER 17

Ellen's anticipation for a chance meeting with Jake created such a sense of excitement that it paralleled the preparation for a date. She tried to restrain her emotions in order to keep some perspective, but wanted to believe that engaging Jake in some personal conversation might lead to a connection to him. Prior to leaving for the high school, Ellen spent extra time to look her absolute best. After showering and washing her hair, she put on a black cotton short-sleeved top and faded bluejeans that she thought would accent her figure. Ten-minutes before leaving, she jotted down a few notes on an index card, similar to what a student would do in preparation for a two-minute speech in a public speaking class. On the way to the high school she stopped at a bakery and bought a pound of butter cookies for the secretaries. Then she reviewed her notes one last time.

> *Be upbeat and positive.*
> *Try to speak calmly.*
> *Tell him how much the workshop helped.*
> *Tell him he's exceptionally talented in his field.*
> *Ask him his opinion of Danny's situation.*

Arriving earlier than she anticipated, Ellen sat in the van, alternately taking sips from a water bottle and reviewing the prompts on her index card. Several moms in their SUVs and vans maneuvered around the front entrance to pick up their kids. Nobody recognized her, and she was glad of it. The last thing she wanted was some PTA recruiting representative with a cheery smile wanting to inquire about why she was waiting there. The afternoon sun was warm and comforting as she entered the front door and made her way down the main corridor towards the guidance office.

Full of nervous energy, Ellen leaned across the counter that separated the secretaries from the waiting area and stood in front of Loretta.

"Good afternoon, Mrs. Marciano. What a beautiful day! Have you been outside today? I guess not. I brought in a special treat for you and the other secretary."

She took the cookies with an impish smile and said, "Mrs. Eastman, you're so very thoughtful. You know, I really don't need this treat, but I can't resist bakery cookies, especially when they're fresh. Often someone will bring in crumb cake or bagels, but personally I love these cookies. Thank you. Anyway, how can I help you? Who...who is it you would you like to see? The bell's going to ring shortly."

Caught off guard by the inquiry, Ellen's mind froze, and she forgot the reason she intended to use for being there. It never came out. Caught in momentary panic, she hesitated for a moment, moved a bit closer to Loretta and politely told her, "Umm...I happened to be in Mr. Carr's seminar. I'm sure you're familiar with the program...right? Do you think I could have a word with him...I mean if he's available? I'd like to thank him personally for giving us such a superb program."

Loretta knew about the chocolates, but she didn't let on. Yesterday, Jake had given her a pick and told her the gift was from Mrs. Eastman. Holding back her curiosity to ask a question about Jake's performance, Loretta was unable to restrain a wide grin. She gazed up at Ellen and said in her best professional manner, "His office is the last one on the right and he should be there. I think he's alone."

Ellen turned away and went where she was directed. Jake noticed her standing alone through the window of his closed door. He waved an acknowledgement and then held up his index finger because he was on the phone. At the same time, Mrs. Fannen also took note of Ellen's presence but was engaged in a parent conference. Uncomfortably, she stood outside Jake's office, pacing back and forth for another couple of minutes. She was feeling anxious. Twice she peeked through the glass door and each time he used the same gesture. After what seemed like an endless wait, he motioned for her to come in.

"Mrs. Eastman, what a surprise! I suppose you're waiting to see Mrs. Fannen? I'd offer you a nibble of the finest chocolate in the world, but I recently ran out. Just kiddin...what a terrific present. Generally I'd prefer a bottle of vodka, but the chocolates were delicious. Would you like to come in for a minute? Mrs. Fannen will probably be free shortly. You need to see her about your son?"

Relaxed by his opening remark, Ellen managed a shy smile and tried to recall the tips on the index card but fell short of remembering them, except the first one about being upbeat and positive. Still nothing came out the way she'd planned it. "I...I really didn't come because of any school business. Not really. I brought the secretaries a treat from the bakery. I really came because I wanted to thank you."

Jake was pleased to hear that she came to see him. Seeing her was a thrill. He'd been thinking about her for the last few days. He turned on his charm and said, "The treat you brought for the secretaries is a far cry from the expensive Godiva chocolates I got. I loved them. I especially got a kick out of the clever way you snuck them into my office. You must have met Hector, the night custodian. He's a terrific fella."

Ellen blushed. She felt completely foolish and was at a total loss for words. Jake sensed her uneasiness and adroitly shifted the conversation. He remembered her comment on the card with the gift telling him, *"You helped me find my way."*

"So Ellen, make me feel important. Tell me. Was the workshop really that beneficial to you? How so? Maybe I should take my show on the road and make a fortune awakening middle-aged boomers to rethink their direction. What do ya think?"

Jake opened the door for a conversation and now it was Ellen's choice to enter or take flight. She told herself to be brave and take a chance. "Jake, honestly, I couldn't begin to explain what the experience did for me. If I was looking for a miracle to happen, and truthfully I was, then it happened cause of you."

"Wow...you trying to knock me off this chair with you generosity? You said a miracle. Tell me this...what do you mean? Did something happen that you can't **explain**? Are you so sure of that?"

"That's exactly my point. I'm not sure how to describe what happened after...after I digested the things you taught me, not only about parenting but...but those final questions that you posed at the end of the group session. Even Linda, that blond woman who's raising her daughter alone, even she said you made her think. Think about things very deeply. Jake, the truth is I've been floundering, going nowhere and then out of that confusion... some things became clear to me. I probably sound so dumb."

Jake knew her letter and the candy were meant to tell him something about her. At first he wasn't sure why, now he though he understood.

"Ellen, it's not complicated and you're not dumb, at least not from my perspective. The whole idea of the seminar was to get you to think about your life as a parent and as a person. Most of the other people at that last session called up afterwards and shared some of their feelings, but you wrote me a personal letter and dropped off the chocolates. Why did you?"

"I suppose it was because you gave me the opening. I wasn't sure I'd ever be able to share anything. Other people seemed comfortable in that group situation. I'm pretty shy. I've always have been that way. But I can tell you this. I am trying to change and I'm sure it wouldn't have happened without you urging me to attend that final session. Your call made all the difference. My God, you really know how to raise a person's self-awareness...far better than anyone I've ever met. The kids are lucky to have you."

He was beginning to enjoy her company. So he decided to let it happen, just like he'd do with a student. He followed his instincts and casually said, "You're very kind to tell me that. Why don't you go ahead and talk. Its ok, I've got the time, and why not? You've come this far. Don't turn back now."

Ellen was sorry she made the comment about being shy. Nevertheless, she felt comfortable enough to tell Jake something about herself in the hope that he'd give her his perspective. "My God you really listen. I'm not used to that. All right, I'll tell you this much. I've lived a pretty isolated existence since I got married. Since I became a mother...it's been the only reason for me to get up each morning a face another day. I'm not at all pleased with how my life has turned out. And when you asked about what we regret...that was an awakening."

Jake was fascinated by the way she synthesized her life so clearly. He thought, T*hat was more of an answer than I ever expected to hear. I better lighten this up.* "So you're a graduate of Middletown High School. When was that?"

"I was in the class of 1977. Everything around here is still pretty familiar to me. Some parts of this school are the same, like the auditorium and the original classroom pods. I think this guidance office was once the choir room. I was in the choir."

The conversation went on for another ten minutes. Jake asked incidental questions about teachers and events, to which she supplied informative and humorous responses, especially about the social scene. The conversation loosened Ellen up more and more. Before long, it became obvious to her that Jake's interviewing skill was masterful. He led her and she followed. He was easy to talk with and more charming than she expected.

"You were an honor-roll student...is that right? I'd bet a case of Molson that you were. And, like you said, you were a member of the drill team, huh? That means you wore a short skirt and a thick white wool sweater while you twirled those dumb wooden guns. The boys must have loved seeing that. Actually, I love all that school spirit stuff. I think it's the heart and soul of one's high school memories. One thing's for sure. I don't see you as a member of the "disco generation" of the seventies. Can you dance?"

That single comment finally broke the ice and whatever was left of her shyness disappeared. Ellen started to laugh and so did Jake. She saw him show another side of himself, outside the counselor. She thought he was engaging, humorous, and personable. Ellen didn't know where it was all going until Jake switched back to the present tense.

"So Mrs. Eastman, how're you doing with what I taught you about the stress of parenting? Somehow I'm not sure you were prepared for some parts of the workshop."

This was a serious question, but Ellen wasn't ready to discuss all that she'd gone through in the past two months. Nevertheless, she tried to give him an honest answer. "You gave every one of us more than enough to consider in the way of parenting and you kept me up late on those Thursday nights wondering what I needed to change about myself. One thing was absolutely clear. I knew I had to alter my expectations. I'm still having problems with my son. I know you may be busy this time of the year, but could you possibly review his record? Maybe you could give me some insight. I'm doing this parenting thing while my husband is away most of the school year."

"There's no quick-fix when it comes to dealing with a fifteen-year-old who has bad habits about learning or, worse, a bad attitude about life. I mean, if he doesn't really care then there's not much that can be done at this time to salvage the year. I'll tell you what. I'll think on it. Is that ok for now?"

The phone rang and interrupted the conversation. Ellen realized that she'd been there much longer than she felt was appropriate and got up to leave the office, but Jake motioned for her to remain seated. While Jake was listening to the caller, Ellen took notice of everything in the room. Both bulletin boards were covered, the one directly behind him with notices, letters, teacher schedules, and administrative memos. There were phone numbers posted everywhere. The other board had nothing school related only snapshots. Many of them were pictures of mountains, rivers, and camping scenes.

Then her eyes focused on Jake who had turned his swivel chair away. She took notice of everything about him. He wore a short sleeved blue shirt opened at the neck. His arms were muscular and well-defined. Compared to other school personnel, he looked more like a fitness instructor than a counselor. He was already deeply tanned and appeared exceptionally well built. When he stood up to retrieve a file, she observed that he carried no extra weight around his waist. The blue chino Dockers fit him perfectly, and when Ellen realized she was "checking him out" she blushed and covered her face.

Jake was ruggedly handsome, and Ellen couldn't dismiss the stirring she felt. Although she acted the perfect lady in his presence, once again thoughts of him woke-up desires of erotic intimacy that were long dormant, or only reserved for late night reading with a glass of wine nearby. During those private times, she'd permit herself to imagine some fictional character like a medieval knight or warrior making love to her.

Abruptly, Jake hung up and turned his attention back to Ellen. "I'm sorry about that, but it was important. One of my students has an intolerable situation with a teacher. I'm sorry. Where were we? I'm really losing it. I guess it's the end of the day."

Instead of finishing with some informal conversation and ending on a positive note, for whatever reason, Ellen reverted back to her problems with Danny. She forgot that Jake had already promised to check into it and should have left it at that. However, this time she focused on Danny's lack of study skills and difficulty with math. After a while, Jake interrupted her. "Tell me, what does your husband think?"

"Remember. He's working down in Atlanta. I'm the full-time mother so I'm supposed to deal with Danny's problems. He expects me to fix things...to stay on top of it."

Within the course of any given month, Jake had heard this type of spousal excuse for not playing a part in parenting a dozen times or more. Her answer angered him and he thought, *I should let this drop right here, right now. I was enjoying this. She's such a nice person. Shit, now this could go to places I shouldn't be visiting with this woman. Danny is Fannen's student and not mine.* But he couldn't stop in mid-stream. "What does that mean, Ellen? What are you supposed to fix?"

"My husband holds me responsible when things go wrong. That's the way he is."

"Responsible. How? In what way? Honestly, it's not that clear-cut."

Ellen felt herself growing tense. Her mouth started to get dry and she worried where the conversation would go next. Jake's mood had turned serious and she felt trapped. Any further disclosure might lead toward sharing her marriage problems and that would open up a door she wanted left shut. But there was no escape. She had no choice.

"He believes I should be able to control Danny and make sure he succeeds at school."

"Is that possible for you to do? Is it? Like I said at the workshop, you've got no control over what happens at school, very little at home and none whatsoever outside on the street. Remember, what I told you? All you have is influence. That's the way it is. I'm sorry if it sounds cold."

"I came to your workshop because I needed help. In spite of all I've done, not much has changed. I wish it was getting better, but it's really not. I'm very worried."

"Now I get the picture. In a goof-proof perfect world you'd simply remind Danny to follow the rules at home. He'd acknowledge your authority and honor your request. Ellen, that's not how it is. Why does your husband think it's that simple? Never mind, I already know the answer. It's easier for him that way, easier to put the burden on you and hold you responsible. It'll never fly. It just won't work."

For the first time, Ellen couldn't contain her frustration any longer and without holding anything back spoke up with a quivering voice. "I'm not sure how to answer you. All I know is…I've tried… really tried to do a good job with the boys, but he finds fault with me most of the time. No, that's not true. He blames me all the time!"

With her emotional reply, Jake knew Ellen had never intended to come in and dump on him. It was obvious from the start that her unexpected visit was simply to connect. Now Jake had heard enough. He saw that Ellen was uncomfortable and unhappy with her situation but knew that nothing he said would change it. Tactfully, he shifted the conversation and decided to share something personal.

"Just so you know my son was a truckload of grief at Danny's age. Now he's leaving for college. I'm lucky I survived. He still gives me lots of grief. He's a lazy senior who was ready to finish three months ago. Honestly, I appreciate your situation. It's hard as hell to get things turned around when your kid has bad study habits or a bad attitude. Hopefully there's some daylight ahead. Summer's almost here and time for change. Are you taking a vacation, or will you be staying in Middletown?"

Ellen welcomed the opportunity to change topics. "Thankfully, we have the use of my in-law's home in Florida for the summer. The boys have friends in the area and there's plenty for them to do. The house has a pool and it's air-conditioned. My husband will spend two weeks with us and then he'll only be there on weekends. I should have some free time to do the things I like… walking the beach and reading. We'll be gone all summer."

"That sounds pretty good to me. Having free time on your own is the best. I know if I didn't have mine…forget it, I don't even want to think about that. Well Ellen, this has been an interesting conversation…actually I've enjoyed it very much. It's late though, and I have to kick you out. Tell you what, I promise I'll talk with Emily Fannen about your son. Maybe between the two us we can find something. It doesn't matter whether you're fifteen or forty-five. Each of us must recognize for ourselves, the necessity for change. That's the indisputable truth. And, that goes for you too, Ellen."

Then he gave her a final word of wisdom. "Let me explain one more thing. I think the best possibility for positive growth occurs because an individual feels pain, inner pain…pain that comes from making bad choices that make for hard times. Try to keep that perspective about change. Maybe Danny will awaken to that reality. I'll tell you this, a kid can get addicted to laziness just like an adult. Danny really isn't that unusual. I believe that if your husband would support you and if you worked together, things could change for the better. I respect your commitment to your family and I promise that I'll help you if I can. You have my word on that."

Ellen was touched by Jake's level of sincerity. Rising from the chair she extended her hand to him. He took it and held on longer than she expected and she said, "Thanks for your time. I suppose you're looking forward to the summer. You like to travel. Don't you?"

"It's true. I count the days from January until I leave on my adventure. Listen Ellen, you're a good person and a loving mother. Remember, I'm here if you need me. I mean it!"

CHAPTER 18

At long last, the school year was finally winding down. On the way to work, all Jake could think about was his upcoming trip. With two weeks left before the planned departure, his wanderlust raced along with the music of David Bowie.

J.D.'s graduation was Thursday at 7 p.m. on the Walden High School football field. Unfortunately, no amount of persuasion convinced his son to attend Project Graduation. Jake wasn't even sure if his son wanted to go out for a dinner celebration, but Sandy wanted things her way and made a dinner reservation anyway.

When he arrived at the office he saw Loretta was sorting out failure notices for the counselors. That meant he had to start notifying parents with the bad news. Even if summer school wasn't available for the subject the kid failed, a parent still had to be notified of any failure. That was department policy. Leaving messages on answering machines wasn't permitted. Today would be a trying day, telling parents about failure and taking flak from them. Jake had to go through his entire stack of blue failure notices, over twenty, and record the date, time, and outcome of the phone conference.

Invariably, the parents would express shock, surprise, amazement, and anger, all combined into a single condemnation of the outcome. Their shock came from the claim that it was a complete surprise to them. They were amazed when they learned that their kid's covered it up so well. And upset, because of the certainty that it would upset the summer plans and cost them tuition money that wasn't in the budget.

As Jake was passing by Emily Fannen's office, he saw Ellen Eastman sitting there. The counselor's face was frozen in delight because on her desk was a flower arrangement. He guessed it was a gift from Ellen, so he continued on his way. Returning with a Pepsi, he began eating his lunch while checking failure lists, but soon lost interest, wondering if Ellen would stop by his office.

After his last meeting with her, he'd promised to check out the situation regarding Danny's academic problems, and he did. He reviewed Danny's record and then discussed the situation with Emily Fannen. Jake respected his colleague and, after ten years of observing her counseling skills, concluded that every possible intervention had been tried to get Danny Eastman on the right track.

Ellen was a woman with a story he wanted to unravel. His attraction to her puzzled him. During the past couple of weeks there were many times when she came into his thoughts uninvited and unexpected. He thought she was very attractive but she was also very different from the women he'd met in the course of his career. Ellen may have been shy in public, but with him she was absolutely enchanting. He was drawn to her because he believed she was going through a stressful period of self-evaluation. Certainly, it was purely coincidental that their paths had crossed. As aware as he was about performing his job in a strictly professional manner, when it came to Ellen, the temptation to know her better was overpowering. Situations similar to this had happened before. In fact several other women had left an opening for a possible liaison but Jake never crossed the line.

No sooner had his thought process concluded, when unexpectedly she entered his office and stood in front of his desk. Jake thought she looked fantastic and was happy to see her. "Hello Mrs. Eastman. Emily might love fresh flowers, but I'll take Godiva chocolates anytime."

"I'm not surprised. And how are you Mr. Carr? That sounded funny. How are you Jake? You've got to be so excited about your trip. As for me, all I can look forward to is a 24-hour drive on Interstate 95. Picture it, one big happy family jammed into a Dodge van with all the luggage and junk necessary to spend eight weeks in Hollywood. You've got the better deal. Mrs. Fannen has just informed me that Danny escaped failing math by a single point. Neither of us knows how the extra point fell out of heaven. Frankly, I'm very relieved. This whole year has been tough. I'm sorry if it sounds like I'm whining, I know how much you hate that."

Jake wasn't paying attention to anything she said. He was mesmerized by the animated way in which she was talking and felt a little smitten by her presence. Turning on his charm, he said. "I'm good. I heard that Danny passed. Maybe he had a guardian angel. So, you want to know how I am. Well, I'm feeling antsy. But I'm ready for adventure. I've been working out lately. Didn't you take notice? I'm ready to be out on my own. I mean, what the hell, if I'm going to be honest with you. I'm dying to get outta town."

Ellen didn't comment right off. She thought he was flirting with her, but wasn't sure. She felt drawn to him and gingerly leaned back in her chair. Jake stared at her and they remained transfixed on each other's eyes. Then he slowly nodded his head up and down while folding his arms across his chest. Still nothing happened and neither one of them spoke.

Finally, Jake turned toward the bulletin board and muttered, "This is real hard for me to say. I mean…I can't even look at you when I say it, but here it goes. Lately, you've been on my mind…coming at me from all angles and whenever you felt like appearing. Yup, you've been right there and I won't pretend it isn't so. It's all crazy and I don't know why. Maybe that's my problem. I should stop trying to figure it out. I guess you're not suffering like me."

Ellen was thunderstruck. At first, she felt embarrassed and she glanced toward the door, not so much feeling afraid or nervous, as feeling completely bewildered by his admission. Nothing came out.

While his face was still turned away, he placed his index fingers on his temples and started moving them in a slow circular motion as if uncertain of what else to say. Nothing came out. Then Ellen pulled her chair closer and joined her hands on her lap. She knew he'd taken a chance. Now it was her turn.

She exhaled deeply and replied, "How strange for you to mention that. I've been thinking a lot about you and, in fact, it got pretty bad last night, so bad that I had to have a few shots of Wild Turkey Rye."

Then, almost on cue, they both broke out in a bunch of giggles like a couple of kids who shared a silly joke. Jake offered Ellen his hand and she took hold of it. Then he said, "Ellen, how are you? Let's toss out the formalities. I really want to know."

The conversation took off in all directions. It was lighthearted and easy, like two friends who met for a drink after work. Ellen kidded him unceasingly about his performance during the seminar.

"You really get into the role! You become Jake the lecturer, Jake the group leader, Jake the wise and powerful. Am I really supposed to believe you're that sure of yourself? Are you ever unsure? Are you? Would you ever admit it to anyone? What's so scary is when you walk around the room while you're talking. Then you stand right in front of some unsuspecting soul and demand an immediate response. You know something Jake; you should have your own cable talk show, or try your luck at being a stand up comic. I'm just teasing. One thing is certain. You're real good at making me think...real good!"

"Ellen, you got me. Truthfully, I've always been confident in my work and in my likes and dislikes. I'm the type of man who likes being an individual and who'll always give you a definitive answer. I can't tolerate people who hedge. I think men like that are gutless. As the jocks might say...they've got no balls. Sorry if that sounds crude. Come on, you remember my number one rule. Say what you mean and mean what you say and say it to my face. Well, I try to live my life that way. Sometimes it gets me into trouble. I meant what I said about you being on my mind. I won't take it back. It is what it is. I think I'm bewitched...how did you do that to me?"

With that said he got up from his chair and walked around the desk.

Ellen rose to meet him. They stood less than a foot apart for half a heartbeat. Then Jake put his arms around her waist, brought her to him, and held her tightly for a brief moment. Ellen felt suspended in time and space as his cheek touched her face. He didn't try to kiss her, although she wished he would.

Very much aware she was in a public place, she whispered in Jake's ear. "I know we'll see each other again. I know it for sure." Then Ellen touched his cheek, smiled and left the office.

Jake plopped down at his desk trying to comprehend what just happened. All he knew was that some emotional force took over him and that it was far stronger than his ability to resist it. He understood that he made the first move. It was his awkward but sincere confession that she was on his mind. Then he offered his hand and she accepted it. Finally, without any hesitation, he held her. It was a moment of romantic impulsivity on his part and she accepted it. It was an inexplicable and spontaneous act, however it was real. Everything that happened between them was real. Jake couldn't account for his vulnerability. He thought that perhaps when he replayed it on his ride home or on his nightly walk, then possibly some insight would be revealed to him. But for the present time, he decided to allow himself to run with it.

One thing was certain. Ellen would be leaving for Florida shortly and he was heading to Wyoming in two weeks. He reconsidered the situation. *Maybe I'm making more of this than was the case. She* mentioned *the possibility of us meeting again. No, no. That's not true. She said, "I know we'll see each other again." Shit, I was too involved with the embrace to answer her.*

It was impossible for Ellen to return home after the encounter with Jake. She drove to her favorite park, a place called Summit Pond. After parking the van, she sat on a park bench overlooking the tree-lined lake. It was 3:30 in the afternoon. Everything she observed, the pine trees, hedges, and the meadow grass, were a shade of spring green that was in harmony with the jade-colored pond.

Jake's words and actions took her totally by surprise, and her response to him was unrehearsed and spontaneous. She wasn't confused or troubled. Everything Jake had said and did was sincere. He was the total opposite of Guy. From the beginning, Ellen believed that Jake was authentic and that the level of honesty she witnessed from him had set him apart from any man she'd ever known. Although she didn't want to admit it, the physical and emotional attraction she felt toward him was overpowering.

Whether she should let go of him because he was married didn't matter.   Common sense should've dictated that she forget what happened, but that was impossible. He'd left her breathless by holding her the way he did.   It was as if by a single act of loving kindness, he released her from a self-imposed emotional exile and brought her back to life.   Her mind shifted to the recollection of his hard chest pressed against her breasts. She smiled when she thought of how difficult it must have been for him to admit his interest in her.   Yet she had responded in the same way to him.

After treating herself to a half-hour of peaceful ecstasy, she decided to walk slowly around the pond to study the reflecting sunlight on the dull green water. A deep sense of satisfaction came over her. She felt nothing they had done was wrong. To her every part of it seemed right. An inner peace took over her and she felt young again. For the moment her life held promise. She felt reborn as a woman and as a person. It was an exciting and all consuming emotional experience. She was energized and aglow, as if a new life force had entered her body. Every concern she had in her head when she awoke that morning had completely disappeared. Tomorrow would have to wait.

For the first time in half a lifetime of waiting, she let herself think about another man, someone with the physical attractiveness, strength of character, and genuine compassion that Guy was sorely missing. And, as if that wasn't enough, she thought Jake Carr was the most fun-loving, entertaining, and spontaneous individual she'd ever met. A chance encounter had put them together.

Ellen was happy beyond words and believed with all her heart that something good would come from the embrace she shared with Jake.

CHAPTER 19

Annie squeezed in between her parents in the packed bleachers of the football field at Walden High's commencement. The processional music was just beginning when she turned to her father as asked, "Dad, can you see him? With all those blue caps and gowns I can't. Where is he?"

"When they enter the field we'll probably pick him out."

There were hundreds of parents and relatives in the audience. Some dressed up and ready for a restaurant party, while others appeared to have come directly from work at a construction site or factory job. The town of Walden was a mixture of working class, professional people, and retirees. It was obvious by the dress and demeanor of those in attendance who was who sitting in the bleachers.

J.D. made up his mind at the last minute not to attend Project Graduation. He was going camping with his friends. He also informed Sandy and Jake that he preferred the company of his two buddies sitting around a fire rather then attending a family dinner in his honor. Very reluctantly, Sandy surrendered the dinner demand but insisted after the ceremony family pictures had to be taken.

As the procession filed past the grandstand, several people yelled out for their kids to look at them for a snapshot. When J.D. passed by, Jake resisted the temptation for fear of aggravating Sandy. He knew she was distressed because of J.D.'s decision not to celebrate in a way that she believed was appropriate. Other than a sign over the entrance to the family room that read ***Congratulations Graduate***, there was little else in the way of fanfare. Two graduation cards were left on the desk in J.D.'s bedroom, one with a $200 check from Jake and Sandy and another with a $25 gift certificate for Old Navy from Annie.

At special times like this Sandy missed her parents immeasurably. During the previous evening, she had spent a couple of hours looking at old family albums when the kids were in their early childhood and Grandma and Grandpa visited for Thanksgiving and birthdays. Sandy remembered them as loving grandparents who doted on the kids. One of Grandpa's favorite rituals was to take his grandchildren to Toys R Us for a hundred dollar shopping spree. J.D. always picked up more Tonka construction trucks and Annie got her choice of a Barbie or a stuffed animal. Even seven years after her parent's deaths, Sandy still exhibited profound grief on occasions that were milestones in her children's lives.

Jake's relationship with his in-laws had been civil but sterile. From the start they considered him an enigma and an outsider. Consequently, their actions toward him were consistent with that premise. Sandy's father had an insufferable disposition, and Jake referred to him in private as "Grumpy." Jake clearly understood that his background fell well short of their expectations but couldn't care less.

Sandy and Jake started dating not long after her divorce. At the time she was teaching at a suburban high school in Edison, New Jersey and living alone in a three-room apartment, still in emotional aftershock from the disappointment of her marriage. Within that first month, Sandy gave Jake a clear picture of her past and the historical background of her marriage.

Sandy dated a young man named Alan Rosberg, who was three years older, all through high school. She was engaged after her freshman year in college and married a month after her twentieth birthday in a black tie affair at a private country club. Alan was clean cut, respectful to her parents, and a Dean's List student. He was Jewish, level-headed, old-fashioned, and could be trusted not to take sexual advantage of Sandy. Alan was always her mother's number-one pick, and she encouraged her daughter to marry him, believing he was the perfect match. Rosberg convinced Sandy to marry after his graduation from NYU, and Sandy, fully aware she'd have to finish her education in the future, accepted his proposal.

Alan had set his sights on working for IBM. His credentials as a top prospect were undeniable, and Sandy looked forward to a comfortable and satisfying life with the first boy she'd ever seriously dated.

However, by the time the honeymoon ended a young woman's dream was shattered. The beautiful, sensitive, and tender-hearted Jewish girl from an upper middleclass background was naïve and completely unaware of her new husband's priorities. He'd kept them private until the flight back from Paradise Island. Twenty minutes before the plane landed at Kennedy he declared his intentions with this remark, "This is the way it's going to be when we get back. The honeymoon is over. On Monday morning, I'm starting out of the gate with a bang. Absolutely nothing will get in the way. I've been dreaming of wearing a gray suit and an IBM security badge day and night for the past two years."

Alan inferred that his first love would have to be his new job, declaring, "It's the only way it can be done if you want to live well and get the things we both desire. I was recruited by 'Big Blue' and I'm going to give a hundred percent to the company. I'm theirs whenever they ask. You can finish school at night and work during the day.

Together, we'll be able to buy a new house within three years. That's the symbol of success and I want it."

Alan's lack of sensitivity and selfishness devastated her. Never once while they dated had he ever given Sandy any indication of his strategy for success until the final months of their engagement, when he was preparing to begin his career. Not long after the honeymoon, Mrs. Alan Rosberg realized that she'd let herself believe in a fairy tale. In reality it had turned into a melodrama of misery. She had played fair and followed his lead, but in the final analysis, he had deceived her into believing she was the love of his life. And Sandy, true to her Jewish upbringing and the solemn promise she'd made to her mother, had saved herself only for him. He'd been her only sexual partner.

In spite of a heroic effort by Sandy to induce Alan to rethink his game plan, Alan's blind ambition took over and the relationship ran out of momentum within a few months. Not only from an empty sex life but because he was a passionless man, a calculating individual who routinely withheld intimacy as a means of control. Alan didn't care about Sandy's sexual and emotional needs; his priority was satisfying the middle-level managers at the company.

Sandy was so ashamed of his treatment towards her that she never shared the truth with her mother and her pride kept her from admitting the mistake to her father. However in public, the Rosbergs had been better actors than Bill and Hillary Clinton and no one in her family had suspected a thing.

At the very end, after seven years of sexual deprivation and emotional neglect, Sandy took the advice of a trusted uncle who told her she had wasted enough of her life. He advised her to ask Alan for a divorce. Uncle Seth also promised that he'd explain the situation to his brother-in-law so there would be no family trouble. Alan, true to form, promptly accepted a fifty-fifty settlement and that was the end of it. He showed no remorse and registered no complaint. His career was still the centerpiece of his life.

According to Sandy, after her first full day of separation, her long period of insomnia abruptly ended, her migraines ceased, and her stomach disorder disappeared.

Jake Carr unexpectedly walked into her life four months later. He was with another woman at a Halloween party. After being introduced, Sandy thought of him as someone as far from the persona of Rosberg as she could possibly get. His flamboyant style, long hair, fringed buckskin jacket, and Frye cowboy boots fascinated her almost as much as the way he talked of his road adventures out west.

A mutual acquaintance passed Jake her phone number and told him

Sandy was interested in meeting him. He called her and she accepted a mid-week date. He took her out for ice cream on the first night and later on, kissed her so passionately that she wished she had asked him to stay longer. Even so, he left her with a feeling that he'd be back. His parting words were, "Sandy, you're a keeper."

ॐ

Unlike the scattered round of applause that followed the reading of a graduates' name, when Joshua Daniel Carr was announced only three people clapped, his family. Whether J.D. even heard them was questionable. Nevertheless, Jake leaned over to Annie and Sandy; he kissed them both, and then held his wife's hand to show his gratitude for helping their son reach this day.

Then Annie exclaimed, "Well you two did the job. Joshua Daniel is a high school graduate, and, even better, he's leaving home soon. Hooray for both of you." Then she gave her mother a hug and her dad a poke in the side.

After the ceremony, J.D. posed for a couple of pictures with his family. Before he left for a night of frolic with his friends, Jake passed on a critical piece of advice. "J. D., I'm proud of you but whatever you decide to do, be careful. I didn't spend eighteen years as your guardian angel to see you end up as a graduation night statistic. No matter what, don't drive if you are gonna drink. You promise?"

"Ok, Dad. I promise not to drive. I'll crawl in my sleeping bag and watch the world spin around while trying not to puke. Don't worry about me. I'll see ya tomorrow."

J.D. tossed his cap and gown to his mother and took off. On the way back to the parking lot Jake offered to take his ladies to dinner, but there were no takers. Sandy sat in silence on the drive back to Treetop Terrace and Jake immediately sensed her disappointment with the whole graduation event. When they got home, Annie left with Jeff, her new romantic interest, and Jake retreated to the basement.

J.D. didn't return until early the next morning, and he was hung over. Fortunately, he was still in one piece and so was his Ford Ranger. Jake, always the first one up, offered to make him pancakes, but J.D. desired coffee and aspirins. Jake respected his request and read the sports page while his son drank his coffee hunched over the kitchen counter, barely able to keep his head up.

Sandy soon joined them and even though Jake motioned with his hand not to bother the boy, nevertheless she began an interrogation concerning his activities of the previous night. Standing beside her son, she inquired in rapid fashion, "J.D. Carr, you look terrible! Where did you go? Was James with you? You didn't drive, did you? I wish you

149

had gone to Project Graduation like everybody else. I was worried sick about you all night while your father slept like a baby. Why didn't you call? Why can't you be like the other kids? I don't know why your father doesn't get upset. What are your plans for today?"

It was a stark reminder of the different parenting styles each of them used. Generally, Jake would get lost when his wife entered "mother's curiosity zone" and conducted the questioning. It was like she refused to allow space to anyone in the family when they needed it most. And, unless they started barking back, she couldn't help herself. Good timing wasn't one of the strengths of her parenting.

"Mom...what's your problem. Leave me alone. All I want is to lie down for a few hours. You're never gonna understand...are you? I did what I wanted. Will you get over it? I'm home, aren't I? The truck's outside...isn't it. So what's your problem?"

Then Jake broke in to put out the sparks before there was fire. "J.D., go upstairs. Now! Look Sandy, you made your point. Whether he was listening...I don't know. Graduation is officially over. The coffee is made, and there's an onion bagel for you. I'm starting my chores. I'll check on the boy later."

After a few minutes, Jake heard J.D. close the door of his bedroom. So he stopped the vacuuming and returned to the kitchen to make Sandy some scrambled eggs. It was another ritual; making his wife Saturday morning breakfast. He'd set a place at the oak dinner table, pour her juice and coffee, place the lifestyle section of the *New York Times* next to her plate, and cook to order. He knew she enjoyed being pampered.

Later that morning, he told Sandy they'd go out for a Chinese food and he would rent a video. He even said he willing to see *Shakespeare in Love*. She told him the proposal sounded good, but she would like to pick the movie. Jake's preference was always action, westerns, or horror flicks. Sandy would compromise once in a while if she liked the actors. Last weekend they had seen a Bruce Willis flick called, *Mercury Rising*. This time Jake figured he'd have to settle for a sappy love story.

After lunch Jake took off for his Saturday afternoon hike. It was a humid June afternoon when he parked the van in a lot at one of Orange County's forest preservation areas north of Walden.

At the start of the hike, he considered how well he had avoided any major family conflicts for the past month, keeping to his daily routines and keeping things running smoothly. He wanted to leave his family on good terms. Both of the kids had summer jobs and Sandy would be done with school on Monday. Additionally, he had paid for a pool membership so his wife and daughter could enjoy a daily swim.

A mile down a trail, Jake removed his tee shirt to get some sun. He wore faded mint green hiking shorts with missing buttons on both back pockets. Sandy had pleaded with him dozens of times to upgrade his hiking clothes, but to no avail. He liked how he looked and felt comfortable. Hikers with upscale "Columbia" outfits along with their "Jansport" stuffed designer fanny packs and backpacks made him laugh. They reminded him of similar types he encountered on the golf course, men with all their expensive equipment who generally shot over a hundred, in spite of their name-brand attire and high-quality custom gear.

Wiping the sweat off his face with a blue and white checkerboard bandana, Jake set off to hike nine miles over the next three hours. With only two weeks left before the trip, he was training harder than ever to get ready. Typically, he exercised three times a week all during the winter. Then when spring arrived, he would gradually increase the use of dumbbells to harden his body. Every night he took Missy for a two-mile walk around the development, but that wasn't the same as trail hiking.

After an hour, he found a spot under some towering pines and sat comfortably on the brown needles underneath. He took a few swigs from his canteen, leaned back against the trunk, and listened to what his inner voice had to say. Over the past few days his focus on the trip and his attention to family matters had been repeatedly interrupted by the memory of his office encounter with Ellen Eastman. He was still unable to decide what, if anything, he should do next and tried to convince himself to put some distance between him and Ellen. He thought. *You know Jake, whatever happened in that office was an impulsive "glitch" on my part. Think about it. All those years of parent consultation and never once did I do something like that. Shit, I've got to admit that it was an admission of interest on my part. For all I know, she probably saw it the same way and she was interested in me. God damn, I hate being in a spot like this...I admit it ,I probably shouldn't have said what I did or held her, but it's too late to change what happened. There's one more week of work left and then I'll be free. Why should I do anything?*

Satisfied with his mindset regarding Ellen, Jake resumed his hike with a clear picture of the coming summer. He would pass the time making preparations for the trip and stay focused on that. Tonight, he had a dinner-movie date with his wife, and tomorrow he would be playing golf with Kevin. His universe was in order, and he felt there was no compelling reason to change things. Yet, in the back in of his mind Ellen remained, showing up too often to be ignored or forgotten.

CHAPTER 20

Guy Eastman returned to Middletown late Sunday night. They didn't get back to their Westgate home until after eleven. He was exhausted and went straight to bed. Ellen stayed downstairs and read well past midnight. Tomorrow was the first day of summer. The boys were finished with school and the family was driving to Florida next Saturday. It was going to be a busy time ahead to get things in order at home and pack for the extended vacation.

Ellen remained detached from Guy for the first few days. With everyone home and making demands, it was easy to stay clear of him. Strangely, there was peace in the house because the family was only together at dinnertime, other than that, the boys were never home. They slept till noon every day, ate a big breakfast and left to enjoy their first week of freedom.

Guy only made one demand and it wasn't for sex. For some inexplicable reason, he insisted that he accompany his wife whenever she went out. That was one of his leftover quirks from when they lived in Atlanta. It used to drive Ellen crazy because he was a compulsive shopper with obsessive "namebranditis." Nothing caused him greater distress than substitutes for name brands, or if Ellen forgot that only BumbleBee solid white albacore in water met his taste requirements.

Now, whether Ellen had to pick up groceries or run an errand, Guy wanted to go. Privately, she believed it was his idea of a date. She hated going to Home Depot for two hours, in search of a new gadget to add to his personal collection of assorted power tools. However, regardless of what she felt, Ellen had no other choice but to resign herself to his company. It certainly reinforced the rationale for her move back to Middletown. She'd been able to escape those inane behaviors of his for almost a year.

It amazed her that Guy was so aloof towards her, treating her more like a neighbor who happened to be available for a trip to town, than a wife of twenty years. It wasn't like it mattered anymore to her; rather, she wondered how he justified such indifference in his own mind. Their conversations were so banal it proved that she was nothing more than a house servant to him.

On Tuesday around mid morning a local landscaper was scheduled to show up for the purpose of negotiating a deal for lawn maintenance during the summer. The Eastman family would be gone for two months and Guy informed Ellen that he would handle the arrangements. Ellen was upstairs changing sheets in Danny's bedroom when she heard the truck pull in front of the house. Curious, she looked out the window and watched Guy walk out to greet the man. Just then the phone rang.

"Ellen. This is Jake, am I glad you picked up the phone. Listen, I'd like to see you. Do you think you can you meet me in an hour?"

Ellen froze up. She never considered the possibility of ever seeing Jake again, certainly not on such short notice. "I want to, I really want to, but it's…it's impossible. My husband's home, and I…I don't think I can get out."

There was a moment of silence before Jake tugged against her heart. "Ellen, you don't understand. I'm going on my trip and you'll be gone for the whole summer. Please…please meet me. I can't explain right now. It's…its real important to me. Please meet me!"

She wasn't prepared to leave the house. Nevertheless, there was something uncharacteristically urgent in his voice. Without thinking, she told him, "I'll try…but where should I meet you?"

"At The Mayfair Farms parking lot. I'll be there at 12:30."

"Jake, are you sure about this? Tell me now…"

"I wouldn't be calling if I wasn't. See you later."

After Jake hung up, he sat for a long while and wrestled with what he would do when they met. Since Ellen left his office last week, all methods of distraction failed to keep her from his thoughts. In spite of an all-out effort, he lost the battle. He recalled that it was like an invisible person was with him all the time, even on Saturday night with his wife. Ellen was there, everywhere, at the Chinese restaurant, on his walk with Missy, watching a movie, and worst of all, in his bedroom. He couldn't make love to Sandy without thinking of her. He was out of sync and confused.

Jake figured his only course of action was to give himself a test. If he was alone with Ellen, even for a brief time, what would happen? What if they were out of his office and in a safe place? Perhaps then he'd be better able to determine what this "thing" really was. He wanted to know the truth and not fool himself into seeing an oasis, when maybe it was only a mirage in a barren desert.

Meanwhile, Ellen put herself in a difficult predicament. Was she willing to toss aside all common sense for a chance meeting with Jake? Why did he need to see her and what motivated him to express it so sincerely? As much as she wanted the rendezvous, she wondered how she could pull off such a daring feat with Guy insisting that he accompany her wherever she went. The clock was ticking and a choice had to be made.

Quickly, she secured her journal from its hiding place and turned to the page that recorded what took place in the guidance office a few days earlier. When she came to the line that read, *He moved through time and space and in between the heartbeats of my soul and took hold of me.* She decided to take a leap of faith. She tossed caution aside and felt the reward was worth the risk.

With whirlwind speed she used the bathroom, brushed her teeth, changed shirts, and grabbed her pocketbook and keys. Then, with the stealth of a secret agent, she snuck out to the van, started it up, and drove up the driveway. Fortunately for her, Guy was in the backyard with the landscaper when he heard the engine. Almost immediately, he came to the front yard to see what was going on.

She was at the top of the driveway when he yelled out. "Ellen, where are you going? I'll be done in a minute. Wait...wait!"

She stopped the van, leaned out the driver's side window and yelled back. "I forgot to go to the bank and the walk-up closes at 12:30. Finish your business with the landscaper." Then she waved as she drove up Westgate leaving Guy seething mad.

Ellen escaped under Guy's nose. Never in her married life had she dared to take a risk like this. The opportunity never presented itself. The consequences of angering her husband with her blatant act of defiance didn't deter her from following her heart. Remembering her decision at Summit Pond, she put her trust in Jake. If he needed to see her, that was a good enough reason to tempt fate.

Ellen was as nervous as a getaway driver at a bank hold-up as she drove to the meeting place. She began telling herself, "He must really want to tell me something important. Be calm and let him lead."

Mayfair Farms was only five minutes from the high school, but the excitement of seeing Ellen caused Jake to lose all perspective, and he literally raced to get there. There was a song he wanted Ellen to hear. It was very close to describing his current emotional state of mind. Right before arriving at the destination, he slipped in the cassette and forwarded it to the beginning of the song. Then he watched and waited for Ellen, hoping she'd come. It was 12:35 and Jake began to wonder. *Where was she? Didn't she think meeting me was as important as I made it sound? Am I nuts for doing this?*

A short time later Jake saw Ellen's blue van pull up next to his Aerostar. He motioned for her to come over to his van. She was wearing sunglasses with a light blue blouse and jean shorts.

"I can't believe you really came. I'm so excited. Bear with me for a few minutes? There's a song I want you to hear. Listen to the words. While the music's playing I'm going to drive us to a place where we'll be alone. Is that all right?

"That's fine, but let's go now. I told my husband I was going to the bank."

Jake drove out and pushed in the cassette for the music to begin.

I'm a million miles from anywhere, where can I be.
Somewhere out on the ocean.
Just take a look at the horizon, what can you see.
There's nothing there for me.
I feel shipwrecked. I might as well be shipwrecked.
I'm hopeless and alone, drifting out to sea. I'm shipwrecked.

Jake turned the volume down after the song played, then reached over and touched her forearm. She felt his warm hand move gently on her skin. It was a very sensual and a tender touch. She still wasn't sure what signal he was sending.

After a moment he said, "That music is from the final album by Genesis, it's called *Calling All Stations*. The song is called *Shipwrecked*. Do you know the band? I have all their music dating back to the mid seventies."

"I'm not familiar with the group, but I liked the song. It was very interesting."

Jake continued, "It's called *Shipwrecked*. Sorry... I already told you that. What's the matter with me! Anyway, I suppose it accurately reflects what I've been feeling since that moment we shared in my office last week. I've been kind of lost lately. I don't know how it happened or why it did. I sort of remember what I said to you. Then...then I held on to you. I remember that hug, for sure."

Ellen had no idea how to respond. Nevertheless, she tried to understand where he was coming from. "That's an unusual title for a song, but I can identify with the idea of being shipwrecked. Are you concerned about the other day?"

"Yeah, I am. It's way out of character for me. I don't say stuff like that and that hug I gave you, it was for real. It happened. Since then, I've been losing it. Do you get what I'm saying? I'm lost...I admit it. I'm going nuts and it's all over you. I can't just walk away from you for the summer. I...I can't do it."

"Jake, you're never lost. And if you are, I'm sure it'll be for a very short time. The truth is... I've been lost for the past twenty years. I've been shipwrecked in a strange place. Can you top that, Mr. Counselor?"

He nodded in agreement because he believed what she said. "Ellen, you're something. That's a hell of a statement...I suppose it would take a while to explain how that happened but we only have thirty minutes. For now, I'm going to a little park. It's a couple of miles away. Hardly anyone ever goes there because it has no restrooms or playing fields. I think you'll enjoy walking around the meadow. I just want to spend some time with you."

"I'm glad you called, and that I picked up the phone. What a stroke of luck that was. Guy was home."

A few minutes later Jake parked the van and opened the door for Ellen. He placed her hand around his right forearm, and they began walking at a slow pace toward a huge grassy field where there were lots of maple trees. The weather was perfect, sunny and comfortable.

Ellen wanted to hear about his trip. "Jake, tell me about your summer adventure. What's it like to travel across the country alone? Don't you worry about anything happening to you? Do you miss your family?"

"Unless you've experienced it…it's almost impossible to explain. I consider the trip to be a pilgrimage. Sounds corny but, somehow I find my other self out there. Frankly, by the time I leave I'm so excited and so up for the escape that nothing else matters. You asked if I missed my family. Oh boy…let me ask you this. If I answer truthfully, will you promise that from this moment on, regardless of whatever happens, we'll always tell the truth to each other? Is it a deal?"

"I'll make you that promise. I'll tell you the truth, no matter what you ask me."

Jake stopped walking and looked toward the trees before he replied, "Ok Ellen…the truth is that I don't miss them at all. I guess that sounds selfish and I should explain why."

"Stop right there. That's enough of an answer. I've got the picture. Now tell me about the road trip."

It was obvious how excited he was when discussing the trip. He proceeded to describe how he'd plan everything during the winter months and why he picked the places he did. Then he talked about off-track camping spots near roaring rivers and beneath the mountains. He told her about the thrill of hiking alone in the wilderness areas and finding insights while on the road.

She knew he was attempting to share a very personal part of him, not the professional counselor or the family man but another identity that apparently was a very private part of him. She could tell that he enjoyed talking about it and told him, "I love listening to you describe that other world of yours. I've never experienced that kind of freedom. I'll tell you this. I'd love to go if I had the opportunity and had someone like you as my guide. How soon will you be leaving?"

"I'm leaving 6 a.m. on July 4th. That's my 'D'-day. I'll be driving about a thousand miles before I pull over at a rest stop to sleep for a couple of hours in central Iowa. Then the next morning, at Council Bluffs I'll head north on Interstate 29, past Sioux Falls, South Dakota before taking Interstate 90 some four hundred miles past the Badlands. Then finally, around mid-afternoon, I'll turn south into the Black Hills and Deadwood."

Ellen started to laugh. How could Jake possibly think she was following his directions with any degree of geographic knowledge?

Seeing her reaction to his explanation and how she laughed stopped him dead in his tracks. Turning to face her, their eyes met and then Jake put his hands on the back of her neck under her hair and brought her closer. He placed his lips near hers so they were barely touching. He wanted to see if his affection would be accepted.

Ellen offered no resistance. She closed her eyes and opened her mouth slightly to encourage him to continue, which he proceeded to do. The kiss was intensely passionate. Ellen thought it was absolutely perfect and for an instant, time stood still. They both seemed to know how precious the moment was and wouldn't let go. Certain that he did the right thing, Jake released her after a minute and looked into her radiant blue eyes. He saw the longing in them, so he kissed her again. This time longer and more fervently by putting his arms around her waist and bringing her body firmly against his.

She felt his hard chest against her taut breasts, and it was extremely satisfying. It was as if their first step toward intimacy, although spontaneous, had been rehearsed a thousand times before it took place. The second kiss was the one she dreamed about before making love to her imaginary warrior. Ellen felt a shudder go up and down her entire body, and in a place where she never believed the ecstasy of a single kiss could reach. It was the most highly erotic moment she'd ever experienced, and when it ended she was blushing and breathless.

If Jake would have taken her, right there on the meadow grass, she would have surrendered. She totally forgot about the rain in her life and felt Jake's warmth.

Without saying another word, Jake took her by the hand and they started walking around the field. She could tell he was in deep thought, so she waited a few minutes before interrupting.

"I really must get back now. I don't want to. I want more of this and more of you. I'm not sure if I can handle what just happened, but I know it was real. I felt it. Now I have to go. I don't want to push my luck. I must get back even though I want to stay with you. You understand?"

Jake touched her face, shook his head and told her, "Of course I understand."

When they were driving back to Mayfair Farms he placed his hand on hers and squeezed it gently. Neither of them seemed to know what to say; two kisses had said it all. As he pulled into the lot at Mayfair Farms, Jake broke the silence and said, "Ellen, I want you to promise do something for me."

"If I can...I promise I will. What is it you want me to do?"

"I know I won't see you for a long time, most likely the whole summer. That's reality and neither of us can change it. I have two requests. Promise me you'll read a book called *The Bridges of Madison County* before we see each other again, regardless of when that will be. And, one more thing, will you write me a letter and mail it tomorrow? Would you do those things for me? It would mean a lot to me."

"I will. I promise I will...please take care of yourself! Remember this. I'll be thinking of you every waking moment. I will. Bye Jake."

After she drove away, Jake sat in his van savoring the encounter he had just experienced. He thought to himself. *What happened in that field? I came here to find out what was going on in my head, and now I'm more confused than ever. Ellen Eastman is too good to be true, or I'm completely bewitched and have lost all perspective. When I think about it, most people live their whole lives and never have something like this happen to them. This is crazy, or maybe I'm so damn miserable that I don't want to believe it's possible. Now what?*

He was so at ease with Ellen. Whatever came out of him was sincere and spontaneous, especially the kiss he gave her. On their first opportunity to be alone and together, within a brief period of thirty minutes, he sensed they touched each other in ways neither of them could have ever anticipated. It was similar to what happened in his office only a week ago. But now it was leaving him wanting her more than anything. Somehow his universe had changed its orbit.

CHAPTER 21

Jake finished a round of golf with Kevin O'Connor at Mountain Manor Golf Club and they both shot respectable scores in the mid-eighties. It was their final outing before Jake left on his trip. Kevin bested him by a stroke with a par on the finishing hole and tossed his partner a wry smile after he sunk a six-footer. In turn, Jake saluted his friend's victory with a tip of his hat and a handshake.

❧

Jake and Kevin became friends almost thirty years ago when they began their teaching careers fresh out of college. They met while working at Webster Junior High, located in the heart of the Columbus Projects in Newark, New Jersey. The year was 1972, a tumultuous time in America. The Vietnam War had changed America forever and the riots which occurred in the large urban cities in the late sixties strained race relations to the breaking point. Jake and Kevin were unshakeable idealists committed to making a difference in an indifferent city school system.

In Jake's opinion, Kevin was the most considerate and generous Irishman the Almighty had ever created. Throughout their long friendship Kevin was always honest, trustworthy, and a straight talker. Both of them knew fifty percent of everything about each other, yet they never crashed into private areas that both guarded so well. They respected each other and didn't argue about race, religion, or politics. Their friendship had endured through good times and bad. They shared the same birthright of a humble upbringing in large families. That was the glue that held them together. Their fathers were blue-collar working men doing manual labor. Kevin's dad was a Newark City employee, a building maintenance man. Jake's dad was a non-union sheet metal worker in a small firm in the same city.

Kevin and Jake worked their way through college with part-time jobs and student loans. Kevin received the better education, graduating with honors from Seton Hall University. He was a full-time commuter student and spent the in-between breaks sleeping in the student lounge or studying at the library. There were no student activities for Kevin. His routine was school, study, and work, with beer blasts on weekends that left him with serious Sunday morning hangovers. He was addicted to sports, not rock music and marijuana; quite an anomaly considering the times.

By Kevin's senior year, he was engaged to a blond-haired, well-built, Polish cutie named Susan Potocki. She was an upstart English major from Elizabeth, New Jersey. Their relationship clicked from the start and for whatever reason, because she wasn't pregnant, he married her right after graduation.

In those days of revolution against the establishment, Kevin played it straight when everyone else was protesting, partying, or running away from responsibility. By all accounts, Kevin missed the campus unrest and didn't give a damn. He got his degree in four years and was proud of that fact. In contrast, Jake was awarded his bachelor's degree from Kean University in Union, New Jersey, or as Jake referred to it, "Poor People's State College." It was the one and only college he had ever visited, and even that was by pure accident. At the time, his girlfriend had an older sister, a math major, who showed them around. It was Saturday morning in late November and afterwards he figured, "What the hell, at least it's cheap."

Jake's college selection process was non-existent, nobody guided him nor did he let anyone inside his head to influence him. The very fact that he secured the loan and went through all the steps involved with the admissions process was a stretch. He did it on his own, and most of the time he wasn't sure if he fit into the college experience or whether he was cut out for the self-discipline necessary to graduate.

He wasn't prepared for college. His study skills were inadequate and so was his vocabulary. He also lacked the ability to construct persuasive essays that stayed on target. Initially, his pride got in the way of using the available resources, whether accessing the professors or begging the junior math major down the hall to explain the vagaries of finite math. Trying to understand the History of Western Civilization only showcased his deficiencies, as did his mediocre research paper on *Crime and Punishment.*

By the time the results of his mid-term exams were posted he considered dropping out, thoroughly disgusted and embarrassed by what he didn't know. The other dorm kids seemed to have an edge, either academically, financially, or socially. Jake was more of a loner. After the first few weeks of school he ignored his spoiled roommate from south Jersey. The kid, who Jake called "Ching," knew better than challenge his sullen leather-jacketed roommate and accepted the territorial lines without a skirmish. For the most part, Ching stayed out of the room when Jake was around, preferring the company of less-threatening individuals who lived upstairs in Dougal.

The breakthrough came when Jake's composition instructor gave him a B+ for an oral presentation about the influence of Bob Dylan's protest music on the youth culture. After experiencing that modest success Jake began to listen better during lectures, take decent notes, and develop a level of self-confidence in writing that was sorely missing from his high school days.

Then one day a history professor, who Jake privately referred to as "Dr. Peabody," pulled the young student aside after class and chided him for not being prepared. Peabody finished the tongue lashing with a statement that proved more of a motivator than anything Jake had ever heard said to him. "Young man, take this for what its worth. **You can make it here because you're not stupid.** You're frustrated because some of the basics are missing in that head of yours. If you want to learn to express yourself better start reading! Read *Time* and *Newsweek*, read *Life Magazine*, read essays and editorials, just start reading."

The force of the professor's words stuck in his head and Jake finally began to read. He also became a campus character of sorts, not because of political activism, but by his blue collar personality. The upperclassmen in the dorm gave him a nickname for his tough exterior and "Don't fuck with me" attitude. They called him "Stone," because he was the consummate individualist. He didn't dress the role or act the role of a collegian because he didn't know how to. He drank himself silly on weekends and danced all night at frat parties. He resented the "haves," and established his own identity on campus.

When sophomore year began the top fraternity heard about the tough kid named Stone and offered a bid to him. That was how Jake Carr became a "somebody" on the Kean campus. He also took the professor's suggestion and went to the college library lounge to read for an hour every day. The academic discipline finally began to pay off, and when sophomore year ended he had a 2.75 G.P.A. Hence, Jake finally let go of his academic insecurity and believed he could finish the race and get a college degree.

At the start of junior year he was an active member of a fraternity, involved in student government, started writing feature articles for the school paper, and began having after class discussions with the professors. He desperately wanted to change the minds of his teachers and classmates about his reputation, and win their respect. Although the nickname never wore off, he eventually made the Dean's list in senior year. It was an honor he once thought was far beyond his capacity to earn.

On graduation day, with the entire Carr family present, his father gave him a hundred dollar bill in recognition for his achievement. Jake knew it was a week's take-home pay for his father and nothing meant more to him than seeing his dad happy on that afternoon in June of '72.

The Carr-O'Connor relationship had endured for nearly three decades because they rarely shared an angry exchange or made a sarcastic remark to each other out of meanness. They both hated phonies, the politicians who started the Vietnam debacle and they had a real disdain for the upper-class. Truly, they were "twin sons from different mothers." Whatever kindness they shared was never taken for granted. They were respectful of one another's individuality and knew the boundaries of their friendship.

When Jake received his Masters Degree in counseling from Kean University, he left behind his urban educational experience at Webster Junior High for a better paying job in the suburbs. Privately, he knew he was burned out from trying to do the impossible, but kept it to himself.

Jake and Kevin started playing golf with garage sale clubs and cheap shoes from K-Mart. Kevin worshipped Jack Nicklaus and Jake loved Lee Trevino's style. They played competitively but never for money, only for the honor of the day. Neither of them could afford playing the better courses and their seasonal "tour" consisted of two or three layouts that they could afford. Through the years they became fairly good golfers and their handicaps were never more than two strokes apart.

One thing was certain. Jake trusted Kevin completely and knew he would be truthful and upfront whenever Jake asked his opinion. They loved each other like brothers and expressed it in their own way, not with corny *Hallmark* cards on birthdays or by bullshit sentimentality spoken on barstools. Whenever they could share five hours on the links, it was the best of times.

❧

As they walked back to the parking lot with their golf bags in tow, Jake tactfully tried to explain his interest in Ellen. "Listen, my Irish friend. I need your advice. I met a woman. You heard me right and umm…I'm wondering what comes next. I think she's pretty special."

"That's it, Jake! Hey, I met a broad too. She served me a coffee at Dunken Donuts. She even commented on my selection, telling me I made a great choice. Jesus, what the hell's with you?"

"Come on Kevin, stop jerking me around. You know those workshops I do every spring to make some golf money? I met her there and we really hit it off. Now do you understand?"

"Jake, for Christ's sake, you meet women every day on that job of yours. Stop the bullshit!"

Kevin instantly wished he hadn't reacted the way he did. So when they reached their vehicles he put his stuff in the trunk and finally gave Jake his undivided attention. "Jake, let's sit on that bench over there in

162

the shade. Tell you what, you spill your guts and I'll listen. I mean it."

As they meandered toward the area, Kevin started laughing and gave Jake a couple of shoves to loosen up him up. He knew that what he was about to hear was something out of the ordinary. Tossing his golf hat at Jake, he got serious and said, "Sorry buddy...Now, what's going on in your life? Who's the woman? Is she married? Is she divorced with troubled kids and wants you to save her? What gives?"

"Give me a break, will you. It's like...I've had this woman on my mind a lot and I can't figure it out. It's not like I had sex with her or something like that. Believe me, she's not a babe, but she's really enchanting. Her name is Ellen, and I suppose I'm kinda overwhelmed by the whole thing. I don't know what the hell I'm feeling. I didn't do anything, not yet, but I wanted to know what you think."

Kevin was flabbergasted and couldn't contain himself. "You're nuts! Let me get this straight. Wait a minute, you skip the essentials and tell me about...about having her in your head. What the fuck does that mean? What's her story? Why is she interested in you? What's she want? No, what's she expect?"

"Kevin, take it easy. Calm down! Ellen's married! Does that answer your question? I don't know much about her situation other than her husband lives and works in Atlanta, but they're not separated. Anyway, I think she's unhappy. She has two sons, one is in Middletown High. The woman came to my workshop and that's how we got connected. We've spoken a couple of other times. What can I say? I like her."

Jake purposely left out their romantic rendezvous at the park. His interest in the woman was genuine and not related to the possibility of a sexual experience since the woman was certainly not a passion craving, bored parent.

Kevin listened with keen interest and gave considerable thought before finally answering his friend. "Let me get this straight. You're married and so is she. Are you crazy? You don't fuck around with someone who...who lives in the town where you work. Shit, you'd be better off falling for a lap dancer. Listen, I know you've been miserable for a long time, even if you won't admit it to me. Let's face it, that's a fact. I remember last summer when Sandy made the starter drive her out to the fourteenth hole, cause she wanted to tell you off in front of us. We were fucking shell-shocked. I felt bad about that, probably because I knew the two of you before you even got married. Back then you loved her...you really did. She was your sidekick and your playmate. You traveled together and got along great. When I think about that day on the course...well I thought you must have blown her off once too often and she wanted revenge.

"Jake my man...you've done so much for your family, and ever since her parents passed away, she's been...difficult. What you won't spill out is that she's been selfish with her time and money. Again you forget, you told me about that inheritance. That shit I'll never understand. You've given your family everything a good man could possibly give. You've been a great father and loyal husband, honestly you have. You think that just because she's working more these days that's a big deal? She gets up early and teaches at that snobby private school. Give me a break. We've known each other for twenty-seven years and we know damn well what real hardship is. Jesus, I'm on the soapbox and preaching."

Jake figured he pushed Kevin too far. The Irishmen was letting it all out, and Jake was beginning to feel guilty for dragging him into his personal problem. They'd spent a terrific day together, but he needed Kevin's advice. He couldn't recall the last time that his friend seemed so determined to give him such a broad perspective of his opinions.

"Kevin, I'm sorry. I didn't mean to put you over the edge. I don't want the day to end like this. I'm leaving Sunday. I guess the thing I'm most confused about is those inner voices in my head. Sometimes I wish they'd shut up and leave me in peace. Last year at this time, all I wanted was to escape and return to the road. Now, because of Ellen, there are too many "what ifs" bouncing in and out of my head. What's crazy about this whole thing is that it's not the way I look at life or make my decisions. You know me. I'm grounded in reality. I've never been a dreamer, but right now you're looking at one. I'm excited about this woman. Something completely unexpected has happened to me."

Kevin sat up straight and turned and faced his friend as if to emphasize his words. "Stop right there! Listen real good...Sandy changed some years back. And whatever her reason was, I really don't know, but you're still the man I met back in the 70's. Maybe not exactly the same regarding the stuff you love; now you're more addicted to Mother Nature and the call of the wild than ever, but what's more important is that you're honest and practical. Listen to me my friend. If this woman...this Ellen, can bring you some degree of happiness, you'd better check it out. I'm telling you it's ok. Just remember that what you're doing is dangerous. Goddamn, you're both married. It's very risky. Whatever you do, make sure it's what you want and she's worth the gamble. Do you hear me? That she's really worth it! Otherwise everyone loses...everyone involved with both of you. You get my meaning? Use that philosophy of yours to guide you. I don't really understand it, but I know it works for you."

"I get your meaning and I get your warning. Tell me. Am I worth it?"

"Jake, you're a great friend and good man. Trust me on this. You sure as hell are worth it. A dozen years ago, when Susan left me, I never thought I'd recover. You were there and saw what it did to me. My kids got through it better than I did. Then, I met Joanie; she'd been through similar shit. Now life is good. It makes sense. Trust me, you're worth it."

"Thanks…Like I said, it's friggin scary to consider the "what ifs." All I keep thinking about are the possibilities. I don't know…I must be really starved. Kevin, I swear to you, I never pursued this. It just happened…it's the kind of dream that middle-aged people always wonder about."

"Oh brother, you make me laugh. You're not too old to dream. Look Jake, it's late and I got to go to my in-laws for Sunday sit-down dinner. Please be careful. Be very fuckin' careful. Take it slowly and give it a chance. That's my advice. Call me as soon as you return. Come back in one piece."

With a handshake, the two friends parted. Kevin drove off, and Jake stayed on that bench to rethink the advice his friend had given him.

Very early the next morning Jake sat at the kitchen counter checking his "things to do before leaving" list, which was essential to complete prior to his departure on the "Montana Express." Tomorrow, the alarm would wake him and he'd begin his second solo journey to the mother of all mountain ranges, the Rockies.

Everyone was still asleep in the Carr house and it was just as well. Jake wanted no distractions as he reviewed the separate categories on his notepad: pay all the bills, inspect the house, change the oil in the lawn tractor, do the food shopping for the trip, pack the equipment in the van, and finally put all the clothes in the duffel bags. Jake took his second cup of coffee to his desk and located his black accounting book and checkbook to begin an orderly process of making payments to utilities, the orthodontist, mortgage company, and anything else that needed attention. A half-hour later the job was complete. Next, he counted out his trip money, $1,000 in American Express Traveler's checks and $500 in cash. He made sure he had his gold MasterCard in his wallet to use for charging any motel costs. He had saved the trip money during the previous school year; half from his monthly personal allowance and the other half from summer wages.

Jake left his desk and went upstairs to ask Sandy if she was ready for breakfast. She was in the bathroom when he gently knocked on the door and said, "What can I make you for breakfast? We have some leftover Challah. Would you like French toast?"

Sandy stepped out of the steam-filled bathroom. She was wrapped in a white bath towel and her hair was dripping wet. When she saw him, she winked, dropped the towel and turned full circle in front of him. Then she leaned up against him to arouse him, which it did. Tonight was their last night for lovemaking for three weeks and she wanted him to think about her during the day.

"Well, how do I look? Are you going to think of me this afternoon? Have I got your attention now?"

She stepped back from him leaving his black tee shirt damp, along with the front of his shorts. Then she let him have a last look at her, this time raising her hands in the air and showing off her butt before she put the towel back on. Jake was amused by the performance and said, "Sandy, damn, you look terrific!"

Sandy was five-foot-four and weighed 110 pounds. She had dark brown eyes to match her hair and a model's face. Truly, she was a beautiful woman, with the compact body of a professional dancer. Whether she wore a business suit, shorts and a halter, or a bikini, she was a knockout and the heads would turn when she was in the company of men. Jake knew her moods well and if she was upbeat and playful, then she was fun to be with. His constant emphasis on physical fitness had taken ten years off her age. And when she felt sexy enough to wear a Victoria Secret outfit, she looked as hot as their catalogue models.

Jake had breakfast going when Sandy joined him. He gave her a kiss and then poured the coffee before placing two slices of egg-soaked Challah in the frying pan. He kept a close eye on the stove while Sandy savored her first few sips of coffee.

"Sandy, I'm going to be busy today. Is there anything you need from town?"

"Not that I can think of right now. Are we going out for dinner later?"

Although he usually went along with her suggestions for dining out on Saturday nights, he felt tonight it wasn't a good idea with all he had to do and hoped she'd compromise. "Umm...If it's okay with you, I'd rather use the gas grill and make a London broil. Honestly, I don't think I'll be able to wind down enough to enjoy a dinner out."

"Then pick up a movie for us. Please skip the death and destruction of the universe tonight, no horror or war flicks. There's already enough of that going on in the world. Find something entertaining, like a love story, or maybe a murder mystery."

Relieved, Jake answered, "That I can do. Listen, I've paid all the bills and I'll be leaving you about six hundred in cash. I put it in the center desk drawer. Use it at your discretion."

"Can you serve me that French toast now? I understand you've got plenty to do. I'll be fine. One more thing, please talk with your son. Let him know what I expect while you're away."

"That, I will do. Incidentally, I appreciated the come on you gave me. Nice show... I'll be ready."

⇨⇦

When they first met, their initial attraction was physical and Sandy knew it. At the time, Jake was fit and virile with long brown hair that covered his ears and neck along with a trim beard. He was the complete antithesis of Alan Rosberg, the man she had been married to for seven years. But that was twenty five years ago and Sandy thought by now Jake would act like a middle-aged professional, even if he didn't look it. Last year when he returned late on a Saturday night in July, she started an argument as soon as he walked through the door by letting him know she wouldn't be left behind ever again. But Jake wouldn't give an inch and reminded her of the agreement they made with the marriage counselor's approval. They talked for a long time that first night and ended with a compromise.

Fortunately, the next morning they were able to reconcile their differences and finalize a mutually acceptable solution. Sandy would plan a mini-vacation and Jake would agree to whatever she desired and promise to give her a good time. Consequently, in August of 1998, they spent three days and nights at a bayside hotel in Newport, Rhode Island. True to his word, they went on a gilded mansion tour, a half-day bay cruise, explored the old colonial city, and they dined at the best seafood restaurants. Jake survived the tourist experience, and Sandy's anger subsided considerably.

During the retreat, Jake made love to her more in three days than most middle-aged women get in a month. There was no denying the fact that in the sexual arena, their lovemaking was superior and their sexual appetite was as intense as it was when they first met in their twenties. At that time, she was starving for affection, and he satisfied her.

During that first getaway, they got along fine and actually made some progress in recapturing the spark that had been out for the past five years. Sandy had felt emotionally secure during the mini vacation and optimistic about their future. For his part, although he was a good companion, he found it difficult to fit into the tourist mold of the Newport crowd. This year Sandy accepted Jake's road trip without any animosity, believing his "free spirit" had to be nourished and only he could do it. She didn't fear that he'd go away and never return. She recalled that after last year's trip he seemed to be at peace with himself and it carried over through most of the year.

☙❧

After looking over the Saturday section of the *New York Times*, which was one of her favorite rituals, Sandy went upstairs to wake the kids. J.D. and Annie shared a bathroom and she wanted her son to use the shower first so she could snuggle with her daughter. It was one of those mother-daughter rituals that began 17 years ago and was still going strong. Regardless of what issue may have caused a strain between them, nothing would prevent Sandy from this show of affection for Annie.

Quietly she opened the bedroom door and peeked into the room. A bright morning sun glistened off the mirror over the dresser but Annie remained still, despite the intrusion.

Annie's room was a "House Beautiful" model. It was wallpapered with two dark green patterns of assorted flowers on vines separated by a border. Fluffy white linen curtains covered two large rectangular windows which faced the backyard. Her short posted brass bed and designer comforter complimented the decorum. All her furniture was solid dark oak with two different style end tables that had antique brass lamps on them. Visitors marveled at how gorgeous and classy Annie's room looked. Sandy would accept nothing less for her "princess."

Sandy pulled back the light pale green comforter and took hold of her daughter. Together, they laid there until they heard the shower cease, then Annie got up and took her turn. Sandy knocked on J.D.'s door to ask if he wanted something for breakfast but he declined, telling her he was already late for work and couldn't wait around.

The kids were off and running in less than an hour, and Jake was at fever pitch taking care of last minute trip needs. Sandy felt rested and mellow. Her job ended nearly two weeks ago and now her time was her own. As of tomorrow, it would be the three of them without Jake for the next three weeks.

Sandy was determined to make a few changes when Jake was gone. First and foremost, dinners would not be on any schedule. They'd eat what they wanted, when they wanted. She decided not to make any unusual demands on the kids other than the basics. Their bedrooms had to be in order and their laundry was to be delivered in clothes baskets to the proper place. If someone wanted to "bitch" or be nasty they had to remove themselves from the premises and take their attitude elsewhere. J.D. was responsible for lawn and car maintenance. Finally, both kids had to keep reasonable curfews so their mother wouldn't lose a night's sleep worrying. Sandy felt the requests would ensure that the three of them could live in harmony with Jake gone.

Jake finished all his preparations by late afternoon. So far nothing surfaced that might cause a postponement in the travel plan. Tonight would be his last dinner at the Treetop estate. He was on schedule to have the meal ready when the kids returned from their jobs. Jake was determined to leave on good terms with his family and if that meant biting his tongue for a few more hours to avoid conflicts, then he would exercise tact and self-control. Tomorrow morning he was a free man.

At dinnertime, when Annie arrived home, she announced that she accepted a dinner invitation with her new boyfriend and would be skipping her father's last dinner. Realizing his daughter preferred the company of a date rather than the family BBQ came as no surprise to Jake, and he accepted her excuse.

J.D., on the other hand, saw an opening to get in his digs and reminded her she ought to feel guilty as hell. Upstairs in private, he scolded her saying, "Annie, Dad's leaving. How could you ditch him like that? Wanna change your mind? Hey, why don't you call up that loser and tell him to come over an hour later. Dad's gonna be crushed that you blew him off. You know he ain't gonna beg you to stay."

Annie wasn't going to allow her brother to lay a guilt trip on her without retaliating. With icy sarcasm she told him, "What a joke, should I remind you of how many of Dad's birthdays you wrecked? Get a grip. On second thought, I forgot you can't get one. You're a loose cannon! Just leave me alone. If you can't grasp that, then just fuck off."

Jake served the meal inside to avoid the bugs, and the dinner was delicious. Although not a big eater, J.D. feasted on the white corn more than the beef and baked beans. During dinner he gave his parents a few laughs with his liquor store stories of the various characters who were regulars and who for whatever reason spoke with the 18-year-old kid like he was their long lost brother.

J.D. expressed himself quite well in relating stories of lottery-addicted working folks who dropped a hard-earned 10-spot and wound up with zero proceeds from the million-to-one scratch-offs. Jake thoroughly enjoyed each of his kids when they were separated and J.D. was in rare form. He spent a grand total of thirty-five minutes at the table, which was quite a feat for a boy who was always busy repairing dirt bikes, customizing his truck, or wheeling and dealing car parts.

Jake cleaned up quickly and took time to wire brush the gas grill. He told Sandy he'd be able to take her on an after-dinner walk later on. Once upstairs, Jake methodically packed his blue duffel bag with enough jeans, tee shirts, underwear, and socks to last two weeks. After that, he put all the necessary toiletries into a small flight bag, along with an assortment of basic medications. Reviewing his checklist, he scratched off the packed items and felt secure he had everything.

Their golden retriever, Missy, happily accepted the invitation for an evening stroll and with her keepers on either side, Jake and Sandy took their final evening trek around the development. With so little time left, they were equally unsure of what to say during this last bit of quiet time together. The walk was the first time in the past two days they had any personal time because of Jake's schedule of trip preparations, house maintenance, and golf outing. The evening sky was beginning to darken when they turned the corner at the bottom of Treetop Terrace.

Then Sandy broke the silence. "How many more of these expeditions are you planning? I mean, before we met, you took off a few time and in the Bicentennial year you drove all the way to the Grand Canyon. I don't remember you doing any others by yourself except one with your old college roommate to Gulf Island National Seashore. Why is it so important for you to have these escapes?"

As usual Sandy's timing was awful, but Jake felt compelled to answer her. "I can't tell you exactly why, but it's important to me. Honestly, it helps me get through the school year. I guess it's a combination of job fatigue and family stress that eventually burns me out by June. I'm sorry if it sounds selfish."

"Why do you have to go alone? What about me? Don't you realize I want to be with you out in the mountains? Remember our trips together, before the kids were born? It's hard to stay behind."

"You got me. I have to get away to the mountains…it's who I am and who I've always been."

"Jake, don't you remember our first trip to Mt. Rainier. I loved that road trip. Remember when I cheered you when you returned from the successful climb. My God, I loved you so much. I worshipped you. You were more of a man than anyone I'd ever met in my life. We were on the road for eight weeks in that summer. I miss those days.

"You took me down the Snake River through some of the rapids in an aluminum canoe. Back then, I thought there wasn't a thing we couldn't conquer together. I lost all my fears because of you. I'd never experienced anything like that. You did the impossible. You climbed to the summit of Mt. Whitney and returned in one day just to prove it to yourself. That ranger said you were crazy. We traveled 8,000 miles in that old International Scout and we hiked in Washington, Oregon, California, and my favorite place, British Columbia. Is all that adventuring over? Tell me. Am I that different now? Do you think I've forgotten all those memories?"

"Sandy, tomorrow morning I'm going. Why are you dumping so much shit on me? For now, I'll tell you this much. I suppose the young woman who went on those adventures is still a part of you, but honestly I don't see her very often. Maybe you ought to think on that."

Sandy didn't respond. She wasn't sure how Jake could possibly compare the "free spirits" they were twenty-years ago to who they were today. She didn't want her husband to leave with bad feelings between them, so she decided the prudent course of action was to let the subject drop. She took hold of his arm, reached over and kissed him, then changed the topic.

"What time will you be leaving? I'd like to get up with you."

"Thanks honey, but it's not necessary. I'm setting the alarm for 4:30 and I'll be busy packing the cooler and gulping down coffee. I promise I'll kiss you good-bye."

Later on that night, Jake found Sandy lying on the bed waiting for him in a black satin Victoria Secret baby doll outfit with black stocking and a garter belt. The house was quiet and the mood was right. He passed her a drink and after some playful foreplay, they made love to each other in the pleasurable ways they both always enjoyed. When it was over, Jake told her she was a terrific lover and a beautiful woman.

Afterwards, Sandy held on to Jake for most of the night.

CHAPTER 22

"The Montana Express" was the theme of the road trip, appropriately named back in February when Jake decided on what part of the country he was going to explore. He pulled the Aerostar out of the driveway as the sun was coming up over the eastern horizon and a dimly lit half-moon was fading fast. He'd slept soundly until three, but his subconscious woke him. It was congested with so many thoughts he couldn't fall back to sleep. Item after item came up like a set of flashcards. The messages popped up in unceasing rotation and Ellen was also there.

As he lay still, listening to the faint sound of Sandy's breathing, he thought of Kevin's advice on Saturday when he warned, "Everyone loses if something goes wrong. Is the woman worth it?" But after all the admonitions, the last thing Kevin said was, "give it a chance." Just before getting up at four-thirty, he made a choice. *I'll take her letter. I swore that I wouldn't, but I can't help myself.*

He was in and out of the shower in ten minutes, got dressed, and was ready to leave when Sandy called to him, "Come here and kiss me good-bye."

He stroked her hair without saying a word. Then she pulled him close for a farewell hug and whispered in his ear, "Your family needs you and I need you. Come back in one piece, that's all I can ask. Want me to get up and walk you out to the van? I will if you need me to."

"Sandy, I'll be fine. Enjoy your free time. Go to the pool, read, take naps, and go to the Jersey Shore. But whatever you do, lighten up on the kids. I'll call you in a few days. Bye, honey; I love you."

"I love you, too. We need you Jake. Please don't ever forget it."

Jake spent a minute petting Missy's belly before he closed the garage door and walked out to the Aerostar. Speaking to the green van like it had the feminine personality; he tapped the front hood three times for luck and exclaimed, "This is it. It's you and me baby for the next three weeks. I know you've got over a hundred K on you, but I've taken good care of you. Now you gotta come through for me."

Then he climbed in and surveyed the interior one last time. All the seats except the front two buckets were removed so the gear was evenly displaced in the rear area, in a space roughly ten feet long from the console to the back door. A small cooler holding a quart bottle of pink lemonade and two cokes rested on the floor. On the passenger seat was a shoebox containing over fifty cassettes that he planned to play one after another. An assortment of state maps, tour books, and paperbacks were in a canvas zipper bag, and the McNally Road Atlas was wedged under the bucket seat.

Every part of the thirty-six hour road trip from home to Deadwood, South Dakota, had been meticulously planned over the past six months. This was Jake's 16th cross country excursion west of the Mississippi but only his second time traveling solo since he married Sandy. The weather was clear and cool driving west on I-80 through the Appalachian Mountains in the eastern half of the Keystone State. The rural landscape of central Pennsylvania was checkered with small dairy farms and picturesque small towns with unusual names like Rosecrans, Yarnell, and Turkey City.

Route 80 belonged to the truckers, and the 775 miles from New York City to Chicago was their exclusive domain. Jake thought they were caravans of commerce much like camels trains in Biblical times. Truckers worked long hours in a monotonous routine of steering a thirty-ton rig and shifting through the twelve speeds hundreds of times a day. Sitting high up in their custom tracker cabs, they talked to their buddies on CB's and listened to country music. Their work was similar to what his late father did, but they made a hell of a lot more money. At least Joe Carr could take a stroll every so often at the sheet metal factory, stop by a fellow worker, and have a word or two about sports or who was on the Ed Sullivan's show. Some over-the-road cowboys got home only two days out of ten. Theirs was a lonely occupation and a dangerous one. The remains of a jack-knifed rig would remind travelers who passed of the consequences of fatigue, bad brakes, or road rage.

Whenever Jake passed by a trucker he'd try to make eye contact and never failed to give a customary salute with his right hand. Usually, they'd return his friendly gesture with a blast from an air horn. Perhaps it was a silly exercise in road fellowship, even childish, but it made Jake feel good and probably made them feel respected. Anything that helps break up monotony was worth the effort.

Without the musical soundtrack, Jake's drive would be intolerable. Riding alone for 1,750 miles required a companion. Rock music was a necessity, as important as taking a cooler full of beverages. The music made the journey interesting and filled Jake's head with memories, some new ones like Ellen Eastman, and some from another time and place. Hearing "oldies" had that kind of effect on Jake. He would sing along with the Eagles, Who, U2, David Bowie, Neil Young, Tom Petty, and an assortment of other musical groups, keeping the beat, by bobbing and bouncing up and down with the base sounds.

The morning sun stayed behind him and rose higher and higher throughout the day. The ride was never boring during the daylight hours when a man with wanderlust appreciated the freedom of the road and the ecstasy of his mind set free from the chaos of his life back home. Jake's thoughts took off in all directions, similar to the way a black crow flies indiscriminately over a cornfield searching for loose kernels, one here, another there, and so on. It never ceased to amaze him that any man would pass through a summer and forsake an opportunity to partake of the American landscape.

Dressed in a faded black pocket tee shirt and cut-off jean shorts, Jake looked the part of the character he liked best, the loner. He was in great physical shape and proud to look that way. For this brief period of time, he left behind the middle-class family man and professional counselor and was in complete control of his own destiny. All the exercise, weekend hikes, golf outings with Kevin, and, of course, the daily walks with Missy gave him the tough appearance of a no-nonsense stranger accustomed to solitary travel like a soldier of fortune. He welcomed the switch of identities with profound gratitude.

On his left wrist was a shiny brass bracelet with a copper insert, a plain Casio sport watch was on his right. He wore a black leather string around his neck with a small white bird figurine hanging from it. Jake, a modern-day sojourner, embraced his rediscovered self with refreshing delight and renewed vigor.

As Jake entered the road congestion near Gary, Indiana it was nearing six o'clock. The whole area was another dismal reminder of urban plight being split down the center by a major highway. There are similar places located on all points of the interstate highway system. Route 495 around D.C. and Route 70 through St. Louis are as bad as Gary. It's simple math. There were always five times as many vehicles as there was space for them to occupy. Consequently, Jake always stopped for gas and a restroom before entering the ramp that led to the four lanes heading toward Gary.

At 6 p.m. on the 4th of July, the Sunday congestion hit precisely as expected, and Jake resigned himself to easing the van along for a two-hour crawl until the road cleared up five miles west of the Illinois border. Passing time through a man-made mess made a weary traveler even wearier. Jake sipped on a coke and tried to focus on the road and not daydream, or he'd plow into the car in front of him, thus putting the trip in jeopardy.

Near Chicago, Jake turned on the AM radio to witness an exercise of American free speech, listening to a mid-west call-in sports talk show. For sure, it's a forum for all athletic enthusiasts to "bitch" about the declining work ethic of multi-millionaire athletes. Invariably, this radio excursion into the soft underbelly of working-class men and their addiction to sports trivia provided Jake with sufficient amusement to make it through the lengthy traffic snarl.

By 7 p.m. he had survived the infamous "battle of the bulge" around Gary. Relaxed and with the traffic buzzing along at a 65 mph clip, Jake let cruise control take over. Jake believed that his decision to buy a top-of-the-line Ford XLT Van with cruise control was one of the smartest purchases he ever made. It allowed him to place his left foot on the dash and vice versa and to stretch any way his body demanded.

The "Three Rivers" rest area was eight hundred miles from home. Jake got there at 8:30 p.m. EST. In reality, he'd gained an hour. So far he'd made very good time, averaging over 60 mph. He took only five breaks, two for gas and three for snacks and exercise. At every one of the highway rest areas, Jake couldn't help but notice the haggard, hot, and hungry travelers that occupied all the picnic benches on this humid, muggy Independence Day. The rest stop was an oasis for frenzied travelers.

As he started eating, he surveyed the families around the area. Then he experienced a humorous sight. Wherever he seemed to look, there was no shortage of overweight adults, with overweight kids, robotically gulping down assorted picnic chow with breakneck speed. Maybe it was his line of sight, but a random check of road voyagers appeared to be entertaining enough for *America's Funniest Video* show.

Jake liked to view people and places in context. Tourists who were visiting national parks and other well-known recreational attractions were strangers at the places they traveled hundreds of miles to visit. The people who lived near the attractions were locals who put up with the onslaught of strangers for the sake of commerce. The Jersey Shore was a perfect example. Some towns like Belmar, Wildwood, and Point Pleasant quadruple with summer population.

The sign on the bridge going over the Mississippi read "Welcome to Iowa!" It was near sunset when the Aerostar crossed the "Father of Waters" around 10 p.m. Sixteen hours and nine hundred miles of travel were completed. At a trucker's gas stop in Coralville, Iowa, Jake filled up, checked the oil, and washed another bunch of insect carcasses off the windshield. There were three more hours of driving to go before he could pullover at a truck rest area.

Those few hours were the supreme challenge because severe road fatigue always arrived promptly around midnight. Even with the windows closed and the air conditioner blowing full blast, it took enormous willpower to keep going until he reached the selected rest site. Music selection was crucial at this time so Jake resuscitated himself by playing the Allman Brothers and Creedence Clearwater Revival. The bands were lifeguards that kept him from drowning in fatigue.

By the time he pulled into the huge unlit trucker area it was 2 a.m. his body was completely shot. There were no washrooms or amenities at the pull-over only areas. Truckers who were overland drivers had latrines and sleeping compartments in their cabs. Jake hated the floodlights of improved rest areas, which was why he chose the dark truck stops and not the safety and security of the regular rest stops.

Walking to a nearby cornfield to relieve himself, Jake listened to the sounds of the Iowa night. It was windless and warm, probably still in the high 70s. Thousands of stars were visible on the eastern horizon. At this particular time of extreme fatigue, he realized he was finally free, and that tomorrow afternoon he would be in Deadwood, South Dakota. He walked to the back of the parked Aerostar, pushed his camping gear to the side, and fell out in a few minutes.

Jake awoke from deep sleep to the caustic smell of diesel exhaust and the accompanying sound of idling engines from Peterbuilt tractors. It was a little before dawn. Without any facilities available, he brushed his teeth using a spare water bottle and located another private spot in the cornfield. Anxious to get going, he did a quick check of his journal notes and realized he had another hour to go before he could buy coffee. Then he stopped for a moment and focused his attention on the emerging sunrise.

The birth of a summer day provided a magnificent panoramic view of the sun breaking over a vast Iowa cornfield. With a mere three hours of rest, Jake was ready to begin the final push to reach Deadwood by four in the afternoon, but first he wanted to take in the unusual landscape and appreciate how peaceful it was in that Iowa cornfield. Ten minutes later he was back on Interstate 80.

Turning into an "American Pie" restaurant a few miles north of Interstate 29, Jake needed decent coffee, not the watered-down crap served at the convenience stores. After using the restroom to rinse his face, he was ready for breakfast. It was 6 a.m. and only a few truckers were there, so he was served quickly. With a 20 ounce cup of Columbian coffee and an oversized blueberry muffin Jake walked back to the van and sat in the rear to eat. Officially, he was beginning day two of his adventure.

He reached the Missouri River Overlook rest area at noon. Towering concrete square pilings formed tee-pee shapes over several picnic tables. The parking area was as chaotic as a shopping mall on Christmas Eve with drivers scrambling to find a spot. But once he parked and strolled a hundred yards to the river, it was obvious why so many travelers stopped to visit. The Missouri River was not the muddy chocolate color that it was by Sioux City. Up at this northern location, its color was a light shade of powder blue. The river flowed quietly beneath high bluffs with stands of cottonwoods, olive trees, and junipers along the banks. The sight was vast in scope and overwhelming to behold. A commemorative sign with raised letters on a bronze plate told the story of how Lewis and Clark had been there.

Rather than use a picnic table, Jake took his turkey hoagie and lemonade to a quiet place overlooking the river. He also took Ellen's letter from the glove compartment. With his tee shirt and sneakers off to cool down, he opened the envelope and read.

Dear Jake,

I enjoyed our walk yesterday, and, as I promised, here is my letter to you. I loved hearing about your adventures on the road and wish I could be the girl in a matching black tee shirt and jeans waiting for you to find me, waiting to be whisked away. I hope you'll be thinking of me whenever you watch the sunsets over the mountains and hike the trails. I wish I could be there. I'm planning to be back in Middletown on August 6th. I'll be alone. I'd like to see you. Please give me a call. Maybe we can go for another walk and I can hear about your trip. Please return safely.

With affection,
Ellen

P.S. I've enclosed pictures of three paintings I've done. A fairy, a wolf, and my dream cabin beneath the mountain. The wolf reminds me of you, wild and free. You already know about the log cabin. And, I guess the fairy is a mystery for you to solve.

A thousand thoughts can occupy a man's mind when he's away from his normal routine, free from the stress of worrying about family, health, job security, and financial obligations. Whether anyone back home understood the necessity for his pilgrimage didn't matter. At this point in his life he had no desire to reconcile his actions. Out on the open road he was the master of time and place, and every day was an opportunity for discovery.

For Jake the unexpected connection with Ellen transcended all reason. Why he was so vulnerable was perplexing to him. He dismissed the mid-life crisis stuff as not applicable to him. He'd read Gail Sheely's *Passages* and respected her point of view. However, he knew better than anyone the difference between theory and reality. He didn't deny that his life was full of passages. For him it was the Tao of living.

Jake was thoughtful and philosophical about living. He had answers or would find answers to questions that troubled him but had gained enough humility over the years to appreciate that there was also karma to consider in everyone's life experience. That was the purpose of his retreat to the mountains.

Walking back to the van he felt a wonderful sense of anticipation for the days ahead and at that moment made an agreement with himself. He'd read the letter when the notion hit him. And in a peculiar way, wished Ellen was with him, dressed similarly and equally anxious to explore the forest trails, skip rocks across the alpine lakes, and watch the sunsets over the Rockies. Maybe it was pure fantasy, but if the letter was to be believed, Ellen wanted to continue seeing him. That situation would be interesting, exciting, and, as Kevin had told him, "dangerous."

CHAPTER 23

Route 16 began in Buffalo and was a Wyoming Scenic Byway that crossed eighty miles over the Big Horn Mountains in the north central part of the state. The road was closed during the winter since Powder River Pass, at 9,666 feet, was impassable. Even in July, there were scattered patches of old dirty snow still hanging around. Road crews were working to move debris and fix bent guard rails. As Jake came to mile-marker eight, a pot-bellied, leather-tanned, veteran flagman stood with his stop sign and held up traffic. Jake's van and a battered Chevy Pickup were the only two vehicles waiting. After a few minutes, the front end loader finished its work and Jake moved on.

Loose cattle were grazing on meadow grass ten miles west of town as the road gradually started twisting its way through the mountain pass. Evergreens, blue and silver spruce, and different varieties of pine and fir trees were scattered on both sides of the road. Wide meadows with dark earth, wild flowers, and pasture grass were dispersed among the stands of majestic trees in the vast Cloud Peak Wilderness. Jake felt increasingly invigorated. He'd waited eleven months to return to the area surrounded by the Big Horn Mountains. This sylvan place was still undiscovered and tourists rarely traveled through Route 16.

Around noon he turned left at milepost 42 onto a gravel road opposite Meadowlark Lake and drove slowly for a mile until he reached Sitting Bull Campground. He figured the spot he desired would be empty this time of day, and he was right. Jake backed the van into site #2. Having finally reached his destination, he shouted a greeting to the foothills. "I'm here… I'm back. I've kept the promise to return."

He had discovered the place a year earlier on his way back from a one-night stay at Cody, which was about a hundred and fifty miles west. Everything about that initial experience left him wanting to return. It had been on wilderness Trail 65 that he had carved his name on a lightning scarred tree, and vowed he would return to this spectacular place of breathtaking beauty. This time, he was more excited than ever to explore more of the area and find the tree.

Setting up the camp was easy and automatic. The Coleman umbrella tent was a 7x7; he wanted it close to the sound of a mountain stream under a canopy of mature pines. First, he placed the ground sheet on a thick bed of needles to provide a softer place to sleep. Then he laid down the tent, inserted the flexible poles, and brought shape to the tent by anchoring opposite corners with plastic stakes while raising it up.

Inside the tent he put his sleeping bag on a foam pad and tossed a small flashlight near his old, flattened camp pillow. Then he unzipped the screen windows half-way down to air out the tent for the first time since last summer, thereby letting the scent of the forest enter.

Jake was a "Class A" wood scavenger. Within a few minutes of claiming the site by posting an "OCCUPIED" sign on the post, he'd drive around the loop of the campground and pick up every leftover fireplace log that other campers left behind. After 15 minutes of site jumping, he would usually have a considerable amount, which he would stack in a neat pile near the fire pit.

Another of Jake's rituals after the camp was setup was his "ax toss." For a reason that only he knew, no matter where he setup camp, he'd look for a nearby deadfall, walk twenty paces from it, and throw his ax. If it landed securely within the first five tries, he would let out a cry of victory like a fieldgoal kicker who scored in a sudden death playoff. If he missed the first three, he'd move a bit closer.

Ten Sleep Lake was seven miles down a rut-filled access road at an elevation of 9,500 feet. The metallic green color of the Aerostar was completely covered in gray and brown dust when Jake pulled into a parking area near the trailhead. With a full canteen of pink lemonade and his walking stick, Jake began Trail 63, which would take him halfway around Ten Sleep Lake and then alongside a winding boulder-filled stream that fed the lake from the winter snow melt up in the Big Horns.

The trail itself was a well-worn strip about a foot wide that was clearly visible from a distance. It looked like a serpent as it wound its way through the high mountain meadows. Rock cairns, which were small piles of rocks, marked the trail in locations where it nearly vanished. As Jake entered the dense forest, he noticed blaze marks of yellow plastic triangles that were placed on the trees to guide hikers.

Again and again, Jake marveled at his recollection of the familiar landmarks on the trail. Immense boulders, some the size of free-standing monuments, seemed to be thrown off the high ridges by the forces of nature. Severed trunks of towering pines appeared to have been blasted by lightning, and their remains scattered. Multicolored meadow flowers, such as Indian Paintbrush and Mountain Bluebells, grew in bunches everywhere. The shark tooth ridges of the Big Horns were still covered with snow and stood as sentinels against the azure-colored sky. All those images created mental snapshots for Jake, pictures that he stored away for other times when he was back east and homesick for the mountains. The natural colors of the area were magnified by the radiant sun and striking to the eye of the observer.

The destination for the afternoon was a high mountain meadow that permitted a full 360-degree observation of the Big Horn range. It was about five miles from the trailhead. Up to this time, he hadn't seen a single other person on the trail, and that was to his liking. There was a strange sense of personal adventure when he hiked in places like this. It provided him the sheer pleasure of knowing he was alone with the mountain spirits and he believed that they'd connect with him if he listened.

Jake kept up a quick pace and at one point imagined himself a warrior, with his stick being a flintlock rifle. Ironically, he did the same thing when he was a ten-year-old boy running through the neighbor's yard or playing war with his companions. He'd transform himself into a character like Hawkeye in *The Last of the Mohicans*, or Lt. Dunbar from *Dances with Wolves*.

He reached the mountain meadow by mid-afternoon. To his utter amazement, a father and young son were fly fishing in the stream that flowed through the center of the meadow. Quickly, he tossed away his disappointment of having company, realizing what a memorable place it was for a father to share with his son. He remembered his own children standing on a snowfield near the Paradise Visitor Center looking up at Mt. Rainier and asking, "Daddy, did you really climb to the top of **that** mountain."

Jake found his own space and rested there. Taking off his Dunham boots and black tee shirt, he stretched out on a flat rock next to the icy stream, and let himself be consumed by his surroundings. In his mind, it was worth working forty-nine weeks to find moments like this where no one could disturb his peace, dictate his behavior, or interfere with his life. The price of admission for Jake to experience this kind of freedom was a willingness to maneuver through the daily crap of middle class living and wait for a chance to reconnect with the mystery of the mountains.

Tomorrow after breakfast, he would revisit Trial 65 and take it past the spot marked with his name on the Douglas fir. Hopefully, he'd discover another "Shangri-La" if he were willing to hike a few more miles into the wilderness. As he was about to begin the hike back, he heard the father and son coming up the trail. Without getting up to greet them, he sat still and waited to see if they would notice him. Much as he suspected, they walked right past him engaged in conversation, carrying their fishing poles and other gear, totally oblivious to the fact that a visitor was twenty feet away hidden by scrub bush.

It was dusk when Jake began placing slender sticks of wood to resemble a teepee, for a campfire. Everything else was in place. His battery-powered cassette recorder sat on a tree stump of some eighteen inches in diameter that he found in a wood pile on the forest access road. The camp chair was an aluminum one with faded yellow and orange webbing that his friend Kevin had given him. Another ritual was to use only one-match to get the fire going.

As the kindling caught and spread to the larger pine sticks surrounding the center, the coolness of the evening descended over the campground. Very shortly, the first stars would appear. And then by 10 o'clock, the moonless sky would gradually burst out with clusters of heavenly bodies.

Every part of the first day went according to plan, and that was the way Jake wanted it to be. The fire was going full blast and gave out plenty of warmth. He sat on his camping chair and finished the first beer within a couple of minutes. Then he put the *Eagles Greatest Hits* tape in the cassette player, opened another bottle of Molson Ice and sang along.

After a few more beers, he began to dance around the campfire, continually lifting his gaze to the incredible night sky. He was full of himself and enjoyed every moment of his antics. It was the sort of celebration he'd waited for during tough times in the previous year. Times when there was nowhere to escape other than the basement. The empty six-pack proved to be the perfect formula for a terrific night.

Before turning in, he walked to the van, opened the glove compartment and took out the letter to read it again. However, this time he allowed himself the pleasure of looking at her picture. She hadn't given it to him; it was a photocopy of her picture in a high school yearbook he found in the school library.

Ellen was seventeen-years-old in the picture. She was wearing a black turtleneck sweater with a pearl necklace. She had the look of innocence on her face. Jake had taken it with him for times like this, when he could forget about the rain in his life and think of her as the sunshine.

A bright yellow sun crept over the mountains and lit up the tent. Jake rolled over on his back and saw that dew covered everything with a uniform mist. Last night's fire left no mark other than a gray pile of ash. Jake stumbled out of the tent a bit stiff and in need of relieving himself. A couple of minutes later, he pumped the plunger on the Coleman stove and heated up two-quarts of water so he could wash up. Then he made his first pot of perked coffee. At 6 a.m. and fifty degrees, nothing jolted his senses as much as strong coffee. While he waited for the brew, he went to the larder box for a soft roll and began to scramble three eggs. His first cup of "Joe" was a treat, and he savored the taste.

Jake's goal was to be at the trailhead by 9 a.m. He completed his camp chores, paid the camp fee, and drove down the gravel road. He was dressed in khaki shorts, a blue tee shirt and wore a windbreaker. The morning was clear with a radiant, powder-blue sky but rather chilly with a moderate breeze. He parked in the same place as yesterday and prepared his daypack. Everything was in order, various snacks, a canteen of pink lemonade, the writing journal, and bug spray.

Unlike the trail he took the day before, Tail 65 went directly through the forest except for one small meadow clearing. Then the trail climbed up the slope, which led to a high mountain meadow near 11,000 feet in elevation. Jake started up the narrow path at a brisk pace, occasionally using his walking stick as a yoke to raise his arms while gripping the ends. He liked to walk that way to stretch his back. The earth beneath his boots was black and everywhere at this elevation the ravages of blizzards and fierce winds left their mark. There were busted evergreens and firs lying everywhere looking like grotesque abstractions of what they once were.

Once in a while, Jake stopped to sit on a rock to catch his breath. Coming from near sea level to over 10,000 feet in a few days was a tremendous adjustment to the lungs, and Jake didn't fool himself into thinking otherwise. Therefore, when his heart pounded heavily and his lungs went into overdrive, he knew enough to stop. Then his breathing would ease back to normal, permitting him to continue his journey. It was stupid to fight that reality. He knew he was a sea-level hiker and not a Himalayan Sherpa.

When he arrived at a clearance beneath the next ridge, he realized he had hiked about five miles. He was completely soaked with sweat from the last half-hour of traipsing up switchbacks, and he knew the toughest stretch lay ahead at the far end of the meadow where the trail ascended through a thick forest. There were no blaze marks, only small cairns to guide him. He stopped and sat on a deadfall to snack on peanut butter crackers and drink from his canteen. After a ten-minute break, he continued his hike with the sun high in the sky and the day quickly warming up.

Soon he had to take off his tee shirt and put on a sweatband. The rendezvous with the initialed tree was about forty-five minutes away. Once he stopped to splash his face in an icy stream, remembering there would be no other opportunity to partake in such a refreshing experience.

He pushed himself up the switchbacks with dogged persistence and was sweating profusely. This was backcountry hiking, it was about endurance and the personal gratification you got from reaching a goal.

Jake kept up a brisk pace, determined to make good time up the trail.

Sensing the location of the marked tree was near, he slowed his pace. A few moments later he stopped short in his tracks when he came upon it. The same tree that he had carved his name in a year ago stood before him. The lightning scars remained but the tree was as hardy as ever. Slowly, he climbed over some boulders to get near it, dropping his gear on the way until he stood a few feet away.

Slowly, he ran his fingers over the dugout letters and marveled at his handiwork. J-A-K-E. He never wanted to forget the pledge he made, that he would return and reinforce his connection with nature. With his back against the trunk and sitting on the needles beneath its boughs, Jake ate two granola bars and drank his lemonade. Soon he would move on to discover what was on the other side of the ridge.

He thought about all the times during the year when he took off for brief intervals to spend a few hours on the trails at the State Parks or when he wandered along the Appalachian Trail near High Point. Somehow, someday, he would take early retirement and leave the congested northeast to spend the rest of his life in his beloved Wyoming.

As he gathered up his gear and prepared to hit the trail, he thought of Ellen stuck in Florida and decided to put her name on the same tree. With exacting precision and a sincere desire for her to share the place, he carved out her name on top of his. E-L-L-E-N. Then he added '99 to mark the year. When he finished the job he stood back and admired his work. He caved her name in the hope that someday Ellen would come to this place and know that Jake thought she was special enough to be remembered.

That night, he wrote the following in his journal.

Each day can be so exhilarating to run with the spirit of the wolf, letting go of society's constant demand for conformity and material gain. I want to chase the scent of the mountain wind. I want to feel wild and free like a falcon gliding across an alpine meadow that chooses his own direction. As I've told my students over the years, knowing others is wise, but knowing oneself is enlightenment. My hike today gave me a sense of peace and balance in a world of chaos and greed. I was where I belonged. I was close to myself. I truly believe that wrong desire is the greatest enemy of happiness. I must never forget that. Today, I realized there's a hidden part of me, a part that I hope to share with someone if my destiny leads me there. That is my only desire. Is it wrong? I hardly known Ellen, and yet, I can't imagine losing her. I wonder if she's thinking of me the way I'm thinking about her.

CHAPTER 24

The air conditioner ran on high as the Eastman van cruised south on Interstate 95 past Richmond on its way to the Sunshine State. The temperature outside was in the mid-nineties; it was a sweltering humid afternoon, but the traffic was moving along at a good clip even if the scenery seemed to be standing still. The boys were dressed in shorts and tee shirts. Ellen wore a modest outfit to ensure Guy wouldn't entertain any interest in her. He wore his baggy jean shorts and purple athletic shirt, which only made his bulging stomach more pronounced. The fact that he wore designer shades only added to the humor of his appearance.

Ellen and Guy took two-hour turns driving. Other than the occasional small talk of families stuck together like cattle in a pen, the ride was uneventful during the first eight hours. Much of the time, she found herself daydreaming about Jake, reliving the walk around the meadow and his passionate kisses. Over and over, she thought of her sexual awakening. From the beginning she thought he was quite handsome, but as he stayed in her mind hour after hour, she found herself filled with erotic fantasies.

Guy kept his thoughts to himself. He dozed whenever she did the driving. Packing for the trip had been exhausting, but the helter-skelter of getting the family out the door generated a dull morning headache for him. Danny listened to his Sony Walkman and was uncommunicative. Joey, as usual, loved sitting up front whenever his dad drove and tried to engage him in conversation whenever something interesting came up along.

"Hey Dad, look over there! That's Camden Yards, right? We should visit there! Dad, what's with all the cigarette factories in Richmond? Dad, how did people get to Florida before the Interstate was built?"

Every couple of hours the Eastmans pulled over to a rest area to give everyone a break from the close quarters and to use the restrooms. Twice they stopped at fast-food restaurants at the boys' urging for a twenty-minute meal. Ellen passed on the high calorie food, preferring a salad and diet Coke. By nightfall the hours took their toll on the family, and tolerance was at a premium. Ellen chose to remain quiet and let her husband direct the dialogue. Her thoughts were still confined to the past week.

During the night while the kids were asleep, Guy brought up the planned repairs he'd promised his parents would be completed during their stay. Ellen's head was resting on a pillow next to the window. She had been in and out of sleep when he touched her. Startled, she sat up straight.

"Ellen, sorry I woke you. Did I mention I told my parents we'd give them some help...with doing a few odd jobs? I mean...nothing extraordinary. Besides, with all your free time, I didn't think you'd mind. After all, it's costing us nothing to stay there. Do you have any problem with the arrangement I made?"

Ellen already knew it would be her responsibility to do the home improvements. Guy had little patience for detail work, and she was handy at interior painting, putting up wallpaper, and doing garden landscaping. Nevertheless, she made no attempt to pursue the conversation or argue about the deal.

"That's fine with me. All I want is one day to recover from the trip, nothing more."

Then Guy mentioned that although he was looking forward to the vacation, he'd be heading back to Atlanta in two weeks, leaving her on her own. "I agree with you. Let's relax for a few days and do the easy stuff first. After that I'll be around for about ten days. Maybe the boys can help...Then I've got to return to Atlanta to meet with some clients. Business is business and it comes first, but I'm sure we'll get a good start on the projects. I'm not worried. My mother gave me a list of things she'd like done."

Ellen tried unsuccessfully to hold back the contempt she felt for her temperamental mother-in-law and told Guy, "Well that was very considerate of your mother. How else would we know what was expected in return for the use of the house? I hope she was very specific about her tastes."

"Stop being like that. You know damn well that they've done a lot for us and she's got every right to expect some show of gratitude."

"Gratitude, gratitude from you or from me? That woman's never been interested in making me part of her family. She's a perfectionist! Look, I told you I'd help and I'll do whatever you promised her."

The only request Ellen gave to Guy was her desire to join a health spa, to which he inquired if it was really necessary since they had a backyard pool and she could exercise in the air-conditioned house. But Ellen wouldn't cave in and let him know it. "Guy, I've never questioned what you do with your free time or what you do to stay in shape. I expect you to support my decision to join a health spa. It's only fair."

He finally relented and blurted out, "All right...that's fair."

They arrived at the Hollywood home right before dawn on Monday. Rather than sleep, Ellen spent the first few hours unpacking and putting the house in order while the boys and their father slept. Then she went grocery shopping to stock the fridge with the kinds of foods the boys liked. After returning from the store she woke them up and served lunch. When they finished eating she told them, "I'll clean up. All of you ought to see about cleaning the pool. I'm sure it needs some attention. Guy, make sure you run a test on the water before anyone uses it. That's important! There're snacks in the fridge... all I ask is that you clean up after you eat. I'm shot. I'll be in the bedroom taking a nap."

The boys cleaned the pool while Guy left to buy the necessary chemicals. By the time Ellen took a shower and crawled into bed, she was totally exhausted.

Two hours later she awoke to some loud music. Still extremely fatigued, nevertheless she was determined to start things off in proper fashion. She put on shorts and a light blouse and walked outside to see what the boys were up to. The steamy tropical heat of the late afternoon was oppressive, and she remained outside only long enough to get Guy's attention.

"I'd like you to pick up some KFC. I don't have it in me to prepare a meal. There's a fruit stand on the way there. Please pick up a watermelon, some pink grapefruit, fresh tomatoes, and some corn."

"I thought you went shopping. Did you forget to buy all that?"

"Guy, look...please go and get it. It'll make my life easier and yours too. I promise I'll cook tomorrow."

Indeed, the first evening was peaceful, mostly because Guy took Ellen's advice and picked up KFC along with a ripe watermelon. Ellen was grateful for not having to cook and served the take-out on paper plates which made cleanup a snap. Considering the last thirty-six hours, all Ellen wanted was to escape and go to the ocean. She invited her husband to accompany her as a formality, knowing full well he had no interest in strolling the eight blocks to the beach in the heat.

"Guy, I'm going to walk to the ocean. Do you want to come along?"

"No, not really. I hate sweating after I eat, and this humidity is like being in a jungle. You go. I want to catch up on some financial news."

It was 7:30 when she left the yellow and white stucco ranch and walked east toward the beach. She had three major concerns on her mind. First, Ellen thought about how she was going to get Guy to let her return home in August like she promised Jake in the letter. Her second concern was avoiding Guy as much as possible. And finally, how could she get in the best possible shape in the event she got to see Jake. That one was settled with the gym membership.

Nearing the boardwalk, she saw the beach was nearly deserted except for a few fishermen who sat on lawn chairs with their surf poles imbedded in white plastic tubes, hoping for a hit. As Ellen approached the edge of the surf she noticed it barely created any waves. Bending down and swirling the water with her hand she realized she longed for that kind of tranquility in her life.

Finding a driftwood log to use as a backrest, Ellen spent the next half hour saturating her senses with thoughts of Jake. Closing her eyes, she remembered the way he kissed her and the way his body felt against hers. The images were so vivid they overwhelmed her consciousness with erotic thoughts about making love to him. In truth, her romantic fantasy was completely out of character because there wasn't a single incident that even came close to her experience with Jake. For the past twenty years Guy had been the only man in her life. The last time she even dated had been sophomore year at college.

Ellen thought she'd been given the chance of a lifetime, a chance to break out of her self-imposed emotional stagnation. The more she considered the questions, the more her anticipation for another chance to see Jake took precedence over everything. Unbelievably, she was falling in love.

It was dark when she returned to the house. The boys were in the pool and their father was watching cable news. She opened the patio door and asked, "I'm back. Would any of you like some ice cream?"

She took their orders and walked back inside to make two hot fudge sundaes and a dish of sherbet for Guy. One thing was certain, Ellen was determined to meet Jake. She wouldn't give her husband any reason to be suspicious, so for the next few weeks she'd keep busy waiting on the family and doing jobs for her mother-in-law. She'd give Guy the appropriate response to anything he asked. It was a game, and she'd play it better than Guy could ever imagine. She would wait until he was ready to return to Atlanta before asking for a week off in early August. Her central argument would be about payback, the way she insisted on going to the health spa. Her resolve would be steadfast. She wasn't going to beg him like in the past.

Ellen served the desserts poolside and returned to the kitchen. After breakfast tomorrow she would go to a bookstore to purchase the novel she promised Jake she'd read. Then, she'd go to Sam Goody's to buy the Genesis tape *Calling All Stations*. On the way back, she would sign up for a six-week gym membership at Bally's and begin exercising in earnest.

For the remainder of the evening, Ellen stayed in the "Florida Room" and read another romantic adventure story called, *Into the*

Wilderness by Sara Donati. Six weeks was a long time, and it would be a difficult period of waiting. But with the possibility of seeing Jake again she'd somehow get through it and hoped with all her heart that he'd be there waiting for her. Although she had no way of knowing what he was feeling for her, it had to be enough to trust fate. Perhaps by buying the book and listening to the music, she'd have some clues about him. Even now, she wasn't sure why he asked her to do those things.

Strangely, after their time in the park together she was certain that a sense of guilt would convince her that falling in love with a married man was morally wrong and she needed to turn back. But those thoughts never entered her mind. For Ellen to drive out and meet him simply because he begged her wasn't foolish. It was hard evidence that suggested Jake really wanted to connect with her. The daring escape to meet him convinced her that he was worth the risk. Even considering the level of secrecy necessary to pursue a relationship didn't frighten her as much as losing the opportunity for a love to develop between them. In truth, the rendezvous would have never occurred without two individuals taking a gamble to reach out and touch each other's souls.

CHAPTER 25

The motel was located on Highway 212, a half mile-outside the town of Red Lodge, Montana. It was mid-afternoon when Jake strolled up to the desk clerk. She was a young woman in her early twenties with a friendly attitude and obviously a "local."

"Howdy! Welcome to Red Lodge. Do you have a reservation?"

"Yes I do. Name's Jake Carr. Pleased to meet you Miss...Miss."

"Sorry sir, its Mrs. Dillon... Joanne Dillon. Recently married and working hard to save up and buy a place near Billings. My husband Lloyd works for Dakota-Montana utilities. He's from up that way. I'm from around here. We're stuck living with my folks for the time being, but I pray that'll change by spring. Will ya fill out this card for me?"

With a wide grin in appreciation for her personal story Jake said, "Well then Joanne, you're the first lady I've met in Montana and you're pretty friendly. I appreciate that."

"How kind of you to say that...this time of day things are slow and I can really talk to people. Then around suppertime all kinds of tourists start checking in. You're early. You ought to use that whirlpool."

"I think I might just do that. One other thing, I'd appreciate it if you would direct me to an establishment that offered a stranger some distraction. Would you know of such a place Mrs. Dillon?"

"Mister, judging by the way you present yourself...umm, I think the Black Bear Saloon is the right place. It's on Main Street; I don't think you'll be disappointed. What'd you have in mind?"

"I'd like to listen to a local band and have a few. Maybe dance a little. What'd you think?"

"Get there around nine, that's when the music starts. Generally speaking, a few ladies are always hanging around looking for someone to dance with. If ya buy 'em a drink and act like a gentleman, you'll have company. I'm pretty sure of that. I can tell you're from back east. What brings you out here?"

"Accent's that bad, huh? I'm from New York. I'm on the road for a few weeks, camping, hiking...kinda vacationing. Hey! Thanks for the conversation. Have a good day!"

Jake turned and left the office. After taking his gear to the room, he undressed, put on his swim trunks, and headed to the pool. After a few laps, he sat in the whirlpool and read L'amour's *Last of the Breed* before returning to the room to take a nap.

He showered and shaved, around six, then got dressed. He wore

Levis, a faded short-sleeved denim shirt, and hiking boots. When he walked to town there were tourists everywhere in sight, parading up and down the main drag, and going in and out of shops. At this hour, Jake knew they'd soon be filling up the local restaurants, rather than standing in line to wait for a table, Jake found a little cafe and sat down at the counter on a red vinyl, squeaky, swivel stool.

Only three customers were there. An older, chubby man in a stained white apron, with faded tattoos and a handlebar mustache, served Jake a glass of cold water and a plastic coated menu that probably hadn't changed in years. Then he stood and waited.

"Buddy, I'll have the BBQ beef with red beans, cole slaw, and some sourdough bread. You better give me a large tumbler of homemade lemonade to wash it down. You know, I can't recall the last time I ate at a restaurant counter... must have been back in high school."

"Mister, there ain't a bit of difference whether you're sittin' on a stool or sittin' over there in a booth. Shoot, as long as the food is tolerable, that's all that matters. Least that's how I see it."

"You're entirely correct! Good observation. I'm hungry. Bring it on."

Jake enjoyed a leisurely supper sitting on that hard stool. It tasted good and that's all that mattered. He drank two free refills of lemonade; but skipped dessert. The bill was seven dollars plus tax. He paid, leaving the old timer a two dollar tip.

After dinner, he strolled around the residential part of the small town to observe what the tourists don't see, the housing ordinary people inhabited. In western towns the homes reflect the culture and lifestyle of the residents. There were no housing developments in Red Lodge. Consequently, every possible type of dwelling could be found and, in many places, a new diesel Dodge Ram truck or Chevy Tahoe appeared to be the most prized possession instead of the home, especially in the trailer park.

Overall, the excursion was enlightening and entertaining. Nobody got rid of anything that was, or could be, useful. The neighborhood garages didn't house vehicles; they were warehouses for more junk. It seemed the residents of Red Lodge didn't pay any attention to city ordinances. The outward signs of financial success and social conformity were missing.

Jake entered the old western saloon as the first set of music was starting. He thought the three wannabe country rock stars were pretty good musicians. Only a few people were in the place. The bartender was a middle-aged woman who wore a cowboy hat and red bandanna around her neck. She moved with grace and purpose as far as Jake could tell from watching her serve a couple who sat in a booth. Jake thought it best to be as friendly as the desk clerk had been to him. He placed a ten-dollar bill on the bar and waited for her to approach.

"Howdy Miss! That band sounds pretty good. Are they local boys?"

"What'll you have Mister?"

"I'll have a gin and tonic."

Jake thought the best way to win her over was to tip her a buck.

"That'll be two dollars. Oh, thank you. I appreciate that."

After listening to some unfamiliar country and western songs, Jake put a dollar in the tip cup sitting on a speaker and requested any Eagles song the band could play. As they started playing "Take it Easy." Jake walked toward two women who had just entered and were drinking draft beers. Without the slightest hesitation, he promptly asked the better-looking one for a dance.

Before she answered, she turned around and checked Jake out for a brief moment. Then, she said, "You bet. I'm ready if you are!"

Jake spent the rest of the evening in the company of the two women. He danced continuously with a 40ish blond named Trish Murphy, an exile from, of all places, Pittsburg, PA. Although she had a rough exterior and ribald sense of humor to go with a gravely voice, she was great company and danced with reckless abandonment. She loved the waltzes and teased Jake into thinking she was easy.

Trish matched Jake drink for drink and dance for dance. He told himself that this experience was all about savoring the moment, and having fun, so he took full advantage of the opportunity. He knew from the start he wasn't heading for a late night sexual encounter because the woman was a local gal and he was a stranger. She'd told him so mid-way through the evening. Reputations mattered, and Trish had lived in Red Lodge for the past ten years. They had grinded a little during the slow dances, but that was more because of the influence of the liquor than any other reason.

Trish asked Jake the basic bar questions: "What brings you to Red Lodge?" "Why are you alone?" and the inevitable "What's a fella like you do for a living?" He gave her the bare minimum and she seemed satisfied. For the rest of the evening, they kept the conversation light in between dances and drinks. Trish couldn't help teasing Jake about his Jersey accent. After buying a last round at midnight, he gave the bartender a five-spot and said farewell to Trish and her shy friend. He was about to walk back to the motel when she offered him a ride.

A few minutes later, before departing from her old Ford pickup, he leaned over and gave Trish a kiss on her cheek. She broke out in a wide grin and exclaimed, "You're a great guy and I had a goddamn good time. You're so easy to be with."

Jake nodded and he gave her another kiss, an innocent one on the lips. Then he said, "So are you, Trish Murphy from Red Lodge, Montana. You've been a terrific date and you're a hell of a dancer!"

Somewhat sheepishly, she touched his face and confessed, "I've been married for ten years, but I swear, I couldn't turn down a dance with you."

Jake felt quite flattered by the remark and thought it appropriate to tell her so. "Trish, tell your husband you met a guy at the saloon from back east. Tell him we danced and I paid for the drinks. Tell him when you get home. Don't be afraid. He'll appreciate your honesty. I'm certain of it. Then, if you feel sexy...go ahead and run with it. He's a lucky man to have a woman like you. Thanks for the company. Good night."

৯৬

Kings Hill was in the Lewis and Clark National Forest off Route 89 in the Little Belt Mountains. Jake picked it for good reason; it was an out-of-the-way place and not a well-known tourist area. Literally, the camping area was completely hidden off a national forest gravel road. There was little probability of any out-of-starters visiting such a remote part of Big Sky Country.

He bought provisions and filled up with gas at Big Timber, a small town off Interstate 90, around noon. Then he took Highway 89 a hundred miles north before arriving at the campground at 2 p.m. As he suspected, only six campsites were occupied, and five of them were RVs with Montana plates. The place was quiet at this time of day. Jake could have fallen out on the picnic table and only the bugs would have noticed him. It was a perfect place to spend a couple of days.

He drove twice around the loop till he found the most isolated site. The best spots were usually the ones at the end of the each loop, because they backed up directly to the forest. Camp setup went smoothly and used up an hour's worth of time. Then Jake took his walking stick and his canteen to survey a trail map that was stapled to the camp bulletin board. He paid the ten-dollar camp fee, checked the time, and figured he had four hours to hike. He took a trail that led to a Forest Service Fire Tower.

The campground was parallel to Kings Hill Summit Pass, which was at 7,350 feet. The tower was listed at 10,500 feet on the topographical map. Before beginning, Jake opened his backpack to make sure he had enough snack foods and a folding windbreaker. The weather was totally unpredictable in the mountains during late afternoons, and it made sense to be prepared for any unexpected turbulence that could develop over the mountains. It wasn't uncommon to be enveloped by an unexpected downpour at this elevation. When that happened, the temperature could drop twenty degrees in minutes.

It was a pleasant afternoon in the low seventies with a cloudless sky overhead when Jake started up the trail. Amazed by the good fortune of finding such a gorgeous place, he sang a song every now and then to make the most of the hike. Today was the eighth day of his road trip, and he was pleased with how the "Montana Express" was going. Unlike the Big Horns, the Little Belt Mountains were covered with standing Ponderosa Pine and Aspen that carpeted the landscape in every direction.

A trail sign pointed off to a small path that led to the fire tower. After another half mile and plenty of sweat, Jake approached the structure standing unobstructed in the distance. To his surprise, there was a faded blue, battered old Subaru parked near the base of the tower. On closer inspection, Jake took notice of the Montana plate, which had the word "Vadar" instead of numbers and letters.

Looking up at the tower, Jake noticed a shelter in the shape of a box at the top. Intrigued and desiring to get a better view of the Little Belts, Jake climbed the steel steps that zigzagged up some fifteen stories. After opening a hatch door, he made his way along the catwalk that permitted the park ranger on fire watch to observe the dense forest in every direction. An entry door to the shelter was slightly ajar. Jake knocked a few times. From inside, a female voice called out, "You can come in."

Over the next hour Jake shared his time with one of the most colorful characters of the road trip. "Lady Vadar" was a recent graduate from the University of Montana at Missoula. She was on a summer work program as a fire observer. Alone for much of the day unless interrupted by a backcountry hiker, the coed was grateful for some company. The "Lady" was a comparative literature graduate who had wanted this type of job to write her first novel. Her genre was science fiction.

As if conducting one of his counseling interviews, Jake won her over in rapid fashion. He also took the time to read the first chapter of her rough draft. In turn, she provided Jake with iced tea, a few Fig Newtons, and conversation about growing up in western Montana. It was a mutually satisfying experience, unrehearsed, and an example of western hospitality on her part.

"Lady Vadar" played a sound track from the movie, *Last of the Mohicans*. She claimed it was the most enchanting music she had with her, except for *The Planets* and she was correct. They listened to the entire score. Neither of them diminished the mood by making useless banter. The student sat daydreaming on her bunk while Jake slouched down on an old shredded parlor chair.

When the music ended, the lady asked Jake a rather probing question considering her youth. "It gets pretty lonely up here and, to tell you the truth, I really miss my family. I don't understand why you're traveling alone. You don't have to answer if it's something personal."

"Young lady, you've been awfully kind to me. I wouldn't think of not explaining. A long time ago, before I settled down to pursue the American Dream, I had traveled all over the country. I was searching for something, something I later learned one can get without leaving home.

"The Taoist masters' claim, *that without going outside the door one can understand all that happens under the sky*. I suppose you can get that understanding without running away. Perhaps you can understand your true self anywhere and at anytime. At least that's what they taught.

"Anyway, a few years ago I felt like I had lost my true self. And, contrary to the Tao, I couldn't find it at home. I don't know why. Maybe I was dealing with too much crap like I said, pursuing the American Dream. Anyway, I asked my wife for three weeks off to hit the road. I think she knew she had no choice if we were to stay married. The bottom line is that I'm on the road doing something that's crucial to my well-being, by getting close to the earth and thus closer to my true self. The other forty-nine weeks belong to my family. That sums up my story. Isn't it amazing how few words a person really needs to describe the truth?"

Jake was certain that his answer was no answer for such a young person. He didn't expect her to reply. But "Lady Vadar" got up from her bunk and sat directly across from him on an old foot stool.

"You may not believe me, but I do understand. My dad is a ranger and even though the Lewis and Clark National Forest is his domain, he takes off for a week whenever he has the chance. My mom and dad are Montana natives; they don't crowd each other or make unreasonable demands. I haven't met many students from back east, but from what I hear, they live in their heads and don't appreciate our way of life. I love this place and I'll always live here. Do you think you'll end up in Montana someday?"

"As things stand right now umm...that's tough to predict. My son is starting college this fall and next year my daughter will be a senior in high school. I've got my dreams on hold for a while longer. Speaking of other things, what's with the license plate?"

"Lady Vadar" explained her total obsession with the *Star Wars*

Trilogy and some of her ideas about the state of the world. Jake listened and then he asked her about her future goals. She told him she wanted to be a writer and, later, possibly a high school English teacher. As the minutes passed, she opened up more and more, as if she had been in solitary confinement.

When it was time to leave Jake requested a simple favor from "Lady Vadar." Would she wave goodbye to him from the catwalk when he was a hundred yards away? He wanted to remember her that way.

∂∞≤

A couple of days later he was in northern Montana at the Cave Mountain Campground in the vast Lewis and Clark National Forest, it was fifty miles south of Glacier National Park. The area was totally deserted when Jake arrived so he set up camp thirty feet from the raging Teton River. Scavenging firewood was unnecessary; it was stacked high near the entrance. Right after lunch he left for a hike into the Great Bear Wilderness. The trail ran next to the river and was used by packhorses.

Every once in a while something unexpected happens on a trail. On this particular afternoon, it wasn't lightning or a hailstorm that wrecked Jake's day. It was mean-spirited horseflies that enveloped him an hour into the hike. Instantly, he assumed a pace fast enough so that the assassins couldn't strike. As long as he kept it up, he wasn't vulnerable. However, as the elevation increased, his pace slowed and the battle of Jake verses the horseflies commenced. Covering his face and swatting for all he was worth, he was no match for attackers, he had to turn back.

Two hours later, he returned to the campground. Bitten all over and disgusted for making such a dumb mistake, Jake stepped into the Teton River to relieve the inching and keep down the welts. However, snowmelt creates icy streams that feed into fast moving rivers. The temperature of the water was only slightly above freezing. Regardless of the needle-numbing pain, Jake soaped up his extremities, held his breathe and crouched down in the river to rinse off. Although it was an invigorating experience, his howling was heard in the Netherlands.

Jake spent the evening in solitude at Cave Mountain. He listened to the symphony of water cascading down the Teton River, while his campfire provided him warmth and a light show. Then he had the ultimate treat. No words could have accurately described the night sky. His neck ached from leaning back in his chair and watching the stars appear filling every crack in the heavens.

Using a sturdy stick as a poker, he sat by his campfire and placed log after log to burn in regal fashion, it was a visual masterpiece. There were bright orange, dull crimson, and brilliant yellow flames dancing together, leaping high into the night, accompanied by the sounds of bursting sap. Taking swigs from a bottle of apricot brandy, Jake sat by the fire well past midnight.

CHAPTER 26

It was a little after sunrise and Ellen was drinking her first cup of coffee. There on the kitchen counter was the ticket confirmation for Continental Flight 845 from Fort Lauderdale to Newark International. The dream of reconnecting with Jake was now a reality. The boys were sleeping soundly and would probably stay in bed until noon. Guy returned to Atlanta yesterday and the morning was hers.

Her spirit was soaring. She felt robust and confident because she had achieved her most important goal. She had her ticket. It was a victory worth savoring; more significantly, it proved that she was clever enough to outsmart her husband. What made securing the reservation so gratifying was that her plan had succeeded perfectly. It was different than when she fooled Guy into thinking she was going to the bank on that fateful morning when Jake called. That experience in late June left her with a feeling of relief, relief because she got away with it. Guy never mentioned to her that he thought it was an act of defiance, and characteristically told her she was stupid for forgetting to go earlier.

Taking the ticket information and the cup of coffee, she went outside, sat on the deck next to the pool, and reflected back on what had occurred preceding her triumph only eight hour ago.

❧

As planned, during the first two weeks of the vacation, Ellen kept busy every day from early morning until she cleaned the kitchen after dinner. She did everything possible to meet the demands of her family: cooking the meals they liked, keeping up with the laundry, and straightening up the house on a daily basis. She refused to ask Guy's help in doing the jobs for her mother-in-law.

In the first week she painted two bedroom ceilings and the outside shutters and trim of the stucco ranch. Right before he left, she even began stripping off the faded wallpaper in the guest bathroom. She coyly told him she was waiting to hear what pattern her mother-in-law had selected from a Home Depot catalogue. She also ran errands without disturbing Guy, drove the boys to the mall, rented movies, and washed and waxed the family van. Everyone's needs were met. And Guy, with typical arrogance, felt he was master of the house once again.

She was constantly on the go for a full two weeks when it dawned on her that if she chose the right time and right mood, she would catch Guy off-guard and out maneuver him. Her behavior during the final weekend became a kind of one-sided mindgame leading up to a Sunday night showdown. The closer it came, the more she was convinced that he'd be hard pressed to reject her request. Moreover, if need be, she was ready to plead with him by breaking down with tears of desperation.

Interestingly, during the entire period prior to making her request, the only time she was ever alone was visiting the health spa, taking her evening beach walk, or staying up late reading when everyone else turned in. She wrote in her journal every day and reread her statements to galvanize her determination. She ended each entry with the encouraging phrase, *I'll never turn back.*

On the night before his return to Atlanta, she knew the time was right for making her move. For the better part of the day Guy had been catching up on his work. After a late dinner, he mellowed out watching *Meet Joe Black* with Joey. On request, sometime after eleven, she took him a martini. After ten minutes passed, she casually entered the hallway outside the bedroom to put some towels away in the linen closet and noticed that he was immersed in reading the *New York Times.* With her heart pounding, she walked into the bedroom and stood by the window so she wouldn't interrupt him while he was reading.

He looked up after a few moments and then she spoke to him with childlike temerity, "Guy, I know you're tired, but could I talk to you for a few minutes before you turn it?"

"I'm sure you want to ask about the wallpaper pattern. I' sorry my mother hasn't made up her mind yet. I'll give her a call tomorrow. I know how much you want to get that job finished, anything else on your mind? Oh, I left you some cash for the week. It's in the center drawer of my desk."

She sat on the opposite side of the bed and calmly stated, "I'd like to take a week off and get away. In fact, I'd like to return to Middletown. I want some time alone…nothing else. I just want to relax, maybe paint a little, walk, and read. Guy, I've been with the boys continuously for a year, and I need a break. I know you can manage the office from here. I'm going to make the reservation tomorrow."

How she managed to deliver the message so effectively was a complete surprise to her. In the twenty years of marriage, she'd never gone on a single overnight excursion much less taken a week off.

"I suppose that's all right with me. It's understandable. Been a long year, huh?"

Concealing her absolute joy, she simply nodded in agreement. Her plan had worked.

Even so, Guy felt inclined to inquire, "Why are you going to Middletown? Why not the Keys or Bermuda? I can afford it. It's no problem. I mean…what are you going to do up there? Really…I'll treat you to a ticket and some spending money to go somewhere else. You've really come around these past couple of weeks."

Her answer was simple. "I'm tired. All I want is some free time. It's been a long and busy year. You don't need to spend any extra money. That's not right. I appreciate the generosity though. Thanks."

Guy left Hollywood the next morning feeling well-rested, and gratified that his vacation plans had not only saved him money but he mistakenly thought that Ellen was back under his control, similar to the way she had been before moving up to Middletown. He felt honoring her request was a necessary trade-off that would keep the current arrangement going, an arrangement that benefited him in ways that Ellen could have never imagined.

ॐॐ

The hazy yellow sun was creeping above the skyline when Ellen left the house for the ten minute drive north to the mall. She took the Genesis cassette out of her beach bag and listened to *Calling All Stations* on the way. Working out at Bally's was a challenge, and this morning was no different than any other. Dressed in sweats and with a towel around her neck, she began the circuit training exercises. The proprietor had told her that if she completed a fifty minute total body workout she would get results.

As she fought against the resistance of the exercise machine, all she could focus on was imagining what her first meeting with Jake would be like. She saw him in her mind's eye as tanned, rugged-looking, and powerful. Above all else, she wanted to look as desirable to him as he was to her. Now that her husband was gone there would be many more times when she was alone. She promised herself that whenever she desired, she'd drift to thoughts of erotic pleasure that never entered her mind prior to meeting Jake. He awakened within her a heightened sexuality that was hard for her to understand, yet it was incredibly real.

She arrived back in time to make pancakes for the boys. Lately, she demanded very little from them except that they keep their room in reasonable order and not cause problems with any neighbors. After she cleaned up the breakfast dishes, Ellen changed into a new turquoise bikini she had recently purchased but never wore, put on shorts and a lightweight black top, and prepared to go to the John Lloyd beach. She took along her journal and a copy of *Bridges of Madison County,* and placed a folding lawn chair, beach towel, and water bottle in the rear area of the van.

At 1 p.m. the sun was full in the sky and directly above. The heat was sweltering with tropical humidity. The fine beach sand was hot enough to cause second degree burns. Finding a spot a few yards from the edge of the surf, she tossed off her clothes and jumped in for a vigorous swim. By combining the exercise at the gym with nightly walks and a swim, she thought she'd make headway tightening up.

Ellen felt refreshed as she toweled off and then she generously applied sunscreen on every exposed part of her body. Then she sat down and started to read the book. After getting through the first half, it became evident why Jake asked her to read it. The story was about two strangers who met by chance and what occurred between them in a period of four days. She loved the novel and the story touched her heart.

After another swim, she thought it was time to express what she was feeling in a letter to Jake.

> *Dear Jake,*
>
> *The last time I wrote to you there was so much more I wanted and should have said. All I seem to be able to do is think of you. I am so drawn to you it's scary. I feel like I've known you for a long time. I trust you. I want you to trust me. I've never known the feelings I'm currently experiencing, but I'm not afraid. I want to know everything about you, what you like, dislike, about your outdoor adventures. I want to know more, much more. Your hopes and dreams. I want to know what makes you happy and sad. Why you need to escape from people and travel alone to your beloved Rocky Mountains wilderness. I want you to tell me the things you feel comfortable in sharing. I want you to believe I would never hurt you. I could never intentionally hurt another person ...especially you. I am not like that and never have been.*
>
> *Right now you are in Montana, I wish I could be with you. I think about you and how peaceful it must be watching the sunset in the western sky. I dream of watching that sunset with your arms around me, just the two of us alone in the mountains.*
>
> *I miss your eyes looking at me and your strong arms holding me, and the way you talk to me, so calmly. Jake, I miss you so much. I can't wait until I see you again, hear your voice, and feel your lips touching mine...our hearts racing together.*
>
> *Love,*
> *Ellen*

She read it over and over, until tears came and went, finally realizing how dreams are born. The truth of her feelings came out in the letter. The words were from her heart and Ellen believed that fate had brought Jake into her life. There was no need for any other explanation. Everything was so right about the way she felt. Again and again, she told herself to believe that when they saw each other again the magic would return. Jake would know what to do, and she would follow him.

Very late that same evening, after the boys went to bed and the house was quiet Ellen prepared a bath. She took a bottle of merlot and a wineglass to the bathroom and placed them on the ceramic-tile floor next to the tub. Then she lit five scented candles and placed them in different locations throughout the room to disperse the light and scent. For music, she chose a CD by Bette Midler called *Bette of Roses.* Then she ran the hot water until the tub was three-quarters full and added a full measure of aloe bath oil, which turned the tap water into a faint shade of mint green.

Ellen had an overwhelming desire for erotic indulgence. She had read about similar scenes many times in romance novels. Whatever fantasy she had about other men was always self-contained and never actualized. Before tonight Ellen had only thought about imaginary lovers. Tonight, she desperately wanted Jake with her. She longed for him and couldn't wait any longer to satisfy that desire. She wanted to surrender herself to him and fantasize that he was in the room with her. Three weeks was too long for her to wait, and in spite of every conceivable method of distraction, Jake never left her thoughts.

After a full glass of wine, Ellen undressed slowly. She thought of Jake sitting nearby and watching her. She placed a mirror on the sink to see herself as he would see her, and that made her heart pound inside her chest. Finally, she stepped into the tub. The bath water was very hot, and the oil gave it a silky feeling on the surface of her body. Flickering candles bounced light off the pale yellow walls as she slowly eased herself into the water until it barely covered her breasts. She kept her eyes open and took in the dreamlike atmosphere created by the candle flames, occasionally taking sips of wine and looking over at the mirror. The mood continued as she finished her second glass, then she poured another and drank it slowly. The music alternated between soft romantic rhythm and blues, to a few overpowering fully orchestrated songs of high energy. The symphonic power made her head sway in time with the music.

Soon, the three glasses of wine lessened what remained of her inhibitions and by the fourth glass she couldn't postpone her desire for gratification any longer. She closed her eyes and let herself think of Jake sitting opposite her in the tub. When she dipped her finger in the wineglass and softly moved it around her lips, she imagined it was Jake using his tongue. When she laid back and let the washcloth drip warm water over her nipples, it was Jake giving her that pleasure. When she held her breasts and slowly caressed them, it was Jake's touch. And when she placed a leg on the edge of the tub, it was Jake she welcomed as she slowly moved her fingers down to her sexual center. She imagined him making love to her and she surrendered to the dream. Finally, with her legs apart and her eyes shut, she felt Jake's penetration, as she reached levels of ecstasy she never had the desire to experience before.

Afterwards, she felt refreshingly beautiful and cleansed from the sexual berating she had endured over the past twenty years. She toweled off and put on body lotion. Uncharacteristically, she decided not to wear a nightshirt. Instead she wanted to sleep in the nude and enjoy the feeling of acceptance for her body, a body that until today had felt undesirable. She realized she was no longer limited in any way. She was capable of being sexually attractive and stimulated. She decided that if and when the opportunity ever came with Jake, she had the confidence to run with it.

The next morning Ellen got up very early, drank a quick cup of coffee, and drove to Lloyd's beach. It was 7 a.m. when she arrived and the place was deserted. She walked to the shoreline and knelt down in the cool moist sand. A stiff morning breeze blew across her face and tossed her hair against her face. The rising sun was just coming up on the horizon, a brilliant ruby red ball of color.

She knelt in the sand, clenched her fists, and declared with the sunrise as her witness. "I'm finished. There's no doubt left in my mind. I'll wait until Labor Day, and then tell Guy it's over. Twenty years of servitude and misery is enough. I've foolishly waited for Guy to love me, respect me, and be loyal to me. It never happened! I was only afraid of finally letting go. I was scared to make it on my own, but now I'm ready."

Although she had some fear about Guy's reaction, she was past caring about what he had to say. Finally, she told herself that Jake had nothing directly to do with her decision. The fact that he had entered her life was pure coincidence. She knew that leaving Guy was the underlying reason for moving back to Middletown. That was the truth. The seminar and group interaction gave her the insight to accept reality. Jake was a separate issue, and there were no assurances their relationship would continue. He was a married man. It was a choice he would have to make.

The last twenty-four hours had been a turning point in her life. She was ready to face uncertainty with confidence. Her faith had been restored and she was ready to break free to seek her destiny.

CHAPTER 27

The "Montana Express" was nearing an end. Jake was in a good frame of mind, notwithstanding the fact that in two days he'd be back in Walden. The temperature hovered in the nineties. It was hot and dry with a hazy sun cooking plants, asphalt, and humans under its rays. Jake found some shade near a bush took off his black tee shirt and began eating his lunch at the Missouri River Overlook.

Last night, after checking into a motel in Spearfish, South Dakota, he treated himself to a KFC buffet feast for six bucks. Afterward, he walked for an hour to the outskirts of town to watch the sunset over the Black Hills. Twenty minutes later, all hell broke out as a set of thunderheads blew in from the north. The puffy gray clouds changed the serene evening sky into a blend of gunpowder black and dull orange, within minutes intermittent lightning lit up the horizon over the hills, accompanied by an ominous symphony of thunder. Some of the blasts struck with deafening intensity. The storm was frightening, an awesome spectacle of swirling wind gusts and pounding rain

For sure, if the thunderstorm stayed on course he was in a dangerous spot. Two choices were available. He could either make it to a covered log framed open shelter that was only a hundred yard sprint, or he could try to high-tail it back to the motel which was a half-mile away. That choice would rob him of the chance to witness the show. He chose the shelter.

No sooner did he reach the shelter when sheets of rain began pelting the metal roof sounding like hailstones. Although still an hour before sunset, darkness covered the entire hillside and the emerging wind gave birth to a sudden gale that pushed against the cottonwoods and wiped them clean of their leaves. Gusts swirled around the playground, blowing dust and rotten mulch everywhere while relentlessly banging the metal swings against each other. The temperature dropped dramatically as Jake sat shivering in a tee shirt and shorts totally mesmerized by the spectacle. He hoped that as fast as it blew in, it would leave, and thought, *This is one hell of a send-off. I couldn't have asked for a better closing act. Damn, Mother Nature's got a temper and when she feels like letting off steam...I guess this is how she does it. This is awesome! Man, what a show and it's free.*

As the storm continued to drench the field around the shelter, thunder shouted deafening sounds as it passed directly overhead. A lone lamp post, probably on a timer, lit up near the shelter and produced an eerie sensation. Jake waited for the storm to pass and reflected on the last few days.

The previous morning Jake had departed from a remote camping area in the Pioneer Mountains near Wise River, Montana. The campground was next to a river and he had pitched the tent ten feet away. The weather was excellent and the two days of hiking were memorable because of three unique experiences.

The first was an old ghost town called "Coolidge," which a forest ranger had given him directions to. Taking a worn-out, dirt road up the mountain, he found the town about a mile away. There he explored what was left of a deserted mining operation from a century ago. Walking among the scattered remains of shelters and shops, he could feel the presence of the miners and visualize them working. High up on the ridge a steel grate covered the mine entrance with all kinds of threatening signs. "Explosive gases present" and "Trespassers will be prosecuted." Inspecting the barrier, Jake figured there was no reason to tempt fate and satisfy his curiosity by attempting to trash the padlock. When it came to spelunking, he had some experience, but lots of things could go wrong traipsing around a mine shaft in the dark.

The second experience was sighting a lone Gray Wolf trotting across a wide meadow. The creature was probably in search of an unsuspecting jack rabbit or field mouse. Never in all his journeys had he ever witnessed a wolf roaming free. Later that same afternoon, on his way back from Cub Lakes, he came upon a ten-point buck and trailed him downwind for almost twenty minutes without being detected. When Jake got as close as possible to the buck, he crouched behind a stand of birch trees. The magnificent creature raised its head from the tall meadow grass, turned, and faced the intruder. There were fifty yards separating Jake from the buck. He held his walking stick to his shoulder like it was a Henry rifle and pretended to squeeze off a shot making the corresponding sound, "BANG!" The buck bounded away in a split second and left Jake knowing he had made the kill.

Finally, he witnessed an eagle flying directly above him holding a twisting brown snake in her talons. It was another "one of a kind" natural encounter, one that left Jake wondering why all those experiences happened in one day. Were they examples of karma or coincidence? The mysterious occurrences were the stuff of adventure tales and left Jake feeling humbled, in awe of the creatures.

One other unusual thing happened during his stay at Wise River. While walking next to the river near dusk on his final night, Jake was hit full force with a personal revelation. It was his "burning bush," that is, in the Biblical sense. There was no voice from heaven, nevertheless, it was an epiphany. The revelation must have been lodged in his subconscious waiting to come out at the right time.

Jake thought the revelation must have come from the spirits of the three majestic creatures he saw that day. They represented symbols and, to his thinking, the mystic power of the eagle, wolf, and buck were, as the Indians would have proclaimed, "big medicine," occurrences which could produce a vision.

He recorded the following thoughts in his journal on the last evening before leaving for home. An evening that Jake knew marked the end of his road adventure in Montana.

MY PERSONAL TESTIMONY

I've had many good days in the past couple of weeks. Right now I'm feeling so alive. Nothing seems to change me more than the freedom and spontaneity of my camping experiences and hikes into wilderness areas. Just like last year, I found that I like this road character (me). Although he's alone, he's quite content. But tonight, thoughts of my life back in Walden started to creep into my head. Initially, I fought them off, knowing I'll have 40 hours and 2,700 miles of driving to think while I travel the interstates from Butte, Montana, to Walden. I'm sure all those miles of driving will allow plenty of time for confusion to enter my head, the stuff I put on hold before I left.

This trip has changed me, far greater than last year and I know it has. I'm ready to start a two-year plan to eventually separate from Sandy. Truthfully, there's nothing keeping me back east except my seventy grand job and the responsibility of getting Annie into college. I've got to stop deceiving myself into thinking there's a long-term prospect of happiness in my marriage. The distance between us is too great. I'm worn out from masquerading and I hate being so dishonest with an honorable woman.

Today, when I was hiking on a trail next to the Wise River I decided enough is enough. I'd rather finish my life in these mountains than anywhere else. I could find a place in a rural area on the outskirts of Buffalo or Sheridan over in the Big Horns. I can live cheaply and travel anywhere I have a notion to go. I love my children, but they're almost adults now. Somehow, I know they'll understand.

I've tried over the last twenty years to follow the American Dream, never sure if the gold at the end of that rainbow was real, or "fool's gold." I'm tired of being a middle-class professional. I've played the role to the max. Sometimes, with regard to my marriage or my career, I sincerely believed it was worth the effort and personal sacrifices. However, in the final analysis, my marriage didn't give me back a fair share of what I put into it, at least not in the past six or seven years. Perhaps I foolishly believed I could conquer anything. I believed Sandy when she said I was superman and that my life would be blessed for following the same traditions she followed. I got lost doing it.

Sandy, I'm worn out. I'm used up and running on empty. You, not the kids, have used me up. You're never satisfied and never know when enough is enough. You've been consumed by your career, worried about material things, and obsessed with your trust fund and the stock market. Sandy, I didn't lose you! **You lost your way and, in doing so, you lost me**. *I'm truly sorry, but I'm not the man.*

He picked up his container of lemonade and tee shirt, and walked back to the Missouri Overlook parking lot. He used the restroom, washed his face and arms, then got back in the van and turned the Aerostar toward Council Bluffs, south on Interstate 29.

The next five hours took an eternity. Every few minutes, thoughts of returning to Walden intermixed with reminisces of experiences on the road. He played a memory game, trying to recall something special about each day of the trip. This was the second road day and another six hundred miles had to be driven. At Council Bluffs, the traffic slowed down considerably as working people crowded the highway at rush hour. Jake planned to stay overnight at Stuart, Iowa, which was another ninety minutes away. He'd made a conscious decision to visit the Roseman Bridge and wanted to get there before sunset.

When he'd told Ellen to read the *Bridges* book, it was on the spur of the moment. When he left Walden he had no intention of taking the trip to the covered bridge. Now, for some reason, it really mattered. Maybe it was the letter he composed at the Wise River, or maybe it was because he wanted to believe in his connection with Ellen. Either way, he believed he'd undergone a change of mind and a change of heart.

Like a man possessed, Jake checked into a Motel 8 at Stuart, showered, changed his clothes, and left for the Roseman Bridge within fifteen minutes. He'd driven continuously for over eleven hours with a minimum of stops, but refused to surrender to fatigue. He took two granola bars from the larder box, a can of coke, and left Stuart. Full of enthusiasm, he turned the van back on Interstate 80 east and exited at

Route 92. After another ten miles driving through endless cornfields, he saw a sign at an intersection that pointed the way to the bridge. Sunset was closing in. He slowed down to twenty mph to avoid creating more road dust, and proceeded on the winding gravel road for another ten minutes until it brought him fifty yards from the historic bridge.

It was half past eight when he parked the dusty van in front of a white plank fence that blocked the entry to the covered bridge. There wasn't a single other vehicle there. Jake walked slowly toward the dull red entrance. A sign at the top of the archway was clearly marked in white letters, "Roseman Bridge." He was surprised to notice a gift shop set back in the woods next to the shallow muddy stream called Middle River. Apparently it was open for business.

He knew there were other bridges in Madison County and they were all tourist attractions long before Waller's novel ever came out. He recalled that all along Vermont Highway 100, there were similar covered bridges off the main road. However, Jake believed that this particular place was special, and he felt it almost immediately.

The bestselling book had been written about the Roseman Bridge in the early nineties. Although some people came to visit as tourists, Jake thought more people came to make a pilgrimage in memory of the fictional characters whose ashes were supposedly spread from the bridge. Though the novel was a work of fiction, when Jake read it, the story left him convinced more than ever that karma, with its emphasis on chance and choice, was part of the theme of the book.

Jake went there because of Ellen. They had met by circumstance and now in some strange way he felt connected to her. Although purely symbolic, coming to the bridge reinforced his feelings for Ellen all the more. She'd been in his thoughts more than he cared to admit. At the entrance, Jake touched the frame of the bridge and then slowly walked from one side to the other as if he was in a sacred place. Dozens of messages were either carved by knife or written in various colored markers on the crossbeams, some dating back more than twenty years.

Pausing for a few moments to recall the characters from the book, he took Ellen's yearbook picture out of his wallet and, using a wad of chewing gum, placed it on the white-trimmed frame around the entrance. Then he snapped a few pictures to remember the place and planned to give one to Ellen. After another fifteen minutes in deep reflection, he felt a quiet calm come over him, and he was glad he visited the secluded place.

Later that evening he called home to tell his family he was on the way back. There were 1,100 miles left to travel and he planned on to drive straight through. He made the call using a phone card from the motel and Annie answered.

"Hi Annie. How're you? I miss you! It everything okay at home?"

"Hey Dad… I'm pretty good. Where're you calling from?"

"I'm in a little town off Interstate 80 in central Iowa. What have you been doing?"

"I'm working as many hours as they'll give me. I've been going out with Jeff and he's been real nice. He's coming over tonight to take me to a movie."

"How's your brother? Is he home? Has he been in any trouble?"

"Dad, it's Friday night! Why would he be home? He's out with James and Matt."

"I forgot. How's your mother? Have you kids been good to her? Have you gone to the pool?"

"Mom's not home. Things have been pretty loose around here. It's different, no schedules. Anyway, the note she left says she went to Rachel's for Friday night dinner. I guess she's all right. With her it's hard to tell. Missy hasn't gone on too many walks. She misses you! Listen Dad, I got to go, got to get ready. I'll tell Mom that you called and you'll be home tomorrow night. Love ya, Dad!"

"Love you, too Annie. Thanks for taking care of your mother. I hope you know I needed to get away. Have fun tonight. I'm looking forward to seeing you. Bye princess."

After the call Jake left the motel to take a walk. On the way out he grabbed a Molson out of the cooler and downed it before he even left the parking lot. It was past 10 in the Central Time Zone, and this was the last night he'd be alone. There were several tractor-trailers in a huge lot in back of the motel. The noise from Interstate 80 could clearly be heard as Jake made his way across the truck lot until he reached a small deserted picnic area. Sitting on a bench with another cold Molson, Jake reflected on the past twenty days. He visualized his campsites in the order in which he had set them up. Sitting Bull in the Big Horns, Kings Hill Summit, Cave Mountain, Glacier Park, and the last one at Lodgepole Campground in the Pioneer Mountains, they were all memorable places.

Jake realized that he'd undergone a dramatic change over the course of the trip. The thought of having to change back to his other self was frightening. How could he re-establish a suitable relationship with Sandy? Was it even possible?

In the short term it wouldn't be too hard. A planned mini-vacation with her would take some pressure off. But after that, when the school year began, he could only hope his home life would stabilize. For the near term he resolved to give it his best effort. Then Jake's inner voice told him, *From the time you walk through the garage door, do everything you can to take care of the family. Somehow and in someway hold on for another two years. Put the kids first.*

Alone in his room, he gulped down a third Molson and read the letter from Ellen again. He took out her graduation picture and gazed at it for a few moments. Whatever he was going to do in the coming month wasn't clear. At the present time, his preconceived idea about holding off the relationship with Ellen had vanished.

Ellen had said in the letter that she would return on August 6th. But would she? If they met, how would she react to seeing him again? Were they both foolish for throwing caution to the wind?

Luckily, he didn't need any answers tonight. As he leaned over and turned off the lamp next to the bed he thought, *I'm beat, but I'm so glad I visited the Roseman Bridge. I wonder if Ellen read the book. Damn, that would tell me a lot about her if she did.*

CHAPTER 28

"You're pretty quiet this morning…something on your mind? Ellen, stop worrying. I'll take care of things when you're gone and I won't touch the wallpaper job until you get back."

"What did you say? Guy, you can leave me off in front of the terminal."

"Are you listening to me?" Her husband said mockingly. They were still fifteen minutes away.

From the time she woke up, Ellen was preoccupied with her trip. Before leaving for the airport she checked and rechecked the things she needed to take; like the *Bridges of Madison* book, her personal journal, and of course, the letter she wrote to Jake. She didn't dare leaving anything behind. Whatever last minute misgivings Guy had about letting her go to Middletown never came up. Last night, after taking a late fight in from Atlanta, he went right to bed and Ellen had slept on the couch.

When she woke him at eight, she made him bacon and eggs, and had it ready as soon as he entered the kitchen twenty minutes later. Naturally, like her other behaviors he had witnessed over the past five weeks, he was completely fooled into believing that she had been transformed into a "good wife."

"Ellen, whatever you do, make sure you give me a call as soon as you get in."

"Guy look over there. There's an open spot near the entrance…right ahead. You see it? Pull over there!"

He dropped her at the curb outside the terminal of Fort Lauderdale Airport. There were no hugs between them and no parting words of love. Ellen hustled out of the car like she was about to miss the flight, when in fact, she was an hour early. From the moment she entered the concourse until the time she took her seat seemed to take forever. She wandered around peering in the shops and looking at the clocks.

The three-hour plane trip was uneventful. The flight was filled with retired people heading north to escape the humidity and heat, along with professional types who looked like they'd rather be somewhere else. Ellen had an aisle seat, next to her was a businessman in regulation garb who began studying a contract proposal and never stopped. The man only spoke twice during the entire flight. Once, to get by in order to use the restroom and the other to inquire what she thought of the chicken salad. She ordered a "screwdriver" after lunch, but passed on another given the fact the first one cost her five bucks.

After what seemed like a space shuttle excursion to the moon instead of a three-hour flight, the plane touched down at 3 p.m. Newark International was packed with commuters because of the weekend. Forty minutes later she rented a new red Mercury Cougar and drove back to Middletown.

Driving the Cougar proved to be a bigger thrill than she expected. It contributed to her sense of freedom and the excitement of being on her own for the very first time since she was married. The ride back took longer than usual because of Friday's rush-hour traffic leaving the airport. The interstate that led to Route 17 through northern New Jersey was also jammed.

She arrived home tired and considered taking a nap, but it would take extra effort just to relax, so she dismissed the idea. The house was in order when she left six weeks ago, and it looked the same now. There was nothing to eat in the fridge and she had no desire for Campbell's Chunky Chicken Noodle, so she showered, changed clothes, and went out to do some grocery shopping.

One encouraging sign was her weight. Unlike in early April when she stood before the mirror and cursed her physical condition, the scale now read 127. And when she looked at her body in the mirror, the image she saw was tight and fit. She even had some distinguishing tan lines.

After an hour of shopping, she walked back into the house for the second time. She unpacked the groceries and made a salad with fresh ingredients, sliced a few pieces of cheddar cheese, and poured a glass of chardonnay. Nightfall was beginning when she lit two white candles and played a George Winston CD. It was a strange atmosphere in the Westgate home with no background noise coming from the boys, their music, or the TV. If anything, she realized how much she appreciated the quiet.

After dinner she took off her shorts and top and put on a lightweight cotton nightshirt, went downstairs, poured another glass of wine, and began reading another romance novel, *The Notebook* by Nicholas Sparks. She thought that Jake might call thinking she was back. After an hour went by, nothing happened. She wasn't quite sure what to make of it. After a third glass of wine, she decided it would be prudent to phone Guy.

"Hi. I just wanted to let you know I arrived safely and that the house is in order. The landscapers did a good job. How are the boys? What did you feed them?"

"We're fine. I made burgers for the boys. Hey, how come you waited so long to call? Why couldn't you be more considerate? I hope you appreciate the time off. It wasn't easy for me to let you go. Now I've got two jobs for a week. What have you done since you got home?"

Guy went on with his cross-examination for another five minutes, going over the same stuff he always did. She let him ramble until she finally had enough and said, "Look, we both know you'll do a good job. I'm sure everything will be fine. Give my love to the boys. I'll call you tomorrow night."

After she hung up, Ellen started second-guessing herself, and questioned if seeing Jake was meant to be. She wondered; *Did I put the correct return date in the letter? What if Jake never received the letter?*

Then she thought, *Tomorrow will come, whether I drive myself crazy or not. I have to believe that Jake will be there. Stop thinking the worst!*

CHAPTER 29

Ellen woke up late and was unable to get moving. Her brain was fuzzy, probably from too much wine, and her head was comfortably nestled in a pillow. Without having the burden of motherhood or doing home improvements, she stayed in that position for another half-hour daydreaming about Jake, while listening to the sparrows chirping outside her bedroom window.

It was a little past eight o'clock when she tossed the covers aside and gingerly made her way to the bathroom. Rubbing away the sleep from her eyes and massaging her neck, she stared at the image in the mirror and declared, "I'd better shake the cobwebs out of my head if I'm going to function at all. Whew, I need some strong coffee before I do anything."

Ten minutes later, she held a mug of fresh brew and walked out into the family room to wait for the caffeine to take effect. She glanced up and, on impulse, turned over an Eastman family portrait that stood on the fireplace mantle thinking, *I don't need any pictures around to remind me of my other life.*

Late last night, fairly blitzed, she'd done the exact same thing to a photo of her and Guy, except in that case, she called him a beast before she flipping it over.

"Well today's the day. I'll take a shower, a very long shower, and wash my hair. That ought to get me going. Then I'll have a corn muffin with another cup of coffee. Maybe I'll put on my new swimsuit and get some morning sun. My God, I've waited six weeks. What's another couple of hours?"

She did as she said, except she finished showering quicker than expected. Around ten o'clock, she made a batch of oatmeal raisin cookies, thinking she'd offer them to Jake. By eleven, she was as restless as a puppy waiting to be walked. She paced around the kitchen, unable to calm down. She thought, *I might as well shed this outfit and get some morning sun.*

Ellen stretched out on a webbed lounge chair in gray gym shorts and a bikini top. Just as she was beginning the fifth chapter of *The Notebook* the phone rang; "Oh boy, this call better not be a call from Florida. P-L-E-A-S-E let it be Jake!"

She felt her insides turn over as she raced into the kitchen to pick up before the third ring.

"Good morning. Ellen, this is Jake. I'm reporting back in your life.

I'm the fella you wrote to in June. You know, the one you sent the pictures to...the wolf, the maiden, and the cabin. Are you okay?"

"Am I okay? What a question. You've come back to me. Wow! I was outside getting some sun."

"Since I got back three weeks ago I've been outside too, doing yard work, waterproofing the deck, and painting the shutters. Now that you're back and I'm back, what happens next? I didn't know if you really meant what you wrote in the letter. Wait a second. That sounded pretty dumb. I confess. All summer I wanted to believe you would return, and I'll be damned, you're here. It's all very surrealistic."

"Surrealistic...huh? Like a weird combination of things. I never thought of us in that way."

Uncharacteristically for Jake, he seemed stuck on what to say next. "You're alone? Is that right? I mean, I hope you're alone. Are you?"

Ellen started to chuckle. "Jake you're really silly. Believe me; I don't have to run off like I did before. I'm alone. I came in yesterday around six. It's what I had planned all along. I thought you might call me last night. It doesn't matter now. My wish has been granted and I'm happy to hear your voice."

Jake was taken aback. For one thing, it hadn't even occurred to him that she'd be returning alone. Then he thought, *Her wish has been granted and now what.*

"Really...You came back because of me? Tell me straight out. Is that what I'm hearing you say?"

Ellen saw no reason to mix words and said, "I think you knew I felt that way. That's what I wrote. Wasn't it? That...that I'd be back in August. I'm just so happy I made it back and you were waiting."

"I get the point. So then, how are you? Is anyone with you? Sorry. You already answered that. Shit, what's the matter with me? I guess I'm speeding. You'd better call me back before I lose the connection. I'm at a convenience store a mile from my house. The number is 342-0879. Call me back."

When she got a dial tone Ellen tapped the number. Jake picked up immediately and replied, "Walden funeral parlor, twenty-four hour pick up and delivery with coupon!"

"Jake, you're nuts. It's great to hear your voice and I'm glad you came back safely."

"Ellen, frankly, I've just been passing time. I guess you did the same in Florida. I've been keeping myself busy doing chores and playing golf. I also did a lot of thinking. Maybe too much but that alone would take three hours to explain. I confess. I think I'm still shipwrecked, if you know what I mean. Only now I know it better than I did last June.

The last couple of days I've been waiting to make this call. So you got me. I have no clue what comes next or what you want."

Ellen plopped down on the couch with the phone. She knew it was her move and she wanted it to come out right. "I've also been waiting. Waiting for your call and hoping you got my letter. Imagine, that was six weeks ago. What comes next? That's a fair question. I'm really looking forward to hearing about your trip. Was it what you expected? Was it better?"

"It was a hell of an experience and much, much different from the previous year. It was an adventure of mind and body. I planned it that way. This time, I did a lot of soul-searching. But honestly, it wasn't possible to call you last night. I'm sorry if you waited up. I'm a terrible waiter, terrible! I did my share of drinking last night to pass the time. The friggin' Cleveland Indians beat the Yankees. Sorry. Would you like to meet me at the Mayfair Farms parking lot? How about an hour from now? Does that give you enough time to put on some shorts and a top so we can walk around the Water Gap or someplace else you'd like to go? It's a beautiful day and I'm free till five. You want to live dangerously or what?"

Ellen could hardly contain her excitement on hearing Jake's proposal. "It's what I've been looking forward to, that is, taking another walk with you. This past month and a half took forever. I missed you everyday. Now you got me."

Jake couldn't resist teasing her and said, "Is that all? You missed going for a walk. What about me?"

"Of course I miss you. I miss you terribly. Is that what you wanted to hear? I'll be driving a red Mercury Cougar. Look for it. See you then. Bye."

❧

Jake returned home with an hour to kill. The regular house chores were already finished. To keep himself busy, he decided to change the oil in the John Deere Tractor and then suddenly realized the Aerostar was filthy, inside and out. Without delay, he drove to the back of the house and used his son's power washer to get it cleaned up in a hurry. Sandy, hearing all the noise, came out on the deck and started waving to him, trying to catch his attention.

"Jake what're you doing? I've never seen you use that contraption before. What's the occasion? Why are you power washing the van?"

"I guess I've finally surrendered to using one of J.D.'s toys. I've abandoned my bucket, soap, and old towel hand technique. Besides it takes too long. Sandy, I'm headed out for a while this afternoon, nothing unusual. I should be back at 5:30 or so. Do you want to go out for dinner tonight?"

Sandy was not about to pass up the opportunity to have Chinese food, "That's fine with me. I could go for some Chinese."

"Oh, I'm real surprised. Ok, we'll go to the Hong Kong Palace. Want to invite the kids?"

"That's a strange request coming from you, but I'm sure they're both busy. I'm going to finish sewing that new skirt I've been working on and then go to the community pool to do my laps. Enjoy the afternoon. I'll see you later."

Sandy went back inside and Jake finished his power wash. Then he took the van back to the driveway to brush out the mats and wipe the Montana dust off the dash from two weeks ago. All that remained was for him to change into a clean tee shirt and fill his canteen with lemonade.

When Jake pulled into the lot at Mayfair Farms he was five minutes early. Too nervous to sit and wait in the van, he started to pace around the parking lot. At no other time in his adult life could he recall the kind of romantic excitement he was feeling. Although he had imagined the rendezvous hundreds of times, now that it was at hand he wasn't sure where it would lead.

At long last, the red Cougar appeared in the entrance to the lot and came toward the van. Jake stood still as Ellen stepped out of the Cougar and walked toward him with a huge smile. Neither one of them said a word as they embraced. Jake didn't kiss her; he only wanted to hold her.

"I guess we did it. Ellen Eastman, we're a couple of outlaws. Aren't we?"

"I don't care. I missed you so much. You look tan and healthy. Look at me. In spite of the power of the Florida sun, I'm still pretty white, but at least I'm a few shades darker."

"Ellen, come on, you look terrific. I'm only laughing because I'm happy to see you. You look like a country club babe with those sunglasses and that sporty outfit. That car is a perfect match."

Jake put his hands on her upper arms and pulled her against him, then he kissed her with such intensity it just about knocked her off her feet. She could tell he meant to give her a message with the kiss, and she knew what it was. Jake missed her too and wasn't shy about demonstrating his affection.

"How would you like to drive over to the Delaware Water Gap and walk along to the river? Have you ever been there? It's real tranquil."

"No, I haven't been there. That's a great idea."

"Follow me to the Grand Union Plaza and park your car. We'll take the Aerostar from there. Let's go."

Fifteen minutes later they were driving south, cruising down Interstate 84 doing 65 mph with the windows open and the music playing. Jake gave Ellen the choice of music, and she picked Tom Petty.

"Ellen, do you mind if I turn up the sound? I love that song *Learning to Fly.*"

"I don't mind. I like this van. I can't begin to imagine all the places it's been."

"Believe it or not, I've put 136k on it since I bought it back in the spring of 1993, when I got my tenure at Middletown. With the four captain's chairs it was perfect for taking family trips. When I went away this summer, I took out all the seats so I could pack all my gear and sleep there if I needed to.

"We should be there in about half an hour. All we have to do is take County Road 521 and it will put us on the Jersey side of the Delaware. I'll find a parking spot and we can meander along the trail for a couple of hours. I see you have on new sneakers. If you're lucky they'll still be white later on."

Jake found a parking space not far from a place called Flatbrook, and they began their second date walking on a well-worn path along the riverbank. Occasionally, they passed fishermen, sunbathers in beach chairs, and a few other hikers. They saw dozens of canoes and kayaks making their way south on the lazy current of the Delaware River. As they approached a shaded area where a fallen trunk of an ancient oak created a comfortable place to rest, they sat down. Only an hour and a half had gone by, and yet they were at ease with each other, sharing their thoughts about the summer.

Ellen loved listening to Jake talk about his "Montana Express" trip because he was entertaining and animated in his storytelling. Every so often they found themselves laughing when Jake recounted one of his unusual "routines." He poked fun at himself for his strange habits on the road and at the campsite. He loved seeing her smile and continued to entertain her as the afternoon wore on. Together, they let nothing interrupt the joy and levity of their date. Neither one made any mention of their spouses, or children. Without ever agreeing to do so, they left their personal baggage behind and focused on the here and now. All that mattered was they liked each other's company and were sharing a good time. That was enough for Jake and more than enough for Ellen.

As the afternoon rendezvous was nearing an end they headed back to the parking area. Suddenly Jake took hold of Ellen and, leaning her against a tree, brought his lips to hers and kissed her. At his advance, she pressed her body closely against his and responded to his kiss fully and passionately while he gently massaged her neck. After a minute, he pulled back and moved his index finger over her chin and then around her mouth while looking directly at her magnetic blue eyes and said: "I've had a wonderful time and I'm feeling so good. I could go on like this for hours, enjoying every second, but there's something I want to show you. You're probably going to think I'm a little crazy. Take a look at this."

With that said he removed her graduation picture from his wallet and showed it to her.

"Oh my God! Where did you get that? I look like a baby. I was only seventeen then."

"I got it from the '77 Middletown yearbook. It was in the school library. You look angelic? Did you ever break away from that image of purity? Know what? I don't think you would have been interested in me back then. No how, no way, cause I was pretty wild."

"Jake, you got it backwards. You wouldn't have given me a second look. I was very shy and innocent. I still think I'm not very sophisticated about certain things. Look at me with that black turtleneck sweater and pearls. I really look sweet, don't I?"

They both laughed about the picture. On this first Saturday of August they appeared to assume other identities. They were happy and perfectly compatible with each other.

When they parted company in the Grand Union Plaza near Middletown, Jake reached behind the seat and gave Ellen an oversized white envelope, telling her to open it later. His last words were simple and to the point. "Do you think I can see you again? How about Monday?"

"Of course you can. Remember, I'm up here alone and you're the reason I'm even here!"

"What did you say?"

"I said I came back in the hope that I'd get to see you again."

Jake was so taken by her sincerity he barely managed to contain his emotions. Whatever misgivings he had about seeing her again dissipated instantly. She'd broken through.

"I've got to confess. That letter you wrote me. I read it plenty of times during the past six weeks. I kept that graduation picture in the ashtray of my van and gave it my attention every day. I can't explain any of this and I don't even want to."

Ellen felt so happy with what he said that she leapt into his arms with a fierce embrace and stayed there until he let her go, giving her a teasing stomach poke on the break. Then he said: "I'll call you around noon Monday. Today was...it was great! You're a treasure. Sounds pretty corny...huh? I don't know how this happened, but I believe it's real, so I'm running with it. I guess I'm reckless and you are too. I know its karma and I don't feel any guilt. What the hell does that mean? The truth is that I don't feel like any part of this is wrong. Not for me. I'm so glad you came to that workshop and I'm so glad you were the only one left to interview. Give me one more kiss. Monday's a long time from now."

She answered his request with joy and told him afterward, "I'll be thinking of you the rest of the weekend. And Jake, I believed in you. That's why I came back."

CHAPTER 30

Ellen was intoxicated with joy after seeing Jake, in a state of mind utterly unfathomable only a few months ago. It seemed as if in a single afternoon she had been magically transformed from being anxious and insecure to feeling empowered with a sense of well-being and hopefulness. The experience brought forth an inner strength that was totally unfamiliar and reinforced her expectation that Jake cared for her.

Full of nervous energy, the first thing she did on her return was to locate her paints, pallet, and assorted brushes, including her favorite fantail. She wanted to paint a romantic image to commemorate the event. She set up an easel in the kitchen dining area and placed a stretched 30x36 canvas on it that had been stored in the basement. Then she took her sketch pad from the bureau and outlined a few ideas.

Ellen was so emboldened from her afternoon date that she wanted to paint a portrait of a young woman with eyes shut and dreaming, standing amid some birch trees in a lush blue gown. The idea had nothing to do with her personal vanity but more of a reawakening of her youth. It didn't matter that they were together for such a short time. Never in her life had she wanted a man so much. Somehow, she needed to capture on canvas what it felt like to be young and desirable. It was to be a picture of a maiden daydreaming of her warrior hero. She put the art supplies in place so she'd be ready whenever the mood took over. Then, still keyed-up but quite worn out, she fell out on the living room couch with thoughts of Jake dancing around her head.

When she awoke, she had lost all sense of time and thought she must've dreamt the whole afternoon episode. Sitting up and gazing over at the clock, she realized it wasn't so. The daylight was almost gone, and her stomach growled.

With a splash of cold water on her face, Ellen muttered, "I'm still out of it. I haven't eaten since this morning, but what a memorable day it's been."

It was dark when she picked up steamed dumplings at a local Chinese takeout and returned home with the dinner, along with two bottles of wine. Before sitting down to eat, she lit two candles for company. While leisurely enjoying the meal, she replayed the date, over and over, until it started to crystallize in her mind. What an unforgettable experience it had been. Jake made her feel so alive, desirable, confident, and most of all, young again. It was as if he single-handedly snapped her out of an artificial identity. Now, more than ever, she realized she'd been through twenty years of emotional neglect, literally growing old with a man who defined everything in her life and stifled her individuality. Jake accepted her the way she was and told her she was a treasure.

Jake didn't ask any questions about the state of her marriage, and she was grateful. Neither did he mention anything about his married life. It would've spoiled the day because she knew she wouldn't lie about it. Dumping her unhappiness on him wasn't the right way to start a relationship. For now, she could only assume Jake wasn't happy with his marriage or he wouldn't have gone as far as he did and take the risk. Ellen felt secure in the knowledge that Jake wasn't taking advantage of her by playing head games. She believed he was authentic and honorable, a very unique individual and a caring man who was outgoing, intelligent, and full of energy.

While she was putting the leftovers in the fridge, she remembered the envelope he gave her and ran to the Cougar get it. With great anticipation, she opened it.

The scene on the front of the card was a reproduction of an acrylic painting. It showed two North American Gray Wolves on a rock ledge with a cascading waterfall as the backdrop. The larger wolf, whom she assumed was the male, was standing guard over the other one, a female that was lying beside him. Inside it read: "Dear Ellen, Sometimes someone touches your heart and stays there forever."

Astonished, Ellen placed the card on the center of the kitchen counter and gazed at the picture, not sure of what to think or feel. Then suddenly she realized the card was a confirmation of his feelings. She thought to herself, *This is more, way more than I ever dreamed was possible. How did this happen?*

Excited by the message in the card, she raised the glass of wine and made a toast. "Here's to the warrior that I've waited for, the kind of man who I thought only existed in my dreams. This I swear, I'll follow you wherever you take me. I'm scared with what I'm feeling and you may be too. But I know for certain it's real."

She lit two scented candles and placed them on each side of the wolf card. Tonight was special. No other thoughts entered Ellen's mind for the next couple of hours. She completely blocked out everything. After another glass of wine she began to pencil in the outline of the forest maiden in her sketchbook. She worked on it for over an hour.

Ironically, Guy never called to spoil her mood on that memorable night. The past twelve hours were unlike any other time that Ellen had ever experienced. Later that evening, when the bottle of wine was empty, she played the piano music of "Yanni" to provide a soundtrack for her mood. Then Ellen grabbed a white silk scarf and slowly danced around the kitchen. It was a spontaneous display of her emotions without precedent. With her arms folded across her chest and her eyes closed, Ellen swayed side to side, dreaming of Jake holding her close and waltzing around the room.

≈∾⊚

As promised, Jake called Monday at noon. He'd just finished an early round of golf with Kevin and made the call from the proshop.

"May I please speak to Ellen if she's there?"

"Jake, you're teasing me again. I've been waiting for you to call."

"Did you like the card? Were you surprised...were you? Huh?"

"I loved the card. You're the best! Where'd you find it?"

"Choteau, Montana. I froze my butt off there. It's a small town fifty miles from Glacier. I camped along the Teton River about twenty miles away. I had a terrific camp site. I've got at least a dozen stories from the couple of days I spent there. I'll mention them later, that is, if we're meeting up again. Anyway, I washed up at the golf course and I brought along a clean tee shirt. If you don't mind me wearing my olive green golf shorts, I'll meet you in twenty minutes at Mayfair Farms. See ya soon."

They went to High Point State Park in the northwest corner of New Jersey. The place was forty-five minutes from Middletown and Jake figured the possibility of bumping into anyone there who knew either of them was remote. Jake entertained Ellen on the way with the story about the horseflies and his river bathing.

"Like I said, there are no words that could describe the icy cold of the Teton River on one's lower extremities. I'd have to tie you up to get you in that river. What a rush! I could have gotten a vasectomy and wouldn't have felt a thing. No shit! Those damn horsefly bites are the worst. They leave a monument on you so you don't ever forget they visited."

"Are you telling me that the mighty Jake couldn't protect me from those nasty bugs?"

"Let me put it this way, they'd smell your sweet skin, and the only way I could save you would be if I put you in a canvas sack and carried you across my shoulder on the trail."

"Would you do that to protect me from those miniature monsters?"

"No way, but I'd steer clear of following fresh dung on horse trails."

He parked the Aerostar in a near empty lot not far from the High Point monument.

"Ellen, if it's all right with you, can we sit a spell on the blanket instead of hiking? I'm kind of tired from playing that hilly Mountain

223

Manor golf course. I'll rally in a half-hour."

"That's fine with me. Let's look for a spot with some shade and no bugs to bother us."

Jake took her hand, and they looked for an appealing place to sit. Then he asked, "Isn't this a beautiful place? Monday's a good time to visit here. It's much less crowded than the weekends. We'll have some privacy, and I'll have to deal with temptation."

Ellen stopped and faced Jake, telling him, "You're my biggest temptation! For two nights in a row I've been thinking about last Saturday afternoon. That was such a wonderful day!"

"You're telling me I was in your thoughts last night. No way! That can't be true!"

"Oh boy, you're teasing me again. Of course you were, and I'm still recovering from a late night party I held without you, although you were there in spirit. I danced with you in the kitchen. I did. I may have had too much wine. See what happens when I don't see you? I hope the skeets leave us alone, because I didn't spray myself with bug repellent. Instead I used a fragrance you might like. Am I gonna pay?"

"I'll be damned. You sound like you're a veteran of the outdoors factoring in the bug repellent. I'd rather smell something exotic on you than bug spray any day."

They walked a few hundred yards to a secluded area not far from the twenty-story granite monument. Jake found an ancient oak tree to provided shade, and placed a worn out blanket on the grass. Then, without giving it a second thought, he removed his tee shirt and stretched out on the blanket.

Seeing him half dressed, Ellen felt a little aroused. She thought his upper body was beautiful. He was very muscular, especially his chest and arms. His legs were athletic and she noticed that his stomach was firm and flat. The sight of him only reinforced the desire she was feeling. Yet, she felt extremely self-conscious about sitting opposite him on the blanket. Nevertheless, she was eager to follow his lead.

After a minute, he took hold of her hand and said, "Would you like to lie down next to me? I promise I'll behave."

She gave him a quizzical look, as if not knowing how to interpret the meaning of his words. He gestured for her to stretch out beside him and put her head on his chest. Then he said, "So what's a nice girl like you doing with a character like me?"

Ellen shot right back with an answer. "You are a first class rascal and you know it. This is a wonderful place. What makes it so special is that I'm with a man who makes me feel good. Even though I'm a nice girl, I won't run away if you make any romantic advances. I'll handle it."

She looked up and touched his cheek with the back of her hand. With that invitation, he bent over and kissed her on the forehead and said. "Frankly darlin', my life has been pretty crazy for the last six years. Now, for the first time in ages I feel like you do. I feel pretty good about my prospects. Of course, I've got dozens of questions buzzing in my head, and I know you do too. Can I ask you one?"

"Jake, I want to ask you a thousand questions. I suppose it's only fair that you ask the first one. But then I want you to tell me what you were like as a child. Will you? Oh, will this be an official interview?"

"Listen Ellen, if I've learned anything about living from the first forty-nine years it's that nothing is more meaningful in forming a relationship then sincerity. I believe that's our guideline in climbing this mountain together. So let's be up-front and truthful from the start. You know something, when I was on the road I thought of you like you were some fictional romantic character. Like Francesca from *the Bridges of Madison County*. But now the woman I imagined has become a reality. That's pretty scary. You want to know about my childhood…how about if I send you something in the mail. Is that all right?"

"So you'd rather not talk about it? Ok, you can mail me something."

Unlike their first date when Jake steered away from anything relating to Ellen's marriage or his own, he sprang a question that was totally unexpected, yet it had been bothering him for some time. "Why on earth did you get married so young? It doesn't make sense, unless you were pregnant."

Ellen had never been asked that question by anyone, much less by the one person who deserved an honest reply. Trusting Jake, she decided to be forthcoming and share her heartbreaking story.

"You're right. I guess we're both making assumptions about each other without knowing enough. Talking about my feelings is very strange and scary. I've never shared them with my husband. This is going to sound unbelievable, but no one, not even my mom or my close friends ever asked me why I got married when I did. The truth is…I've covered it up and buried it, mostly out of shame. I suppose I've never forgiven myself for being so afraid. Over the years I've tried to look forward and not back. It hurts too much. I've come to realize looking back is a futile and frustrating exercise. Nothing can change what happened back then. I don't want to look back because my heart breaks whenever I do. I don't want to analyze my past. It's gone and I can't change what I've done. You may, or you may not understand what I'm saying. You just mentioned that your life's been, what did you say, crazy for six years. Jake, believe me, I lost all my trust with my husband in a matter of weeks. This is tough to admit, but his interest in other women began during the first year of our marriage and never stopped. Hard to believe, isn't it?"

Jake understood and he felt she deserved an honest response.

"Ellen, we're here because our belief in the people we married is either dying or already dead. You're telling me that for you it's been dead from the beginning. I'm so sorry that you couldn't have escaped sooner and started over. Why didn't you? I'm sorry. Maybe you'll share that story with me someday. But I'll tell you this much. I don't believe that love can exist without having a sense of hopefulness. Being hopeful is being alive, and trust is the bond of a loving relationship. I think trust is simple to explain…it's believing your partner has your best interest in mind. When trust is broken it's like knocking the keystone out of an archway. The love is destroyed and the bridge to the other person is broken. Listen, I learned back in my childhood to look out for myself. I had no other choice. More importantly, I learned from the pain of my mistakes, by falling down and getting up again. At this very moment I'm trusting in you because I think this is a beginning."

Ellen stared up at the monument. The only sound came from the wind and a couple of loud crows who balked at the presence of humans near their corn field. Jake wasn't sure where the conversation was going. Nevertheless, he wanted to hear more of Ellen's story, so he waited patiently for her to continue.

"Like I said, I've never talked about this before, because I'm ashamed. I guess it all happened because Guy wasn't satisfied with just living together. It's hard to remember all the specifics. I knew him when I was a senior in high school. We worked at the same place and I thought he was arrogant and spoiled. Actually, I turned him down a few times when he asked me out. At the time, I had a boyfriend who I liked a lot. We were going steady, but that's another story.

"Here it goes. When my parents got divorced I never saw it coming. I was blindsided so to speak. My mother was a mess after my father left and I had no financial support to continue going to school. Sometimes it's all so clear and other times I can't make any sense of it. It's a blur. Anyway, at the time Guy was at Emory. He said I could get residency if I moved down there and that I could apply to Georgia State in the fall. It all sounded doable at the time. He invited me to move in with him and work during the summer. When I agreed, I never thought of getting married. I still had two years left of college. I believed him. Whatever his motivation was at the time, it doesn't matter now. Like I said, I trusted him and went along with his plan."

Jake gently put a finger over her lips. Then he got close and kissed her lightly on the forehead. "That's one hell of a beginning," Jake commented. "So what happened next?"

"I didn't get a job in Atlanta that summer, and I found myself totally dependent on his financial support. I was so stupid. I thought I had only one choice and that was to go along with the marriage. It should've never happened. It was my fault. Neither of us was ready, and I really didn't know him."

Jake sat up as if bitten by a rattler. As a counselor, he'd heard it all before. "Stop right there. Determining fault doesn't mean shit. I've been boxed in and scared a time or two in my life. Nobody was around to drag me out of the quicksand or point the right path. I think a young kid at twenty is as stubborn as a mule that won't pull a plow without being beaten. If you made your choice because of fear, that wasn't a choice at all. Honestly it wasn't. You both were naïve. Did you hear me? Both of you were innocent victims of your own foolishness.

"I'll grant you this. Some young men use a persuasive sales pitch when they really want to possess a woman. As a counselor, I know the power of words and he must've really made the plan sound appealing. Yeah, that's what he did. So your family and friends didn't step in with a viable alternative. Shit, someone should have interfered. Both of you were way too young. His parents, they went along with it? You must be kidding?"

"Jake, we secretly eloped. His parents didn't know. No one knew. He wanted it that way. Within a month I knew I was hopelessly stuck. Truthfully, I haven't been independent since that time. Only since moving back to Middletown have I been able to think about the future. I want to get a job, find a place to live with the boys, and start over. That's why I moved back. I don't love him and I probably never did. My marriage is a lie, and what's worse, I'm the one responsible for keeping it going for so long. I'm ashamed of myself, but I'm glad I told you about it. I never want to be dishonest with you."

Jake had heard enough. Her story was a tragic one, one he could identify with to a certain degree. Perhaps she gave more of a picture than he bargained for. However, at this early stage of their relationship it wasn't his intention to do any counseling. It was time to drop the subject.

"Come on Ellen. You answered my question. Let's take a walk up to the monument. There's a restroom and water fountain there. I want to splash some cold water on my head. It's sizzling."

He placed Ellen's hand on his forearm and they began to walk up the path to the restrooms.

"Is this as tan as you get? Yikes, I'm ten shades darker than you my little angel."

He put his tanned arm next to hers and they both started laughing. Then he put his leg next to hers, gently squeezed her butt cheek, and ran off. She caught up to him near the water fountain, but he got there first. As she approached, he swatted water at her and took off again. She followed him, screaming, "You're a double bunch of trouble. I knew it the first time I met you."

"Hey pokey, just try and catch me! I'll give you one of my patented take-your-breath away passion kisses if you can. Come on, make some dust and catch me for the reward."

At that precise moment in time, she knew she loved him. The feeling was exhilarating. He had the ability to make her feel young again. Indeed, Jake was her warrior.

"I've caught you, my handsome prince. What about my reward?"

"As soon as we get to the blanket, can you wait a couple more minutes?"

"No, I won't wait another second."

He took hold of her and kissed her passionately, his bare chest against hers, and his leg nestled between her thighs. She felt him getting excited and the sensation got her deeply aroused. Finally, he broke the embrace and took a handkerchief out to wipe away his sweat.

"Damn Ellen, you're a great kisser. Are we ever gonna get to the blanket? I gotta cool down. I mean, it's noticeable, isn't it? See the effect you have on me! Bet you feel pretty full of yourself? You got me boiling. Now, let's cool off and walk, so I don't catch on fire."

As they strolled down the dirt path and passed the park monument to where the blanket was, Ellen knew more than ever that her decision to take the gamble and spend the week in Middletown was the right one. She was in a state of ecstasy.

Neither of them said a word as they started to make-out. Jake kissed Ellen again and again. Then he pulled her on top of him. She felt him aroused again and moved her lower body slightly side to side, to acknowledge what was happening. After a minute of intense mutual pleasure, he stopped abruptly.

Moving her to his side he said, "You're really an angel. I thought of you so much driving through Montana. Did you know that state is called Big Sky Country? Back in July, on a particular gorgeous morning, you were there. I was pretty scared thinking that I'd ever lose you."

"Jake, it's strange how we experienced the summer. Unlike you, I was trying to do everything possible to make time go by. Your image was always there, though I think it was your counselor image. Now I have another image of you. You're not the counselor to me anymore. You're my warrior."

She traced her fingers over his chest, chin, and face as if she were a blind girl and wanted to see him using her touch. Then she told him, "Jake, I hope you're ok with the things I told you today. You really listened before giving me your thoughts. I'm not used to that level of consideration."

"I'm glad you shared your past with me. Maybe I should have told you more about me, but I was selfish. I wanted to feel closer to you. Ellen, please listen very carefully to what I'm about to say. I want you to be real sure that this is what you want! Trust me. Nothing will be easy for us if we continue seeing each other. Absolutely nothing! Life is short and now I can appreciate how stuff like this happens. People read about it in romantic novels or watch a movie and then they wonder; what choice would they make? Somehow, I know we're both moving in the same direction. I just want you to be sure…real sure."

Ellen took Jake's hand and kissed it. Then she held it to her breast and said, "Jake, there's no way you can begin to understand what our time together means to me. I feel reborn! I've never been this certain of anything in my life. I'm not afraid of what's ahead. I believe in you with all my heart."

Jake believed everything she said. He smiled, holding her against him; he stroked her hair, while kissing her one last time.

‽

On the way back to Walden, Jake's mind was in turmoil. The situation was dicey at best. There was no denying what he was feeling in his heart and soul. He liked everything about Ellen. Although they had spent only two afternoons together, he knew that if it went much further the whole thing would take on a force of its own. The "Law of Unintended Consequences" would turn their worlds upside down. And, for a man who deplored chaotic situations, Jake was definitely putting himself in jeopardy.

There was no denying the fact that he had been on the receiving end of some intimate information this afternoon. He was the one who put forth the marriage question. She answered, but she didn't ask him about his married life. Why didn't she? Was the answer that obvious to her? Perhaps it was.

CHAPTER 31

There were two days remaining before Ellen's return to Florida. After a light breakfast of two cups of coffee and a granola bar, she continued to follow a strict routine of exercising. After a thirty-minute workout she took a long shower and, depending on the weather, went for a walk, painted, read, or straightened out the house. It made her feel proud knowing she had the self-discipline to stay on track with her diet. Since the Chinese dumplings on Friday night, she ate nothing other than a low carb array of salads, along with a yogurt a day. Whatever caloric intake the wine produced she conveniently dismissed as a trade-off for giving up ice cream and chocolate.

Jake seemed to be a constant part of her thoughts. The past two dates had filled her with erotic thoughts and an intense curiosity of what Jake was all about. He did answer her question about his childhood by sending her a poem that left her wanting to know even more.

My Beginning

There was a time long ago, in my childhood, when the only thought of the future was where and when I could play in the forest. The choice of adventure was mine and mine alone. I might decide to defend the Alamo or drift down the Amazon with Tarzan. Near falling asleep every night, my last thought was always in another place I wanted to explore.

I loved the woods because old oak trees were the ramparts of ancient castles. My imagination left the steel cage of the classroom everyday, and it ran down the wayward path of a young boy's adventurous mind.
I loved running, leaping, climbing, chasing, and swinging air born over fallen limbs and fences that blocked my path. I tumbled full force into the walls of hedges that kept me out of magical kingdoms, and I stamped down on puddles to watching them exploded under my powerful foot.

Was I really a boy, or some unusual Disney character from Adventure Land? No, it was me!!! I loved carrying sticks. They would become my saber, Kentucky long rifle, or a walking companion to talk with. Many a dead limb was severed by my hand. I loved to throw crab apples at assorted targets, be they the brick walls of Harrison school or the center of a tree trunk in a vacant lot near the tracks. I'd watch them burst into oblivion and knew I was a great warrior looking to save the kingdom.

Occasionally my travels would take me to where the world seemed bigger than it was the day before. Perhaps the city park had expanded during the night without my knowledge. The old crumbling stadium was a mammoth concrete and ivy fortress waiting to be stormed. The gray and white pigeons were soaring eagles to me. I loved to be alone in that place, and I learned to overcome the fear of walking in the dark shadows of the dingy locker rooms and dimly lit corridors.

Looking out my attic window, the one in my bedroom, I was hypnotized by heavy falling snowflakes, the sound of thunder, and the dull pitch of a downpour on the roof. I was enchanted by multi-colored maple leaves blowing carelessly down Third Avenue. I remember it all.

Yet in all of those moments of time gone by, one thing stands out. I got along pretty well with myself. I wasn't afraid to be me. I was easy to be with, in my outside adventure world, away from the house I lived in. I was content, for each of those days of childhood meshed into each other without interruption. I had a child's heart and, it belonged to me. There was an innocence that defied reality and, there was no measure of time.

Ellen read the poem several times and concluded that Jake had presented her with an intimate look at himself, preferring to write about it in a cryptic manner, instead of explaining in person. She accepted the fact that whoever he was back then, he must have already known he was different.

The portrait of "The Forest Maiden," was coming along. It wasn't a frontal pose, rather a slight profile of a young woman leaning against a slender white birch in a stand of similar trees. The figure wore a dark blue, low-cut gown with long sleeves, and revealed a hint of cleavage. The maiden's eyes were closed as though she were making a wishing or was in deep introspection. Ellen did a commendable job with the maiden's hair by painting it with thick dark brown stokes and exaggerated curls that flowed down her back. The maiden was holding a small bouquet of purple violets in her outstretched arms.

Nothing disturbed the wolf card and two candles on the kitchen counter. When Ellen ate, she sat in the formal dining room or snacked out on the deck. She wanted the painting area left the way she had set it up last Saturday evening. She called Florida every night to check on the boys. Each time the conversations were short, consisting of a report on their activities and the weather. It didn't matter with which son she spoke. If either boy actually missed her, they forgot to mention it. Oddly, it didn't bother her at all. Maybe they needed a break from her as much as she needed it from them.

Ellen reasoned that for all she knew her husband was occupied with a female client or some other lady friend. But now she didn't give a damn. Meeting Jake didn't change her feelings about Guy. On the one occasion when they spoke, Guy inquired how she was spending her time. Although she wanted to propose the same question to him and prove her new independence, she let the opportunity pass. She figured if the boys were ok, then she didn't care who Guy spent time with. Instead, she gave a simple, but sanitized, explanation about her activities. He accepted her response without question.

When Jake called again on Thursday, Ellen was out shopping. He left her a brief message. "This is for Ellen. I hope you get this and not your cleaning lady. I told my family I was going to some horror movie in Middletown. I knew nobody would be interested in going with me. Meet me at the Shell station opposite Montgomery Manor at seven o'clock. I'm looking forward to seeing you."

Ellen picked up the message when she returned home and literally jumped for joy. Like a cheerleader after the home team scored in the final seconds of a football game, she paraded around, picked up the wolf card and spoke to the picture. "I get to see you one more time and I'm finally going to tell you about my feeling for you."

Jake arrived first at 7 p.m., corresponding to the show time of the movie. This would be their final time to be together before Ellen left for Florida the next morning. She was ten minutes late when Jake walked over to the red Cougar. "Hey my Montana angel, you look pretty hot with that black top and short skirt. Would you like to go for a drink with me? I also have a gift for you."

"Come on in handsome. You said we only have two hours. Let's go!"

He leaned over, gave her a kiss, and directed her to a small pub called, "Henrys" fifteen miles north on Route 6. On the way there, he placed his left hand on her inner thigh and started teasing her by sliding it up past her knee. He left it there to see her reaction. Ellen's face blushed but she didn't make a move, instead she released a groan while telling him, "If you keep that up I'll be in no condition to get out of this car. Are you having fun teasing me? How much can I stand?"

"Ok, I'll stop. I just wanted to know if you missed me."

"Jake, I missed you every waking moment. Are you happy now? Is that what you wanted to hear? I must tell you something. I loved the poem you sent me about your childhood. Don't worry. I won't probe any deeper. But you certainly knew yourself in a...in a very special way."

"Thank you for the observation. I'm so glad you enjoyed it. Please lock it away. It's a very personal world for me to share with you."

They sat opposite each other in a booth that had red vinyl benches and knotty pine dividers. The pub was noticeably empty. A waitress came over right away to take their order. She gave each of them a once over and smiled at Jake.

"Evening folks, you two look happy. Did you win the lottery or something?"

"Nope, we're just in a good mood. Could you light this candle for us? Then please bring two Absolute Vodka and tonics. Thank you Miss."

Jake reached over and held Ellen's hand; he broke into a smile, nodding his head up and down as if responding in the positive to the proceedings without saying a word. Ellen returned a similar smile and neither of them said a word until the waitress returned with the drinks.

Then Jake asked, "So tell me. What did you do for those six weeks in Florida before you came up here?"

"I did some swimming and I loved walking the beach, especially at dusk when the sky turns colors. I kept my promise to you and read *The Bridges of Madison County*. I also wrote in my journal from time to time. Oh yeah, I joined a health spa too."

Ellen made no mention of her plans to end her marriage. Instead, she kept it short and simple. "I'll be there for two more weeks. Then I'll drive with the boys back to Middletown. I've got a few more things to do before I leave Florida, nothing big, just some wallpapering and a little painting. What about you Jake? What's ahead?"

"Actually, I'm taking my son to college at the end of the month. I'll be working at the high school the week before Labor Day. How will I know when you return? How can I contact you? Would you drop me a line and mail it to the high school?"

"That's a good idea. I'll write before I leave."

They spent another hour at the pub, and Jake told her some interesting stories about the summer road trip. As they left, Jake left a five-dollar tip for the waitress.

Returning to the Montgomery Manor parking area, Jake told Ellen to wait in the Cougar; he walked to the Acrostar and reached under the front seat where he had stored the gift. It was a silver-foiled wrapped package, the size of a paperback novel. Holding it behind his back, he walked to the open window of the Cougar and said, "Ellen, this is for you. I hope it shows that I thought of you a lot during my trip. You can't imagine what it was like for me to bring you along in my head for those three weeks."

Ellen tore away the wrapping paper. There were two separate envelopes and a CD. She looked at the CD. It was the soundtrack from the movie, *The Last of the Mohicans*. She hadn't seen the movie nor ever heard the music. Then she opened one envelope. In it was a bunch of pressed, dried wild flowers. In the final envelope were three snapshots. One was of the Roseman Bridge with her graduation picture posted on the entrance. Another was her name and the date carved in a huge tree trunk. And the last picture was a shot of a lush meadow surrounded by snow-capped mountains.

He noticed a look of delight in her expression and begged, "Well say something! Do you like them?"

"I don't know what to say to you; this means so much to me. I love the gifts. What can I say?"

"Listen Ellen, don't be afraid. Don't be afraid of me or what tomorrow may bring. If there's one thing I've learned in life, it's that life is full of mystery, and my life has never stopped being anything other than an incredible journey. I'm glad I made you happy. That matters the most to me. Tonight was a very unusual experience for me, going to a public place. I wanted to do something different. Anyway, I feel like we've known each other for so long...like we're totally separated from our other worlds when we're together. Do I sound strange? Are you coming out of that car to kiss me?"

They stood together and held each other as long as they could. Then Ellen placed a letter in his hand as she gave him a farewell kiss.

৵৽৻

Jake knew something about the movie plot if Sandy asked, but he was a half-hour late and a little concerned. Admittedly, he should have left Ellen earlier but he couldn't let go of the moment. He decided to take another chance, so he pulled over and read Ellen's letter.

Dearest Jake,
You couldn't have improved on the two days we spent together this past week. You truly are my magnificent and mysterious Warrior Wolf. Don't ever let anyone change you. Thanks for trusting me. You are a very special person in my life. You care, you listen, and you make me laugh. I'll always keep you in my heart. I love you just the way you are - wild and free. I loved every moment we shared together. I'm sitting at the kitchen counter looking at the wolf card and wishing I could be in your arms. Tonight, I promise to dream of you making love to me

whenever I listen to the CD. I want to surrender myself to you. I'm ready to make this dream a reality. I still find it hard to believe how we met and what has happened since that first interview at the workshop. I love being with you! Finally, I want you to know that I love you with all my heart.

> *Forever yours,*
> *Ellen*

He put the letter in the glove compartment and started to worry. Although he thoroughly enjoyed their time together and planned to continue seeing her, the letter was perplexing. He understood that she was probably through with her marriage, even if she didn't exactly say so.

As he neared his home, he thought; *So now Ellen loves me. Even so, I don't want to be the primary cause of her marriage falling apart. Then again, twenty years of being trapped in a life of unhappiness is enough pain for any woman to endure. This relationship has moved too fast and I'm still trying to comprehend what it is. She makes me happy but loving her is serious business. We promised the truth. I'm not afraid of that. I guess I'm just not as certain as she is. Maybe I'm a little scared. I'll have to wait.*

Jake didn't consider uncertainty in such serious matters to be a bad thing. He believed that people seeking a different path had the right to feel ambivalent about that choice. He couldn't recall giving Ellen a clear picture of his own marital status. However, the fact that he'd made advances proved he was unhappy; if his marriage was solid, he wouldn't have secretly met her on four different occasions.

Jake was certain that Ellen's love for him was caused by the consequence of things he did and the words he had said to her. In the days ahead, he reasoned that he'd replay the past week until it made some sense to him, and go forward from there.

CHAPTER 32

The long-awaited day of J.D.'s departure finally came and the Carr family, minus Annie, left after dawn for the six-hour drive to Vermont Technical College. The Aerostar was packed with the necessary things their son needed to set up residence in the dorm, plus enough goodies to open up his own snack bar on the dorm floor. Jake also managed to squeeze in two suitcases for his mini-vacation with Sandy.

Dense morning fog covered Route 52 for the first thirty minutes until a dull red sphere came up on the horizon and burned off the haze, opening the curtain on a gorgeous day. The ride north was uneventful, and for a Friday morning rush hour they breezed through Danbury without interruption. J.D. sat in the rear snoozing on and off for most of the trip through Connecticut. Sandy occasionally conversed with Jake about the passing scenery and her vacation plans following the college drop off.

Getting there was simple: Interstate 84 north to Hartford, to Interstate 91 all the way to White River Junction, and finally 89 to the college. It was a scenic trip through Connecticut, Massachusetts, and the verdant Vermont countryside. They stopped twice to use the rest areas, and Jake let J.D. take over the driving at the Vermont state line.

As the van drove through the front entrance of the college, Sandy's prior enthusiasm faded away in a matter of seconds. Whatever she saw apparently didn't match up with her expectations. J.D. parked in the designated area for new students and led the way.

True to form, Sandy couldn't contain her misgivings and questioned her son immediately. "J.D. is...is this the whole campus? My God, there aren't too many buildings. It's so small. Where is everybody? Do you know where you're supposed to be?"

"Mom, chill out! I know where to go. You forgot, today is freshman orientation. The sophomores are coming tonight and tomorrow. School begins Monday. Let's go."

Jake, sensing that his wife might derail J.D.'s attitude, took Sandy's hand and let the boy go ahead. He stopped outside the front door of the administration building and calmly explained.

"Sandy, take it easy. He'll check-in and we'll make sure he gets what he needs. Look, it's a beautiful campus and J.D.'s orientation begins at four o'clock. We've got a couple of hours left so right after he picks up his student ID and schedule, let's have some lunch at the college cafeteria. Then we'll get him set-up. You can do this."

"I should've come up before, but I left it up to you. I'm not sure about this place."

"Let's see how it goes. Give it a chance. We're going on vacation...relax. He'll be back soon."

"How'd it go J.D.? Do you have all the stuff you need? What'd ya say we go to the cafeteria and have some lunch? Got your meal ticket?"

"Dad, everything's cool. They gave me a photo ID and meal ticket so I guess I'm set. You know, I was too nervous to eat before we left this morning and I didn't sleep much last night. My friggin' brain wouldn't shut off. I knew it was my last night in my own bed."

As they waited in the cafeteria line, along with dozens of other freshmen and their anxious parents, Jake spoke to Sandy out of earshot from others telling her, "During lunch please try to keep your opinion about the place to yourself. I know it's not exactly your idea of what college should look like. But honestly, J.D. will have a chance to grow as a person on a small campus like this. The people are friendly, the classes are small, and the Profs are accessible."

Initially she responded to his comment with a blank stare, but then reconsidered. "You made your point. I'll be quiet. It's done. I just wasn't quite prepared for this. Why do those brochures always make colleges seem so big and attractive?"

"Are you kidding? Shit, that's like asking why travel brochures always show smiling faces in perfect weather with no crowds!"

Unlike some sappy Disney movie, the final parental farewell was not quite a tearjerker. Jake shook his son's hand and told him to make the most of the opportunity while placing a fifty-dollar bill in his son's pocket. However, he did want the last word.

"Listen J.D., I was scared as hell when my father left me off at a state college thirty years ago. My mother stayed behind. Anyway, he wasn't much of a talker. When I think back to that time, I didn't have much. Not a radio, phonograph, or even a spare pillow. My father just said, 'Good luck.' I don't remember anything else. But I want you to remember something. Luck isn't enough to cut it in college. You're only lucky if you get enough sleep and you don't get the flu or mono. J.D., you got to want this to work. I've only got another minute, but I want you to know something. You've got my support. I believe this will be good for you. Now whatever you do from this day forward, try to be a nice guy. You heard me! Another thing, you're gonna find assholes up here just like any other place. Take my advice and let 'em alone...whether they're kids or adults. You understand me?"

The boy had given his father the courtesy of listening. Now it was his turn. "Dad, I'll be fine. You and Mom go. You're heading up to Burlington, right? Dad, one more thing, set the John Deere for a two inch cut, and whatever, use regular fuel."

"Gotcha, two inches it is. Oh yeah, whatever you do, don't try and match these Vermont boys, beer for beer. You'll not only lose, you'll be huggin' the toilet bowl all night. Take care of yourself son. Work hard and remember you're loved. We'll miss you. Bye."

As Jake turned to walk away, J.D. grabbed his arm and said. "Dad, make sure you keep close tabs on Annie. She's sneakier than you think. Mom's got no clue. Thanks for the extra cash. Bye Dad."

Jake waited in the van as Sandy walked over to her son and hugged him. He glanced over a couple of times and could tell it was tough for Sandy to say goodbye. A few minutes later, she sat next to Jake with wet eyes and a sad face. They left the college hopeful that J.D. would make the transition from his otherwise carefree high school years to an acceptance of his new identity as a college student.

⇛ⅎ⇝

Sandy's mini-vacation plan was for them to spend two days sightseeing around the lakeshore town of Burlington that was home to the state university, and then drive south to the Lake George area of New York State. According to the AAA tour guide, the lake region was surrounded by gorgeous scenery, state forest preserves, and quaint rural towns with the local color of hometown eateries, various curio shops, and antique emporiums. All of which interested Sandy. Much of the conversation during the ninety-minute drive to Burlington was devoted to an exercise of maternal speculation. Sandy mentioned several concerns she had about J.D. being away from home and what calamities and temptations would confront him like drugs, alcohol, and coeds with loose morals.

Whatever concern she raised, Jake reassured her that the boy was ready to be on his own. "Listen Sandy, you have to believe that J.D. has enough common sense and that he'll settle into college life within a week or two. I'll admit I'm more concerned than I let on. I really am, but it's time for him to make his way in the world. Of course it'll be hard for him at first. We'll just have to wait and see. Sandy, you've done a great job!"

Still, it was a hard sell and Sandy continued to share her worries in spite of whatever Jake had to say. Whenever she got fixated on worrying, he'd just let her talk.

"All I can think of is how I felt when I went away to U Mass. My parents left me in that humongous dorm which of all things was called 'The Tower.' My roommate was a night person. I didn't get any sleep for a month. My boyfriend, who I depended on for support, was four hours away at Syracuse. There were only two pay phones on the floor. God, it seems like a century ago. You know at the time I never felt so alone in my whole life. I finally realized how overprotected I was by my parents. You couldn't appreciate that kind of innocence. The university was big and impersonal. My first class was in a lecture hall with three hundred kids. They forgot to mention that. I was scared about the whole idea of leaving home and being on my own. Not about the learning. I was able to handle that part. Do you understand what I'm saying? No you don't. Do you?"

She stopped in the middle of what she was going to say next, looked over at Jake, and started to cry. Jake turned down the sound of U2 and waited for her to continue.

"Everything challenging is an adventure or a test to you Jake. You're strong willed and sure of yourself. You've always been like that. Remember when we met. You overwhelmed me with your ways. My father warned me and said you'd never change. He was right. I'm not like you. Not in the least. You'll never understand a Jewish mother's heart. When Annie was sick I thought I'd lose my mind. Now she's so much tougher. She's your daughter, self-reliant and determined to succeed."

Jake felt that if he let her go on much more the vacation would be a lost cause. "Can't you let it go? We've done our job. Now it's his turn. Sandy, snap out of it, will you? I thought you looked forward to this vacation in the worst way. Let's try to have a good time. Maybe the weather will cooperate and we'll be glad we took this trip instead of going to the Jersey Shore or Virginia Beach. I hate those places with their traffic jams, no parking signs, and unruly crowds. You liked it here back in the summer of '95 when we visited the Green Mountains. Well it's still the same place. We've got good memories. Relax, Joshua Daniel will be fine. We'll be in Burlington is half an hour."

They arrived in Burlington by late afternoon and checked into a Best Western not far from the harbor area. Sandy had reserved a room with a king-sized bed. After taking a nap, they both showered and the vacation officially began. Sandy was dedicated to making the most of their four days together and was absolutely gratified with what Jake told her.

"You decide what you're in the mood for. I've had my adventure; now it's your turn."

She stopped brushing her hair and walked over to the bed, sat next to him, and pushed him down to hold him close for a few moments.

Then she ran her hand across his cheek and spoke with tenderness in her voice. "Thank you for giving me the luxury of making the plans. For now, let's find a good seafood restaurant. I'll ask the desk clerk where to go. I want a steamed lobster. After dinner, let's walk by the harbor. That would make me real happy."

"Good idea, even if we have to wait in line for a table I won't mind as long as the food is good. Take a jacket in case the evening gets cool."

After satisfying Sandy's desire for a pound-and-a-half lobster during a leisurely dinner, followed by sharing a slice of key lime pie, they strolled along the Burlington wharf. Thus far the evening was proving to be "good medicine" for both of them. Jake was on his best behavior. They got along well because he let her set the pace. That was the deal he promised, and Jake had no problem with complying with her wishes.

Unlike the time they spent in Newport a year earlier, which followed some intense marriage counseling, Sandy felt a greater sense of urgency about rejuvenating the relationship this time. She knew it was crucial to put some romance back into their lives. The past school year had increased the space between them and something needed to change.

Considering the dozens of recreational places they explored on their previous road trips around the USA, Burlington was on par with Portland, Maine, but certainly not Seattle or San Francisco. In town, there were shops for Sandy to visit, and of course, the famous Burlington town square bustling with tourists and UV summer session students. There were street vendors, musicians, jugglers and groupies of all types. There were even leftover hippies who apparently chose to hold on to the lifestyle of the late sixties. It was definitely an above average "people watching" venue.

By ten o'clock Sandy was ready to call it quits. Under a pale white crescent moon over the lake, they slowly walked back to the motel. Sandy held on to Jake's arm and felt reassured about the evening, even if she was extremely fatigued. "Jake, thanks for a terrific evening. What a day it's been. I feel like I've run the gamut of emotions. Right now, I'm ready for bed. I hope you're not disappointed. I promise I'll be available tomorrow night."

"Sandy, I don't think I've asked, but thanks for the signal. I'm pretty tired too. I'm glad you got out of the doldrums. Tomorrow we'll start fresh. Everything up this way depends on the weather. We'll see."

On Saturday morning the weather was spectacular. A stiff breeze blew in from the lakeshore, but it was warm outside with little humidity.

All in all, it was going to be a terrific day for being outside. Jake managed to get Sandy up by 7 a.m. and in the lounge by 8 for a continental breakfast. Even before they drank their first cup of coffee he offered a suggestion concerning the day's activities.

"I know I promised you could make the plans, but may I share an idea I have for the start of the day? Not the whole day, just some prime daylight hours."

"Jake, I think I've heard this routine of yours before. But go ahead. Tell me what you've got in mind, as you said, for the daylight hours."

"Well, there are a couple of terrific state parks on Route 2. They're on Grand Island, which is right in the middle of Lake Champlain. I asked the desk clerk, and he said there were great hiking trails that overlook the lake. If you're up for it, I'd love to spend a few hours up there hiking, nothing too strenuous. Later on, we can come back to the motel, have lunch, and maybe take advantage of the hot tub and pool. What do you think about my proposal? Pretty nifty huh? Can I get you a cheese Danish while you consider?"

"You'd do anything to get out of town. Just like Newport, you think browsing at antique shops borders on Chinese water torture. All right, I'll go along with your idea. It is a gorgeous day. But you've got to make me a promise. When I tell you I've had enough that definitely means it's time to get back and crash. Another thing, last night we were exhausted from a long day. Tonight I'd like some fun and you know what I mean."

"You have my word. I promise. If you're in the mood, I'll give you a very satisfying experience. Right now, let's finish eating and get out of the city. Grand Island State Park is forty minutes away. Aren't you glad you brought your hiking boots?"

Sandy called Annie before they left for dinner to remind her to follow the checklist on the fridge; locking the house, feeding and walking the dog, getting the mail, and taking accurate phone messages. She also made it perfectly clear that there was to be no entertaining while they were away. Annie could have a girlfriend over, but that was it. The phone call was a reminder in case of adolescent amnesia.

"Mom, you and Dad forget about me and have some fun...I promise I won't disappoint you."

Jake stretched the hiking time till noon. On the way back they stopped for a slice of pizza and then returned to the motel to wash up and change. When they hit the shopping district of the town square, it reminded Jake of Colonial Williamsburg without the costumes on the store clerks. Saturday afternoon tourists were everywhere.

Sandy asked, "What happened to all the college kids we saw

hanging around last night?"

"My sweet innocent college coed from U Mass, they're all crashing from partying last night. This is the time of day the older generation takes to the streets to do the thing they love best...browse the shops, eat ice cream, and pick out where to fill-up later."

"Is this really so hard for you? I played fair this morning."

"I don't mind it for an hour or two. Remember when the kids were small and we visited places like Estes Park and Disney World? It was a real pain dragging them around. Now, I actually think of it as a form of entertainment. And this euphoria, pardon the word, that people exhibit, shit, it goes on everywhere. Hey, the only difference here is the fact that Burlington's a college town. Honestly, I prefer this to snobby Newport."

"You don't have to come in all the stores, just the ones you want to. Is that fair?"

"That's sounds fair to me. When we hiked over at Grand Island I hope you enjoyed it. You looked pretty relaxed to me. Remember honey, that's what a vacation is for."

"You're right. Good thing I'm still able to keep up with you, well almost."

After a thirty-minute wait they had dinner at a place called The Cellar Pub. It was down a side street and two blocks from the square. The pub was recommended by a store clerk. He told Jake not to be discouraged by the looks of the outside storefront.

Sure enough the advice paid off. The creamy clam chowder was heavenly and the stuffed shrimp outrageously delicious. Plus, the portions weren't tourist size. After dinner Sandy had told him, "That was the best seafood dinner we had since staying in Newport."

Later on, they made their way back to the harbor park where they sat together in a gazebo overlooking Lake Champlain. As darkness came and the lamps along the walkway lit, Sandy startled Jake with a provocative question concerning their relationship.

"Jake, we've been married almost twenty years. It's hard for me to imagine what we'll be doing five years from now. By that time Annie will be graduated from college. Will you be ready to retire? Where will we be? I'm anxious to hear what you think."

"Wow! A minute ago I was sittin' here with a full stomach and a clear head and now you drop a bomb on me. Why ask me now? Why tonight?"

"Truthfully, I planned to ask you this when you returned from your trip. Anyway, when you were away things went pretty smoothly, but I felt very unsettled. At certain times, I felt like you were gone forever, gone to live your life away from me and the kids. I felt alone for those three weeks. I'd wake up and you weren't there. The coffee wasn't made. Missy didn't get walked. Everything seemed different in my life. What I'm saying is that I don't know what my life would be without you. How I could finish raising the kids? I realized more than ever before how much our family depends you. What do you think?"

Before answering, Jake thought, *This is fuckin' crazy. I'm just trying to get through this vacation and she lays this crap on me. Christ, she wants a guarantee about the future.*

Feeling the pressure he told Sandy, "You're asking a lot, too much at one time. Don't get me wrong. I heard you. You want a look at our future, huh? Let's start back. Let me think on it rather than speculate off the top of my head."

Sandy thought it odd that he dodged the question. Jake wasn't in the habit of being unsure about anything. Rather than accept his excuse, she decided to repeat her question. "Well, I'm sure you have some thoughts on it. What are they?"

"I have only one of the answers. Contrary to what you think, the kids are finished being raised. I know it's the Jewish mother thing, but that's your hangup and not mine. As for the other stuff; all I can say is, as usual, your timing is nothing short of...I'm sorry Sandy. That wasn't fair. You have your reasons, but it's past nine, we should head back."

Sandy accepted Jake's answer because they weren't back home sitting in the kitchen or on their nightly walk. As much as she longed to hear what his plans were, she conceded that Jake was right about her sense of timing. And rather than miss the lovemaking by ruining the mood, she let the subject drop. They walked in silence until they reached the motel entrance.

Then spontaneously, she whirled him around and hugged him, saying, "Hey Jake, you're my hero. Still have some energy left? I miss you? I brought along something special to wear. You won't be disappointed!"

"**Mrs. Carr, you're a piece of work. You really are**! Five minutes ago you scramble my brains into an omelet about the future. Now you tell me to come back to the present and make love to you. It's a good thing I can switch circuits in my head. Ok, since you brought the outfit along and you're willing to wait for some answers to your cosmic questions, then there's no reason why we should lose the opportunity to please each other. Now that the air's clear, let's walk a little faster."

🔊

Sunday morning the weather changed dramatically; it was foggy and a dreary shade of gray outside the big bay window of the lounge at the motel. As planned, they checked out of the motel by nine and left for Lake George. Jake figured it would take a couple of hours to drive through the flat spacious countryside along Route 7 in the sparsely populated area of northwestern Vermont. They would spend the second half of the mini vacation at a tiny lakeshore town called Huletts Landing.

The drive was interesting in spite of the threatening weather, especially a short detour to visit historic Fort Ticonderoga. They rounded the southern tip of Lake Champlain before reaching scenic Route 9 that hugged the western coastline of the huge lake. There the speed limit dropped to 30. The road bordered an extensive state forest that attracted tourists and hikers for its waterfalls, trails, and trout brooks. It was a single lane that twisted and turned around the lake shore. There were several turnouts that offered superb views of the lake below and trailheads for the Tongue Mountains.

Unfortunately, the weather didn't improve, but luckily Sandy hadn't made any motel reservations. She figured that finding a place early on a Sunday afternoon wouldn't be a problem. Around one o'clock they stopped for lunch at a lakeshore restaurant called George's Landing.

No sooner had they finished sharing a slice of carrot cake when a downpour began and shattered any hope for outside activities. Jake ordered a second cup of coffee and they both sat quietly and waited, waited for the deluge to cease. It didn't happen.

"Sandy, there's no reason for us to check into some motel and for me to pass the time watching golf on TV or you reading all afternoon. Neither of us is any good at killing time, not like that. Do you think it would be better for us to drive back home this afternoon and take a rain check on this part of the trip? We'll be home around seven. I really wanted to hike the trails around here, or rent a canoe, but the damn weather isn't cooperating. Actually it's shitty. We could visit the Jersey Shore for an overnight on Tuesday. I only owe Middletown High two more days of work. Listen, whatever you decide is fine with me. While you were in the shower I watched the weather channel. The forecast doesn't appear promising for the next couple of days."

"All right then. I was thinking the same thing. It makes no sense. We'll try the shore, but before we leave I'd like to visit a couple of shops in town. Is that ok with you?"

"You go ahead. I'll read in the van. Let me give you a fifty?"

"No, I have what I need. Jake, wait a second. I want to say something. Look at me. Yesterday was fun. It reminded me a lot of the past. I enjoyed hiking with you, although you were pretty quiet and in your own world. Actually, I got the feeling you were somewhere else and not there. But there's one thing I want to say. You were so good to me last night. I knew you didn't want to answer my question about our future. Thanks for being patient. Last night I needed to be spoiled and you came through. Not only once, but more times than I could count. You took care of me. Why can't we have that at home? I get so caught up with work and school. Last night I was someone else."

"I'm glad you enjoyed it. You looked pretty sexy in that red babydoll outfit and those fishnet stockings. Shit, when you took it off slowly, piece by piece, it was a complete turn on for me. That's why the lovemaking went on for so long. Sandy, you didn't hold back. You let yourself go and I followed your lead. I took you where **you** wanted to go. Shit, I'm just glad I had enough self-control to hold on until you were really cooking. I've told you your timing is usually off, but not last night. You were great.

"Go find some treasure to bring back. But please don't get me another tee shirt. At this stage of my life I prefer black pocket tees, not advertisements for Lake George. Take the umbrella. See you later."

Jake paid the check and Sandy took the umbrella and began walking south toward the shop.

๑๛๑

The driveway was vacant when they returned. Missy began barking when Jake opened the garage door. The place smelled of stale beer and cigarettes. When Sandy lifted up the lid from one of the garbage cans, it was filled with party trash. When they entered the house their vacation ended abruptly. On the kitchen counter were bottles of vodka, gin, and rum; in the fridge were two cases of Bud.

After resurrecting their relationship and sharing an intimate experience last night, Jake and Sandy were derailed with an unexpected crisis. Sandy was beyond disappointment and went into an excited state of justifiable indignation. As she vented her rage, Jake kneeled and stroked Missy to calm her down.

"How could Annie do this? How could she put our home at risk like this? This is more than I can handle, how selfish and how stupid. Look at this place. This is my home! Wait till she walks through that door! I never did this to my parents! I'm shocked. You hear me Jake? She's not going to get away with this deceitful act. We trusted her."

Seeing her reaction, Jake told Sandy, "Let me handle the prosecution and sentencing. Believe me, Annie will take full responsibility and accept her punishment. I'm not gonna argue with her. Her behavior is reckless and indefensible. It's pretty obvious to me that Annie's friends were taking advantage of the situation, but still, that's no excuse for using such poor judgment. She put our home in jeopardy.

Shit, I'm angry and I'm disappointed, very disappointed. Listen Sandy, when Annie comes home we'll give her a chance to explain. Not that it will change anything, but we'll give her the opportunity."

Jake hit a raw nerve, one that he didn't know about. Sandy went ballistic. "No Jake! No way! Not this time. Are you listening? Don't you dare let her think she's entitled to an explanation! She's ruined everything. I don't want to hear any of her excuses. I'm ashamed of her and she's turning over her freedom. She's grounded, period. I'm disgusted. I won't ever trust her again."

"Ok Sandy. You're right. Just one thing, please try to do this without making too many threats. Screaming won't help. But if you must, you must. I'll understand."

"Damn you Jake! There you go again with that bullshit…like you understanding Annie better than me. I didn't hurt my parents. I was a good kid and they have put us through hell!"

Afraid to say another word Jake walked outside to the deck with Missy and waited. Sandy's despair was evident, and he realized that this time Annie had gone too far. It surprised him that the neighbors hadn't called the cops.

After five minutes passed he went back inside to find Sandy vacuuming the family room rug, and cursing with every push of the machine. He took the plug out of the wall, took Sandy by the hand and led her to the couch to let her vent some more. But only tears came. Jake tried to comfort her just the same.

"Sandy listen, Annie is seventeen and she's basically a good kid. Granted, she used bad judgment. Hitting her or screaming will make you feel better, but it will only make it worse. We caught her lying. She was deceitful. I want to give her a chance to be remorseful. That's all I want. As soon as she sees the van she'll know it's over for her."

"You're right. I'm too angry and distraught to have any control. I'd probably slap her and I wouldn't feel guilty. My mother gave it to me a couple of times for far less crimes. Listen Jake, J.D. was enough to deal with. I won't let her take advantage of me. She's a liar!"

Ten minutes later, Annie walked through the kitchen door, not knowing what to expect. She saw both her parents sitting at the counter. Jake could tell by her ashen face that Annie wasn't prepared to deal with the grief she was about to receive. Sandy moved to the kitchen table and sat there, looking outside, unable to face her daughter. Jake wanted to remain even tempered, but he couldn't. He pointed to a seat and Annie took the hint. Then he raised his voice and let her have it.

"What the hell did you think you were doing turning our home into a frat house?"

"Please Dad, don't yell at me. Please Dad...I'm sorry."

"Sorry won't help Annie! You're too smart to be so irresponsible and reckless. Why? Why?"

"Everybody does it. There are parties every weekend. Just because I've never done it before..."

Jake wouldn't tolerate the "everybody does it excuse." He lashed out even louder at her. "I don't give a shit what everyone else does, and you know I don't. You're my daughter. Mom's devastated, she's heartbroken, and I'm blown away by your actions. Weren't you satisfied with getting away with it once? That was dumb. Now do what I say. Pick up the phone and call your guests."

Annie didn't move so he raised his voice and shouted the command. "Annie, do it now or I'll call their parents myself. Goddamn it. Take your pick!"

"Daddy, please don't make me do this. I'm sorry. I really am. I'll never lie to you again."

"No good Annie. Call them...call them now and tell them you got caught!"

With a trembling hand and a whimpering voice she made the call. "Jackie, this is Annie. My parents just got home. They know about last night. I'm in big trouble. Call the other kids. Please hurry and do it. My Dad's really pissed and he'll squeal on you. I'm screwed."

After she hung up, Annie started to walk away, but Jake blocked the passage. "Wait a second young lady. Give me your car keys. Lucky for you there's only a week left before school starts. No driving privileges for a week. You're also housebound. It's not negotiable."

Annie was too ashamed to face her mother. She stood with her head hung low like a convicted criminal after the pronouncement of a guilty verdict. Jake walked over to Sandy and put a comforting hand on her shoulder and barked out.

"Annie, go to your room and think on this. I'll be up in a few minutes. I want to know who bought that liquor. You're getting up early tomorrow to clean up the house."

Sandy was satisfied that Jake handled the crisis properly. However, her upbeat mood and sense of optimism was torpedoed by her daughter's reckless behavior. She felt betrayed by someone she loved. Even worse, Annie's thoughtless act had doused the fire that had been rekindled in Vermont. Only a few hours ago, while on the way back to Walden, she had relived the passion of the night before and planned to seduce her husband again to keep the momentum going. Now, all she felt was anguish and self-pity. In her mind she was cheated, and the setback was more than she could handle.

CHAPTER 33

Ellen and the boys left Florida on a Thursday morning intent on staying ahead of the Labor Day weekend traffic going north. After a grueling eleven-hour drive up Interstate 95 with an overnight stay in Florence, South Carolina, they entered the D.C. beltway around four the next day. Two hours later and forty miles before the Delaware Memorial Bridge, the traffic began to crawl. Ellen wanted to stop for dinner, but there was nowhere to go.

"Mom, why'd you take this stupid road? I'm friggin' starving and it's your fault that we're stuck in this mess. There's no cold soda left. This sucks big time. Can't you do something?"

Without hesitation Joey snapped, "You're a jerk! Leave Mom alone, it isn't her fault and you know it. We're stuck, same as everyone else. What'd you expect her to do? Drive on the shoulder?"

"Shut your mouth or I'll stuff my fist down it. Mom, when the hell are you gonna feed us? We haven't moved a mile in the last fifteen minutes. You said if we left a day early we'd miss this traffic. Dad wouldn't have made such a dumb mistake. Can't we get off and at get some McDonalds? Come on!"

Somehow Ellen held her temper in check, notwithstanding her son's ill-mannered, fresh mouth. "Danny, stop complaining. You made your point. Now sit back and listen to your music and wait till the next exit...My God, can't you see everybody's in the same situation as we are. And your Dad would be in the same situation if he were driving back with you."

"Hey Danny, I'm hungry, but you don't hear me whining. Do ya?"

Hearing that stinging rebuke, Danny turned around and punched his younger brother with a stiff shot in the arm, and then yelled angrily. "Joey, you little turd, you're lucky I'm sittin up front or I'd pull you out of the van, throw you on the highway, and rub your friggin' face in it for giving me your shit."

Ellen tolerance was now stretched to the limit. A day and of half on the road with the boys had taken its toll. Moments before she was about to ignite, she noticed an exit sign. "Stop it Danny, and leave Joey alone. There's the exit ahead. Both of you keep quiet."

Ten minutes later, she sat with Joey eating a salad, watching him eat chicken nuggets and fries. Danny ignored his mother's invitation to join them and took his food over to a deserted table and gobbled up two Big Macs without raising his head.

"Mom, why does Danny act like that? What's his problem? Sometimes he's such a jerk. Boy, I hope I'm not like that in high school. You know Mom, coming down was a lot faster. The trip back is taking forever. What do you do...I mean while you're driving? What do you think about? I've run out of stuff to think about."

The truth was that she mostly thought about her experiences with Jake during the week she spent in Middletown. However, she took a different approach to his inquiry.

"Danny doesn't like school, and the thought of going back isn't too thrilling for him. Actually, I was the way you are. I couldn't wait for the school year to be over. And then by the end of August I was ready to go back. You know Joey, looking forward to something special or exciting happening in your life is a wonderful feeling. When I was your age and visited my cousins in Galveston for the holidays, all I thought about was opening gifts and playing games with my cousins, Robin and Becky. We loved staying up late and talking girl talk. With you and your brother it's pretty much the same. Both of you were looking forward to being out of school, getting away from home, using the pool, sleeping late, and just being free. Some things never change. Now we're heading back and it's what they call, anticlimactic. That word means, after the main event happens and all the rest is, well is sorta less important. Do you understand? When I was away for the week and you were with your father, were things that different?"

"Dad was out of the house most of the time. He said he had appointments. A few times he left us money for pizza. I guess he really didn't feel like cooking. I watched a couple of movies with him, but that was it. I didn't see him working much around the house. That week was weird. I missed you, but I didn't hear Dad mention you, at least not to me. Mom, did you miss me?"

"I won't lie to you; I had to get away because I needed time to think. This past year a lot has changed, and I have some important decisions to make. I know that's difficult for you to understand."

Joey had hoped to hear a different answer, that his mother missed him. "Mom, I know you're not happy with Dad. When I was little, I didn't pay any attention to how you and Dad got along. Now, I'm going on twelve and I guess I notice stuff that sometimes I wish I didn't. I get scared sometimes wondering about us. Do you think Dad will ever be moving up north with us?"

"He hasn't made up his mind yet. His business is doing well from what he tell me. Who knows?"

"I thought maybe you'd know his plans. Guess not. You want me to take the trays back?"

"Thanks sweetheart. We should be home around eight. I think the traffic will be moving when we get on the Jersey Turnpike. Do me a favor, tell your brother to meet us out front in five minutes. I'll fill up with gas across the street and pick up a six-pack of Pepsi and a bag of corn chips. Both of you use the restroom. It's time to get moving."

❧

The twelve-hundred miles of driving had drained Ellen, but as usual, she was up at six the next morning. By noon, she'd unpacked the van, had done three loads of laundry, dusted the furniture, vacuumed the downstairs, bought groceries, and was going through the mail when the phone rang in the kitchen. Instinctively, she knew it was Guy.

"Hi Ellen, I was going to call last night, but something came up with a client. How are things at the house? Is everything in order?"

The next couple of minutes of conversation were as one-sided and impersonal as ever. It was as if he was reading from a checklist.

"Is there any water in the cellar? **I didn't check.** Why not?"

"Did the landscapers do a good job? **Yes they did**. You sure?"

"How much money was left over from the trip? **About fifty dollars.**"

"Did you pick up the mail? **Yes, I went early this morning**. Good."

"What're you doing today? **Why is that important to you?** Huh?"

"I have a right to ask. **No you don't.** Yes I do!"

"Are you hiding something? **Are you?** Forget it!"

"Are the kids ready for school? **Joey's excited and Danny's isn't.**"

"Did you check their schedules? **I always look out for my kids.**"

"I won't be back for three weeks. **That's fine with me**."

"I'll call you tomorrow. I love you. Bye. **Ok. Bye.**"

"Ellen, why don't you ever tell me you love me anymore?"

"That's simple, I don't love you and I want a divorce!"

When she dropped the "bomb of deliverance" it was a spontaneous reaction to his high and mighty attitude toward her, and her response came without the slightest bit of hostility. On the other end of the line, Guy wasn't sure what she just said, or what he thought she said.

"Ellen, what was that you just said…what did you say?"

"Guy, you asked me a question and I gave you an answer. I told you the truth. I said I'm through with you. I've had enough. The marriage is over and I want a divorce. I'll take care of the boys and you…you'll finally have your freedom. You can do whatever you want. That's what you've done for the past twenty years anyway. Move back up and get a place of your own or stay down there. What's the difference? Like I said, you've done whatever you wanted all along. At least now it will be legal. I'm through wasting my life. I should've left you a month after I married you, but that doesn't matter now."

She didn't give him time to respond to her biting remark before she struck again. "Here's the point, I'm not discussing any details over the phone or arguing with you over alimony and child support. My lawyer will advise me on those issues. All I want is to take care of the boys and start a new life without your interference. I hope you're listening? There's nothing to argue about and there's no promise you could make to me that I'd believe."

If Guy was shocked by Ellen's last comment, he didn't let on. Instead, he tried to restrain his anger and rage for her ditching him with such ease. "Wait a minute, Ellen…hold on now. Maybe we should see a marriage counselor. Didn't we do that once before? Didn't it help? You can't walk out on me like this?"

"Stop playing mindgames with me. At this point, it's way beyond that. Why don't you just accept the truth? You've stepped on me a thousand times. All these years I've had to do whatever you wanted. No, I take that back, whatever you demanded. I'm through with accepting that kind of treatment from you or anyone else. I've learned a lot about myself this past year. I know I can live without you, and frankly, I'm not afraid. Not any more. All you've ever done was to criticize me, finding fault with everything about me. I never looked good enough for you. You made me feel bad too many times to count. And worst of all, you never respected my opinion about raising the boys or anything else for that matter. I feel nothing for you. It's over. I'm finally wise to you and, and another thing, I'm not one of your female clients that you can manipulate with your mouth or your American Express card. Don't worry, I'll tell the boys tomorrow. And whatever you do, don't call back tonight. I've said everything you need to know."

Ellen hung up the phone without waiting for his rebuttal. Sure enough, the phone rang ten seconds later. Certain it was Guy; she gave in to her curiosity and picked up.

"Ellen, don't you dare hang up on me. Now it's my turn. You better shut up and listen."

"Why should I? I already know what you'll say. You can call me tomorrow night and not before. There's nothing more to discuss. Why don't you just accept the way it is? Is it that difficult to believe?"

This time, she placed the phone on its back and heard the repetitive warning buzz until she buried it under the pillow. Ellen may have felt unsure about her immediate future, but this time she wasn't going to back down. She was emboldened by her own show of strength. Her actions proved that she was indeed capable of giving back to Guy what he had dished out over the past two decades.

Walking out to the deck to gather her thoughts, she felt immense self-pride and jubilation for turning into a *terminator*. The last time she tried to leave was two years earlier. But without any support the separation lasted only a couple of months before she foolishly believed Guy's promises for things to change and an apology for his past infidelities. That time, Guy had played on her insecurities convincing her that the boys needed a father and would suffer irreparable damage if the separation continued.

Now the situation was entirely different. He was down in Atlanta, and the boys liked living in Middletown. Ellen's intention was to get a full-time job as soon as possible. Guy would have to pay alimony and child support based on New York State law.

Ellen took out a pen and pad and wrote her priority concerns. First, she needed to hire a lawyer in order to find out what level of financial support she could expect. Perhaps an initial consultation would be free. Next, she would sit down with the boys and give them the news, answering any questions they had. Finally, she must begin working on a job resume and start the search. At the top of her note pad Ellen wrote these words. ***Twenty years is enough! No turning back!***

Satisfied with her performance on the phone, Ellen wished for nothing other than a quiet Saturday evening. Perhaps she'd read or bring out the canvas of the Maiden and work on the forest background in the privacy of her bedroom. She decided that after dinner tomorrow, she'd tell the boys. She would conduct herself honorably without condemning Guy. She also knew that Jake would be returning to work on Tuesday, and she would tell him about the situation at that time.

The next day Ellen searched for the right words to share with the boys about her decision to seek a divorce. While taking a walk late in the afternoon, one of the statements Jake used in the group process popped in her head out of nowhere. "Say what you mean, mean what you say, and say it to my face." Ellen reasoned there was more wisdom in Jake's directive regarding group dialogue than she previously understood. In fact, without knowing it, she had spoken to Guy about getting a divorce in that manner. She though; *It's probably best to do the same thing with the boys, no matter what they ask.*

As Ellen scraped the plates and put them in the dishwasher, she glanced up at the clock and realized that the dress rehearsal was over. It was time to tell the boys.

Ten minutes later, with the dishwasher humming and the kitchen in order, she was ready. Ellen wasn't sure what their reaction would be but decided to speak with them in a reassuring manner that wouldn't be a condemnation of their father. She felt over the past few years they'd witnessed enough conflict between Guy and her. Moreover, Ellen believed if there was going to be an amiable divorce settlement it would be wise to keep the boys out of it. And above all else, keep them from taking sides.

Although she hated Guy, she didn't want to share that with the boys and didn't want them to know about their father's affairs. She refused to drag them through the mud and poison them. Her mother did that to her when she was in college, leaving her forever estranged from her father.

Danny and Joey were in the basement when she went downstairs and asked them, "Would both of you please come upstairs? I'd like to talk with you about something important. It's not about school or anything like that. Turn the TV off and come upstairs."

Ellen took a seat at the head of the dining room table and waited. Joey came up first and kissed her on the cheek. He already knew what was coming. Danny sat at the opposite end of the table with his arms folded across the chest in a defiant pose.

"Yesterday, I told your father I wanted a divorce. I'm not going to tell you all the reasons why this is happening. Both of you have your own opinions. During this past year I've thought about this a lot, and now I'm certain it's the right thing for me to do. I hope you believe me when I tell you that this didn't happen overnight or as a result of any one single thing. It's complicated, and yet it's not. Your father and I don't love each other. As far as I'm concerned, we are staying in Middletown. Both of you like it here, and I'm near the job market. You'll see your father as much as you do now. That's all I have to say for the present time. I wanted both of you to be aware of what's going on."

The boys sat still for a few moments; Joey with his head down and Danny staring at the ceiling. Finally, Ellen could tell neither of them wanted to ask the first question.

"Danny, is there anything you'd like to ask me? Do you understand what I've said?"

"Mom, I don't know about this. You told Joey and me the same thing a couple of years ago when you left Dad. What makes this time any different?"

"Look Danny, I've told you the situation is different now. I'm not turning back. What more can I say. We're staying here and I think that's important. What about you, Joey?"

"Mom, I'm just glad we did this without a lot of yelling. I'm happy we don't have to move. I like it here. I guess I'll be all right. I know Dad will make sure we're ok."

Ellen got up and walked over to Danny, who seemed to be in deep thought, but wouldn't let out a single hint of what was on his mind. She sat next to him and took hold of his hand, then motioned for Joey to come over. Then she made them a promise.

"Boys, please believe me. We're going to be fine. I know how to take care of us. It will be easier on me if you watch over each other and help out around the house. Wednesday is the first day of school. I know the three of us have to adjust to the early schedule and start the year off right. I'll be looking for a job after you're both settled. I promise we'll be all right. All I need from you is to be responsible and honest young men."

After listening to his mother, Joey's eyes began to tear. He swallowed hard and muttered, "Mom, don't worry, we won't let you down." Then he turned to his brother and said, "Will we, Danny?"

Danny didn't answer. He let go of Ellen's hand, stood up in front of her and said. "I'll speak for myself. As far as I'm concerned, I'm on my own. You got your reasons, and I don't care what they are. That's your business. Right now I don't plan on giving you any grief as long as you give me my space. That's all I really care about."

"I understand. You're both free to go. I'll bring down some ice cream later."

When she took her nightly walk in the Westgate development, all she could do was wonder about what the months ahead would bring. In the course of a single year, her life had changed dramatically, but it had changed for the better. If she hadn't moved back to Middletown she might never have been able to end the marriage. But the separation from Guy convinced her they could live without him.

She had two major concerns. Would she have to fight a battle for adequate support? And how could she pay a retainer for the legal services? Tonight she didn't have answers to either.

Just before she was ready to take a shower the phone rang.

"Glad you picked up the phone. I'd like to get a couple of things straight. First, did you already tell the boys about the divorce?"

"Yes I did. I told you I would, and I wanted to get it over with."

"How did they react? Did you blame everything on me? I bet you did. You're the reason Danny and I don't get along. Well, did you put all the blame on me?"

"No, I didn't. What good would that do? We both know this

divorce is long overdue."

"I think I should've been there to have my say. I know they'll believe me. I wanted to tell them my side of the story. Jesus, I can't imagine the shit you told them."

Ellen grew more agitated by the second. She thought, *What a beast.* Then she lectured him. "There are no sides. Those kids have seen and heard enough over the years to know we don't love each other. Actions speak louder than words, and your behavior toward me speaks for itself!"

"You're an ingrate and a sick woman! I thought last year went pretty well for us, and we had a good arrangement. In fact, I thought it was the best year of our marriage. I gave you what you wanted. Christ, you didn't even have a job! You liked doing whatever you felt like while I was working in Atlanta. I was supporting you. How did I know you were unhappy? You sure you don't want to go for counseling?"

"Guy, you still don't get it. I'm finished with you. I've been satisfying your needs and trying to keep you happy since the very beginning. Year after year I've tried to stay out of your way because I was afraid of your temper and your sarcastic mouth. The kids felt the same way, but you don't want to believe it. It took a while, but I finally realized I've surrendered too much of me. That's it in a nutshell. I'll repeat it one more time. I have no intention of changing my mind. All I want to do is get a job and take care of the boys. You're no longer a part of my life. It's over. Now, what is it that you still don't understand?"

Typically, Guy wanted the last word. He didn't appreciate hearing her condemnation of him. "Let me tell you something. Don't think you're going to continue living in that house and take all my money. Ellen, it's not going to happen. You go ahead. Do whatever you're planning on doing. Just keep that in mind. You're not taking advantage of me. You're not milking me dry. Do you understand?"

She hung up the phone and felt nothing but contempt for him. Leaving the bedroom, she went down to check on the boys. They were still watching TV.

"Can I get you anything? Want some ice cream?"

"We had chips and salsa a little while ago. We're cool Mom." answered Joey.

Ellen retreated back upstairs. She realized that Guy was absolutely true to form, antagonistic and brutish whenever she didn't agree with him. The fact that she took the initiative about the divorce was a devastating blow to his ego and was something he hadn't planned for.

Hearing the neighbor's dog barking, she looked out the bedroom window. She started to laugh a little thinking; *The idea that he assumed it was the best year of our marriage is totally asinine. It only proves how warped his view of our relationship actually is. I suppose he thinks it's true because I've been away from him for so long. He has no clue of how much I despise him for the way he's treated me. He thinks of me as the woman who takes care of the kids and keeps the house in order. He is a beast. What a night! At long last I feel free from his domination. After the boys are in be, I'll take out my journal and write a congratulatory letter to myself and commemorate the event.*

CHAPTER 34

Middletown High School welcomed the staff back with warm bagels, assorted Danish, fresh fruit, and a choice coffee. The three male administrators were outfitted in business suits, while the teacher corps was dressed down. Appearing like a pro golfer, deeply tanned and looking fit, Jake stepped onto the spit-shined waxed cafeteria floor and circulated among the faculty, exchanging greetings in a lighthearted manner. After a few minutes of working the room like a politician, he spotted the teacher he most respected on the faculty, Jim Van Ness, and strolled over.

"If it isn't the top biology teacher in North America, how goes it Lord Jim?"

"Jake Carr, here we are again for another year. You look well, like you belong at the country club. How come you're aging better than I am? It must be genetics."

"Maybe so but it's probably my addiction to hiking, golf, and exercise...and of course, staying away from Entenmann's crumb cake."

"You know, you're making the rest of us older bulls look even older. Where did your adventures take you this summer? You were going to Montana, is that right?"

"You bet! I got lots of stories to share, animal stuff that would interest you...about a mangy moose, my first lonesome wolf, a herd of roaming Elk, and a pair of shaggy mountain goats up on the ridges in Glacier Park. Some of my pictures tell the story. I had a terrific time out west. What about you?"

"Unlike a man with your wandering spirit, I'm still paying for my divorce. Imagine, three years ago it ended. The attorney fees have sucked me dry. The head custodian, Frankie, gave me a job here doing maintenance. I helped out for twelve bucks an hour. It wasn't too bad painting classrooms and waxing floors. Jeez, you oughta see the crap these kids leave in their lockers, toxic stuff, like moldy lunches. The kids left piles of trash, hundreds of missing textbooks, and foul-smelling gym clothes. I think we should have burned it all. So, how's your family? Did your son go away to school?"

"Yup, I took him up to Vermont Tech last week. I can only wait and see what happens. Annie's fine, other than her mom is still pissed off about walking into a surprise party before the guests arrived. You know, when parents are away the kids will play....whatever. I spent a couple of days up in Burlington with my wife and visited Grand Island State Park.

It's a fair sized island in Lake Champlain. Ever been up that way? It's real pretty country, sparsely populated, except for the college kids who camp up there. For a lover of nature, when the hell are you going to the far blue mountains?"

"Damn you Jake, you never stop reminding me of what I'm missing. Well, at least I have the calendar pictures of the parks you visited. Jake, you're the only man I know around here who can literally mesmerize the kids telling them about the places you've camped. That office of yours is a shrine to Mother Nature. You're right! I still haven't crossed the Mississippi River. I know it's shameful. Look, it's getting late. I've got to sit with my fellow colleagues. You have a good year! You're a good man! You know, Jake, I don't how you're not burned out yet, considering the problems you deal with."

"Jim, always remember this. You can't be a victim of burnout if you were never on fire."

"As usual, you never fail to share your unusual insight into the human condition."

For the ninety staff members at Middletown High, it was time to begin another tour of duty; a time to burst out of the starting gate and win over the minds and hearts of adolescents. The "rollover" of classes was complete, and the new freshman class of '03 had already been through orientation. It was indeed twenty-four hours to post time when all the textbooks and lesson plans reverted back to page one.

After an hour of eating and renewing acquaintances, an announcement was made to report to the main auditorium. Slowly, the masses found their way to the place where invariably, a select group of veterans who had heard it all before sat in the rear. To the casual observer, it seemed like only the rookies and the supervisors occupied seats directly in front of the podium.

A hundred or so staff members listened attentively, or acted like they did, to the opening remarks by the superintendent, Dr. Romanov. His secular convocation was a necessity, one of those speeches that was meant to provide overviews and objectives, but wouldn't be remembered next week. After him came the principal, Dr. Augustine Moore, who gave a dramatic introduction of the new faculty.

"Would David DeSantis please stand. David is a dean's list student who comes to us from of Marist College. He's volunteered to be our newspaper advisor and will be teaching American History. Let's welcome him to our family at Middletown High."

Mild applause followed and the pale-faced rookie stood alone for three seconds of recognition until Dr. Moore gave him the nod to sit down, then another rookie was announced and followed the same script.

After that ritual was completed, the featured guest, usually a college professor from SUNY Binghamton or other such teacher prep institution gave a rousing Pentecostal sermon on rededication to the mission of teaching and the critical importance of demonstrating positive attitude. The crowd was exhorted to "stretch" their capacities and "turn on" young minds with curiosity and a love of learning.

By 10:30 the proceedings were over and everyone got down to the business of preparing for the opening of school when thirteen-hundred students would report to their designated homerooms. Usually it went well, except for the kids whose schedules were incomplete or inaccurate. They'd be restless and worried, standing in line in the guidance office waiting for a consultation to resolve their problem.

After the faculty meeting, the year officially began for Jake and his fellow counselors. For the next two hours they tried to fix problems in rapid fashion, handling one scheduling conflict after another. It reminded him of a crowded emergency room following a chain reaction highway crash. Everyone had to wait their turn, but eventually they got help.

An enormous pile of requests for schedule changes sat in the middle of Jake's desk, and his voice mail had twenty-seven recorded messages. The mail was overflowing in his box, and to confuse the situation even more he was already scheduled to meet with two new students who were entering Middletown High. The new school year started as always, with a measurable amount of chaos.

The counseling team was a collection of individuals that had little in common, but were united in the common goal of helping students successfully maneuver through the perils of adolescence. Surprisingly, none of the members socialized with each other on the outside, and yet, while working together, they were a team. Each person did his or her job differently but effectively, in their own style, and the staff and the students knew it. They were contemporary crusaders who fought for their students when the cause was just or the consequences of being defeated were unacceptable.

Overseeing the counseling crew was Bob Washburn. A former all-star athlete in high school and college, he was formidable in his physical presence, six foot two and over 220 pounds. He spoke and acted like a supervisor, and never lectured or bossed anyone around. Bob wore a sport jacket and tie every day to fit the role. He was mild mannered, perhaps to a fault, level-headed during a crisis, conscientious about timetables, and a master of diplomacy. Washburn was well-suited for the job, a thoughtful and careful individual who never bothered anyone if they did their job and acted like a professional.

William Robertson was the "Senior Fellow" with forty years of experience and a wealth of knowledge about college related information. Already eligible for social security, Bill truly loved his job and announced he'd stay as long his wife permitted. He had more field training with parental disputes than the five principals he'd served under since he began while Eisenhower was still president. Bill lived in the community, was active in church, and knew the town culture better than anyone in the office. His connections were limitless and his former students were now the parents of some of his kids.

Derek Andrews was next in line with seniority in the school system even though he had half a caseload of students. Before his counseling career he'd been in the social studies department of Middletown for twenty-five years teaching American History. He was small in statue, but more than made up for it being an erudite intellectual through and through, with a burning commitment to fairness and justice. Jake referred to Derek as the "mayor" because like Mayor Koch, he was the voice of reason.

Emily Fannen was an outsider who came to Middletown a year after Jake. She was a happily married middle-aged professional and a "lady" in every aspect. However, when it came to the well-being of her students, she was as fierce as a lioness protecting her cubs. She was educated in Catholic private schools from kindergarten through her Masters Degree. Emily was polished and unselfish, with a set of Christian values that permeated through her counseling. With Emily, there was only a limited amount of gray area. She was a highly emotional woman who took everything to heart and made no excuses for being that way. She mothered the kids and they all knew it. Of all the members of the team, she literally lived the role of counselor.

Rosalyn Hopkins was the newest member of the team. She was the "rookie" and this was her second year. Emily and Rosalyn were close in age and Emily had helped her through a tough transition period. She had worked in the private sector and also taught as an adjunct instructor at Orange Community College. Best of all, she was computer literate way beyond everyone else in the office. She was a straight talker, and had little patience for slackers and bull-shit artists whether they were fifteen or forty-five. Jake liked Rosalyn because she had spunk, a rare commodity in the field of counseling.

Jake believed there was a tremendous difference between counselors and teachers. He thought of himself as a resource person, but held the view that the teachers were the superstars because they delivered the curriculum. Although some members of the faculty believed counselors had it easy and said so, that never bothered him. He knew it was pure bullshit and he didn't try to win them over, which annoyed Washburn to no end. Unlike the rest of the team who seemed to care what the teachers thought about their profession, Jake figured if they didn't respect the job he did, then "screw 'em."

ॐ�

Jake was back at work after lunch trying to get a grip on things when Loretta buzzed him.

"You have a call on line three."

"Middletown guidance, Jake Carr speaking, may I help you?"

"It's me, Ellen."

"Where have you been? Why didn't you write me? Shit, you picked a terrible time to call. Honestly, I'm as busy as hell. What's up? It seems like it was another lifetime when we were together."

"Slow down. I got back with the boys last Friday. Are you ready to be back?"

"Not really. But it's already started. I got a shitload of work to catch up on and not enough time to do it. So, how're you doing? How did the rest of the summer go for you? I took my son to college. It's pretty strange without him around. I've been playing golf with Kevin and working around the house the past few weeks. I guess I'm kinda adjusting to his absence. I think even the dog misses the boy. I bet you look great. So darlin', what's happening in your world?"

Ellen didn't know how to answer him in view of the turn of events. She knew this wasn't the time to talk, and had hoped he'd ask her to meet. Instead of waiting, she put the question directly to him. "When do you think you'll be able to see me? I've got time this afternoon. I need to see you."

"I don't have a toothbrush. I'm not dressed for a date. I'm too nervous. You... need to see me?"

"Jake, you're so silly. Only you would answer me like that. Yeah, I do. It's important."

"All right, let me think for a second. This request of yours came out of the blue; all I want is to get through the next two hours. So you need me, huh? Tell you what. I'll meet you around four at Montgomery Manor. Is that ok? Hey, how will I recognize you? I know what you should do. Wear a disguise, a moustache and a black derby."

"You're crazy, but I love that about you. I'll see you later."

ॐ�

Jake had thought about Ellen every day since they last saw each other. At times it was both aggravating and satisfying, depending on where he was. He worried about it because he was starting to like her. And based on her last letter, he knew Ellen was falling fast. The problem was that things were stable at home and Sandy was ready to forgive Annie's party mistake. He knew the next chapter with Ellen was about to begin. However, his inner voice kept telling him what he didn't want to hear. *You asshole, why put yourself in such a risky situation? Ellen is married! You hear that? Are you supposed to believe that she's stuck in a sinking ship like you are? Ok, so you had some good times. But you still haven't crossed the point of no return. You keep thinking about how happy she makes you feel, but a shitload of trouble awaits you if you keep this up. The bottom line is what Kevin told you. Is Ellen Eastman worth it? Jake, your problem is simple. You can't contain your interest in this woman. If only you could keep it all from getting out of control, but that's impossible. You're a fool! You've forgotten where the limits are. That goddamn letter! She tells you she loves you. How can that possibly be true? Why isn't she afraid? Why is she willing to let it happen and why are you so scared? You're wise enough to know that love isn't practical and love isn't predictable. If you don't put up some boundaries this afternoon then you're heading for a world of confusion and a world of worry. For now, go and meet her. Listen to what she has to say and see what happens.*

CHAPTER 35

Whatever ambivalence happened to swirl around Jake's head from listening to his inner voice mysteriously evaporated when he met Ellen. Without a doubt, his feelings of desire took over his rational thought processes. He was twenty minutes late when he arrived at Montgomery Manor, but Ellen didn't look disappointed as much as she was amused. On seeing him, she grinned and shook her head while making a teasing hand gesture at her wrist watch.

She was dressed in a short denim skirt, white sneakers, and a yellow cotton top. Right off, Jake noticed the sunshine in her face and he swallowed hard to maintain his composure. He walked over, swaying side to side until he was a couple of feet away.

"This isn't fair. Look at you! You're a few pounds lighter and maybe a half shade darker since I last saw you. At least do a three-sixty for me. Come on."

Ellen accommodated Jake and turned full circle with a huge grin.

"Damn, you're irresistible, and I look like I work at *Sears* selling appliances. You're a fox! Wow!"

He could tell Ellen was eating it up so he laid it on even thicker. "Ellen, you look fabulous or as Billy Crystal would say, you look simply M A R V E L O U S!"

She put her arms around him and held on tightly before planting a kiss right on target. Then she confessed, "My God, I've missed you. I've missed you more than you'll ever know. It's been a long time since we sat at the Pub and held hands."

"You're still holding on to me so I guess I believe you," replied Jake. Since he was in a teasing mode he kept it up. "What! That's the last thing you remember about that night? I thought it'd be the gifts I gave you when I said goodbye. I suppose I can forgive you. Guess you forgot. You know, I've had a rough afternoon, listening to all kinds of gripes and whines from students and their parents. It makes me yearn for my days on the road. Shit, I've still got a hundred eighty-three work days left before the next trip."

"Hey, how about another hug? I can't get by with only one. Come on. Then let's go someplace where you can leave the job behind and rest your weary head on my lap. You can tell me you missed me."

"Ellen, any place we go better be private. Ok? And, it suits me fine to put my head on your lap."

"That's what I hoped you'd say. You're right about the need for privacy. A lot has happened in my life since I last saw you. That's why I called, but let's save it for later. Anyway, you don't look dressed for the trail. Do you have a quiet place in mind, not too far away, but safe? I have to get back by six."

"Me too, I think we should drive up to High Point. Remember the place? I'm concerned about inadvertently bumping into someone we know. That would be disastrous. I'm worried and I can't help it."

"I understand. It's not worth the risk. That was a great afternoon. You played golf before we met that day and it was hot out. You made out with me on that old lime-colored blanket like we were college kids. I saw that mighty chest of yours. Do ya still have that blanket?"

"I carry it in the back of the van for the purpose of taking advantage of situations like the one you're proposing. Are you saying you're in a smooch mood or what?

They both started laughing and Jake poked Ellen in her sides to make her laugh even more. Then he kissed her. With reckless disregard for anyone who may have been watching, he placed his hands over her butt and let her feel his excitement at seeing her again. Without speaking a word, each of them realized they were right back where they were in mid-August. When he pulled back after the kiss, he noticed her nipples were visible under her yellow top but thought better than to tease her about their appearance. Instead, he beckoned Ellen toward the van, opened the door, and gave her a squeeze on her ass, which produced a squirm and a giggle.

She turned around and stared at him holding up her fist and said, "My goodness, you're a rascal! You really are. Know what? You're the first fella who ever did that to me. I suppose you think I'm easy. With you, I probably am."

"I can't help myself. It's your outfit. I'm really shy around beautiful women."

"Sure you are. You know exactly what you're doing. Come on, confess."

"I won't confess anything under duress. Ever heard of Bruce Springsteen? There's a song called *Hungry Heart*. Anyway, he sings the words *'everybody's got a hungry heart.'* For you, Ellen, my heart's hungry. Am I corny or what? How about some music? Would you like to hear anything in particular?"

"Jake, you pick. I'm not any good at that."

"Listen my little angel, if you're gonna travel with me you gotta love music. How about some Don Henley? I've got *The Age of Innocence* cassette."

"Who's he?"

"He's the lead singer of the Eagles. I'm sure you've heard of *Hotel California, Peaceful Easy Feeling,* and *The Best of My Love.* Sit back and listen."

Jake put *The Age of the Innocence* cassette in the slot and they took off for High Point State Park a half-hour away. Ellen got a kick out of watching Jake making time with the music. She loved the unique way in which he expressed himself, whether in words, or physical expressions.

They parked in the monument lot like they did back in August, Jake still had no clue as to what was on Ellen's mind. Sensing the time was right, he gave her an opening to begin.

"Do you want to sit on the blanket and talk or would you rather walk? I'm cool either way. Listen, whatever it is that you need to get out, just do it."

"Let's walk for a while. As much as I want to hold you and feel you next to me, I have something I need to share. Something you're not expecting. I hope you're still interested in me after today. My life is getting very complicated. Come on."

They started walking on the path that went around the monument. Ellen didn't open up, so Jake amused her a while longer by talking humorously about the opening of school. He mimicked the parent's absurd demands for teacher changes and their ridiculous requests for lunch period changes. The five-minute monologue gave Ellen a look at the comical side of Jake's counseling job. After a momentary pause in his act, Ellen pulled the curtain down. Without breaking stride, she broke the news.

"I told my husband I wanted a divorce. That happened last Saturday and I still feel the same way today. I'm sure it took him by surprise and...and it just came out of me. That's why I needed to see you."

Jake couldn't temper his reaction to Ellen's disclosure. He wasn't ready for it. "Shit! You really know how to lighten up a conversation. What did you say to him? It's not your run-of-the-mill request from a disgruntled wife. Did he expect it? Do you think he took you seriously? Are you sure it's what you want? Forget that...I'm sorry. Have you told the boys yet? How are they coping with it? Shit, I'm speeding again. Ellen, you dropped this on me out of nowhere. I mean, you only told me a little about your past, like why you got married so young, but you didn't say much about him. I mean, I figured you weren't happy. Did he push you too far? You had enough, huh? Please, please tell me I'm not responsible for this? Believe me darlin', **I wouldn't like that! Not a bit.**"

Ellen had rehearsed the impending conversation with Jake for the past three days and was prepared to give him a clear and honest explanation for her decision.

"Getting out of the marriage was in my plans long before I met you. One thing's for sure, he didn't expect to hear it, certainly not the way it came out. He's the know-it-all type. When he hit me with a barrage of his inane questions, for whatever reason, he pushed me over the edge. So I told him that I'm finished. Then I had to tell him twice more. He actually suggested we see a marriage counselor. Jake, I've heard all his excuses before. He still doesn't get it. In fact, he thought things were going great in our marriage. He actually had the nerve to suggest the past year was the best. Can you imagine that? He's so self-centered it's ludicrous. That's how distant from me he really is. Obviously, things were going great for him because he wasn't around me or the boys. He was living the life of a bachelor down in Atlanta."

Her last two sentences hit Jake like a stiff left jab to the chin and he told her, "I can appreciate that, out of sight, out of mind. When I was away, honestly, I hardly thought about stuff back home. I'm sorry I interrupted. Go ahead; tell me more."

"I was pretty emphatic about my decision. I don't think he was ready for me telling him I didn't love him anymore. He became sarcastic and antagonistic, but that's not your concern. The boys seem all right, but maybe it hasn't sunk in yet. I mean, they've lived a year with only seeing him occasionally. Danny acts like he couldn't care less. Joey's very different. I'm not sure what's going on in his head. I assured them that we'll be fine, but I couldn't give them any specifics since I'm not sure exactly how the pieces will fit. Honestly, I don't know what Guy will do. I keep telling myself that I'll survive. Well, that's what I wanted to share with you, but it's not the only reason I'm here. I hope you know that."

Jake thought, *Holy shit, this is just what I was afraid of. I can't believe this is happening.*

"Mrs. Eastman, I've got to laugh. I came out here thinking one thing and now…now I don't know exactly what you want from me. I like you. Shit, I like you enough to take some risks. However, in view of this change of circumstances…well you'd better give me some time to let this sink in. Does that sound fair?"

Ellen didn't kid herself into thinking Jake would get the whole picture in five minutes. His response was serious and she knew that he had changed back into the counselor. She didn't like it.

"Stop it Jake! Stop it right now. If you read my letter, you know how I feel about you. I haven't asked you to do anything for me, have I? I thought I could share this with you and that you cared about me. Was I wrong? Are you feeling like I deceived you or something like that?"

With that stinging indictment, he stopped walking and turned to face her. Instead of saying anything, he tenderly kissed her cheeks, her forehead, and finally her lips. This kiss was sincere and spontaneous, jolting Ellen's senses. She knew he had answered her question in his own way and his actions made her feel secure once again.

Then he looked at her and said, "Ellen, I'm not afraid, but enough of this. I heard every word you said. It's a lot for me to consider, in fact, more than enough. Let me go get the blanket. Then you can talk some more and I'll listen. Wait for me under that old Chestnut. Then you can tell me what's on your mind. I'll be right back."

A few minutes later he spread the blanket on the soft grass. Both of them sat cross-legged facing each other as Ellen began telling her story.

"I've been planning to leave my husband for over a year. It was one of the reasons I moved back to Middletown. No use pretending it was any different. When I told you why I got married so young, I left out part of the story."

"Ellen, believe me, you told me more than you think. Remember, you said you eloped and blamed yourself. I told you that fault didn't matter. Sorry, please tell me whatever else you need to."

"I was the perfect child. I wanted to be that way. All through elementary and high school I did all the right things. There was no backtalk in me. I was always obedient. My parents were devout Catholics. All my life I went to Catholic schools until I moved to Middletown and began tenth grade at the public school. My mother used to say I was 'too good for my own good.' Anyway I've always been shy and very modest about my body. I liked being in my own world. Compared to other high school kids, I lead a very sheltered life. You may not believe it, but I never gave my parents any reason to worry. When I left for college I was innocent and unsophisticated. I thought I was going to be successful as a business major.

"When my father left us I didn't understand why he did. I was mad and I took sides with my mother. When I finally got a chance to question him about his affair, he got angry, and told me it was none of my business. That was the end of my relationship with him. Even now, he won't have anything to do with me. I haven't seen or spoken to him in many years. Anyway, my mother used to call me four or five times a week at school. She was so needy. Truthfully, I was just as needy. What I so desperately need you to understand is that before I met Guy I never learned how to be independent. I wasn't prepared for the breakdown of my family and to take responsibility for myself. All I remember back then was that I was scared to be on my own. Now it's happening all over again and I'm scared."

"Can you hold your next thought for a minute? I'm gonna get a couple of cokes that I brought from school. They should still be cold. Give me a minute and then please continue with your story. You're filling in the missing pieces."

A minute later Jake returned with the cans. Sitting opposite Ellen, he opened them up and proposed a toast. "Well Ellen, let's toast the virtue of innocence. Sometimes I think it's more of a curse than a blessing. You married a young man who promised you a safe haven in a storm. He didn't come through, and now you've got to make it on your own. So I think your course of action was long over due."

"Jake, the truth is that I've never been able to recover from that awful mistake. I was so stupid!"

It was painful to hear her bring up the past again, always with regret. Then the counselor came out. "You know Ellen, at the first sign of trouble we either fight or take flight. It takes enormous courage to go it alone when you think you have no other choice. Listen, you compromised your future out of fear and you made the wrong choice. Shit, you can't begin to calculate how many baby-boomers did the same thing. Our generation's hung up on pursuing the perfect version of the American Dream. I'm no different. It's a weird trip. I've since learned from my own circumstance that it's not for everyone. But getting back to your past, how in the hell can a twenty-year old possibly know the right course of action in a situation like yours? All of us tend to take the path of least resistance, meaning the path that presents us with the least amount of hardship. That's what you did. Listen, running away because you're afraid of what lies ahead is not only dangerous, but it leads to catastrophic consequences. Forgive yourself and let it go."

Ellen thought back to that summer of 1979 and knew Jake was right. She did run away and it had bothered her everyday since she married Guy.

"I told you when I went to Atlanta to live with Guy it was supposed to be about getting a job and gaining residency so I could attend Georgia State. But somehow while I was there he convinced me it would be the proper thing to marry him. Do you hear me? I said the proper thing! Damn the proper thing! The next part is hard to admit."

"I know...I know, you've already told me. It's gonna be ok. You're gonna make it. Let-it-go!"

But she couldn't. Maybe because she was now changing course she wanted Jake to understand why. "When Guy said he'd take care of me, I believed him. I was so stupid. I've never been able to forgive myself. We were a bad fit from the start. We had nothing in common. I think he stopped loving me within a month, but he wouldn't admit that he make a mistake, not to me or his parents. I knew it was all wrong. I'm telling you that I knew it was wrong, and I didn't change a thing. God, that really hurts. For so many years I accepted my fate as a punishment for being stupid. I need you to understand. Looking back, I can't ever remember him treating me like he loved me. He said it over and over, but it was a lie. He said it to keep me where I was. I think he has always blamed me for us getting married, and I'm certain that he's resented being stuck with me. Maybe he's right. But like I said, he'd never admit he made a mistake. All these years I hated knowing I was to blame."

Jake remembered that she had told him the tragic story of her secret marriage back in August. Even so, in view of her decision to finally break free from Guy, he figured she needed to complete the story. He sympathized with her. His own memory was polluted with mistakes he made in his youth.

"Ellen, young people make choices on blind faith, especially when they're naive. A twenty-year old is a dreamer. I was born a hardcore realist. You're not like me because you inherently believe in the goodness of people. I'm tarnished. We've all got some unresolved family issues. You and I both do, and most likely, so does Guy. You can choose to let them burn a hole in your heart with toxic memories of childhood and adolescence, or you douse them with reason and let 'em be. You admitted you didn't know much about Guy. The truth is...he didn't know much about you. You made a mistake, and so did Guy. It wasn't because of stupidity. It was because of innocence. I'm not excusing your foolishness, but I am sympathetic to the problem you created for each other. Now that I've listened to your explanation, I'm not surprised at all about the divorce. It probably should've happened before your kids were born. I mean, you both knew you were incompatible. But like all things regarding pride, people can be stubborn for a long time. Wait a second, I'm still missing something. I understand your lack of sophistication and innocence, but didn't you ever have a serious relationship before you met Guy?"

"Jake, can we start walking?" She wanted to answer him away from the blanket where she felt enough was discussed about her past.

"There was another person in my life before Guy. He was a classmate of mine named Robbie Carlson. He was my first real boyfriend. Of all places, we met in chemistry class as lab partners. Pretty silly, huh? We stared dating and went out from junior year till the fall of my sophomore year of college. Then he started losing it...smoked pot and partied night after night. Before that we did the usual things. We loved skiing and we hung in a large group of kids. He always respected me, and my mother liked him. Robbie knew I was a good girl and he never tried to take advantage of me. If you ever saw our prom picture you wouldn't need an explanation. I wore a white satin gown. I was the epitome of innocence."

On hearing that last description of Ellen, Jake clapped his hands and said, "Congratulations! I sure didn't want to believe you fell for the first young man you ever kissed."

Ellen didn't appreciate his sarcastic remark and let him know it. "Jake, stop that! You're being to sound like someone else I know, and I don't like that at all."

Hearing her reaction, he instantly knew he must have said the wrong thing, "I'm sorry. Ellen, I didn't mean to sound... that was a dumb thing to say. I apologize!"

"No, it wasn't Jake. That's the point. I never did anything bad at a time when everyone else was getting drunk, stoned, or were having sexual experiences. I wasn't and neither were my two closest girlfriends. It's hard for me to explain. You probably started early. I mean...doing it. Am I right?"

"Good thing you didn't know me then. For sure, you wouldn't have let me anywhere near you."

Ellen was correct in her assumptions regarding his sexual experience. He was going to let the subject drop, but the counselor in him wanted to know more. So he raised a sensitive issue.

"Ellen, are you telling me you were a virgin when you started dating Guy. Is that why he wanted to marry you? Holy shit, now I get it. He thought you were untouched and he was going to show you the way. Your story is absolutely fascinating. I knew a couple of fraternity brothers who wanted the same thing, the perfect girl who would be all theirs and nobody else's until death do us part. What bullshit."

"Only you would understand it that way. I never thought of it like that. I guess he thought I was a virgin. My biggest secret was that I slept with Robbie a few times during the two years we went out. Even then, I don't think I knew what I was doing, much less what I was experiencing. I was so modest. What can I say? I know, you think I'm nuts, but I was afraid of getting pregnant. It was a curse left over from Catholic school guilt. I don't think the idea of pleasure ever entered my head, or my body for that matter. Besides I was always too tense to actually enjoy it or know what I was doing. It's all lost...lost in my memory. I did like making-out and...a little touching. All right, Mr. Carr, I confess that Robbie Carlson was the first. Does that sound dumb? Imagine all those memories had faded away."

"Ellen, do me a favor. Give me a few minutes to think about what I've just learned about you. Maybe I can give you some insight. You mind if we walk back to the blanket in silence?"

They returned to the tree and finished their drinks. Then Jake began. "Here's my take on your story. At this time, I still know very little about Guy. But I believe you both made a tremendous mistake back in the summer of '79. Hear what I said? You both screwed up! Your parents or his absolutely should've had the marriage annulled. You told me you don't love each other.

"Listen. Some young men dream of possessing the perfect girl, one that's virtuous and modest. When and if they find that so-called fairy princess, they won't let anything get in their way of having her. Anyway, I'm positive he felt like you were some unspoiled treasure that he had to possess. For all you know, maybe Guy, for whatever reason, wanted you to be his and only his in body, mind, and soul. So you became dependent on him, and that's exactly what he wanted.

"Some people marry their high school sweethearts and live happily ever after. However, I think in your case your marriage began under false pretenses. Not so much a lie as a whole lot of misconceptions. Nothing has changed since then, except you feel like you've lost twenty years of your life. For all you know, maybe he feels the same way. Did you ever consider that? Now, you're gonna need all the strength and courage you can muster to start over. And I'm not tossing those words around because they sound appropriate. Based on what you've told me, it will be a hard road ahead for you. How he will feel about losing you, that's anybody's guess. I'll tell you this much. Getting divorced will cost a bucket full of money. And always remember this, alimony and child support can turn a mild-mannered man into a fire-breathing dragon. That's the truth!"

Ellen believed that Jake understood Guy more than she did with regard to their marriage. Everything he explained made sense to her. But now she realized that figuring out the past had nothing to do with the present. She needed Jake's support to make it on her own, at least in the beginning.

"Jake, will you help me? I love you...even if I can't have you. If you can help me get my new life started, it would mean everything to me. I know you're married and it's risky, but I don't care!"

"Ellen, my sweet Ellen, I think I've proven that I'm not trying to possess you or take advantage of you. Christ, I haven't even tried to make love to you. Have I? So far I've taken some risks, but they're risks I could handle. Listen to me very closely. You can stay being Ellen Eastman, or you can learn to be an individual. I think you know what you want. You certainly made that clear to Guy. You have my promise that I'll help you turn your life around. I do care about you very much.

But I'll admit, at this moment in time caring about you is scary. That being said, there's one thing you've got to accept and respect. Ellen, I have another life. So please don't ever lose sight of that."

CHAPTER 36

Early autumn in Orange County is picturesque and a delight to observe. Spectacular foliage decorates the countryside in various shades of bright red and yellow gold wherever the hardwoods grow. Outside the city, away from the malls and pavement, the landscape is fluid with ever-changing tides of windswept leaves blowing wherever they choose. Only the spruce, fir, and pine trees remain unchanged, with their dark green needles providing the only color during the bleak months of winter.

On Saturday afternoons, Jake took Ellen to the safe confines of the state forests when the weather permitted. The routine began after the start of school, and it gave them time to learn about each other in an environment they both loved. Jake had told Ellen, "You'll learn that the forest is Mother Nature's way of providing a retreat from the crazy world. There are no trail signs to guide your thoughts or anyone to block your way when you walk along the path. I believe it was intended by the Creator to be a place for reflection long before any 'self help' books and TV evangelists told us how find peace."

Each time they hiked together, Ellen shared another piece of her life with Jake. Her story was a grim reminder of the price that some women will pay for the sake of their children and to perpetuate flawed relationships that really weren't meant to be. Always the realist, Jake thought it best to establish a few ground rules if they were going to continue their relationship in secret. Above all, neither of them was to discuss their connection with anyone. Since Jake had already told Kevin O'Connor about Ellen, he was the only exception. Another covenant made at his insistence, was not to discuss their children. Jake wanted the kids strictly out of bounds and in the domain of their other world. He felt they had no relevance in the relationship.

Jake phoned Ellen whenever the opportunity presented itself, but generally it was in the morning and from his office. He'd signal the call by letting it ring twice. Then he'd hang up, count to five, and call again. That way Ellen knew it was him. He also made it plain that he wouldn't give her any advice regarding the divorce settlement until the final document was ready for review. He claimed it was the attorney's responsibility because they were paid to secure the best possible deal.

During their first few dates, Ellen learned bits and pieces about Jake's past and present, but especially how his philosophy of life deeply influenced him. Ellen never probed beyond what Jake was willing to share and instinctively knew he closely guarded whatever ambivalence he had concerning his wife and family. Yet, over time, it became apparent to her that his dissatisfaction with Sandy was long-standing. She had no doubt that Jake cherished his role as a father and loved his children dearly. Ellen also came to appreciate that when Jake focused on problem solving, nothing could distract him.

The first Saturday in October proved to be a dramatic turning point in their developing relationship. Jake had called Ellen a few days earlier to explain that his wife would be taking Annie on a college visitation to Penn State at College Park, Pennsylvania. Mother and daughter would be gone for most of the day; thus he and Ellen could spend the day walking the dunes and the shoreline at Sandy Hook. For her part, all Ellen had to do was get someone to supervise the boys. She couldn't pass up the date and reluctantly called the only acquaintance she had made since returning to Middletown. Her name was Lucy Capone, her son Larry was a friend of Joey's. Ellen told Lucy she would be attending a job fair in the City and that she would return the favor when Lucy needed time off. Lucy agreed to the deal, and much to Ellen's absolute delight, the shore date was set.

They met in the parking lot of Montgomery Manor at nine and lucked out with an Indian summer day. It was a gorgeous morning with a bright lemon-colored sun in a cloudless blue sky. The temperature was in the mid 70's. They arrived at Gateway National Seashore before noon and found an isolated area near the hard-breaking surf of a high tide. There were no more than a dozen fishermen spread along the expansive beach and only a few other couples soaking in the rays. It was relatively quiet, with only the sounds of the sea and the breeze blowing in from Raritan Bay.

Ellen looked radiant and happy. She wore a sleeveless black cotton top and a pair of gray cotton running shorts. It was obvious that she'd lost weight since they first met, probably ten pounds or more. Naturally, he wore faded khaki shorts and a black tee shirt.

After they found a secluded spot on the beach, he set up the folding chairs on each side of a small ice chest, then he took off his shirt and sneakers. Ellen followed suit, except she wore a sleek looking black bikini top to show off her reconstructed flat stomach. Jake took Ellen's hand and they began walking ankle deep in and out of the cold surf of the shoreline. He'd been there many times and pointed out the landmarks such as the Fort Hancock Lighthouse and the tide pools.

Since last week there was something on his mind, but he steered clear of it until he thought the timing was right. Then it came out of him, spontaneously and sincere. "What a beautiful day! I'm not nearly as much of a beach person as I am into the mountains, but I'm always in awe of it whenever I visit. Ellen, I'm here, and yet, I feel like I'm a thousand miles away from my other world. These past five weeks have given me time to know you better. It seems to me that whenever we're together, our secret life actually makes sense to me. I know it sounds crazy because how can I make that claim, after what, thirty hours? Doesn't sound like much time, does it? In the beginning, all I was doing was looking over my shoulder, waiting for shit to happen, for this affair to blow up in my face. But today I have something to confess. I've wasted precious time worrying and that's not like me. I'm sorry. I swear to you, from now on I'm not letting it take over again."

Ellen found it incredible that Jake would admit to being afraid of anything. However, his disclosure made her understand that she didn't know him as well as she thought.

"How can you feel like that? We've been so careful! I'm not afraid and I can hardly wait for the time I spend with you. Jake, every morning I wait for your call. It means the world to me because it means I'm in your thought and that you care. Nothing we do is ever wasted. You touch my soul whenever we're together; you stay with me through the day and night until I hear your voice again the next day. I think we've been very cautious and I'm not worried, neither should you."

Jake wanted to believe every word but thought she missed the point he was making. He thought maybe his message came out scrambled.

"Let's sit here for a while and I'll try to explain."

They sat facing the bay, and Ellen knew Jake was struggling to find the right words. The lemon colored sun was high in the sky and glistening off the ocean surface.

"You don't understand! I'm having an affair with you. It's that simple. I've been worrying, worrying way too much about someone catching us instead of getting closer to you. That's what I mean. Lately I've been fighting it so much I'm weary. Ellen, you're in my thoughts all the time, in spite of a painstaking effort on my part to hold you at bay. I'm so tired of it. Now I want to run with it."

He kissed her twice, tenderly and lovingly. Then he said, "Ellen, I'm not running away from you any more. Nothing is going to interfere with this awakening. For once my heart is overruling my head. That's a first. I know this is very dangerous, maybe more for me than for you. But I think this is my day of liberation. I think it's my beginning and the first day I'll let myself be transported to another time and place. I don't want to be your friend today. That's always been my way of keeping my feelings in check. Today, I want to feel how close we are."

Ellen waited a moment. She repeated some of his words in her head before giving him a reply. Pressing against his bare chest she whispered. "I knew this would be a special day and I didn't want to miss it for anything in the world. Jake, I'm all yours. It's our time and I'm not afraid because I believe with all my heart that this is what you say it is, and you say its karma, it's our destiny. It's the consequence of letting each other enter our souls. Let's walk on the beach and watch the waves."

The barefoot beachcombers strolled for an hour. They walked in silence, taking in the visual display of the breakers pounding against the jetty and listened to the squawks of the white seagulls that trailed overhead wherever they walked.

When they returned to the chairs, Jake opened two cans of Pepsi and declared, "Should I close my eyes or what? What did you make for lunch?"

"That's not necessary. I hope you like olive loaf on Russian Rye. I also brought some potato salad and sour pickles. How's that sound?"

"I was hoping for a roast beef sub. However, my second choice was olive loaf with honey mustard."

His reply brought a frown to Ellen's face, and then she burst out laughing. He poked her in the ribs and she did the same to him. They were like two kids teasing each other.

"Jake, I've come to believe it must be destiny that brought us together."

"Destiny? Wasn't it the workshop? Just kiddin'. I've also thought about that a lot. So if it is inevitable, then this is the beginning. Isn't it?"

Ellen nodded and keeping the mood light she added, "It's also because I've made a list of things we both like and you'd be amazed how long it's getting."

"You did...I never thought of that. What's at the top of your list?"

"That's easy, kissing. Come on, you can't dispute that fact. Since coming here I think you stopped five times to give me one of your kisses."

"Angel, when you wear a sexy black top and look as sweet as you do this morning, shit, it's a wonder how I've restrained myself from making love to you right on this beach. I've thought about it."

"Why? Why have you been that way? Why haven't you taken advantage of me? I've had so many passionate thoughts about you. To me, you're the sexist man alive!"

Ellen had him in the uncomfortable position of explaining why he didn't make the move. "You mean that? How am I supposed to eat now? Seriously, the reason I've kept my desire in check is because I know there's no turning back once we cross that line. I don't know it's not something I take lightly. No way! Believe me, I've thought about it plenty of times, too many. I think it's the legal definition of going over the edge. I've never cheated on Sandy. Was it the same for you? Did you ever cheat on Guy?"

"Never! It was the other way around, but I'm sure you've had many more opportunities than me to misbehave like that."

"You're pretty astute. I suppose I've been waiting for a signal from you about moving in that direction, and now you've given it. Maybe it will happen when we least expect it and then we'll be stuck with the consequences. It's not making love, but the consequences of making the choice. Believe me; the passion is there, pounding away at me from all angles. Shit, I'm worried about imploding from all my desire for you. Well, there you have it. Remember, always say what you mean and mean what you say when you talk to me. Imagine what a world it would be if people followed that rule. Can we eat now?"

"Not yet. First let me get this settled right now. Jake, look at me. I'm speaking from my heart. I'm ready to make love to you. I've been ready since that day at Summit Pond before you left on the trip. I've thought about it a thousand times. My only fear is that I'll disappoint you."

Jake put the sandwich back in the cooler and sprang up from his beach chair as if a sea monster snuck up from behind, snarled a hungry growl, and was ready to take a bite out of him. He raced down the beach a few hundred yards. Then he sat on the warm sand to give his mind time to digest what Ellen had just revealed. He didn't understand why she was so fearful of disappointing him. From their very first kiss, he'd felt nothing but desire for her. Similarly, he understood they'd reached a point where having a sexual encounter was inevitable. Did he love her? He knew he was falling fast, and yet there were so many loose ends. Ellen's divorce was proceeding on track and she'd be free in a matter of a few months. In contrast, he was still leading a double life and he hated it. It seemed everything about loving Ellen involved conquering impossible obstacles, some real and some imagined.

It was an undisputable fact, he was having an affair. Yet in his mind, he hadn't gone the full distance, it hadn't reached official adultery. Nevertheless, he knew if Sandy found out about it, there would be serious problems. On the other hand, Jake believed sexual infidelity would be totally unacceptable to Sandy and would surely lead to a divorce. Moreover, he felt if the situations were reversed, and Sandy had the affair, the outcome would probably be the same. He'd dump her.

Ellen had no clue what was going on in Jake's mind when he returned.

"Sorry babe, I guess I experienced system overload. I'm gonna scoff down that sandwich now. After lunch, why don't we continue to explore this place and walk the trail through the dunes?"

"Jake, why did you run off like that? That's pretty strange behavior for you. Wouldn't you say so?"

"I suppose I was upended by your offer. Making love to you would be my ultimate fantasy come true. Anyway, I was too excited to keep sitting there. It wasn't like you were discussing the weather."

"I think I understand. Actually, I was surprised by my own honesty. I want you to know that admission came out because I love you. Let's finishing eating, then a restroom break would be good. I want to rinse off my face and hands and then we'll walk the beach."

☜☞

The afternoon at Sandy Hook proved that the bond between them was undeniable. They liked each other and got along exceptionally well. He was complimentary about her looks, which made her feel desirable and motivated to keep working out. Ellen had caught him staring at her several times and she was gratified all her workouts had made a difference. It was late in the afternoon when Jake suggested they have a seafood dinner at one of the local restaurants in Atlantic Highlands.

At a small table overlooking the Highlands lighthouse, they ordered their first dinner and drank a toast to celebrate the wonderful afternoon they spent at the beach. Jake felt himself weakening as he held Ellen's hand and had to fight off the urge to tell her what he was feeling. His affection had grown faster in the past eight hours than at any other time. He had fallen in love. Looking at her, he tried to get it out.

"Ellen, my angel, I have no idea what's ahead for us. You're much more of a woman than I ever thought. Since that first encounter at the workshop, I can see and feel changes happening to us. You look great in spite of all the turbulence in your life. What I'm trying to say is that I love our time together and don't want it to end. I haven't been this content in a long time. I don't want to lose you."

She held his hand and brought it to her lips. Then she told him, "Jake, thank you for telling me! Every moment we've shared has been absolutely the best. You have an ability to take me away, far away from my other life. Maybe that's what happens to you."

☜☞

During the two-hour drive back to Middletown, Jake played the *Moody Blues, Concert at Red Rock*, Ellen sat peacefully alternating a touch of his right arm and shoulder with a rub on the back of his neck. Ellen was more certain of her love than ever before. And Jake finally realized that Ellen seemed to bring out the best in him. He let down all his natural defenses whenever he was with her.

It was dark when they got back to the Montgomery Manor parking lot. Although they were tired, they didn't want the day to end. Jake opened the van door for Ellen, embraced her and said, "Thank you for the best time I've had in a long while. I'm gonna remember this. I wish we could go somewhere... somewhere with scented candles and a comfortable bed. I'm not going to apologize for wanting you. I'm trying my best to cope with this insatiable need I have to have you."

"Listen, my warrior wolf, I want you as much as I think you want me. Remember that! It's your choice. I'll wait for you for as long as you want. I mean it. Think of me tonight and know that you'll be in my thoughts. Good night, my darling."

CHAPTER 37

In the weeks following Ellen's "Declaration of Divorce," she didn't give Guy any indication of changing her mind, in spite of repeated inquiries from him. The best evidence of the finality of her decision was that following the shore date with Jake, she single-handedly moved Guy's belongings out of the bedroom and put a lock on the door. The following Friday, Guy called around two in the afternoon from the airport. He figured Ellen would be there. However, Ellen went out for the day and was shopping at the mall.

When he arrived at dinnertime the first words out of his mouth were, "Couldn't you have picked me up? It cost me thirty-five bucks for the limo. I had to share the ride with a bunch of strangers. How could you do that? For Christ's sake, it took an extra two hours to get here. Where's your consideration?"

Ellen snapped back like a trail lawyer during a cross examination. "What's your problem? I forgot and that's all there is to it. You can use the extra bedroom while you're visiting. Your things are in there."

"What do you mean... my things are in there?"

"You're not using my bedroom or my bathroom!"

"So this is how it's going to be,...huh? Goddamn it. Why didn't you tell me the other night on the phone so at least I would have known what to expect."

"What to expect! Why would you think any differently? I don't want anything to do with you."

Like a spoiled adolescent, he took his suitcase upstairs and went down the hallway to the spare room. There, he saw his underwear and socks piled high on the twin bed, along with a cardboard box that held the odds and ends from his top dresser drawer. It was quite a shock for him to find things that way. Ellen was in the kitchen waiting when she heard him yell out from upstairs.

"What's this note on the mirror that tells me to use the kid's bathroom and do my own laundry? Don't you realize I'm still paying the mortgage on this place? Shit, we're not even divorced yet!"

She walked over to the stairway and spoke just loud enough for him to hear her. "Guy, it would be helpful if you could keep that bathroom in order. You know, the way you always expected me to have it for you, no toothpaste left in the sink and the towels hung up. The boys will be home for dinner any minute. There's a casserole on the stove."

Guy was ready to implode with rage. Surrendering to her wishes was equivalent to being castrated. Ellen knew his fuse was burning down to the powder, so she left the house and went to a movie.

As she pulled out of the driveway, she realized that Guy's behavior was a grim reminder of everything she hated about him. Their marriage had always revolved around him, with Ellen constantly seeing to his needs, trying to meet his expectations, and placating him whenever he was unhappy with her or the boys. He was as self-indulgent as ever, regardless of their impeding divorce.

Fifteen minutes later, she purchased a ticket to see *The Green Mile* and for the very first time it hit her, she had left the house without giving Guy her destination or when she'd return.

∻

Ellen retained the services of a local attorney with money she borrowed from her mother. The attorney, Ms. Judith Clark, came out of the Yellow Pages, a random selection based on gender preference and a three-by-three "Divorce Specialist" ad. After the preliminary interview, Ms. Clark assured her that she'd receive adequate child support and alimony based on New York State guidelines. The assurance of financial support made turning over the thousand-dollar retainer less painful.

That legal maneuver caught Guy by surprise, and he bristled with the notion that his timid, non-confrontational spouse was represented by a Cornell Law School graduate who introduced herself through "a notice of representation" letter that he had received two days ago. He wondered how Ellen got the money to hire the lawyer and challenged her about it when she returned home after the movie.

"I hope you didn't use my American Express to purchase the services of that upstart attorney of yours. Cause I'm not paying her. I'm starting to think this thing was in the works a long time ago."

Ellen's reply was short and to the point. "How I secured the services of an attorney is none of your business. I'm simply expediting the process. It's not that complicated to resolve, and the boys don't need the hassle. You wouldn't want our problems spilling over on them. Would you?"

"You must be kidding. Everything you've done since you made your intention known indicates we're going to be at each other's throats with this divorce. That's the message you're giving me."

"You're dead wrong! All I want is to get it over with. I expected you to feel the same way. It's in the best interest of the boys. Contrary to what you think, people get divorced all the time."

"Wake up, Ellen. You're a fool. You caused this to happen, I didn't. You better understand I won't make it easy for you. Why should I? And, how do you know what's best for the kids?"

"I'm not going to argue. I'm going upstairs. Please don't bother me for the rest of the evening."

The boys believed that they'd be staying in Middletown, and for the present time their father gave them no reason to think otherwise. Guy spent most of his time with Joey and took the boys out for dinner on Sunday. As far as they were concerned, there was no reason to worry. They believed their father would pay child support and alimony, just as their friends had told them he would. Meanwhile late that Sunday night, Guy told Ellen he would be staying in the Westgate home during future monthly visitations, claiming it was better for the kids and easier for him. Ellen had no choice but to agree. However, she made it clear that once the divorce was finalized, he'd have to make other arrangements.

❧

During their Saturday date, Ellen implored Jake to break one of their rules, regarding the discussion of their kids, due to the circumstances. Sensing the level of her anxiety, Jake made an exception and gave her some advice regarding the boys.

"Ellen, whatever you do, tread very lightly about the subject of blame. Leave the boys out of the mix. Throughout my counseling career I've seen some tragic results whenever kids are forced to take sides. Regardless of what you know about Guy's other side, keep it locked up. Children absolutely need to believe in the inherit goodness of their parents. Demolishing that image is an unconscionable act of selfishness."

Then Jake spoke in the strongest terms when he warned her, "Truth means nothing in situations like this. It's all about perception. Whatever Guy says or does, don't bring out the past because in the end, the boys will suffer. I've seen it happen so many times."

Since their day at Sandy Hook, Ellen's feelings for Jake were stronger than ever. She loved him and told him so many times. However, he still withheld any long-term commitment. She knew Jake was embroiled in his own marital problems and that in time he'd tell her about it.

Nevertheless, he was emphatic when he told her, "You swore to me that I wasn't a part of your divorce and I believed you. You have become a part of my life, I'll admit that, but it's your responsibility to settle with Guy."

❧

Three weeks later during Guy's next visit "Murphy's Law" took over. Everything that could go wrong did go wrong. Night after night Danny refused to come home at a reasonable hour. Some school nights he'd walk in at ten o'clock with no excuse other than he was with his friends. He wasn't doing his homework or doing his chores. Ellen even suspected he might have been truant based on a call she received from the high school attendance office. In spite of Ellen's efforts to keep him under control, she was losing the battle. Whenever she tried to confront him, it went nowhere and he'd walk away. She anticipated a showdown when Guy returned for his next visit.

Guy arrived on the last Saturday in October. He took the airport shuttle, and by noon he was sitting in the kitchen having lunch with Joey when Danny walked in. At first, Guy said nothing. Danny looked disheveled and it was obvious that he'd been out late last night and slept over a friend's house. That wouldn't have been a problem, except he never called home to tell Ellen where he was. Danny greeted his dad with a couple of questions instead of acknowledging his presence.

"Are you staying here for the weekend? I thought you weren't coming till next weekend."

Before his father had a chance to answer, Ellen walked into the kitchen and opened fire. She was determined to get some answers with Guy present. "So where were you last night? You didn't call, and we had an agreement that you would if you were going to be late. I waited for you and ended up sleeping on the couch. How could you be so thoughtless? I've told you a hundred times you can't live without rules. You have to be responsible for your actions. I'm glad your father's home. Maybe **he** can get through to you in a way you'll understand. For whatever reason, you won't listen to me. Tell him. Why didn't you come home last night?"

Danny wouldn't answer, and stared defiantly at Ellen. There was no way he was going to be yelled at in front of Joey, so he turned on his mother in a vicious manner. "You're not telling me what to do. I have to put up with my teachers doing that all week. By Friday I've had enough. I don't have to listen to you. You got your own life, and I got mine. As soon as I eat some lunch...I'm out of here."

Guy stood by silently and didn't interfere. To his way of thinking, if Ellen was going start an argument, then Danny was her headache. Meanwhile, Ellen waited patiently for Guy to intervene, but he didn't.

As a result of his silence, she abruptly turned to him and asked, "Why are you just sitting there? Say something? Can't you see, Danny's out of control!"

"What's the big deal? So he was with his buddies. He's ok. Leave him alone. Danny, get cleaned up before you have lunch. You can tell me your side of the story later."

Ellen couldn't believe what was happening and physically blocked Danny's exit and yelled, "No! Now you listen to me. You can eat your lunch, but you're not going back out. I want you to clean your room and bring your laundry down. You're not leaving. This is my home, and there are rules. Rules your brother must follow and you too. Danny, you're grounded for the rest of the weekend!"

"Bullshit! I got plans for today, and I'm keeping them." Danny barked back like a caged animal.

Ellen realized the situation was reaching a meltdown. A year ago, she would have walked away and swallowed her pride. But now her credibility was at stake, and considering she'd be a single parent in a few months, Ellen knew she had to take a stand. To compromise would be unthinkable. It was a defining moment; and there was no turning back. She faced off with her son, and as stern as she had ever been, told him, "Maybe you think living with your dad would be better for you. Is that's what you want?"

Danny said nothing. He turned away, opened the refrigerator door, and took a couple of swallows of orange juice. If he was intimidated by Ellen's last statement, he didn't show it. Guy was completely surprised by Ellen's reaction and told her so.

"I don't understand. Why are you making such a big deal about this? You act like the kid is some kind of juvenile delinquent. He's your son. Christ, what the hell is wrong with you? You made your point. He stayed out last night without calling. He's fifteen. I thought you took that parenting course. Didn't you learning anything?"

His sarcastic comment was stinging. He was as disrespectful to her as Danny was. Ellen was ready to draw the line. She stood opposite Guy, who sat with a smug look as if he knew he'd beaten her. He was wrong.

With her heart pounding and her voice quivering, she raised her voice and said, "Listen to me, Guy. Danny has some serious problems. I think he needs professional help. You obviously don't agree. If you can do a better job with Danny, then say so. Go ahead! I'm not fighting with you about this. It's your decision. The way I feel right now, I don't care! I'll drive you down to Atlanta tomorrow and save you the airfare."

Guy got up and started to walk out of the room. Ellen felt herself losing control and screamed, "You're not making me look like a fool in front of my son. **You're not...do you hear me?** You have never believed me when it comes to the welfare of the kids. You think you always know best. You've bribed and spoiled that boy since he was a baby, and it has done him no good! Can't you see he's got problems and they're not going away simply because you're ignoring them. If you want to take care of him, I'll pack up his clothes and you can take him back to Atlanta. Well?"

Guy was feeling the pressure. Ellen had never talked to him like that. "I'm sure I can do a better job because I can relate to him. This is interesting...so you made up your mind, you're gonna toss us all out. I got some news for you Ellen. I'm not backing off."

‽‽‽

The die was cast and Ellen didn't fully appreciate the consequences until later that evening.

"Mom, it's me, Joey. Can I come in?"

Ellen unlocked the door and asked her son to sit on the bed. "Joey, I'm sorry that you had to witness Danny's behavior. This has been a rough day for me. Please...please don't ever treat me the way your brother does."

"Mom, you know I'm not like Danny. What's going to happen? Dad won't say."

"Unless I hear differently, tomorrow or the day after, I'm taking your father and Danny to Atlanta. I'm sorry, but it has to be that way and I believe it's for the best. I can't control your brother nor can I get your father's support. He won't listen to reason. I'm sorry. I'm really sorry."

"Mom, help me. I don't know what to do. I'm confused."

With her heart about to burst, somehow she held back the tears and asked the ultimate question. "Do you want to stay with me or live with your dad? Joey, you'll be going back to your old school at East Point. Do you understand?"

Joey got up from the bed and walked over to the door before he answered. "Mom, I love you, but I want to be with my brother. They need me, and I need them. I can't imagine being without them. That's not what I'm used to. Mom, please...please let me go."

Ellen hung her head in disbelief. This wasn't supposed to happen. She was losing the boys. Somehow, she mustered the courage to make the hardest choice a mother could ever make.

"Joey, I don't know if you'll ever be able to understand this. As much as it'll hurt me, maybe it's best for you and Danny to live with your father. I'm not going to break you up. That's not right. Someday you'll appreciate why I had to stand up for my principles. Always remember, I love you. My God, I wish it never came to this. Believe me, I never thought it would. Let me hold you for a minute" She held her son and tears came to both of them, tears of grief from Ellen and tears of uncertainty from the boy.

The next day, Guy made no attempt to change anything, and offered no alternative. He thought Ellen would back down. By Sunday night, Ellen thought she would confront Guy one more time since he wasn't coming to her. All day long she had considered the choice. He was watching TV when she sat down in the living room to see if he had

285

anything to say.

"Guy, I assume you've spoken with the boys and you're taking them. I don't understand. Why didn't you stick up for me? You knew I was right! Danny broke the rules; he didn't accept responsibility for his actions. Why can't you see that he's failing and maybe something even worse is going on in his world that we don't know about?"

Guy was so angry at her; he refused to give her the satisfaction of his agreement. "Ellen, you made the call, and I accepted your challenge. Like I said last night, I can handle Danny. Besides, it'll be cheaper for me in the long run. Go ahead. Pack us up. Do it! We'll go whenever you're finished. There's one other thing. You better get yourself a job real soon because you're not using my credit cards and living off of me much longer."

"Is that all you can say to me. You think this is some kind of game!"

Guy didn't answer, and rather than say another word Ellen walked out to the deck, and stood facing the chill of the evening. Looking up at the crescent moon she had to admit she was terrified. Her world was crumbling, and she had set everything in motion by standing up to Guy. If ever Ellen faced a moment of truth it was now.

The choice was simple. She could beg Guy to reconsider; telling him she just lost it and explain her position, hoping he would listen. The other choice was to hold fast to her principles. Then it came to her, something Jake had taught at the workshop about taking responsibility. She thought,

Why should I change the consequences of Danny behavior? It was Guy who acted improperly. Giving in to him would be continuing to live the same lie as before. The boys made their choice. Whatever was left of my personal integrity and self-respect was at stake. There's no turning back. For the time being, I must accept things the way they are and move ahead with my life, with or without the boys, and without Guy's financial support. Whether Guy thinks I'm serious or bluffing doesn't matter. I've made my choice.

Ellen started packing that very night and Guy made no attempt at any resolution. Moreover, he went to bed fully confident that his wife would back down the next day. Much to his surprise, early the next morning his sleep was interrupted by the sound of footsteps outside his bedroom. Ellen was carrying the boy's bags down to the foyer.

CHAPTER 38

If indeed "ignorance is bliss," then Jake was feeling somewhat short of blissful because of the missed opportunity to see Ellen since she hadn't answer the signal when he called. Regardless of the disappointment, he was still determined to get away on Saturday afternoon.

As hard as he tried to maintain some perspective, he was finding it impossible to bail out of the relationship. Literally, she was always on his mind, and he knew he was falling in love with her. But true to form, he tried to look at the future prospects objectively. Of course, that only led into a maze of possibilities, each of which was blocked by uncertainty at the end of the path.

Meanwhile, the distance from Sandy was growing week by week. Jake was beginning to feel like they were strangers who crossed paths a couple of hours every day. Things were stable, and life went on in the usual manner, but that was all. The marriage was sinking under the weight of Jake's withdrawal and Sandy's full-time schedule which kept them apart. Their relationship was frozen beneath the civil language of two people trying not to upset a delicate peace, two detached people who for different reasons knew they were holding on for the sake of the kids.

Often he found himself contemplating various scenarios for the year ahead. Of all things, the unexpected destruction caused by Hurricane Floyd to the entire northeast was a concrete example of how Mother Nature could turn a world of serenity into a world of devastation. If the hurricane had turned toward the Atlantic, possibly thousands of homes and businesses would have been spared destruction. Similarly, Jake believed that if he pursued the wrong path with Ellen, he would end up in catastrophic circumstances. He bounced back and forth. At times feeling committed to Ellen, and then once in a while, he would get hammered by an aggravating sense of ambivalence.

As he took to the Appalachian Trail heading south, Jake was positively sure about one thing, he wasn't getting into a world of chaos and financial instability if he could avoid it. He'd measure his steps carefully to avoid injury, especially because their kids were involved. The affair wasn't about sex, at least not on his part. The desire was there but was cemented in Jake's compartment of postponed gratification, a mindset developed through years of separating need from want.

One of Jake's primary guiding principles, which he referred to as "Jake's Law," was often taught to his students, *"If you can get most of what you need and some of what you want, then there's no reason why you can't be satisfied."*

When he examined the facts, neither Sandy nor he was getting much of what they needed, much less a piece of what they wanted. Thinking Ellen was the answer to his discontent, after such a short period of time, was childish thinking on his part. He wasn't even sure if he was crestfallen by pure infatuation, particularly after such a long period of prolonged stagnation with Sandy.

Over the years, Jake had held his temptation to stray in check. Sandy was a beautiful woman and a caring mother. She also was a terrific lover when she was in the mood. Then again, Jake never met anyone he felt was worth the risk. He knew having sexual intercourse with Ellen would be too much for Sandy to forgive. He knew if he were going to cross the line, it would be because he loved Ellen.

After hiking about three miles, Jake took a break and sat alone on a flat ledge against a pine tree. With so much on his mind, he took out his personal journal and began writing.

I shouldn't look too far ahead. Yet, all I seem able to do is look that way. I know the wisdom of waiting, of being patient. I'm stuck in an emotional tornado that swirls around my head and my heart and won't let go of me. It grows in size, in strength, and in speed. Am I to let it go unchecked? Pretty soon, by not passing time with inner harmony, I'll lose the direction in my life. The force will drive me away from Sandy and to Ellen.

As my children grow older, they're not factors in my plans. Not now. They must learn to make their way in the world by using their heads and by overcoming obstacles the way I did. That's what I've done my whole life, and that's what I've tried to teach them. When I think of Sandy, and what I'm feeling, I see little hope of us making it together over the long haul. I'm not the man who can make her happy anymore. I'm not the man she needs. I've become estranged. Nothing is going right for us. I feel empty and detached. But I'm also sorry. Not for what I've done, but sorry that I couldn't have just walked away from Sandy sooner. I've stayed for the kid because I needed to be around for them. In staying, it's become worse...

I know there will be a period of never-ending struggle if I continue this affair with Ellen. Should I accept what fate has given me, what karma has ordained? Should I runaway from the truth and continue living a lie? Is my desire for Ellen's love the wrong desire? That's what frightens me the most. Looking too far ahead is bad karma, and I accept that fact...I'm losing the center. I cannot deny my own discontent. It's been seven years since the birth of that discontentment. Over 2,500 days have passed and my love for Sandy is gone.

In the final analysis, there is only the self and one's attitude about the self. Am I being true to myself? I've always believed that life is about finding little moments of joy in the routine of living, and about being full by being empty. Where is the joy with Sandy? I've been disconnected from her for so long that maybe I've lost the ability to reconnect. If that's true, I'm on the wrong path and should alter my course. However, there's uncertainty either way I go.

As Jake spent the rest of the afternoon hiking, his thoughts bounced back and forth, advancing forward to Ellen, and then retreating back to Sandy. As much as he cared for Ellen, the upcoming divorce from Guy would burden her with responsibility and family commitment. His inner voice questioned him. *Do you believe that having an affair with a woman with two sons is a wise choice? Where would it go after a few months? You know that meeting in secret isn't going to work forever.*

Jake tried to step back and view things as an ideal observer, looking at the facts. Ellen was waiting to finalize her divorce and he was passing time in a deteriorating relationship. They both had two children to worry about. He had a professional career, a solid reputation in the community, and a good paying job. Ellen was going through a transition period of uncertainty. The facts were obvious. All the evidence suggested their affair was facing hard times. And, regardless of his initial good intentions to help Ellen, what long term outcome could he expect?

Time was running out. In spite of all his efforts to think through his situation, Jake reached no specific conclusion on the trail. On one hand it was disappointing, but on the other it meant that what was at stake required a better understanding and that would take time. He also understood that the only cure for ambivalence was patience.

As he drove back to Walden, he felt disgusted, knowing in a couple of hours he'd be having dinner with Sandy. That meant shifting away from Ellen and back to his other world. Sandy would be sitting across from him eating Chinese food. She'd discuss the kids, concerns about her job, and when they'd be getting together with the family for Thanksgiving. In short, everything except their marital problems. He'd listen and comment at the appropriate time, with the appropriate response. Later on, they'd watch a movie and then make love around midnight.

He really was shipwrecked. Something had to give and he had to make a choice, a choice that would certainly alter the direction of his life.

CHAPTER 39

The Eastmans left Middletown on a dreary overcast Monday morning. Guy's mood was sullen when they began the trip, and he immediately turned on news radio to keep his mind occupied. Ellen sat next to him, detached and indifferent though quietly engrossed in her own thoughts. Danny and Joey slept at first and then listened to their individual Sony "Walkman" to pass the time. During the first few hours family interaction was limited due to the tense circumstances of the unexpected exodus. Other than Joey calling attention to road signs and making idle conversation, not much was said between the parents. An unsigned truce appeared to keep the peace. Danny was indifferent, immersed in his own thoughts about returning to his old home town.

By noon, the boys started nagging for food, so they stopped at McDonalds in a sprawling rest stop complex south of Baltimore. Guy gave the Danny a ten-spot and said he'd join them inside in a few minutes. When they left Ellen braced herself for the worst and she was right.

"Ellen, don't go in yet, I want to talk to you. You're really something, pushing us out of the house and forcing the boys to leave their home. You're selfish and completely irrational. You've been like that ever since you told me we were finished. I didn't start this, you did and I don't know where you're coming from. I know you can't make it on your own. You never could, and what's worse is that you think you're so damn justified with your principles, as you call them. You tried to make a fool out of me, claiming I can't look after the boys without you. That's bullshit and we both know it. I can handle it!"

Ellen had heard enough. When she started to open the van door he stopped her by yelling, "I'm not finished...wait a minute. You think hiring a smartass lawyer will do the trick. Last night I realized I've always made things too easy for you. Know something...you haven't worked in over a year. I've supported you! You have no money and no one to stake you. Did you tell the lawyer that? Did you tell her that I bought that damn house up in Middletown because of you? Did you? It was your idea to move up here, not mine. Remember what you said, that the boys would be better off going to school up there instead of Atlanta. What horseshit that turned out to be. All I've ever asked was that you take care of the kids and live on a budget while I was hustling, busting my ass to make a buck in a tough market. You couldn't even do that right. Now you're putting me through this crap. You still won't answer?

Huh?"

She hated him, everything about him, and refused to answer his charges. She just stared straight ahead, watching droplets of rain run down the windshield instead of facing the man she despised.

Guy still wasn't through. However, he toned down his anger in order to get her to respond. "Come on Ellen, admit it, it was never hard for you. You can't even tell me why you were so unhappy with me. Go ahead, make you're case! I'll listen. Like I said, I thought things were great last year. You're sitting here acting deaf and dumb with your eyes turned away because you know I'm right. Why don't you look at me when I'm talking? You're nuts!"

Frustrated by her silence, and realizing he was getting nowhere, he opened the van door to leave. But before departing, he leaned back inside the van and gave her one more volley aimed to disable her. "I might as well tell you this. I'm actually glad to be rid of you. Now maybe I can look for someone...someone who'll look after my needs. You sure didn't! You're a waste and that's a fact."

Ellen's reply consisted of one sentence, which she delivered with the accuracy of a brain surgeon removing a malignant tumor with a single burst from a laser. "You're dead wrong, wrong about everything, and we both know it." Then she left and slammed the van's sliding door for effect.

Guy never came into McDonalds; instead he went for pizza to avoid his wife and children who were sitting together. Twenty minutes later when they returned to the van, she told Joey to sit in the front so she could stay out of Guy's line of sight. It was better for everyone that way, and besides she wanted to nap. When Guy came back, he began driving without saying a word.

Shortly after, with the boys engaged in their games and the radio on, Ellen closed her eyes and tried to sleep. Intuitively, she realized that her hatred for Guy was finally equal to his, but she wouldn't give him the satisfaction of knowing it. His vicious diatribe only provided more evidence of his total lack of respect for her. When she gave him her retort and left the van, she was more certain than ever that she'd never let him get to her again. She thought he was arrogant, self-righteous, and ill-mannered.

∽∾

After a grueling eighteen-hour drive, they arrived at Guy's East Point apartment early in the morning. Everyone was exhausted from the discomfort of sleeping in bucket seats and driving through the night. Danny and his father left the van immediately and crashed in the master bedroom. Ellen refused to surrender to fatigue and emptied the van with

Joey's help. A spare room that was used for office files and storage was converted into a makeshift bedroom for the boys.

After unpacking, she took Joey for breakfast at Dunkin Donuts and then they went to a nearby Wal-Mart to buy cots for the sleeping bags they brought with them. It was a well-meaning gesture to give the boys some comfort until other arrangements could be made. Then Ellen stopped at the grocery store to pick up some basics. When she returned, she placed their clothes bags inside and put the food away.

Satisfied that things were in order, she spent a few final moments alone in the kitchen with Joey, reassuring him that he'd be all right and that she was sorry she had to leave him there. The boy listened intently but didn't answer back.

Just before gathering her things to driving back, Ellen heard Joey open the door to the master bedroom and wake his father. She stood quietly outside the door.

"Dad, Mom's leaving. Do you want to say goodbye? Hurry up! She's ready to go. Please get up!"

Guy listened to Joey's plea. Reluctantly, he got up and walked into the kitchen without saying a word. His face was unshaven, his hair was disheveled, and his eyes were cold and expressionless. He'd emptied his anger and frustration at the McDonalds lot the day before and had given her the silent treatment since then. Even with Joey holding his mother's hand, Guy didn't alter his attitude. He stood with his arms folded, waiting for her to say something, perhaps even beg for his forgiveness.

He was wrong. She held her ground and said, "I'll call you when I get back. I think I've left things in order. I bought some food for you at the grocery. Their clothes are in the bags. I think they have enough for school. You can register them tomorrow. Please, please watch over them. They're going to need time to adjust. Keep Danny on a tight leash, and be patient with Joey. They can call me whenever they need to talk. I hope that's all right with you. One more thing, could you give me a hundred dollars? I don't have enough cash to get home."

Still half asleep but capable of sensing the importance of the moment, he leaned against the fridge and muttered in a "matter of fact" kind of way, "So you're really going to do this? My God, I thought by now you'd come to your senses and apologize for all the trouble you caused your family. I suppose you're not going to do what's right. Well that's your decision and you're gonna have to live with the guilt. **You're gonna regret this**. That I can promise. I'll give you the money, but you'd better start looking for a job. That's all I can say. Joey, go get my wallet off the dresser in the bedroom."

A few seconds later, his son handed over the wallet. Guy put five twenties on the kitchen counter, and walked back to the bedroom, closing the door behind him. Joey appeared transfixed by the scene; his head fell down in disbelief from what he just witnessed. He had prayed to God for a miracle to happen.

"Joey, I'm sorry things turned out this way. I'm going in the bedroom to say goodbye to Danny. Lay down on the couch and I'll cover you. I'll be back in a minute."

She opened the door and even though Danny was fast asleep she touched his face and whispered; "I love you." Guy's back was turned away and he didn't move. When she stepped back into the other room Joey got up from the couch for a final hug.

"Mom, please be careful driving. I'm worried about you. You look so tired."

"I'll call you tomorrow, I promise. Look after your brother. I love you."

Just before she pulled away, Joey ran out and waved to her. That last glance of her son was heartbreaking, and it was all she could do to drive away without cracking. She began to whimper, fighting back the tears from the only life she had known for the past sixteen years, being a mother.

Two blocks away she waited for the red glow of the light to change. At that spot, despite a flow of tears brought on by Guy's insensitivity, she clenched her fists in anger and banged the steering wheel. "I won't surrender! I won't ever! Let this be a lesson for Guy."

Twenty-eight hours after first leaving Middletown, Ellen was back on the road making the 900-mile trek on her own. To her knowledge, this was the first time she ever had to drive that much distance alone. Nevertheless, she was undaunted by the challenge. In fact, she wanted nothing more then to be alone after the trauma of leaving the boys. The whole tragic episode was almost surrealistic in retrospect.

Ellen's maternal emotions didn't fully come forth and burst until she pulled into a rest stop off Interstate 20 just north of Augusta. It was there, during a restroom break that the full impact of the separation smashed into her. The anguish she felt was overwhelming and her tears were unstoppable as she sat bent over with her hands covering her face, drowning in despair. A few people passed by, but they either pretended not to take notice or didn't care to intrude. Finally, a woman with her young daughter stood nearby, and waited for Ellen to turn around.

Then the woman spoke softly and kindly. "Miss...Miss are you all right? My daughter noticed you were crying, and it frightened her. Are you in trouble? Are you ill? Is there something wrong with your car?"

Ellen glanced over to the woman, trying to hold back the tears, and then she composed herself enough to answer the inquiry. "You're so kind. Thank you. And you're daughter is very thoughtful. I'm sorry if I caused you any concern. I've...I've just had a very tough morning. I'm driving back to New York and...I suppose I'm worn out. I've had some family problems and right now I've got a lot on my mind. I'll be fine in a few minutes. Thanks for stopping by to help."

The woman came closer to Ellen and the picture was worth a thousand words. "I think I understand. I'm just getting back on my feet after a difficult divorce. I never thought it would end up being so difficult. My daughter is the joy of my life, and she's been an anchor for me. Now it's just the two of us. Her father's still in the picture but, thank the Lord above, he's not causing me trouble. All I can tell you is that without my parents helping me out, it would've been impossible. I hope you have someone to depend on. I know right now things look terrible, but it will pass...Good luck, Miss."

During the previous two days, regardless of the mind games and sarcastic comments made by her husband, Ellen held on to her dignity, determined not to give him the satisfaction of seeing her overcome with fear. She had no one to call for sympathy, guidance, or companionship and was too embarrassed to phone her mother or sister. She dealt with the crisis alone, like she always did.

Guy had taunted her several times by saying she was too dependent on him and would never make it on her own. At times, Ellen was certain the boys heard the mocking, but they didn't interfere. During the drive to Atlanta, they seemed detached, or pretended to be from the dramatic turn of events. And, given the circumstances, they didn't want to incur the wrath of their father. All that mattered to Joey was for him to stay with his father and his older brother. All that mattered to Guy was not to back down from Ellen. And Danny, whose behavior had caused the trouble, absolved himself of all blame putting it instead on his parents.

After ten minutes, Ellen returned to the van still tearful, but no longer sobbing. She remembered what Jake had taught her about the importance of being thoughtful during a crisis and to wait for some insight. With that mindset, she continued on the interstate to Columbia, South Carolina, and the turnoff for Interstate 95. To distract her from her anxiety, she listened to the Genesis tape *Calling All Stations*.

Soon the familiar songs provided an escape from her thoughts of separation. The music took her back to Jake and miraculously, within a short time, the sadness subsided and Ellen rediscovered her determination to continue her journey into the unknown.

It was around one o'clock when she decided to call Jake from a rest stop. Loretta transferred the call immediately as if she knew that something unusual was going on. She heard the desperation in Ellen's request to speak with Mr. Carr.

After a second to transfer the call, Ellen heard Jake voice, "This is Jake Carr. May I help you?"

"Jake, this is Ellen. Please listen. I've taken the boys to Atlanta. They're going to live with their father. It's very complicated. Danny stayed out all night and the next morning things got out of control, way out of control. I couldn't convince Guy to back me and then…"

"Where are you Ellen? Are you all right?"

"I'm on the interstate in South Carolina, north of Columbia. I just stopped for coffee and a sandwich. All I want is to get home. It's been a horrible few days. I'm sorry, but I needed to know that you're there for me. I can't help it. So much has happened. Can I call you tomorrow?"

"Of course you can. When you didn't pick up on Monday morning I wasn't concerned. I figured Guy might still be there. But when I didn't hear anything from you the rest of the day, I guess I started to worry. Now I know why. Listen, you've got a long way to go. We'll talk after you get back. Promise you'll spend the night somewhere. Don't try to drive through. It's not worth it. Ellen, promise me!"

"I promise I'll stop. I know you're right. Thanks for caring."

"I care very much. Call me when you get back. I'm here for you."

∂∽⑤

When Jake left work that afternoon he knew Ellen's world had been turned upside down. What had happened in that Westgate home over the Halloween weekend, he could only guess? His knowledge about family "meltdown" was both professional and personal. Without knowing all the facts, he surmised that Ellen probably had gone over the edge. Considering what he knew about Ellen, making such a bold move must have taken incredible courage. He doubted if she had ever wanted this to happen the way it did. Everything she told him up to that time suggested the boys would remain with her.

His job was obvious. First, he'd give her encouragement but not specific advice because she'd already moved the boys. And second, he'd keep her focused in the present so she could choose the right direction. That path had to be Ellen's choice and not his. He would listen to her plans, and as long as they were reasonable, he'd back her. If he thought her choices pointed toward disaster, then he would intervene. Finally, Jake believed Ellen had to grow her own wings and learn to fly. He was willing to teach her how and that would be his objective.

∂∽⑤

Over the next two weeks, Jake checked in with Ellen every morning. They also continued to meet one weekday after school, even if only for an hour. They were limited by time and had to end the rendezvous by 4:30. One hour was never enough. Fortunately, they still kept their Saturday afternoon date, and by that time Ellen was wound pretty tight so Jake treated her with compassion and with love.

Overriding every other issue was the pending divorce settlement. When Judy Clark, Ellen's attorney, told her that things would be financially secure, it was based on the fact that Guy would be paying child support and alimony ordered by a New York State judge. That would have permitted Ellen and the boys to remain in Middletown for the foreseeable future. Now with the children living with their father, Ellen could only anticipate getting some alimony money.

Another unexpected turn of events occurred when Guy offered Ellen a no-fault divorce settlement. He was willing to pay the legal fees in return for her cooperation. He was a resident of Georgia and could prove actual separation to comply with the time requirement. Since Ellen had no financial resources, she had to accept the deal. Consequently, he offered her a proposal. If she did the necessary repairs and painting, then he'd continue paying the mortgage and also give her some money to live on.

She accepted the arrangement, and spent the first few weeks following the separation busily preparing a resume, checking the want ads, and fixing up the house. She also tried to keep her mind occupied by reading, exercising, and taking long walks. But some days were much harder than others. On those dismal rainy afternoons, she missed the children more than she ever thought was possible, especially when she heard the school bus stop in the neighborhood.

CHAPTER 40

Jake planned to give Ellen a very special forty-first birthday dinner, so he sent her a card with a handwritten invitation inside. On the front cover, there was a black and white photo of two small children playing together on the beach building a sand castle. Inside there was a brief message.

Dear Ellen,
Join me at a private dinner party in your honor and hosted by yours truly. I'll see you Thursday night at 6 p.m. in the Montgomery Manor lot. I promise you'll have a wonderful birthday and a night to remember.
> *With love,*
> *Jake*

For the occasion, he chose the Red Pheasant Tavern in Newburgh. The place had the intimate atmosphere of an old colonial inn that made it the perfect choice. His explanation to Sandy was that he'd be attending a surprise party for one of his counselor colleagues celebrating the half-century mark. It was a rock solid-alibi. He wanted to give Ellen a romantic evening, a sumptuous dinner with lots of laughter, and a chance to dress up.

At 6:30 they entered the restaurant. Jake asked the hostess for some privacy, so she led them to a candlelit table separated by a partition from the entrance lobby and bar. In a chivalrous manner, he took Ellen's winter coat off her shoulders and saw that she looked absolutely stunning in a red satin corset top with a gold dragon pattern, revealing just enough cleavage to catch his glance every fifteen seconds. She complimented the provocative top with a tight fitting pair of black silk pants that accentuated her figure perfectly. Jake was so taken by her glamorous appearance that he stumbled over his first few words.

"Are you the same shy young woman I met at the school library back in March? I'm...I'm tongue-tied and astonished. Ellen...wow, you look terrific."

Jake knew full well he was being as charming as Rhett Butler from *Gone with the Wind* as they stood by the table.

She played the part perfectly and said, "Mr. Carr, this is the very least I could do to show you how much I appreciate your company. Why sir, you look pretty snazzy yourself dressed all in black."

"I confess. It's the outfit that makes me feel like I'm ready for anything. Right now, all I'm missing is a heavy gold chain, a pinky ring, and patent leather loafers to go with this shirt and pants."

When Jake moved behind her he caught a faint whiff of some exotic perfume and shook his head while exhaling. Then, he pulled out her chair and waited for her to sit. When she did, he bent over and kissed her on both cheeks.

"Happy Birthday! I'm glad we can share it together."

They ordered vodka and tonics. Then he toasted Ellen with a double bang before making a proclamation.

"I wish you all the good fortune you so rightly deserve and hope you always remember this birthday. Remember, if happiness is in your destiny, you need not be in a hurry. So please be patient."

Ellen nodded in acknowledgement and tapped his glass twice more saying, "I've looked forward to this more than you'd ever know...tonight you're mine."

During the prime rib dinner, Jake was as entertaining as a medieval knight in pursuit of the heart of a fair maiden. The food was prepared well, especially the stuffed mushrooms. They ate at a leisurely pace and thoroughly enjoyed the fact that they had time to share without watching the clock or the crowd.

Later on, the choice of dessert was difficult to make because they were filled to capacity. But Jake wouldn't accept any excuse for passing it up. He told the waitress it was Ellen's birthday and ordered a piece of cherry cheesecake. When the dessert arrived with one pink candle on it Jake and the waitress sang "Happy Birthday." Ellen was delighted and clapped her hands in appreciation for all the fuss.

While they were having coffee, he presented Ellen with an envelope. He waited and waited, but she had him right where she wanted and sat still without opening it.

Unable to restrain himself another moment he pleaded, "Well, do you think you could open it and read it...like now?"

At his request, she opened the envelope and read it, while Jake sipped his coffee.

Dear Ellen,

Happy Birthday! I wish I could give you a chest full of gold coins, but I haven't pillaged any kingdoms as of late. Instead, I'm offering you my support in the days ahead. I'm aware that some days will be filled with turmoil and uncertainty. But you will make it! I promise that you will. You need to believe in yourself. Then and only then, will you learn to be independent and make your way in the world. You can do it with your intelligence, wisdom, and sheer willpower! On this special day, at the start of your new life, I offer you the most valuable gift I have, my support, my understanding, and my affection.

I take this commitment very seriously. On my honor, you have my promise I'll be there for you, whether in the best of times or worst of times. I love the time we spend together. I am your servant.

Love,

Jake

Ellen felt both puzzled and pleased. Jake's words were thoughtful and sincere, yet the message lacked the passion she wanted to hear. She looked up and smiled, then leaned over and took hold of both his hands. He didn't know what was coming next.

"Jake, you've proven over and over again that you'll be there for me. I appreciate the promises you made. I really do. Of course I'm depending on your continued friendship, but I want you to listen and listen very carefully. You're not my servant. I am in love with you. Tonight you've made me so happy. Now please take me home and give yourself to me. I want you. Are you ready to love me?"

Jake was totally taken by Ellen's comment, and was aware for the first time, that he was being too timid with a woman he wanted so badly.

"Ellen, I am at your service! I'm ready. Let's go."

They left the restaurant without a restroom stop and drove back to Montgomery Manor. Then, they both got into Ellen's van, and she drove home. Jake had never been there before, believing it was too much of a risk if anyone saw them together.

Twenty minutes later, Ellen opened the garage door with the remote and pulled the van inside. Initially, Jake felt awkward when they took off their coats and sat at the kitchen counter. If either of them was nervous, it was camouflaged in the dim light created when Ellen lit two large candles on the counter.

"Jake, would you like a drink? Vodka and tonic…right?'

"That'd be great. You gonna have one with me?"

"It's hard to believe that this is the first drink I've ever made for you. You like it strong, don't you? What did you tell me, a fifty-fifty mix?"

"You bet. I'm used to it. I'm reckless; what can I say?"

Ellen opened a cabinet and took out a new bottle of Absolute Vodka and made the drinks. Jake thought she looked as sexy as hell doing the bartending. Sitting opposite one another, they took a couple of sips in silence.

Then Ellen questioned him, "How are you set for time? You're not going to run away, are you?"

"I'm good. It's only a little after eight and I'm here to celebrate your birthday and take you up on the offer you made at the restaurant. What about you? Have any second thoughts about it? You took me by surprise, but honestly it's what I've longed to hear."

"Jake, you're the only one I've ever offered myself to. I've been alone for so long. Then you came out of nowhere and gave me hope. You've been with me every day since the first time I met you. Imagine, I fell in love with you right after that first walk we took. Everything...believe me, everything about us has always felt right. We were meant to find each other. It's our destiny. Jake, I've waited long enough for this to happen. Give me ten minutes to get ready and then come upstairs?"

"I hope I don't have to wait any longer or I might go crazy."

After she left, Jake stared at the candle flames and realized that five months had passed since he first held Ellen in his arms that day in the office. Since that time, every word and every action eventually lead to this moment. He knew that once he ascended the stairs, it would be a turning point in his life. He had not made love to any other woman except Sandy for the past twenty years. Nevertheless, his feelings for Ellen were so strong that he knew it was impossible for him to turn back.

When they went to the shore in early October he knew he loved her. But it was so frightening to him that he backed off telling Ellen. He was sure of the love, but was scared of pursuing it.

He rose from the stool and silently declared in the presence of the burning candles, as if it was some sacred fire on which to make an oath, "I accept the love I have for this wonderful woman who has totally captivated me and made me feel appreciated and loved. I wanted this to happen and it did."

Then he called out to Ellen in a jovial manner from the staircase. "Hey up there. May I come to the party now?"

"I'm almost ready. Bring the drinks, and wait for me on the bed."

A few moments later he entered the soft light of the master bedroom. There were scented candles everywhere, six in all. Dark blue sheets were on the queen-sized bed with four fluffy pillows propped up against the dark mahogany headboard. Ellen was still in the bathroom. Jake took the hint and took off his clothes except for his blue boxer shorts. Then he sat on the edge of the bed and waited.

Just as Jake was wrestling with his decision a short while ago, Ellen faced her own feelings of uncertainty, but her thoughts centered on overcoming nervousness. Unlike Jake, who appeared confident and ready to make love, Ellen felt the opposite way. She worried about how she looked and if she could perform well enough to please the man she loved. There were only a few moments left to exorcise the feeling of inadequacy that had been cemented in her consciousness during twenty years of married life.

The anticipation of making love to Jake that had continually filled her mind with visions of romantic and erotic fantasies disappeared. Now she bordered on being terrified, and felt ashamed for leading Jake on when she felt far from ready to take the plunge. But it was too late to back out. All she could hope was that Jake would know what to do, and deliver her from the paralyzed state she was in.

He sensed her apprehension the moment she stepped into the dim light. Her facial expression left little doubt how anxious she was standing there barely ten feet away. She was dressed in a sexy black satin floral lace chemise with a sheer mesh g-string. There was a red satin ribbon tied around her neck that formed a bow under her chin. She stood motionless, with her arms at her side as though frightened by her own boldness. Jake realized she needed encouragement, so he spoke to her calmly and persuasively.

"My God, you look beautiful. May I ask for one thing? Just do this. Try to smile and slowly turn around so I can love you with my eyes before I taste you with my lips."

Somewhat awkwardly, she honored his request. Then he said reassuringly, "Ellen, I've waited so long for this moment. It'll be fine. You're beautiful...you're absolutely beautiful."

He got up and removed his shorts in the candlelit room and stood naked. Then he walked slowly toward her. Ellen's innate modesty kept her eyes from wandering to his manhood. Suddenly they were embracing. The first kiss was so intense and satisfying she responded by pulling him tightly against her. He kissed her neck and shoulders repeatedly, and Ellen felt him harden against her. It was like she was dreaming. Then he began a slow movement of his hips side to side while he moved his hands in a circular motion across her lower back. It made her breathing increase in rapid fashion.

Then he broke off, glanced over her entire body and said, "Well birthday girl, are you where you want to be? Would you put some music on? You pick the music you want to hear and I'll roll with it. Go ahead. I'll wait on the bed."

Jake rested on his side, with his head on his hand. He watched Ellen place a CD in the portable boom box that was on the nightstand. Never once did his eyes move off her body. Her black lace G-string was a complete turn on. It aroused him even more. Then the soundtrack of

The Last of the Mohicans started to play. It was perfect music for the mood. Ellen paused by the bedroom mirror and looked at herself.

Then Jake asked her, "Are you going to talk to me while I'm making love to you?"

She turned around and tried to prepare for the next moment telling him, "Everything happening is a new experience for me. You're the one who's enchanting. I've never been here before, not with a man I truly love and desire. I bought this outfit just for you, only for you. I'm not sure how I look in it. It doesn't feel like me, not yet, but I'm glad you like me in it. Jake, more than anything in the world I wanted to please you and now I know it was the right thing to wear…Is this really the new me?"

"Only you can answer that. Ellen, you look very sexy, honestly you do. Come over to the bed and let me love you the way I've dreamed about loving you. I'll tell you this, it'll never be in the dark."

Ellen walked to the bed and took her place next to him. He waited to see what she'd do, but all she could manage was to lie there with a sheepish grin. Another few moments went by and still nothing happened. It was exactly what Jake had suspected. Ellen's sexual communication was non-existent, he realized more than ever that he loved her dearly and there was no reason to hide it anymore.

He thought there was still so much innocence in her. Yet she was seductive enough to arouse him. Whatever flirtations she had made during the past few months were always hidden with a measure of insecurity. Making love to her was going to be a wonderful experience because it was an act of love, not just having sex. He believed that when love and passion came together it was the most exquisite of all physical and emotional experiences. Jake decided to take Ellen to uncharted places. He wanted to satisfy her completely. First he'd get her used to seeing him lying naked, and then he would teach her to fly.

"Babe, I love looking at you. So this outfit is just for me…huh?"

They began their lovemaking slowly, Jake taking his time and Ellen responding to each caress with barely a whisper. First they kissed over and over, then he gently rolled her on her stomach. Beginning with her shoulders, he placed his hands under the lingerie top and, using his fingers, traced outlines of figure eights in various wide and narrow curves over her back, hips, and upper thighs. Ellen responded to his touch by moving ever so slightly after each caress. Then he positioned himself on top of her while anchoring his weight with his arms, letting her feel his naked lower body moving across her exposed buttocks while he spoke softly to her.

"You feel so good and tonight you're enchanting. Is this what you wanted?"

Ellen was near the point of sexual ecstasy when Jake asked the question. She turned over, touched his face and whispered, "I'm with my warrior and my dream finally came true...we're together."

Jake didn't remove her g-string or black satin chemise. He felt they gave her a feeling of sexuality. Instead, he moved his right hand to rest on her breast, while moving his index finger in a small circle around her nipple, as he continued kissing her. Ellen was getting hotter and hotter, and once again close to reaching climax.

"Ellen, you're so beautiful...you're a goddess, my goddess."

He continued using his hands, this time on her inner thighs. When he moved his mouth from her lips to her nipples, she began to moan in a barely audible tone. He shifted his tongue from one breast to the other, continuing to arouse her all the more till he knew she let herself go. Then she abruptly pulled him on top of her. Jake knew Ellen was in sexual freefall and was rushing to reach the next level. Breathing heavily, he rolled off and took a moment to speak to her.

"I'm not ready, not just yet. I think I want another drink. Do you want one, too?"

"Don't leave me...come on Jake, I want you right now. Please."

"Why rush? I'm as hot as you are, but I need a break. I'll be back in a minute."

As Jake got up from the bed she looked at him for the first time, all of him. To excite her even more, he walked to the large dresser mirror pretending to check his hair, and passed right in front of her on the way downstairs. Her eyes followed him to the door. In truth, she previously had only seen two other men naked in her life. So it was an erotic experience to enjoy the pleasure of looking at Jake's muscular body and the fulfillment of a sexual fantasy that she had envisioned since their first kiss.

Jake's physical presence was overpowering to Ellen. She had to admit she loved seeing him au natural, and even if she couldn't force herself to compliment him about his manhood, it didn't matter. He looked solid, his stomach was flat, and he was well-enough endowed. She marveled at how he was completely comfortable with his masculinity, whether dressed or undressed. After a couple of minutes, he reappeared at the bedroom door with the drinks.

"Here I am. I brought you another drink to toast your birthday."

"You're the best thing in my life. Let me toast, to my warrior and my prince."

"Whoa darling', there's no way I'm a prince. I'm not the type. But tonight you're the star. May I start kissing you again? Where can I?"

This time with patience and with great skill, Jake took Ellen past anything she'd ever experienced. He touched and stroked her beneath the g-string in various ways that brought her to climax repeatedly. She fought back every inclination to scream out. For the first time in her life she mumbled an exclamation of ecstasy, it came through her rapid breathing and the trembling of her lower body.

"Oh, my Jake…oh, my darling, it's so good…so very good."

Jake kept up the stimulation until her soft crevice was abundantly wet from his touch. Then, without so much as a minute of repose, he slowly brought her upon him. With her body in a crouching position, he slid the passion-soaked g-string to the side and gently placed himself inside her. Within three breaths, they found a rhythm that was exquisite.

The lovemaking continued uninterrupted till Jake asked Ellen to open her eyes and look at him. He spoke softly while caressing her breasts tenderly, all the while moving his lower body up and down.

"You're wonderful, you're beautiful, and you are my angel. Now my darling, you have wing."

Jake couldn't hold on any longer, it was his time and she responded by moving her hips slightly faster, which intensified their pleasure and enabled her to match his climax. When Jake released, he whispered enthusiastically a simple expression three or four times in a row, like a kid on a descending roller coaster ride.

"Wow, wow, wow…you're the best. That was awesome."

After a few minutes they separated and tried to catch their breath. Holding her next to him he said, "Ellen that was so satisfying. I feel great. How are you feeling? Are, are you satisfied?"

"Jake, it was beyond anything I've ever experienced. I love you."

They had taken a chance, each in their own way, and they conquered whatever remaining doubts stood in the way. How and why they found each other was a mystery. Was it their destiny or mere coincidence? On this particular night, all the concerns about their other worlds were forgotten. It was the inevitable conclusion to the choices they made that finally brought them together.

Right before leaving the parking lot at Montgomery Manor, Jake told Ellen something he felt she needed to understand. Holding her close, he poured out his feelings to her. "Ellen, never forget… loving in secret will be hard to do, but its still loving. I think that sacrifice in the name of love is noble. Believe me the months ahead will be filled with many obstacles, so expect them to be in our way. But I promise you that we'll overcome all the roadblocks if we have patience and hope. Unselfish love demands that kind of commitment. We'll be together some day. It may take longer than we want, but we'll get there. It's in our destiny and you have to believe in that."

"Jake, I'm sailing away on a cloud and I've never been so completely happy in my whole life."

Following the farewell, Jake remained in the parking lot. It was late, but somehow he didn't care. He wanted to internalize all that happened, and waited for his inner voice to speak.

Jake, you've made your choice so don't look back. No explanations are necessary. It was karma. If you truly loved Sandy, this never would have happened. That's the truth and there's no denying it. You love Ellen, and this wouldn't have happened if it didn't feel right. So, whatever sacrifices must be made in the future, make them and listen to your heart.

CHAPTER 41

It was Thanksgiving eve and Jake waited up for J.D.'s arrival from Vermont. Near midnight, he heard Missy barking and the garage door rattle. In walked J.D., looking exhausted after his seven-hour drive. Jake welcomed his son with a handshake, while Missy jumped for joy upon the return of her friend.

"Man, I hope I look better than you. I guess the driving took its toll."

"Dad, you can't believe the friggin' traffic! What a mess in Hartford. Shit, I'm glad to be home."

"Relax. Take off your jacket, use the john, wash up, and I'll make you a sandwich? I'm gonna have a Molson. You want one?"

"I'll take you up on that. How about making me a couple of grilled cheeses? I'll tell you, the dudes up there drink Coors Light in the woods around a fire, even when it's freezing outside."

"What'd ya expect? They're born and raised up there and you're not. I'll get your sandwiches made in a few minutes then we can talk."

As J.D. was washing his face and hands in the hallway bathroom he yelled out, "How's my grilled cheese coming? I'm starving. Hey Dad, where's everybody?"

"It's after twelve and today was a school day. I waited up because I'm nuts...just teasing. I promised your mother I'd be here for you. Besides, I wanted to find out if this Vermont thing is still on track. It's not like we know how you're doin', I mean, grade wise. All I know is what you tell me."

Jake opened up two Molsons and put the sandwiches on the counter, J.D. sat beside him.

"Listen, every two weeks I send you seventy bucks, but apparently that's not enough incentive for you to give me a status report. Are you learning much in Auto Tech or did you already know most of it? How's the social life? You meet any girls?"

Originally Jake planned to get his son settled quickly, but now he found his curiosity getting the better of him. J.D. finished his first grilled cheese and answered.

"Good news Dad, it's not a waste of money. I'm learning from the best teachers, so put your mind at ease. The social life is bullshit, only thirty percent of the kids on campus are girls, and most of them are locals with boyfriends. That's it!"

"I'm sorry about the social scene. What about Andrew?"

"My roommate is breezing by in the academics. We're not tight, but I guess we're cool."

They shared another round of beers and exchanged news about their lives. Whenever Jake tried to pry out any specifics, academically speaking, the young man managed to skirt the inquiry and deftly elude his father. Even when Jake attempted to discuss plans for the next semester, the boy sidestepped. After fifteen minutes, Jake saw the boy was completely worn out.

"It's late. Finish that Molson and go to bed. I'm glad you're home. Get some sleep."

৵৽৶

Annie and her brother slept late, which allowed Jake and Sandy time to talk. The two most pressing concerns were Annie's college search and J.D.'s upcoming semester at Vermont Tech. After filling Sandy's coffee cup a second time along with his own, Jake opened the touchy subject of Annie's plans for college. He took a diplomatic approach keenly aware of his daughter's preferences.

"Where does Annie want to go to school? Has she told you?"

"Remember when you gave her that initial selection list over a month ago. She crossed half of them off within a week. Lately she's been researching on her own and talking to her teachers. I think she's narrowed the field. She realizes that Cornell is out of reach. You told her that didn't you? I hope you realize she took your assessment as an insult. I have a college viewbook I want you to look over."

Sandy went into the dining room and brought back the catalogue.

"We've already visited Penn State, Delaware, and SUNY Binghamton. Annie didn't like any of those schools. I really wanted to take a tour of Hofstra, out on Long Island, and I thought that would be fine with Annie, but she said "no way." Take a look at this. It's from American University in Washington, D.C.

Taking the glossy brochure from his wife, Jake scanned through it and stopped at the page regarding college costs. It was excessive, but Jake refrained from commenting. A full price admission ticket to American would cost thirty-two thousand dollars, not even counting a monthly expense allowance. Before he could offer an opinion, Sandy quickly noticed his forlorn expression and chimed in.

"Jake listen, this is the type of school I think we should check out. Don't you agree? Anyway, I'm taking Annie for an open house next Friday. I'm using a sick day. I already told her, and she's up for it. What do you think?"

Jake wanted to be tactful, especially because it was a holiday. He thought there was no need to upset his wife with negativity of any kind.

307

"Sandy, that's a good idea. I think she deserves to go to a top school like American. Please remember to stop by their Financial Aid office. Take her report card and SAT scores. My problem is that without some merit-based assistance, I don't think I can make it work for eight semesters. But go anyway. American has a lot to offer."

"Thanks honey. I'll tell Annie later. I'd better start cleaning the turkey. Will you please do the guest bathroom and put a sign on the door so the kids leave it alone. I'd like Annie to set the table by noon. I'll put the china and crystal out for her."

"I'm looking forward to my brother's visit, and so are the kids. I hope I can get him off the couch and tear him away from the Dallas Cowboys. He's a member of the brotherhood of couch potatoes. I'm gonna get started now."

They both went their separate ways to get the house in shape. Sandy did most of the food prep and Jake did the house cleaning. The kids slept past eleven, but neither parent cared. They were grateful they had time to prepare the holiday meal and get the house in order. The mood in the house was upbeat and positive.

☜☞

Ellen left for Summit Pond as soon as the weather warmed up. This was the first Thanksgiving that she was spending alone, and she was feeling very unsettled. Just yesterday, Jake had told her the critical importance of getting out of the house and taking a long walks to keep her head clear. Admittedly, she missed the interaction with the boys. Her twice-weekly calls to East Point weren't enough to satisfy an emotional need to stay connected. Most of the conversations were limited to casual updates about school or their activities, and not much else. What saddened her the most was that neither boy called her that morning to wish her a Happy Thanksgiving. She knew that without Guy's urging, they probably wouldn't.

After half an hour at the pond her mind wasn't clear at all. It was saturated with worry, not only about the boys, but about her own survival. At water's edge she noticed the wind created small waves of turbulence on the surface of the pond and it reminded her of the ambivalence she was feeling.

She'd finished her resume and for the past couple of weeks had been knocking on the doors of recruiting agencies and sending out letters of introduction to banks, financial services, and upscale retail outlets. In spite of the time and energy she spent, no concrete offers came back, which further increased her insecurity. The reality was that for the present time she was still dependent on Guy's financial support and he could end it at any time. There was no legal binding agreement in force.

308

Ellen was vulnerable and she knew it. Fortunately, the other day she had received a letter from Guy saying he would agree to pay for the divorce in return for a no-fault settlement.

Ellen believed that the boys would continue to stay with their father because Joey told her that they would be moving into a three-bedroom townhouse the first of the year. She feared that any active role in their lives was coming to an end. Hence she wondered, would her boys think she was a bad mother for giving them up without a fight? Would Guy tell the boys that she abandoned them for selfish reasons? Would they believe him? Would she get to see them for Christmas? But there simply were no answers.

Yesterday, Jake worked a half-day. The weather cooperated, so they went to Bear Mountain State Park. While on a walk, he shared his thoughts about the difficult times that were coming.

"Ellen, if we're only focused on our fears about the future we'll be robbing each other of hope. I've come to believe that wherever there's misery, you'll find the absence of hope. Personally, I think the loss of hope is actually the abandonment of our dreams. In a symbolic way, I truly think that hope is our mother, she's nurturing and kind-hearted. So no matter how scared we get, we have to believe in hope and that our destiny is to be together."

Ellen found the wisdom of those words to be prophetic because during the past two decades, the one feeling that overwhelmed all others was her sense of hopelessness. It amazed her how complex and mysterious Jake was. On one hand, he could be very entertaining and humorous, but when he was serious and philosophical, he became another character. To her, he was a mixture of warrior, medicine man, and shaman. He exhibited an intense desire to clarify the most perplexing problems, using Eastern philosophy, Taoist teachings, or the wisdom gained through the heartbreak of mistakes. Jake seemed able to simplify the most troubling issues. The best example was helping to cope with the anxiety she felt about the boys being raised by their dad. He offered her the following insight.

"I think if Guy was intelligent enough to graduate from Emory and smart enough to know he should be in business by himself, I'm quite sure, that he'll know how to find answers. Obviously, they're all going through a tough transition, but eventually things will level off."

Jake also encouraged her to visit the boys in December, even though she initially believed it might be a trap to lure her back. "Nonsense," Jake had told her, adding, "The past eight weeks should tell you that Guy's much better off having the boys with him. Don't forget, a New York judge would've forced him to pay alimony and child support to the tune of four grand a month."

Until Jake explained the situation in such stark terms and exposed the money angle, it never really occurred to her that Guy had an advantage.

Ellen spent most of Thanksgiving afternoon thinking about her future. She had complete trust in Jake but didn't trust herself. Too many bad decisions during the tumultuous years of her marriage had taken away her confidence. Tomorrow she planned to try an employment agency and see what it offered. Even without job security or a place to live, Ellen still felt optimistic about her future. Although she missed the boys terribly, she could depend on Jake, and that was enough to make her believe in the promise of tomorrow. She knew he was right; to lose hope is to abandon your dreams.

❧

The company came an hour later than expected, which was typical for Jake's older brother and his wife, Marie. Skip brought Sandy a bouquet of flowers, which prompted a comment from his nephew.

"Uncle Skip, couldn't you have brought me a case of Coors or something like that. What's with the flowers? You must be hoping to take leftovers home with you."

"J.D. you don't need the beer, but I happen to know your mother appreciates beautiful things. Now young man, why don't you build us a fire? Make yourself useful."

Missy's barking brought Annie down from her room to welcome her favorite uncle with a warm hug and a kiss. Marie stood silently by and watched her husband of seven years turn on his charm, complimenting Annie on her appearance.

"Well I'll be snake bit, you're a beauty! I'll tell you this. If I was your father I'd never let you out of my sight. I'd send you to community college so I could keep my eye on you!"

Uncle Skip was a genuine character, possessed with humor and a working man's appreciation for hard work, common sense, straight talk, and good food. He was well-liked by everyone who knew him, whether on the job or in friendship. Whenever he visited, it was always a treat for the kids since he was a superb storyteller and self-effacing man. Jake loved his older brother but tolerated Marie, who usually had a hard edge about her at family gatherings. She was a professional hairdresser, paid to listen to bullshit from her clients for a decent tip. Jake thought Marie was argumentative by nature, and lacked a sense of humor.

Sandy and Jake served the turkey dinner at four. The food was scrumptious. Following the feast, everyone relaxed for an hour watching TV before Sandy brought out her homemade apple, blueberry

310

and pumpkin pies. The desserts brought raves from everyone, even Marie. As with most families, there were many ongoing conversations around the dinner table, some pleasant and some controversial.

When the last cup of coffee was finished and the conversation died down, Jake rose from the table and began to clear off the dishes telling the family, "Go find a comfortable place in the family room and relax by the fire. J.D. has it all set up. I'll do the cleanup. Come on, move out."

"Listen to my younger brother. He always likes taking charge. Nothing ever changes with him. Jake, go ahead and clean up the mess. I'll entertain the ladies, and your son will take care of the fire. You don't mind if I watch the game, I don't need the sound so don't worry."

"Go ahead. I'll be coming for you after I finished the cleanup."

An hour later, Jake signaled his big brother it was time for a walk. Skip, well-fed and rested, took the cue, got dressed in his leather overcoat and scarf, and met his brother in the garage. When they turned to start down Treetop Terrace, Jake began.

"Did Marie enjoy the dinner? She's pretty detached. Sometimes I think she has trouble with family conversation. I mean when Dad was alive, we sat together at a holiday meal and everybody had two cents to say about everything. You know what I mean? Remember when the ole man used to cut up a twenty-five pounder and sit back and listen to the insane ramblings of the brood. God that man loved to preside over holiday meals! When we were kids, we ate the best meals during those times. That's what made the holidays so special. You know Skip, I think about him every day, and he's been gone for twenty years. He was a hell of a man, a real man. No bullshit allowed. Do you stay in contact with Florence?"

"Yeah, I call her about every two weeks, but her health is deteriorating with that Alzheimer's. I know you don't think much about her. You got your reasons, and it's cool with me. I don't know about the rest of the clan. It's a damn good thing that she's with Kathy. I hear her kids take real good care of Mom."

When Jake didn't ask anything else about Florence, Skip knew better than to push it any further.

"Jake, Marie has no clue about family stuff. She was an only child, and it must have been pretty lonely for her growing up. Then again, her father was an alcoholic and left her mother when Marie was pretty young. She doesn't talk much about him. I think he lives somewhere in Europe. To be honest with you, I don't know how I've lasted this long with her. Sometimes, I try to figure out why I got married at all after twenty-five years living a life of freedom. Shit, it's all lost to me."

"Bullshit! You got scared when you turned fifty, and she was available. Now its seven years later and I'll bet you've regretted that decision a thousand times. Do you even like her? Forget I asked that."

"Jake, you may not look it, but you're gonna be fifty next year. You really shouldn't be questioning me about how I panicked at fifty and married Marie. Is your future that solid? Cause I'll tell ya, I've known you and Sandy since you started dating, and you're no facsimile to that couple. So who are you kiddin? It's all show between you and her. Don't get mad, I'm not knocking you. This…this is what you wanted. You got your career, a big house, beautiful wife, and wonderful kids. You've provided everything for your family, but I think it's been at your expense. I've never second-guessed you. You're the educated man, not me. As you would say, I'm a grunt. But for a long time now, you and Sandy have just been passing time. So don't lecture me about Marie. Enough said, let's get off this shit. What's new?"

"Annie's going to be choosing a college in the next couple of months. Frankly, I'm worried about paying for it. Sandy wants her to attend a big-name school, and having two kids in college is a financial nightmare. But Sandy's right about one thing, Annie deserves the choice."

"Here we go again. I've heard all this shit before. Why does everything always fall on your shoulders? Doesn't Sandy have inheritance money? Could she help you? You told me she made a bundle in the market. I don't understand. Why doesn't she part with some and contribute to make up the shortfall? What's the problem? That ain't fair!"

Skips comment hit home, and it embarrassed Jake. "Look Skip. The bond fund was set aside to pay for college. Sandy has made it clear to me that the money she inherited isn't for the kids. It's hers and most of that cash is in the market. I suppose that's my fault. Maybe I should have made some demands. I don't know. That goddamned money has been more of a curse than a blessing. You have no idea…none. It's my shit to deal with. Fuck it!"

"You're goddamned right you made a mistake. You should've never agreed to that. I mean, you're gonna tell me her father told her on his death bed some bullshit about how his money should be spent? Sandy's foolish, and in the end this is gonna come back to haunt her. I don't know how or when, but if she wants Annie to go to a big name school…Let's drop it and keep walking. I'm getting pissed."

The brothers returned to the house to attend to their spouses. Skip sat between Annie and Marie, and did a curtain call with another half-hour of personal monologue, stories about his job, gambling, movies, and political commentary. Jake sat with Sandy enjoying his brother's show. It was obvious, Annie and J.D. loved their uncle and they begged for more. After a while Marie had heard enough, and began hinting every five minutes that it was time to leave until Skip finally gave in.

Jake walked Skip and Marie out to their car around ten. He opened the passenger door for Marie and gave her a kiss on her cheek.

"It was great for you to join us for the holiday. Thanks for coming."

Then Jake proceeded to shake his brother's hand, placing a twenty-dollar bill in his palm. The modest gift to his brother was Jake's custom whenever they were together.

"Well Skip, another Thanksgiving is over. All I can say is I'm grateful we're still connected, and glad you made the long trip to celebrate it with us. Stay in touch."

Later that evening when the house was quiet and the last embers in the fireplace were dull red, Jake sat alone reflecting on Skip's visit. He cursed himself for letting his brother know about his financial worries. Recently, Skip went through bankruptcy and for him to complain about money for college was uncalled for. He resolved to call him tomorrow and apologize for his bitching.

Just before midnight, J.D. entered the family room and sat opposite his father. Jake was surprised to see him, and started a conversation.

"Did you enjoy seeing your uncle?"

"I swear he never changes. It's hard to believe you're brothers."

"Well there were four brothers, all trying to get by. I was always close to Skip, maybe because he dropped out of school at seventeen and joined the Marines. As far as my other two brothers....whatever. Anyway, how's school going? Did you register for next semester?"

"That's why I'm sitting here. Dad, I know how hard you pushed to get me into college, and I really appreciate it, but I don't want you to pay for next semester. I've decided to quit. It's not for me. There's nothing wrong with Tech. Maybe you can help me figure out what's next for me, but I'm failing math and without passing it I can't move ahead."

It was a long day and Jake was too tired to argue, reason, or come up with the right response for his son's declaration. Admittedly, he felt foolish for not seeing this coming. Like most parents of a first semester freshman, he hoped his son would stick it out until the end of the year.

"Are you sure about this? I mean...maybe you'll change your mind?"

"Dad, I won't let you throw your money away. You worked hard for it. Use it for Annie. She's got the brains and the drive. I know you'll figure something out for me. That's what you do best. I've had this on my mind for over a month. I'll tell ya, I'm glad I finally got it out. I'm gonna up to bed now. Let me sleep late tomorrow. Night, Dad."

"Wait a second. You didn't tell your mother? Did you?"

"You kiddin', that's your job."

CHAPTER 42

Ellen's big break came when she least expected it. After attending a tedious day long job fair at the Marriott in Newburgh, she drove back to Middletown feeling frustrated and tired. Five minutes after getting in, she noticed a phone message on her answering machine. Figuring it might be news about the boys, she hit the play button.

"Ms. Eastman, this is Century Personnel. My name is Gail Sanders. I may have something for you. The number is 346-4280."

Ellen checked the time, 4:45. Maybe she could reach the agency before it closed for the day. Without hesitation, she dialed the number hoping someone would pick up.

"Hello, may I speak with Ms. Sanders? She left a message to call."

"Hold on. I'll see if she left for the day."

"This is Gail Sanders. May I help you?"

"This is Ellen Eastman, I received your message and…"

"I'm glad you called back. I think I have something for you. Can you get here by 9 a.m. sharp tomorrow morning? I'll prep you for an interview at a financial firm that needs an Administrative Assistant for one of its investment specialist. Your resume looks promising. Generally, I have good hunches about these things and I think you might fit their needs. Are you still looking for a job?"

"Yes I am, and I've been hoping for an opportunity like this. Where are you located?"

"1100 Main Street in Middletown, it's the corner brick building."

"I'll be there at nine. Thank you so much."

"Ms. Eastman, one more thing, they're willing to cover the fee."

With only two weeks until the New Year, the opportunity couldn't have come at a better time. Too excited to eat, she undressed, put on her workout sweats, and exercised strenuously for an hour, all the while worried about tomorrow. When it was time for dinner, she used the microwave to nuke a *Weight Watchers* chicken dinner, but was scarcely able to eat it. Her stomach was in knots, so she decided to walk around the neighborhood. Although it was a chilly twenty degrees outside, it didn't deter her.

Over the course of the evening her mood swings were in full gallop and the "what ifs" flowed in and out of her consciousness, interrupting her ability to focus on the prep for the interview. By eleven-thirty she finally surrendered, dropped the note cards on the end table, and poured a large glass of merlot to calm her nerves. In the final moments before she fell asleep, all she kept thinking was, *I've got to get this job...I've got to.*

When Jake called the next morning she couldn't contain her excitement, "Jake, today is my big day! I've got an interview at 9 with a recruiter at Century Personnel, in Middletown. She's prepping me for a job as an Administrative Assistant at a firm in Newburgh. Last night...My God, I could barely think straight. What are my chances? What do I need to know?"

"Hey, take it easy. Just slow down! Your luck has finally changed and your chances are excellent."

"Jake, tell me I'm going to be make it happen. Why am I so nervous? Please tell me I'll be fine?"

"Ellen, honestly, I was the same way when I interviewed for the job at Middletown. I think it was because I wanted that particular position. When you have time and money on your side, it's a lot less stressful but in a situation like yours you've got neither. Yeah, I bet you're nervous. Now listen. First and foremost, follow the specific advice the recruiter gives you. They know what there're talking about. Believe me they want the commission. Stay calm and listen attentively. Your overall demeanor will be assessed in a matter of minutes. No matter what the personnel people ask you, answer in a professional manner. Whether you're a hundred percent sure or not, don't let them suspect you have a down side. In a job like that, they're looking for a confident individual. Men in business world expect their support people to handle their clients. Get the salary parameters from the recruiter. Same thing goes about medical benefits. The recruiter has the answers. I'll call you tonight. It's time to grow your wings. Good luck!"

Gail Sanders turned out to be supportive, kind, and articulate. She knew her job and her attitude, enthusiasm, and self-confidence were an inspiration to Ellen. They were nearly the same age and she also mentioned that she was divorced and living with two daughters. The two women may have been complete strangers, yet they managed to connect and broke down the formalities quickly.

After thirty minutes of strategic advice, Ellen felt prepared for the big challenge only an hour away in Newburgh. Some parts of the advice were repeated for emphasis. As they both got up from the interview, Gail walked Ellen to the lobby to give her one final suggestion.

"Make sure you keep eye contact at all times. Be conscious of your body language and speak clearly without using any slang. Speak and act with confidence. Good luck!"

Linda Williams, the personnel manager at Horizon Financial

Services seemed pleased with the candidate sitting opposite her following a brief period of reviewing Ellen's resume.

"I think you're the person we're looking for. Is there anything you want to add?"

Ellen remembered Jake's advice. *Say nothing personal during the interview.*

"Ms. Williams, everything on the resume is accurate. I'm prepared to start whenever you want. There are no extenuating circumstances that would change that."

"Thank you for being candid. You'll be having an interview with Mr. Spano in fifteen minutes."

"Ms. Williams, could you direct me to the restroom. I'd like to freshen up."

"It's down at the end of the corridor on the left."

Ellen excused herself and appreciated having a few minutes to gather her thoughts. As she looked in the mirror for one last check, she was nervous but ready for the task at hand. She repeated Jake's words of encouragement before she left to face Mr. Spano. "Be confident and be calm."

Jake kept his promise and called Ellen that same night. He used his daughter's phone line while she was watching TV in the family room. Ellen picked up after a single ring knowing it had to be Jake.

"I got it! I got the job. I start the first of the year. What a Christmas present. I'm so excited!"

"Like I've told you before, you're growing wings to fly on your own. I'm so proud of you. I knew you would succeed. We'll celebrate on Saturday afternoon. Can you believe it all happened so fast?"

"It was like one moment I was lost and wandering on the beach, then the fog lifted and I found my way. Instead of hiking on Saturday can we come back here? I have a surprise for you."

"Are you sure? I mean in the daylight. What about the neighbors?"

ॐॐॐ

They couldn't help but burst out laughing when the electric garage door closed behind them. "I feel like a kid back in high school, trying to get make some out time," Jake said as he jumped out of the van.

The weather was cold, gray, and blustery so it was just as well they skipped the forest. It had been almost a month since the birthday celebration, and the back of the Aerostar wasn't conducive to serious lovemaking in freezing temperatures.

"Do you want your surprise now, or would you rather wait?"

"My darling Ellen, believe me, just being here to celebrate with you is a surprise. I can't imagine how you even got any sleep last night."

"I didn't. Hey, let me show you the treat I made for us."

Ellen took Jake's hand and let him into the kitchen. There on the counter sat a homemade blueberry pie. She kissed him on both cheeks and then said. "I bought some Haagen Dazs Vanilla ice cream to go with it. Well, are you surprised? I think this is the best way to celebrate. Should we have it now or would you rather go upstairs? I bet the pie will taste much better later."

Ellen didn't have anywhere near the level of anxiety she had the night of her birthday dinner. This time, when Jake waited for her, she stepped into the bedroom and leaned against the door frame in a teasing pose. She wore an unbuttoned long-sleeved denim shirt with plum colored bra and matching thong. As she walked casually to the edge of the bed she dropped the shirt and turned a full circle.

"Ellen, getting that job loosened you up. Yikes, you look terrific!"

"It's been a long time and I've missed you something awful. I understand the limitations of that old van of yours and I'm going to make up for it right here and right now. Come and kiss me."

This time, their lovemaking was supercharged with passion and erotic anticipation. Ellen took an active role from the start and never let up. Her kisses, her touches, and her level of desire matched Jakes. When she shed her remaining garments, it wasn't in the dark. She wanted him to gaze at her because she was comfortable with the way she looked and she was confident being the lover she was. Occasionally, they would stop caressing areas of maximum pleasure and just hold each other.

When Jake took the initiative and brought her upon him, she responded with a moan and then told him, "You're so good to me and you never put yourself first. What a wonderful gift you've given me."

As they accelerated their rhythm, the lovemaking rose to the extreme limits of satisfaction. Once again, they climaxed together. He kissed her again and again then told her, "Darlin', you were absolutely the best. You're so sexy when you're looking down at me biting your lip."

"You're my warrior. I'll never want another man."

"I believe you. Umm…what about the pie? I'm starving'"

They both laughed. Jake's sense of timing and humor were contagious. They gobbled down the pie with an appetite that lovers have. Jake ate another piece without the ice cream just to prove his appreciation for her baking skills.

"Jake, what's the winter going to be like? I mean…will I ever get to see you during the week? I'm going to be starting my new job soon.

Will we only see each other on Saturdays?

"Shhhh…Are you happy right now? Are you satisfied? Are things looking up? Answer me."

"I'm the most happy. My life is finally coming together, and it's making sense."

"Then my darling, things are hopeful and that's the best feeling in the world. We'll find our way. Every phone call and every moment we have together will fill us with the knowledge that our lives are connected. I'm so happy you've turned the corner and you can see some daylight ahead. You'll be a working girl in a short time. Boy, will your life be different then. Isn't it great to be in control of your own destiny? I hope I'm not too far behind you. Shit, it takes a hell-of-a-lot of resolve to wait."

"What about your situation Jake/"

"No more talk. Moments like this are very rare in the scheme of things. Let's just enjoy it."

CHAPTER 43

The sun came up at 7:16 in Orange County, New York and the New Millennium began without the institutions of the United States coming to an abrupt halt. All the dire predictions about power blackouts, computer collapse, terrorist attacks, and commuter chaos proved to be false. Planes took off on time and trains left their terminals without a glitch. Investments weren't deleted from crashing data banks, and nuclear missiles remained in their concrete silos. Common folk returned to work after celebrating New Years, and among them Horizon Financial Group's newest employee Ms. Ellen Eastman.

At 8 a.m. on January 2nd, Ellen started her job as the Administrative Assistant to one of the top producers of the firm. Joe Spano was her boss, and she took orders directly from him. Working with Ellen was Marybeth McMahon, a part-time college student and clerical worker who was efficient half of the time and lost in post-adolescent space the other half. To suggest Marybeth was scatter-brained would be an understatement. She was plain "ditzy." Nevertheless, Joe Spano liked her in spite of her shortcomings, and Ellen was given the responsibility of keeping her focused with assorted secretarial tasks. Ellen's only problem was being able to find her, because she managed to sneak away and socialize whenever an opening appeared. Not surprisingly, supervising the post adolescent wasn't mentioned during the interview. However, Ellen was determined to keep a close watch over Marybeth.

Ellen's office was a windowless cube directly outside of Joe's spacious mahogany paneled kingdom. She had at her desk a new Dell computer, loaded with Microsoft Office XP. It was a fully functional workstation with fax attachment and laser printer. There was also a phone system capable of handling eight incoming calls. All customer information regarding investment status, insurance inquiries, or any pressing concerns from Spano's clients were directed to her from the main switchboard. She had to be diplomatic as well as knowledgeable when dealing with the clients, especially if she got the impression they were anxious about their investments.

Ellen was a graduate of Georgia State University with a business degree, but that sheepskin was awarded nearly twenty years ago. Consequently, she began the job with a sustained level of trepidation due to her long absence from the world of finance. It wasn't that she didn't know the fundamentals or that she lacked sufficient people skills, quite the reverse. However, from day one it became evident there was too much to know and never enough time to learn it. Unfortunately, the woman Ellen replaced gave her only a week of indoctrination. Consequently, Ellen's level of job stress at the beginning was excessive, and she resigned herself to climbing the mountain of knowledge one step at a time. That was Jake's advice. He also told her to stay focused on each task and stop thinking her boss carried a stopwatch and was spying on her.

Spano was a fair but demanding taskmaster. He was a perfectionist, relentless about time management, organization, and getting things done properly. Moreover, he wanted production without ever having to raise his voice or display a short fuse. Direct eye contact was his instrument of intimidation, and he knew how to use it effectively. He rarely lectured Ellen on office protocol or made her feel inadequate in the first couple of weeks. But, if a letter to a million-dollar investment client wasn't absolutely perfect in format, spelling, and grammar he called her in and personally pointed out the mistake. At first, Ellen worried way too much about his criticism or indignant stare. Then gradually, after a few weeks of daily exposure to Mr. Spano, she began to handle his comments in the proper context.

Ellen never second-guessed him and performed her job in a strictly professional manner. She remained calm when Spano was agitated and cooperative when he lost all patience. Even when he sent her across the street to get him lunch, she just did it and didn't get hung up about women's rights. By the end of the first month, Ellen thought she was well-suited for working with Spano. The problem was that so far, he'd given her no indication of her job performance.

Her level of anxiety gradually diminished during the first week of February. After a month Spano began to loosen up and, although their relationship was still very formal, she thought he was satisfied with her job performance. The affirmation finally came when he stopped by her desk to inquire about a misplaced file.

"Ellen, did you locate that Johnstone file? I need it now."

"I haven't found it yet, but I have Marybeth checking with the insurance people to see if it's over there. I'll stop what I'm doing and look myself if you need it in the next five minutes."

"Ellen, would you come into my office and bring a pad with you"

Sitting across from him, Ellen's heart was racing well above idle speed worrying about the file.

"Ellen, maybe that file was sent to the equities department. I'm sure it's probably there. Relax for a minute, will you? Before I give you some notes on the Sullivan investments, I want you to know that I'm very satisfied with how things have worked out since you came onboard. I know I'm demanding, but you seem to fit in quite satisfactorily. I think it's about time you ease up. How do you like it here?"

"Actually, I'm pleased with the way things have gone so far, and I appreciate your patience with me. As you know, this first month had been hectic…a lot goes on every day, and the clients are used to getting their calls answered promptly. Sometimes you're not available, and that's challenging. Each day I learn a little more and I expect to improve. Thanks for giving me your vote of confidence. I needed it."

Spano liked her, especially because of her work-ethic and professional demeanor. He then said, "I know things get pretty crazy around here but you've handled my clients very well. I've also heard good things from the insurance people regarding your work. One more thing, please continue monitoring Marybeth. I've noticed some improvement lately. I appreciate that very much. Keep up the good work!"

Ellen was careful not to discuss anything of a personal nature at the workplace. That was Jake's advice and she stuck to it from day one. When she sat with the other office personnel during lunch, she listened to group gossip, but rarely engaged in any discussion. Strange as it seemed to her fellow employees, her reserved behavior worked to her benefit. By never taking sides in office politics, bashing fellow employees, bad mouthing her boss, or tossing rumors around, the staff accepted her within a few weeks, and Ellen's dedication and professional demeanor was obvious to everyone.

She settled into her workweek routine quickly. She got up at 6 a.m. to make coffee, exercised for fifteen minutes, drank a cup, showered, dressed, and sipped the second cup while watching the morning news on TV. She left by 7:15 so she could get to work a few minutes early. Her day usually began by checking a voice mail system Spano used to set up the day. The tape gave Ellen the priorities for the day. Soon she acclimated herself with no problem to his style of management. Her predecessor had told her Spano was very predictable, and that his moves could be anticipated and planned for. The information turned out to be a godsend.

Most of the time, she returned home from Newburgh by 5:30. Gradually, she fell into an evening routine that flowed smoothly. First, she'd get out of her work clothes, put on jeans and a sweatshirt, prepare a meal, go for a thirty-minute walk, and read, watch TV, or work on a painting. Every single night she looked forward to hearing from Jake. He had promised to try to reach her between 8 and 10 p.m. Generally, connecting with him even for only five minutes, made the rest of her evening go by in an acceptable fashion, but she missed him terribly. Of course, waiting for Saturday afternoons took every bit of her patience, just as Jake had predicted it would.

❧

Unlike Ellen, who was getting acclimated to her new lifestyle, Jake was constantly challenged with family issues. January proved to be a turning point in ways he never thought were possible. First and foremost, it became clear to him that his marriage was living on borrowed time. The arctic like cold of a New York winter was similar to his feelings about Sandy, and lately the kids too.

A measure of the depth of Jake's disconnection occurred when the first major winter storm hit in late January. With the schools shut for two days and the Carr family stuck in the house with no possibility of escape, it became an unbearable nightmare for Jake. He recalled years ago, when the kids were younger, that a three-foot blizzard gave them time to play together, whether outside or inside. Sandy would bake cookies and J.D. and Annie would sleigh-ride all afternoon. Now six years later, the glue that once held them together had lost its bond. Whenever they were stuck in the house, cabin fever hit them all. If not for the size of the house, another crisis would have developed.

On the plus side, Jake fortunately was able to use his connection with a fellow counselor at Orange County Community College to get J.D. enrolled for the spring semester. The fall spent at Vermont Tech had sufficiently changed J.D. to push him forward in his auto tech education, but he still remained a problem at home. His moods would vary with the success or failure of his latest project, whether it was fixing an old Ford Bronco or busted 4-weeler. Now that he was living at home, it became an ever-increasing challenge for Jake to make concessions, especially with the junk piling up in the garage and spilling out on the driveway. Regardless of how many times he reprimanded his son for his lack of consideration, the boy continued to disrupt the family peace.

There was only one place for Jake to hide during the winter and that was the basement. After taking Missy on her nightly walk, regardless of the weather, he'd retreat to the comfort of his recliner to plan his next summer road trip, read a novel, or watch a documentary on PBS. Whenever it was safe he called Ellen to let her know she was in his thoughts.

In February, he ordered a Ford 150 pickup from a dealer in Middletown. Jake was the counselor for the owner's son and had assisted the student throughout high school. The senior had applied for early decision to the Arizona State and had gained admission. In appreciation, the father permitted Jake to pay only three hundred dollars over cost. The vehicle was due to be delivered in March. As was his way with all financial planning, Jake had saved seven years for his dream truck so he would own it free and clear.

Annie continued working part-time at a local Italian restaurant and kept busy at school with National Honor Society commitments along with her job as editor-in-chief of the school literary magazine. As the winter progressed, it became evident that mother and daughter believed American University was the perfect choice. The cost was roughly three times that of any SUNY school and would drain every dollar from the bond fund. Regardless of Jake's financial concerns, Sandy gave Annie the final approval to go. Her anticipated acceptance on March 1st was fast approaching and a meltdown was in the works.

The college decision to attend American wasn't fully supported by Jake, and Annie knew it. He wanted her to go to Penn State, SUNY Binghamton, or the University of Delaware. What Annie didn't know was what her mother had told Jake when he had asked Sandy to contribute.

Jake thought he knew what Sandy might answer, but wanted to believe it would be different. One night in late January after dinner they were having coffee when he posed the question. "Sandy, I hope Annie gets some merit money to offset the costs, but it may not be enough. How do you feel about contributing from your inheritance? After all, you were the one who guaranteed her choice. I thought it was out of reach. Will you help?"

She looked across the dinner table at him and without hesitation told him bluntly, "I believe it's our responsibility to pay for Annie's college education with the money we've put aside. You can't expect my inheritance to pay for it. My father didn't want it used that way. I'm sorry, but that's my answer."

Stunned by her icy response, and full of resentment for how she used her dead father as an excuse, Jake stood up and began to clear off the table without saying another word. He hated her for that.

Later that same evening, while walking Missy in freezing weather, Jake knew it was over. He'd been walking the edge, and Sandy finally had pushed him over. Strangely, as he turned to head up Highland Road, the wind blew fiercely and made the tears of disappointment sting his cheeks as his inner voice spoke to him. *Jake, you've got to accept that this is karma. Goddamn her father and his fucking money. First, the kids suffered from Sandy's extended grief and now, eight years later, the shit is still coming. First, it was her indulgence and now it's her greed. Sandy, I don't even know you anymore. I'm sad because it didn't have to be this way. When we first met, and even when the children came along, less was always more as far as I was concerned. All right, Annie will go to American. I'll make it work. But tonight you knocked out whatever was left inside for you. I'll hang on. I'll play the game and get Annie settled in college. Then I'm going to pack it in. To go wrong and not alter one's course can truly be defined as going wrong.*

ঙ্কৃ

When February came, it brought some joy back to Jake's world when Ellen picked up her new Jeep Cherokee. Previously, they had gone car shopping all over Orange County, trying to broker a deal. The best advice Jake gave Ellen, concerning the new purchase, was to ask her married sister, who was well-off, to provide her an interest-free loan. She knew about Ellen's strained financial situation and sent the check within a week. That money, along with the trade-in value of her van, allowed them to make the deal. It was the first new vehicle Ellen ever owned, and her name was on the title.

Only two hurdles remained for Ellen, the alimony settlement and finding an affordable place to live. The divorce was on the docket for March, which meant Ellen needed to be out of the Westgate home thirty days after the decree. Whatever equity she would receive for the house was still undecided.

A week before Valentine's Day, they met in the usual place and returned to Ellen's home. She had her Jeep, reasonable job security making thirty thousand a year as an Administrative Assistant, and the long-awaited divorce was pending. On this particular day there was every reason to be hopeful, yet Jake surmised something was wrong.

"Ellen, I know it's been a tough month for both of us. You look troubled. Am I getting a pink slip? Did that anal boss of yours blow up over something?"

His comment brought a smile to her face and reminded her why she loved him.

"Jake, you're never getting fired. What would I do without you? It's nothing that concerns you. I can't shake it. I got a call from Atlanta last night."

"Are the boys all right? Did your husband lose his business? Come on, tell me."

"Nothing like that…The boys are fine. They like the townhouse and especially the freedom he gives them. It seems like whenever I call, the message is always the same, things are good. Anyway, I got the word that I've got to be out by April."

"Ellen, shit, that's no surprise. Why does it matter? Let him have his house. We'll find you a place for you to live. I'll help…Really, it's not a problem. It is what it is."

She was surprised by his curt reply. It sometimes bothered her that he always saw things so clearly whenever they applied to her, but he kept very private about his own problems. Pausing for a moment, she shared her concerns.

"Jake, don't take this the wrong way, but you have no idea what I'm going through. You really don't. I love you, but until you're in my shoes in this divorce game, you'd better stop acting like it's all so simple and so black and white. You oughta realize that this isn't a parent workshop with you directing the blind and disabled to the Promised Land. Come on, for once, try and put yourself in my place?"

Jake sat motionless, as if he'd been zapped by a stun gun. It was the first time she'd ever called him on anything he advised. Like a wounded animal, he wanted to run and hide but he couldn't. He remained quiet until Ellen continued.

"That's not the only thing. Basically I have a take it or leave it property settlement. If I refuse, the divorce will stall. It's not what I expected. I actually thought he'd be more generous considering our twenty years together. That didn't happen. You know I can't afford to contest this in court. Now what do you think? It's not so simple is it? I wasted twenty years of my life and all it's worth is a few hundred a month. Now do you get it? Do you think that's fair? You haven't answered. What do think, Mr. Carr?"

Jake felt she had every reason to be upset with him. He thought, *Every fuckin' problem in the universe is always about unmet expectations. Shit, even my own. Will it ever change?* But Ellen was right. He wasn't living through her experience. Even so, he wanted to explain his position.

"Why would you expect anything to be different? The plain fact is that he's responsible for the welfare of the boys and that's a hell of a responsibility. He thinks that since you have no one to support but yourself, why he should pay you any more than the bare minimum. He's got all the headaches. I know it seems unfair. But sooner or later you've got to accept reality. What's a few hundred either way? Terminate the relationship, accept the settlement, and free yourself once and for all. That's what I think."

Later on that afternoon they snuggled on the couch while listening to *The Last of the Mohicans*. Their world was back in order, but she wanted to know when he'd open up and share his world with her.

"What about you Jake? What about your happiness? Lately, you won't even talk about your other life, the one with your family. You're always focused on mine. What can I do for you? Tell me!"

"This relationship has been about helping you find your way. Tell you what, after you get settled in your own place then we'll see where my path takes me."

CHAPTER 44

Annie received her letter of acceptance to American University on March 1st, just as Jake had expected. Immediately, there was a noticeable change for the better in her attitude, and with only fourteen weeks till graduation, she was easier to live with. Another visitation to AU was planned to take a closer look at the college and possibly secure a merit grant based on Annie's academic record. Meanwhile, Sandy spent all her spare time working on new curriculum with the intention of increasing her course selections at the private high school. He could see the road ahead and wanted her to be financially secure if and when he left. Until Ellen's divorce was a reality, Jake put his future plans on hold.

At home he continued following his daily routines, and never gave Sandy any indication of his intentions. Moreover, she never had any reason to suspect that Jake was unfaithful when he did his disappearing act on Saturdays. One change Sandy did notice more and more was that Jake seemed unwilling to share his thoughts with her. It wasn't as if he was purposely avoiding her, but more like they had fewer conversations about anything. When they happened to talk after dinner, Jake preferred to respond to her concerns about her job or her worries about J.D. and Annie. Although Sandy appreciated those conversations, they never were about their faltering relationship. Typically, if she questioned him about anything serious such as, where they would be in five years, or why they don't seem to be as happy as they once were? He would answer, "I'm fine, maybe a little tired, but things are ok with me."

In Jake's mind, Sandy's talk about the future was premature. Maybe that was his way of keeping his choices open. One thing was certain, if Sandy ever found out about his relationship with Ellen, his world would come crumbling down upon him. At the present time, he wasn't prepared for that to happen. As March began, things were stable. And Jake resolved to keep things that way as long as he could.

❧

On the morning of March 17th, Ellen called Jake from work to announce her divorce was finalized. She settled for a few hundred a month in alimony and an equity check based on a real estate appraisal of the Westgate property. Guy accepted custody of the boys, with Ellen having reasonable visitation rights. She was so excited when she called that Jake had to put her on hold and ask the student to leave for a while.

"Ellen, thanks for waiting. Holy shit, from now on your

Independence Day will be celebrated on St. Patrick day. My buddy Kevin will get a kick out of the coincidence. When I think of all the changes you've gone through...wow! There's no need to give me the grim financial details. I'm sure Mr. Eastman made out pretty well. Then again, you got the freedom and he's got the responsibility. Try to think of it like that and you'll see it's an even split. So you're feeling pretty good...huh?"

"Well, I've got to be out of the house by April 15th, but I can accept that. Jake, I can't even begin to thank you for your support all these months. Do you believe it's almost been a year since we first met at your workshop? Imagine, who would've ever thought that by attending your seminar it would change my life forever. How was it possible for me to find someone like you? Karma...right?"

"That's the only answer I can come up with. You know, you're making me feel like a knight of the round table who saved you from a fate worse than death. How do you know I don't feel the same way about you? Remember that first time we secretly met and I played the song *Shipwrecked*? In a way I guess you've been coming to me and I've been waiting. Problem is...I'm still stuck in the final act. Anyway, I like the sound in your voice. Now you appreciate how important it is to have hope. There's still one more piece of unfinished business. This Saturday, I'll help you find a place to live. When that's complete, your new life will officially start. I'm very proud of your accomplishments, and you should be too. Take this for what its worth. Never look back and never second guess the decisions you've made. And like I told you a hundred times, Guy won't let anything go wrong with the boys, so rest assured they'll be fine."

"Thanks for reminding me of that, though I still worry about them. But you're right. Guy might hate me as much as I hate him, but he's a proud man and I suppose he'll do a good job with the boys. Saturday can't come soon enough. I love you so much. I wish you could come over and spend the night with me."

"I know you're happy. It's been a long time coming. What a hell of a story...probably would make a great movie. There have been plenty of women who've been in chains at some time in their lives. I think they would enjoy seeing a sister break free. Would you do me a favor? Write me a letter and put your thoughts and feelings down. In that way we'll always know how you felt on your day of independence. Listen Ellen, I really gotta go. You've waited twenty years to turn your life around and now you've succeeded. I think there's not greater sense of satisfaction than conquering our fears and moving ahead instead of standing still."

Jake received the letter two days later. As usual, it was hand delivered by Loretta. Then he went outside to read it in the solitude of the football bleachers where no one would disturb him.

My Dearest Jake:

Tonight I want you to know how I am feeling and what I am thinking. Thank you for sticking with me through all the ups and downs. I love you completely. I'm glad the legal part is finally over and I'll feel completely free once I'm in my own place. I still worry about the boys and wonder when I'll get to see them again. The last time I spoke with Joey he seemed fine. As far as Danny, I can only hope he learns to take responsibility for his actions and his father keeps a light leash on him. I must confess there are days when I miss them so much. And yet, I've come to understand there was no other choice for me. Guy planned it that way just as he controlled everything else in the family. Looking back, I feel the choice regarding the boys was a turning point in my life. I stood my ground and wouldn't surrender. All I wanted was to be treated kindly and with the respect that I thought I deserved. I don't regret taking the path I chose.

I feel like I've known you a very long time. You're kind, patient, and always considerate of my feelings. I love everything about you, your smile, your touch, and the feel of your body next to mine. I love every moment we spend together. There aren't enough of them. I can't imagine my life without you.

I knew from the very beginning you were special, a mysterious warrior from another time and place who just happened to come into my life by mere circumstance. I know, you call it karma. I loved you after the first time we were together. Something about you is so familiar and so comfortable. You're someone I can't do without. You are my soulmate. The one I have been searching for all my life.

Jake, I am convinced we were meant to be together. It's our destiny. You have my heart and I am yours forever. However long it takes, I will wait for you. I haven't forgotten your birthday is coming. I have something special for you.

With all my Love,
Ellen

CHAPTER 45

Of all the apartment complexes in Orange County, none was as attractive or well-maintained as Chestnut Hill Gardens, located a few miles south of Montgomery off of State Road 6. Although higher in rental fees when compared to the others they visited, it was Ellen's first choice.

They met with the rental agent on a dismal Saturday afternoon and took the tour of the one bedroom model. Ellen thought the apartment was well-suited for her needs. Sliders in the master bedroom led to a small deck that overlooked a spacious tree-filled courtyard. The living room had a wall of windows with blinds and a small dining area adjacent to it. There was space in the den for a piece of exercise equipment, her desk, and her easel. Other amenities included central air, a walk-in closet, and a new dishwasher in a Pullman style kitchen. It was seven hundred dollars a month and worth every cent.

After the mini tour, Ellen immediately asked for an application declaring to Jake emphatically, "This is the place. This is where I want to live." Five minutes later as she signed at the bottom she realized it was the first time she had used her former last name, Douglas, since back in college. A short time later when she introduced Jake to the agent as her "boyfriend," that was also a first.

After a cursory review of the application, the rental agent spoke in a reassuring manner to Ellen. "Ms. Douglas, everything is in order. Your salary is above our requirement for the lease. However, there's only one problem, I'll have to put you on our waiting list. If a two bedroom is what you wanted, we have one available. It seems that single professionals are always looking for the one bedroom units. Hopefully, some tenants will be moving by April 15th or May 1st. Why don't you call me next Saturday and I'll give you an update. You might get lucky, who knows. Will both of you be living here?"

Jake broke in before Ellen could answer. "The rental is for Ms. Douglas, just like the application indicates."

"Indeed it does. Is there anything else you want to know?"

"How much security deposit will Ms. Douglas need to secure the lease?"

"She'll have to bring me a certified check to cover a month-and-a half-along with the first months rent. That will be 1,750 dollars. Will that be a problem?"

Ellen responded instead of Jake as she extended her hand to the rental agent. "No it won't. Thank you so much for your time. I hope something opens up soon."

They left the rental office to survey the outside of the complex. It was immaculate. The grounds were superbly maintained and the landscaping first rate. There was a well-lit parking area, laundry facilities, and a large swimming pool. Most of all it was clean, quiet, and safe.

When they returned to the van, Jake looked around one more time thinking about the future. With a look of satisfaction on his face he said, "Angel, if I were looking for a place, this would be my first choice. When you consider how the model was setup, it's perfect in every way. I like that deck. One thing's for sure, you'll have to follow up on this every week. Do you have the money for the security deposit and rent? I'll help you if you need extra cash cause I want you to live in a place like this."

Gratified by his generosity, Ellen replied, "Luckily, I've saved twenty-five hundred. I think I'll be able to cover it. I've got to leave Westgate pretty soon. Jake, you've been so patient. Thanks."

"You're so close now. I've got to believe you'll end up here. I'm hopeful it will all work out."

"Jake, I want to have a place, a place for us. Somewhere you'll feel comfortable living."

"Well that may be in the cards, but we'll have to wait a bit longer. Anyway, how much time did Guy give you before he wants you out of Westgate? Is he asking or demanding? There's a difference."

"I think he'll let me stay a while longer. Then again, I can always beg. I've been doing jobs around that house every weekend. I've spackled and painted all the bedrooms. I even packed up the stuff in the basement and marked the boxes. I want to believe he'd do the right thing by me. Who knows?"

He didn't like Ellen's remark, not one bit. Whenever Ellen took the smallest step backwards to her former submissive self, it made him angry, but he decided to let the comment slide.

"Darlin, if you have to beg Guy for some consideration, well then, it's not worth it. I guess I think differently from you. What's it to him if you stay a couple more weeks? Did you ever consider that he owes you a little consideration, maybe some payback for sticking with him as long as you did? Anyway, please don't tell me about begging. I can't handle it. You've more than covered the rent by doing the painting and packing. What about shampooing all the rugs? Enough...I'm sorry for going on like this. There is a place called Eagle's Nest up in Newburgh that we should check into. Let's go."

Ellen thought better than to continue trying to explain what she meant by begging. Jake was a fair and unselfish man and couldn't fathom why Guy was unreasonable. So she changed the subject.

"What about your birthday? It's tomorrow. Anything planned with your family?"

Jake wanted to pass the day without any reference to his other life. Now he was cornered.

"There're two reasons why I'm not into it. Tomorrow when I get up...I'll be fifty years old. Things are shitty at home and it's not the place for celebrating anything. What I'm trying to say is...I'd rather not even be there. For the past few years I've had no cause to celebrate anything. I'll enjoy the teasing from the kids. I'm sure Annie will make the day special for me. J.D. will probably give me battery cables or a flashlight. Sandy wanted to take me out but I told her I'd rather be home with the kids. Turning fifty is strange, very strange. When I got your card at work it made me real happy. And the letter you sent me last week touched my heart. I love the fact that you care about me so much."

Ellen felt awful after listening to Jake. He hardly ever mentioned anything about his other life, hearing the truth made her realize that he faced daily struggles in ways she didn't fully appreciate.

"Jake, you're the most unselfish person I know. You gave up your day to help me. We should be making love at the house and celebrating your birthday. I feel sorry for you."

"Ellen, you don't ever have to feel sorry for me. I'm so fortunate to have you and my good health. That's more than enough. But I wish I could fast forward time so I could exit my other world with some peace of mind. The problem is that it's very bad karma to think that way. I can't teach young people to view their life as a blessing and then be so hypocritical as to want to wish away time. What bothers me so much is loving you in secret. I hate it! As many times as my inner voice tells me about the Tao of life, there are times when I come up short and remain confused. The Tao teaches that the wise person avoids extremes, indulgence, and complacency. Frankly, I should've learned this by now. I still feel out of balance, sometimes in the extreme. I hate it! I've seen you grow so much in the past year, but what about me? Have I changed into a better person? Am I worth the love and devotion you've given me?"

Ellen squeezed Jake's hand and for the first time, she saw tears in his eyes. She knew he was on overload worrying about making things work out for his family, and concerned about her. Their roles were reversed, now it was her turn to give Jake the feeling of hope that he'd given her over and over during the worst of times. She ran her fingers through his hair, touched his cheek, and said.

"Jake, look at me, I'll wait. I'll wait for you no matter how long it takes. You'll see, I'll get the apartment for us. My job is ok and the last I heard, my boys are fine. We're soul-mates…we're meant to be together. I'll always love you. Tonight, when you go for your walk, look at the stars and know I'll be thinking of you. We will find our way! Remember what you taught me, if you lose your hope you lose your dreams. I've got enough hope to carry us through."

He kissed her without saying a word, and he knew he loved her with all his heart.

⁊⊶⥸

Two weeks later, Jake waited as usual in the Montgomery Manor parking lot at noon. Ellen didn't show at 12:15, 12:30, or at 1 p.m. Concerned, he strolled around the parking lot over and over like he was doing guard duty at a secret military installation. This had never happened before, and he thought the worst. Maybe she got in an accident or something had occurred with the boys? His brain was getting frazzled and he felt his patience waning as each car pulled in the lot and Ellen wasn't in one.

Finally, he saw the black Jeep approach about 1:30 with the driver waving at him frantically, trying to get his attention. Before she even pulled in a space, she started yelling out the window.

"I got it. I got it. I have the key. We're moving. I'm finally free!!"

She jumped out of the vehicle and wrapped her arms around Jake.

"I was beginning to wonder about you. I thought you ran off with a salesman. But I guess you still want me on the payroll. No pink slip today? Seriously, you scared the shit out of me. So you got it?"

"Do you want to see the place? I signed the lease an hour ago."

"Wait a second! First I want you to see something."

In her excitement Ellen had failed to notice the brand new Ford truck that was parked nearby. "Oh my God, you got your dream truck. What a stunning color! Is that metallic red?"

"You like the color? Well, it looks like we have two reasons to celebrate, don't we?"

Jake gave her a mini inspection tour of his new truck, pointing out how the eight foot bed provided a cargo area for cross-country travel, and how spacious and comfortable the front cab was.

"What do you think of my 'Red Dragon?' That's what I'm calling her. I'm already planning my next adventure! This is my high-powered covered wagon. I'm ordering the matching cap next week."

"Well Jake, what should we do for the rest of the afternoon? Visit the apartment or would you like to take me for a ride in your new truck?"

"I miss our walks. I'd rather drive to the Delaware Water Gap, than visit an empty apartment on a sunny day like this. Are you interested in taking a maiden voyage with me?"

"I am, but I'm hungry. Can we get an ice cream? There's no better way to celebrate than with a double-dip, chocolate chip cone."

"Interesting offer, but I don't know about that. There are other ways to celebrate that don't involve ice cream. Personally Ellen, I'd rather take a bite out of you."

As they drove south to the Gap, Ellen related how she decided to stop by the rental office to check on the status of her application. Out of nowhere, the agent had offered her a place that became vacant the day before. Without even inspecting the apartment, she agreed to sign the lease, site unseen. However, the agent required a money order or cash for $1,750 that day. Ellen had twenty minutes to get to the bank before closing, so she begged the agent to wait and left immediately. She returned five minutes before the office closed. That was how she secured the apartment.

In Ellen's mind, she understood the significant role that Jake had played in her life. He was her catalyst for change. He'd always told her to believe in herself, to have hope, and to grow wings and learn to fly. Today, her task was finally completed. Her life had changed dramatically over the course of a single year. She finally had a place of her own, a place to cultivate their love and watch it grow.

CHAPTER 46

When Jake finished the final session of the parent workshop he didn't invite the participants to sign up for the additional group experience. Either because he felt the right chemistry wasn't there, or he just wasn't up for it. For the first time in doing the seminars, Jake felt changed by the experience. More than ever, his own words about the marital stress of adolescent parenting had laid bare the senselessness of his own marital situation. He concluded it would be hypocritical for him to share his beliefs any longer.

Oftentimes, while addressing his audience or visiting the groups following his lectures, he found that he was facing the same introspection and self-evaluation as the participants. That reality, plus the fact that his own kids were moving beyond adolescence, convinced him that he was in his own state of transition. It wasn't that he didn't give the workshop his best effort, he did. Anything less would have been unacceptable to him. As usual, his dynamic presentations provided stimulus for discussion. However, this particular group had more than a fair share of outspoken parents who didn't shy away from tough issues. He had particularly enjoyed their engaging arguments involving "parental rights."

On the final night, Jake left the high school and visited Ellen instead of going home. Something was on his mind that couldn't wait another day. He didn't care that it was 10:30 when he arrived at Chestnut Hill. Ellen had moved there only a week ago.

He knocked three times before she came to the door. Ellen looked through the peephole and opened the door; she was wearing reading glasses and an oversized black athletic shirt with an Atlanta Falcon's logo on it. She was surprised but worried by his late night appearance.

"Jake it's so late! Are you all right?"

"I need to be here with you tonight. I'd sure like a cold beer?"

Ellen went to the fridge, took out two Molsons and gave him one. "Jake, you look like you need a hug. I know you, and this is not what you do."

He kissed her on the forehead, downed half the bottle and then leaned against the doorway as if trying to decide what to do next. Finally, he put the beer on the table, sighed and opened up. "Ellen, I've something to confess. I hate dumping this on you, but my situation at home has become a goddamned nightmare. It's a bunch of things, not just one. I've made it a point to keep stuff like this away from you. But I can't anymore. Things really suck. I feel like a stranger when I'm there. Without the basement to hide in and the dog to walk...there'd be nothing. Somehow I've got to hold on until my daughter leaves for college. I feel like that's the only honorable thing to do."

When he finished, Jake hung his head like a beaten prizefighter.

She brought him over to the couch and stroked the hair above his neck. Then she spoke very softly to him without looking up. "Jake, you've always been there for me. Whatever's bothering you just let it out. It's my turn. Please trust me. Whatever's hurting you, share it with me."

"Shit, I'm tired of the whole reality at home. There's no joy for me there. All I do is put in a day's work, then go back home to some ongoing crisis. The other day I paid my income taxes; the shortfall was over seven thousand dollars. Can you imagine that? It was because of Sandy's capital gains. She acts like it's nothing and expects me to take care of it. She's nuts! Lately, J.D. is bringing home more and more junk and has turned the garage into a disaster. The neighbor is constantly complaining about the noise from his joy rides around the property on a dirt bike. The bastard threatened to call the cops if I don't get the boy under control. I'm barely getting along with Sandy. There's no middle ground left. I don't even like her. I suppose I'm really over the limit. I'll tell you, without Annie, I swear I'd pack up and leave. I didn't even have it in me to facilitate the extra group activity this year, and I don't even know why. I hate living in this chaos. I'm sorry for bleeding like this. It's just that...I need you."

Ellen's heart was about to burst. Jake was a tower of strength to her, yet she felt he was falling apart. She remembered what he had told her when she was at her lowest point. "Listen Jake, we are gonna get through this. Remember what you said, that the road ahead will be filled with obstacles and we should expect it to be that way. I believed you, and considering all that has happened in the past year it was a prophetic statement. All you need to know is that I'm here for you."

Jake snuggled up close to her and told her what had been on his mind for months. "Listen to me. A year from now, when Annie's finished with her first year at college, I'm leaving Sandy. I'll try to do one more year for the sake of the kids, but that's it. I'm counting down. I'll save all the money I can and do the necessary planning for the event. You can count on it happening."

Ellen didn't know what to say, so she waited for Jake to finish revealing whatever else he needed to. Nothing she heard really shocked her; she believed this must have been building up for a long time.

Then Jake put his hands on her shoulders, looked in her eyes, and said. "Would you like to go to Wyoming, Montana and Idaho this summer? Do you think it would be something you'd like to do? Are you up for a road adventure with me? I want you to go with me."

The invitation, coming out of nowhere, made Ellen spring off the couch to face him. "Oh my God, you're serious! There's absolutely nothing in the world I'd rather do than go on an adventure with you. What should I do? What do I need to bring? I have no boots. I need a sleeping bag. My God, you mean it…you really do! When are we going? You like going alone but you want to take me. I'm astonished…I am."

Ellen was too wound up to stay in one place. She walked into the kitchen, then paced the living room. Jake started to laugh at the site of her so beside herself.

"Calm down babe. I'll fill you in on all the details this Saturday. I've decided the trip will give us a perfect opportunity to learn more about each other and leave this world behind. That's what I want. I promise you'll have a hell of a good time."

"Jake, you've already given me more than I could have wished for, but this invitation is beyond my wildest dreams. I don't know what else to say. I'm so excited."

He knew his offer was the only way he could survive the next couple of months. Ellen reacted with the enthusiasm that he needed to galvanize his resolve to make it through.

"I've got to go now. Don't worry. When my mind is made up, that's it. We're going. We're going to have our first adventure together. So put in for vacation the first two weeks of July. Do it tomorrow! I've got to go now. I hope you're happy. Goodbye."

The next morning, on the way to work she realized her relationship with Jake had entered another stage. Jake had made two defining choices. He was taking her on an adventure and he had declared his intention to leave Sandy by next year. The faith and trust she had in him gave her an indestructible sense of optimism about their future. Now everything they planned was more meaningful than ever before.

One thing that bothered her was the hardship they faced in being separated for another year. She knew better than anyone what it was like to live with someone you didn't love. Unlike her solitary confinement of the past twenty years, she knew that Jake had his career, the love and respect of his children, a trustworthy friend in Kevin O'Connor, and a core philosophy that guided him. Ellen had survived all those years without the benefit of anyone or any career. Up until last night, Jake had never complained about his home situation, now Ellen hoped he would share his world whenever it was troubling him. She wanted him to have that much faith in her.

❧

A week later, Ellen returned home after work. Without giving it a second thought, she tapped the play button on the answering machine thinking it was Jake.

"Ellen, this is Guy. I'm moving back to Middletown. I have a good deal on an office lease and will be expanding the business to the metropolitan area. Fortunately, I didn't accept the last offer on the house. The boys are looking forward to seeing you. We should be there late tomorrow evening. Bye."

Unsettled by the news, she left the takeout order of Chinese on the counter and went to the bedroom to consider the implications. What would happen now that the boys were returning to Middletown? The call caught her by surprise because neither the boys nor their father had given any indication of the impending move. She believed the move was probably because of Guy's business which was the explanation he'd left on the message. Her appetite was gone, at least until something popped in her head to clarify the situation. She was worried. Would Guy reverse his decision and ask that she take over custody of the boys? Would the boys want that? Was it possible that after six months as a single parent he'd rather pay her child support even if it would cost him dearly?

Critical times like this made her appreciate how important Jake was in her life. They'd be meeting tomorrow at noon. Most likely Guy wouldn't be back by then. As her anxiety calmed down and she realized there was nothing to do but wait, she went back to the kitchen, and ate the lo mien. It was another obstacle they had to face in order to keep their relationship moving ahead.

The next morning the phone rang fifteen minutes before noon, as Ellen was packing some lunch for the trail. Reluctantly, she answered the call.

"Hello Ellen. We won't get back until Sunday and I was hoping you could help me register the boys at school on Monday morning. Is that possible?"

"How are the boys doing? Is everything all right?"

"I think things will be better when they're back in Middletown. Joey was doing fine, but not Danny. Anyway, what about the registration? Will you help or what?"

"It's impossible. I can't take off on Monday. There are things on my desk I'm expected to have ready for my boss and I'm still new on the job."

"So you're telling me the answer is no. Is that right?"

The tone in his voice turn nasty and it brought back memories she wanted to forget, so she remained quiet like the hundreds of other times when something didn't go his way and he got frustrated.

"Know something Ellen, I wish you could be there when I tell the boys what you said. Now I can see that your job comes before your children. Is that it? You're too busy to be a mother."

"Guy, you don't understand. I can't take off on such short notice. You can do it. It's not a big deal; the secretaries at the school will help you register the boys. For Pete's sake, stop being so difficult!"

"You bitch! Who do you think you're talking to? I've been raising the boys alone and doing a damn good job of it. You've seen them only once since you kicked us out, and all I asked was for a little of your time. How selfish can you be? Step up to the plate and do your part."

"Let's get one thing straight. You took the boys away from me to prove a point, and now you have the nerve to ask me to accommodate you on a moment's notice. Divorcing you was the smartest thing I ever did. You're unreasonable and an insufferable brute."

She slammed the phone so hard on the receiver that it jumped off and bounced on the floor.

In the space of two minutes, she realized that Guy spoke to her in the same way he always did, and it reminded her of why she left him. He was as sarcastic as ever and she reasoned it was foolish for her to even consider he'd change his mind about custody, especially when it involved money, the use of the house, or the boys having a stable relationship with her. The best option for her was to leave things alone. Guy would call back sooner or later, and then she'd visit the boys."

A few days later Ellen received another message from Guy. She could visit the boys on Mother's Day. When she entered their former home to pick up the boys, she saw Lucy Capone sitting in the kitchen. Ellen had no desire to make small talk or inquire why she was there.

When she took them for pizza, the boys took turns talking to their mother. As Jake suggested, Ellen let them talk. Danny made it clear that the time he spent in Atlanta was ok but the school situation wasn't to his liking. He had been absent a lot and some of his grades were down.

Then Joey told his story. The weather was way better in Atlanta, but he spent too much time being alone. One thing was obvious; he missed the calming influence of his mom, especially her patience with regard to doing homework. He also missed the kids in his class and his friend, Anthony Capone.

Their first pizza outing lasted a little over an hour and Ellen felt relieved knowing she had re-established a connection. Joey told her he loved her and gave her a Mother's Day card, but Danny ended the visit with s brief message. "See ya, Ma."

As Ellen was about to drive away, Guy came out of the front door and handed her an alimony check through the driver's side window of the Jeep.

"Take this. I wouldn't want you to report me to the court for being in arrears. Tell you what...I'll be in touch when I need you. I'll call you at work."

"No you can't, and you know it! You can call me at home and leave a message."

Guy swore bitterly under his breath as Ellen took off down the road.

CHAPTER 47

"You're gonna do what? Are you out of your mind? Jesus, I thought I knew you, but this is nuts…taking her along with you on the trip. You simply can't push your luck, not that far."

"Kevin, what the hell is your problem? I better buy you another beer, maybe a shot of *Old Grand Dad* to go with it. After thirty years of friendship, now you're gonna start telling me what to do? Is that it?"

"Then why did you tell me your plans? Jake, let me get this straight. The two of you are going out on the road for two weeks in July and you want my…my blessing. You're fuckin' nuts! Why push it to the limit? Too many things could go wrong. Think about it for a minute. If either of you gets sick or you have a freak accident of some sort, how would you explain it to Sandy? I know her. She'd throw your ass out on the street, and you couldn't blame her. Want me to go on? Listen to me, you jackass, I don't like it because you're being so reckless…this could end up crashing down all around you."

"You want another one my fine Irish friend? Why are you arguing with me? Bartender, I'll have another Molson and bring a Becks for my friend."

"Hey Jake, you asked my opinion, didn't you? You wanted the truth. I'm not trying to wreck your plans. I've known all along that this woman is really important to you. I knew it last year. What's so different now?"

"Stop right there and listen to me. I love her…period. My marriage is over and you know it is. Of all people don't tell me you've forgotten what its like to fall in love a second time. Remember, I was at your wedding six years ago. Let me refresh your memory. Joanie was recently divorced from an asshole that practically ruined her emotionally when you started dating. Isn't that right? Didn't you come into her life knowing there'd be potholes on the road? Didn't she have two kids? The bottom line is that you stayed with her in spite of all that shit. How do you figure…was it love? Well, answer me!"

"Jake, you're leaving out one important difference. You're still married and I wasn't, neither was Joanie. What the fuck is wrong with your thinking? You told me you'd just pass the time till Annie's was away in college. Don't take Ellen with you…don't."

"Goddamn it Kevin, I'm gonna take her. That way I'll know for sure if it's meant to be. You don't understand. I'm burnt out! Ya hear me? I'm burnt out at home and at work. I've got to get away and I'm taking her...cause I need to. I'm sharing this with you because I trust you and wanted you to know my plans. I can tell you're not gonna change your attitude. Fuck it. Let's drop it."

Kevin had given it his best shot and lost. In his heart, he loved Jake and didn't want anything to go wrong. But he knew that when Jake's mind was made up, it meant the end of the conversation. He downed the Becks, ordered another, and then turned to other things.

"Jake, I think I'm gonna take early retirement. I'll work a couple more years and get out with thirty. That'll give me half-pay. Christ, didn't the time fly by?"

"Kevin, I like your plan. You're right. It all went by too quickly."

O'Connor had to give his friend one more thought before he left and so he told Jake. "This woman, this Ellen, I think she's been good for you. Remember when I told you that if you had a chance of finding some happiness to take it. Remember that? Didn't I tell you to give it a shot? So now you're gonna give it the ultimate test, common sense and good judgment be damned. Good for you."

"About time you gave me what I needed to hear. Yeah, things are better for me. At least I got some hope for the future. Enough said. I see you're finally using the new golf balls I gave you for your fiftieth birthday. How come I still beat you today?"

"Cause you were lucky. So Jake, how do you like being fifty? Sucks don't it. Tell you this, I hate to admit it, but you still look fit...no beer gut, plus you got them big arms. Still doing your pushups? Shit! On top of all that, you got most of your hair left...mine's almost gone, plus I got a tinge of arthritis."

Jake enjoyed the compliment and gave Kevin a punch on the arm while telling him, "Kevin, you ain't as handsome as you used to be, but you're still shooting damn good golf scores. And as far as being fifty, there's nothing I can do about it. Besides, being fifty is a hell-of-a-lot better than being sixty!"

CHAPTER 48

It was the birth of a new day when Jake left Walden and turned the "Red Dragon" in the direction of Chestnut Hill. He knew he had crossed over the threshold of fear. In less than ten minutes, he'd pick up Ellen, and they'd begin their journey. Jake's head might have been on a loose swivel a few days earlier, but now it was at rest. During their last evening together, Jake went through the motions and Sandy did the same. They played out the final scene like a couple of veteran stage actors who had performed the drama a hundred times. The conundrum was that the production was a marital tragedy without a denouement. Sandy had learned to master her lines as well as Jake; their timing and delivery were convincing, but shallow in substance.

When Jake got in the truck a note from Sandy was in the sun visor.

Dear Jake,
I wish you the best as you begin your third road trip without me.
I had hoped you might change your mind and offer to take me
with you. I waited and waited and never got the invitation.
Whatever you may think, I still love you. There's no way the
children would have made it without you. I'm grateful for all
the things you do around the house to make our lives better.
You kept your promise and didn't leave me, even when I knew
you weren't happy. I'm thankful for your act of loving kindness.
Raising the children without a father would have been a
disaster. Please come back. We all need you. Be safe!
> *Love,*
> *Sandy*

When Jake finished reading her letter, he placed it in the glove compartment to remain undisturbed. Then he muttered under his breath, "What a sad situation for a man to be needed just to keep things in order. I should feel guilty for keeping the charade going for so long, but it's too late for that now."

As he neared the apartment complex, Jake's state of mind exited from the last traces of apprehension, and he assumed his colorful road character identity. Hundreds of times in the last month, he'd questioned the wisdom of making this decision. Each time, his inner voice convinced him it no longer made any sense to deny his feelings. In the final analysis, he believed it was karma. In short, it was meant to be.

He pulled the truck alongside the two-story apartment building just as Ellen descended the stairs carrying a large black duffle on her shoulder, holding the strap with both hands like a she was boarding a troop ship to go overseas. She wore a black sleeveless cotton top and new, olive green hiking shorts, and new Nike sneakers. Jake beamed up a smile when their eyes met. Leaving the truck engine running, he shifted to park, pushed down the emergency brake, and jumped out to help her with the gear.

"So my little traveler, did you get any sleep last night or were you too wired?"

"Hi handsome, I was too excited to get any rest. I'll bet you didn't get much either. I can't believe today is finally here. The weather looks promising…good sign, isn't it? I think I remembered to pack everything. We'll have to wait and see. I called the boys to say goodbye and told them I was going to Steamboat Springs on vacation with a friend from work. They didn't ask me anything. Guess they're busy with their own summer activities. I didn't want them wondering where I was. I'm all set, let's go."

"Listen to you, my firstmate giving the orders! You're something. Hand over the duffle bag, I'll stow it in the back and we'll be on our way. Take your backpack up front."

Jake placed Ellen's bag in the last remaining open spot in the truck bed, then opened the passenger door and pointed.

"Here's your spot! You'll be sitting there a very long time. It's now five minutes to six on a beautiful Sunday morning and our adventure is about to begin. Having any second thoughts? You ready to follow me anywhere?"

Ellen shook her head in disbelief. Then she pointed to her temple and said, "Second thoughts never entered my mind. Let's go captain!"

They began the trip in high spirits, and she listened as he delivered his orientation speech for road travel. She instinctively knew it would be coming as soon as they reached the Interstate. Throughout the month of June, he had sent her at least fifteen e-mails describing the places they'd visit, and the order in which they'd occur. He also told her what to expect during their travels like the crowded rest stops and the few congested areas along the interstate. In that way, he succeeded in keeping her interest percolating while preparing her for the regimen of the actual trip.

After a short time, they took 209 running parallel to the Delaware River and picked up I-80 in East Stroudsburg. The weather was delightful, in the mid-sixties with little humidity. The golden sun was rising directly behind them, and Jake let the cruise control take over.

Jake poked Ellen with a finger on her thigh, smiled and said, "We're going to be together in this truck for the next thirty-four hours. When you consider that's equal to the entire time we spent with each other in the month of June, you'll realize how important it is that we agree on a few things. Does that make sense?"

Ellen appreciated the words more than Jake could possibly know. It was one of those things she thought about a lot because she wanted the adventure to be a success.

"It makes sense to me. Go ahead. Tell me what I need to know about traveling with you. Am I allowed to voice reservations, or must I surrender to your rules?"

Jake turned and looked incredulously at her for the smartass remark. "Hey, I'm gonna issue you a fine right off the bat for being a smart aleck. Seriously, what's really crucial is that we leave our other lives behind us. We should experience the present and take in the sites. Of course we can talk about any part of our relationship. But, honestly, let's leave the rest back in New York State. What you think?"

Ellen nodded in agreement, saluted, and poked him in his side. "What else, Captain? That can't be the only thing on your mind…what else?"

"No matter what, let me know your needs, whatever they are. I know my own because I've done this many times before. I don't want you holding back. Whether it's food, rest, quiet, privacy or relieving yourself, make sure you tell me. In a couple of days, it'll all be second nature to you. We'll mesh together like a team of mules hauling a wagon. Get my message?"

"You have a way of putting things in quite unusual terms. You're turning western on me already and we're not even through Pennsylvania."

"I'm into my road persona. The counselor has disappeared."

She grabbed her camera from the backpack and took the first shot of the trip. It was of the strange man with the black tee shirt and shades, behind the wheel of his new truck.

"Hey kid, put that map case on the floor and park your butt next to me. It's time for you to pick the first tape of our trip. So go ahead and set the mood."

Ellen shoved a Santana tape into the cassette slot and Jake started tapping his foot to the beat.

❧❧

Thirty hours later they reached the Missouri River Overlook. Ellen came through the ordeal much better than Jake had figured and they were compatible road buddies. After finding a parking spot, they took turns using the restroom facilities, and met back at the truck to prepare lunch.

During the break Jake entertained Ellen with his commentary on the cultural significance of rest areas while they ate subs at a shaded picnic table. Afterwards, they walked along the high bluffs that overlooked the river, and he took some photos of Ellen with the muddy Missouri in the background.

When they returned to the truck, Jake turned over the driving to his co-pilot. "Darlin', I'm pretty exhausted. Do you think you could let me crash for an hour? Stay on I-90 west. Its 12:30 now and we should be in Deadwood by four. The speed limit is seventy-five. There's no need to go any faster. Sometimes a gust of wind will come out of nowhere; be ready for it. Slow down a bit and keep both hands on the wheel. I've got to crash. Driving the truck in cruise control is a snap."

"I'll be fine. I'm utterly amazed how you drove as long as you did. You let me take three or four catnaps. What a difference that makes. Grab a pillow and try to sleep. I'll wake you up in an hour."

She drove over the flat rolling plains of South Dakota for over three hours and made it to the Wall Drug parking lot before Jake finally woke up. Wiping the sleep from his eyes, and feeling hot and clammy he was grateful for the break Ellen had given him.

"Man, was I wasted. I can't believe we're at Wall Drugs already. You did great! Shit, all we have left is two hours of driving. Let's get some ice cream to celebrate and then I'll take us to Deadwood."

"I've got to pee right now. Please get the cones and I'll meet you back here."

"I got the message. Go already! Then we'll have a treat."

As they drove through the Black Hills, Ellen watched the transformation take place in Jake and it amazed her how excited he was as they entered the old western gambling town nestled in a valley. After checking in at the Motel 8, he took the duffle bags to their room and they both collapsed on the bed laughing. Immediately Ellen rolled over on top of him and began kissing his neck.

"Whoa, Darlin', I think I smell a bit stale…sorry but I got a get out of these clothes this second."

Jake sprang up and completely disrobed like it was nothing. They hadn't been together in over a week and the sight of his naked body, clean or not, turned her on.

Then Jake piped in, "Hey Babe, how's this sound? You take a long shower while I go for a swim. Then I'll come back and take mine. We'll lie down for an hour and then get dressed and walk to town. It's only about a half mile down the road. I'm taking you to the Silverado Casino for a prime rib feast. Tell you what…I'll even give you a roll of nickels for the slot machines. I'll show you around town, and then we'll finish the evening at Saloon Number Ten, where Wild Bill got shot. What do ya think?"

Ellen thought Jake acted as though he were a movie director describing the next scene for an actor. Roles reversed completely and she took control and let him know it. "Forget your swim and make love to me. Jake, I'm not on your schedule. That wasn't the deal."

Instantly, Ellen slipped out of her shorts and top, and tossed her bra aside. Her spontaneous offer did more to excite him than the sight of her looking seductive, and it showed. She took him on, right there and then, and they went at it like it was the last bit of lovemaking they'd ever share.

She loved everything they did that first night, especially visiting Saloon Number Ten, where they drank beers, listened to a cowboy band, and had enough energy to dance four waltzes. When they returned to the motel around midnight, Jake's eyes were glazed over with fatigue, but so were hers. He apologized as he turned off the lamp saying, "Forgive me, but I don't have anything left."

Ellen snuggled next to him, kissed him tenderly whispering, "I love you so much. You gave me a perfect evening and some fabulous lovemaking. I'm here when you want me, anytime you want me."

⌘

Two days later, they setup their first campsite at Sitting Bull campground in the Big Horn region of north central Wyoming off Scenic Byway 16. It was the same #2 site that Jake used the past two summers. Patiently, he explained the reasons why he did each part of the setup.

"Ellen, watch how I do this in case you ever leave me…just teasing. First, we've got to place the ground cloth and tent in a way that will prevent runoff from a rainstorm making its way inside. But before that, we'll check for small stones and exposed roots because you would definitely feel them through your sleeping bag, and that would rob you of a decent nights sleep. Truth is you can't fix something like that in the dark, especially if you had too many Molsons and wanted a poke."

"What did you say? What do you mean by a poke?"

"That's having sex. I first read that expression in *Lonesome Dove*. Will you allow me to use it? It's not very romantic, however, classically western."

"You're silly. I guess it suits us. From now on, we'll call it a poke."

Other tidbits of camp setup involved common sense, like leaving a full water container in sunlight to warm it up all day. Another, was never to leave the cooler outside of the truck overnight, it would be an open invitation for a black bear to whisk it away. Then there were Jake's customs that brought laughter to Ellen, such as his ax toss ritual.

"Grab that hand ax from the wood pile and let's see if we can locate a deadfall."

"Sorry, you got me again. What do you mean by a deadfall?"

"It's when a gunfighter gets shot through the heart. Then the sorry dude has a deadfall. Get it?"

"That's not true. Jake, you're teasing again! You keep this up and there'll be no poking later."

Jake started to belly laugh and couldn't contain his delight as they walked next to the streambed on a well-worn dirt path.

"A deadfall is a downed tree. Get it? It's one that's been leveled by lightning or blown down during the winter. Look there...see that tree? It's a yellow pine. Follow me."

Ellen watched in admiration as Jake walked off ten paces from the tree trunk, used his boot to make a mark in the dirt, and got in position to throw the ax.

"Ok Darlin', this is my ax ritual. Check this...I've got to stick this ax in that deadfall given five chances and no more. If I do, well that's 'big medicine.' Now don't ask me what that means. I'll tell you. 'big medicine' brings us good fortune, like secing a rainbow after a storm or catching a glimpse of a pair of moose munching in a marsh. Hey that sounded pretty good. All right...here I go."

He rehearsed the motion three times before letting go of the ax; it looked like he was throwing an overhand fastball, except the motion of his arm was slower.

"Holy shit, I missed! It must have been a gust of wind or maybe the stump moved. Yup, the wind affected the throw. Let me fetch it and try again. Be patient now."

Ellen covered her mouth with her hand and spun around in a circle, desperately trying to hold back from bursting out laughing. Then she gave him a cheer of encouragement. "Come on, Jake. Stick it in that monster deadfall. Hooray for the great warrior!"

This time Jake practiced the ax toss twice and moved in half-a-step before he let it go. With a dull thud, it landed flush in the tree. He danced a jig for a second and then retrieved the ax, handing it to Ellen so she could participate.

"I'm not doing it! That's all there is to it. It's something you do, not me. You didn't even take notice my own camping ritual, did you? I put wildflowers on the picnic table, Indian Paintbrush and Bluebells. Now let's hear it for my 'big medicine."

Silly with laughter, Jake carried Ellen piggyback to the campsite. When he noticed she had placed the flowers in an empty water bottle on the picnic table, he gave the high sign with his hand.

Jake assigned Ellen three jobs on their first day and said she was responsible for doing them for the rest of the trip: to setup their 7x7 master bedroom with sleeping bags and pads, bring anything else they needed for comfort inside the tent, and never leave the screen windows open more than a few inches when they were gone for the day. Her second job was to collect twigs and kindling wood for the nightly campfire. The last job was to help him straighten out all the gear stored in the truck bed every few days.

Later on that same afternoon he learned there were two tasks Ellen flat-out refused. They had to do with fishing. She wouldn't put a live night crawler on the fish hook and wouldn't take a twisting trout off the hook even though she caught it. Those were jobs exclusively for Jake. Despite all his assurances, she professed to have a squeamish stomach.

The weather was perfect for a hike during the mid-afternoon on their first day in the Big Horns. Jake took Ellen for a three-hour, eight-mile roundtrip hike into the Cloud Peak Wilderness. He wanted her to get acclimated to the altitude and see her reaction to the natural surroundings. He was fairly quiet on the trail and appreciated the effort she made to "feel out" the activity.

After the hike, they tried their luck fishing for German Brown Trout at Ten Sleep Lake. Ellen won the dollar fishing derby by landing a big game fish. However, it weighted less than a pound and measured less than a foot, obviously not a keeper, but she was still the winner of the first fishing contest. Jake had been continually worming one hook after another for her, due to the uncanny ability for worm snatching those trout exhibited.

Jake made chili for their first meal and served sourdough bread with it. For desert, he divided up a large can of sliced peaches with oatmeal raisin cookies. When they finished eating, he gave her a suggestion, "I'll clean up the dishes. You take some time for the next hour. You could read, write in your travel journal, sketch, or do whatever you choose. Later on, I'll take you for a loop walk, and then we'll have our first fire. Wait until you see the stars come out, usually around ten. You're in for some kind of thrilling experience. Maybe we can waltz around the fire. Maybe even have a late poke…see ya later."

Everything he planned went exactly as expected. Around midnight, when they turned in, she zipped up the mummy bag he brought for her, and in total darkness leaned over to say good night.

"I've never experienced anything like this in my life. The joy I feel being with you is better than I ever expected. I could do this the rest of my life. What about you?"

"Sounds like you're making a proposition to me after only one day. Tell you what. Ask me on our last day on the road, and then I'll give you an answer?" She kissed him tenderly and they both fell out with the sound of the stream singing a lullaby.

Early the next morning they took Trail 65 into the Cloud Peak Wilderness. Ellen wasn't prepared for such a strenuous hike, but it was the most breathtaking mountain scenery she'd ever seen. Jake was considerate of his novice traveler, stopping as frequently as she needed to catch her breathe, take a few sips of lemonade, and wipe away the sweat. Although she thought her exercise and nightly walks had prepared for the ordeal, it soon became apparent that wasn't good enough. At an altitude of nearly 9,000 feet, the continuous uphill trail of switchbacks began to wear her down. Jake continually encouraged her by saying, "Just a little while and the trail will take us above the tree line." Whatever that meant, didn't register with Ellen. The back of her cotton top was soaked with sweat, and the weight of her daypack made her neck muscles tighten. Jake took notice of her obvious discomfort.

"In a few more minutes you'll see the monument. Remember what I told you?"

Ellen was breathing hard when she stopped to reply. "Yeah...you told me you put your name...you carved your name in a tree up here somewhere...that right?"

"Well it's just up another hundred yards. I'm gonna do a mad dash for it. I'll wait up there for you. I know, you think I'm wild. Guess I'm excited about the reunion."

Jake bounded up the last stretch like an Indian following the trail of his prey and disappeared somewhere up the rocky path. Ellen reached him in about five minutes. He was sitting on a rock ledge directly in front of a towering fir tree and waved to her.

"Put down your pack and walking stick. I've got something to show you."

He took her hand and led her toward the back of the tree. Sure enough, carved in the trunk above his name was hers, E-L-L-E-N. Then he brought her hot body next to his, touched her cheek and said. "I carved your name last year, never knowing what fate had in store for me. I had you in my thoughts a year ago, and you've never left, I love you, and I am so thankful we found each other. This place is very special to me, and now I want it to be a special place for us...a place that we'll come back to again and again."

Ellen was touched by what he revealed and astonished to see that her name was carved a year ago, when her life had been full of turmoil and uncertainty. Unable to control her emotions, tears came to her eyes and she was only able to mutter a few words to Jake. "This is our destiny. I swear I will always love you."

During the next fifteen minutes she sat and watched him patiently carve out what appeared to be two wing-like creatures on both sides of their names. Then, with even more patience and precision he carved the name S-K-Y-E under his, along with the year.

When Jake showed her the completed carving, Ellen was puzzled by the name. "I've never had a nickname and now you want to call me Skye, is that it?"

"Only if it's what you want. It's your choice."

"Thanks for giving me that choice. I love it and I want you to use it, but only when we're alone."

They spent the next couple of hours wandering along a creek that twisted and turned through a vast mountain meadow that eventually led to a waterfall on the slopping edge of a ridge. Ellen thought of the wolf card Jake had given her last summer. On a soft bed of grass, near the mist of the cascading water, they made love with a passion equivalent to the power of the raging mountain stream.

❧

The Scenic Byway through the Big Horns on Route 16 gave Ellen an appreciation for the wonders of nature beyond anything she'd ever experienced living on the East Coast. There were National Forest signs next to geological formations that gave the ages of the rocks; "Big Horn Dolomite 435-500 Million Years Old." Jake gave his take on the info with the following observation.

"Makes you kinda wonder about the Creationist Theory, huh? I don't know how it all happened, Big Bang from the Almighty or not, it sure makes you feel small."

Three hours later, Jake took her to Yellowstone Falls and the experience was breathtaking. They stood on the trail alongside the Grand Canyon of Yellowstone and felt that the rainbow below was a personal gift from Mother Nature. When another appeared on top of the first, Ellen was amazed to observe her very first double rainbow.

"Look at those colors. I couldn't possibly capture them on canvas. The view is beyond words and the mist from the falls...I can feel it."

A couple of hours later, Jake parked the truck to permit Ellen to view the magnificent vista of the Tetons on a clear summer afternoon from the shore of Jackson Lake. Nothing could have matched the first moment she saw the jagged mountain peaks against the powder blue sky. It was then that she clearly understood why Jake loved the mountains and she was saturated in awe by the image of the majestic scene. Jake broke her trance by putting his arm around her.

Then he declared with complete confidence, "I know this sounds crazy, but someday I'm going to live within a few hours driving distance from here. Probably near the Big Horns. I love Wyoming and never tire of visiting this state. You know Ellen, I mean Skye, I've probably spent fifty or sixty nights camped beneath these mountains over the past couple of decades. Tomorrow, I'm taking you to the hall of the mountain king. We'll hike up Cascade Canyon. The day after that, we'll take a white water rafting trip down the Snake River. Tonight though, we're going dancing at the Million Dollar Cowboy Bar, after eating at Bubba's."

"Are you teasing me again? What kind of a place would be called Bubba's?"

"When you see the line waiting outside...you'll know why I'm taking you there."

"Let's stay here for a while longer. I can't leave. It's too beautiful."

After two more days, Ellen was a convert and learned from first-hand observation, about Jake's intimate relationship with nature. The man he was during the first half of the trip was an extension of the person she fell in love with back in Middletown. She was more taken with him than ever. If he ever asked her to join him and start a new life out west, she wouldn't hesitate to go. Now his dream was also hers. Every moment they shared only reinforced their love for each other. She thought he was larger than life. Of all the experiences they shared together in Jackson and Teton Park, the most extraordinary for Ellen was the time they spent dancing at the Million Dollar Cowboy Bar.

The plain truth was that Ellen never danced to anything other than a slow waltz at the proms in high school. Jake managed to break her resistance, and the new experience made her feel certain that the person she rediscovered in herself was someone she really liked. Jake did for her what she wasn't able to accomplish alone. He brought back her youth. He believed in her, loved her, and played with her. He encouraged her to try new things and made her laugh more than at any time in her life. He was considerate of her feelings and needs. But above all, he made her feel desirable and worthy of his love.

☜❧

On Tuesday and Wednesday of their second week they camped along the Wise River in the Pioneer Mountains in southwestern Montana. After that, he planned to finish their adventure at Redfish Lake in the Sawtooth Mountains of Central Idaho.

Wise River was an isolated and out of the way place. Only two other sites were occupied in the Lodgepole Campground. Jake placed the tent on the river bank, only eight feet from the swift running water. He thought it would give them the sensation of traveling on a raft when they were in the tent in the black of night. At first, it was scary to Ellen who thought if a cloudburst occurred they would be pulled into the river. However, Jake reassured her he knew what he was doing and they'd be fine.

On both of the afternoons at Wise River they went for long hikes deep into the National Forest. On the first hike they came upon a Montana moose mother with her young calf trotting alongside a game trail that ran parallel to the path. Ellen tossed her camera to Jake and he ran after them in hopeless pursuit trying to get a picture. He also took her to the abandoned mine he had visited the year before.

On the second day, both of them had an endurance challenge that they were unprepared for. What was supposed to be an enjoyable eight-mile roundtrip hike to a place known as Bobcat Lakes turned into a trek in the Himalayas. The trail never stopped climbing through a vast, dark forest. Trail 65 seemed like a bunny slope to an experienced skier in comparison. Moreover, Jake called it, "a double black diamond hike," a never ending, inclined trail that bordered a ravine and went through a vast stand of Aspen. The mountainside was a forest of incredible beauty, complete with ferns and meadow grasses that gave it the appearance of a place from *The Lord of the Rings.*

Thankfully, Jake had some Advil in the truck when they returned to the trailhead. They were exhausted and smelly from sweating which prompted Jake to suggest they immerse themselves in the Wise River.

"We've got a treat waiting for us back at the campsite."

"If I drank a cold beer I'd collapse. What is it?

"Well...you and I get to wash up in the river. You'll be experiencing a first. We'll take a skinny dip and you can wash my back and I'll wash your butt...sound ok?"

"I know you. There's got to be a catch...there's something you're not telling me."

"No way! You mean to tell me that you'd rather use that warm water than have an Indian style bath? Come on...we'll take off these stinking clothes, step in that cool water, and you'll get refreshed in a jiffy."

"When you put it like that, I suppose I can handle it, if you can."

Thirty minutes later...

Undressing behind the tent was the fun part, complete with giggles and pinches. However, all of that euphoria evaporated when Jake grabbed Ellen's hand and they stepped into the icy water. She went as far as her knees before she let him have it full bore by splashing him with a vengeance as she screamed out, "You...you son of a skunk! You tricked me and I fell for it...some bath! I'm shriveling up and goose bumps have taken over my entire body. How can you stand there laughing without freezing solid?"

❧❧

Redfish Lake was the last place they camped and in some ways proved to be the most enjoyable, probably because they savored every waking moment of the experience knowing their time was running out. Since leaving Middletown, as each day passed, they were more and more comfortable and compatible with each other. The camping routines and road travel became second nature to Ellen.

On their final camping day, after a pancake breakfast, they took a three-hour hike to reach an isolated alpine lake beneath Mt. Heyburn, the highest summit in the Sawtooth Range. After snacking on wheat thins and cheese, Ellen sketched a picture of the pristine place while Jake walked the shoreline. When he returned, Jake waded into the frigid water to get a yellow orchid from a lily pad for Ellen. Then they cuddled on a bed of pine needles, reminiscing about how they met in the spring of '99.

Ellen confessed, "When I saw you standing in front of the group, assigning pairs to do interviews, and you motioned for me to come over, I thought I'd die. You know, if it hadn't been for Mrs. Fannen, we probably would've never met. She told me you'd be interesting. That's an understatement!"

"My darlin Skye, chance is part of the mystery of the universe. Honestly, I don't think of things the way you might. You'll lose your mind if you're always trying to figure out every angle of the human condition. What matters to me, is that somehow and someway, in this crazy world we found each other."

They shared their scariest times during the past year that night. Jake admitted how frightened he was during May and June, fearing that once she was on her own working at Horizon Financial and living alone that a younger man would come along and take his place.

"I'm almost ten years older than you. That indisputable fact has swirled around my head about ten thousand times. You're a beautiful woman. Shit, I don't know how you kept the gents at Horizon Financial from making a move on you."

She laughed and answered his question. "Remember when I took that picture of you at Sandy Hook, the one of you standing next to the pilings with the surf breaking behind you? That picture is on my desk.

When a couple of the single guys in the office saw it, they figured I had a boyfriend. Maybe they took a look at you and it scared 'em off."

Ellen confessed that her worst nightmare was how self-conscious she was just before they made love the first time. They looked back and laughed about their worries. Ellen telling him, "Jake, no one could ever take your place. Age doesn't mean a thing. Promise me, you'll never let that enter your head again."

He nodded in agreement, but it still bothered him.

Later on that night, they sat by the campfire listening to Tom Petty. On their last night camping together they drank too many Molsons, and following each one by downing a shot of blackberry brandy. The combination of alcohol and dance music got them really soused. After burning up a huge pile of firewood, they walked around the loop and waved goodnight to the stars. After he took her to the restroom and returned, they barely managed to get out of their clothes and into their sleeping bags.

The following morning, Jake made cowboy coffee when the bright sun woke him shortly after six o'clock. Both of them had super-sized hangovers and had a tough time getting started. Ellen took twice as long packing up the sleeping bags and pads, while Jake didn't start packing the truck till after breakfast. The camp gear was stowed by eight, and they were on State Highway 75 traveling south to Twin Falls.

The scenery along the Snake River Valley was awesome. They both knew this was the last full day on the road, so they stopped twice for breaks to check out some interesting viewpoints. Tomorrow, Ellen had a 10 a.m. Continental flight from Salt Lake to Newark with a brief stopover at O'Hare. Already, the return to reality was creeping into her thoughts; she was feeling depressed knowing only one day remained of her time with Jake.

They arrived at a Motel 8 near the airport by late afternoon and decided to shower and crash. According to Jake, other than the Mormon Cathedral and the Union Pacific Station the town was usually in a comatose state, except for the Mormon missionaries on street corners offering redemption. He said if they were lucky, they'd find a decent steakhouse and have some prime rib for their last meal.

Parking the Red Dragon was a problem; luckily, they found a spot without a meter off Main Street only five blocks from the Temple Square area. The whole place seemed to be under construction as they maneuvered around wooden barriers and roped off crosswalks. When they turned a corner, Jake stopped and directed Ellen's attention toward the magnificent structure ahead.

"The figure at the top of the cathedral is the angel Moroni. Look at those elaborate spires? Quite an impressive site, don't you think so? There's also a museum across the street and beautiful gardens. Let's walk for a while, see the sites, and then we'll find a place to eat downtown. Is that ok with you?"

"After sitting in the truck for six hours to get here, I'd love to walk around. I think I'm still recovering from last night. Thank God you let me sleep in the truck."

The temple closed at six, which gave them less than an hour, but that was enough time to get inside and view from behind a glass barrier the largest pipe organ in the western world. It was quite an impressive musical instrument, even if it was turned off. After touring the museum with its array of life size dioramas portraying the history of the Morman people, they decided to walk downtown where they found JW's Steak House.

Five minutes later they were seated with the early Saturday night diners. Jake ordered two Molsons. When their waiter returned, he placed an order for prime rib, one king-sized and one-queen sized. Jake seemed to change moods while they waited for the order. After finishing his beer he spoke in an unfamiliar fashion to Ellen.

"Tomorrow morning you're taking the airport shuttle to catch your flight back to reality, and I'll be heading for the Wasatch Mountains. That means I'll be alone on the trail up to Bald Mountain while you're on the plane looking out at the clouds. I know nothing will be the same without you. Shit, I'm already missing you and you're sitting right next to me. I don't want this to end...it all went by too fast."

Jake rested his forehead on his hands and looked down like a sad puppy. Ellen wasn't sure if he was done talking, so she waited a couple of moments then moved her thumbs slowly in the palm of his hands. She knew there was more as he slowly raised his head and searched her eyes for a sign.

"That night...when I came over after my last workshop ended, I admitted that my life at home was going nowhere and made no sense...well, I guess it was a turning point for me. I was falling fast; there was no joy in me. Anyway, I want you to know I'm planning to leave Sandy next year, probably around April or May. You've kept our agreement and never asked me about Sandy, and I've tried to stay out of your former life. Right now, I'm so glad we spared each other. Shit, so much has happened in the past year. My sweet darlin' Skye, I want you to know I loved every moment we've spent together on this road trip. I'm so damn glad I wasn't afraid to take the risk, cause now I know, with absolute certainty that we're so good together. Regardless of what happens when we get home, I wouldn't have missed this chance to find out the depth of my love."

Ellen felt the deepest love she'd ever experienced in her life, and her eyes filled with tears. Jake had opened up his heart in a way that was most unusual for him, throwing caution to the wind. After hearing his words, she intended to give back an equal measure of commitment.

Leaning over the table, she held his hands tightly and said, "I've never been treated with the kind of consideration and love that you've given me during this trip. Everyday we've laughed so much. You've let me inside your world where there seemed to be no measure of time. Through it all we were playing, always playing. I've never been so completely free. And now, more than ever, I feel like I really know you. I know the things you love and your spontaneous reactions to nature. I've loved all that you've shared with me. I finally found what I was looking for and it was you. I've been waiting for you all my life. Jake, do whatever you need to do for your family. I'll wait for you as long as it takes."

"Well darlin', we've both let our hearts speak for us. Good thing! Now let's enjoy our dinner."

Jake snapped out of his funk and returned to his former entertaining self. They thoroughly enjoyed the meal, especially the pie and coffee. Then they walked around the Temple Square until dusk. Jake interrupted their travel several times to hold Ellen and kiss her.

After Jake parked the truck at the motel he suggested they change into their swimsuits and use the spa. However, while they were changing, their primordial instincts took over. Instead of frolicking in the pool, they took their first shower together and followed that by an hour of exquisite lovemaking.

CHAPTER 49

"Hey Dad, Uncle Skip is on the phone." Jake tossed the remote on the recliner and left the basement to take the call in the kitchen.

"How's it going, Skip? It's kinda late for you to be calling on a weekday night."

"When did you get back from your trip?"

"Last Sunday...I'm trying to get back into the flow. What's up?"

"Mom died in her sleep this afternoon. Kathy said she had been in the last stage of Alzheimer's and passed away peacefully. Imagine, she was eighty-two years old. Anyway, her body will be cremated and the ashes will be brought up for a memorial service at St. Helen's Catholic Church. It's the one she attended since Dad died, in Brick, New Jersey. Kathy took care of the arrangements and has asked that each of us bring a seven hundred dollar check to help cover the funeral expenses. I don't know any more then that at the present time. If you want to give your sister a call, I'd wait till tomorrow morning. I've got to call Joe now. I guess I'll let you know the day and time of the service when it's set. Take care."

"Thanks for calling, Let me know the plans as soon as possible."

"Will do, brother. Regards to Sandy and the kids."

When Jake related the news to his family, it was more like a news report from a TV announcer than a son's sorrowful disclosure about his mother's passing. If their grandmother's death didn't appear to disturb the children, it was probably due to the fact that for the past ten years they had very limited contact with her. Also, their father acted almost indifferent, as though it wasn't a catastrophe.

Before Jake's sister had taken her in due to her deteriorating medical condition, she had lived independently in a one-bedroom apartment at a retirement complex called Leisure Village, not fifteen minutes from Skip. Jake used to take his family for a visit two or three times a year to pay their respects. The children didn't know much about grandma Florence during their childhood, and by the time they reached adolescence, they were well-aware of the distance between their father and their grandmother.

During the first few years following the death of her husband, Florence continued to live in the modest home in Brick, New Jersey. Her children visited frequently, all except Jake. Nevertheless, he made monthly contributions from the time of his father's death. Those checks were paid in respect to his father's memory and were made in his honor.

Jake and his family sat in the second pew at St. Helens and listened to the eulogies delivered by Kathy, his brother Joe, and three of Kathy's children. Annie stood next to her father, occasionally checking to see if he expressed an outward sign of grief. She saw nothing other than his blank expression throughout the entire service regardless of what comments were said by members of the family. Annie finally understood what she'd suspected all along, that her father was more of a private person than she had ever thought, especially when it came to discussing the memories of his childhood.

Annie took her father's hand and held it tightly when the Deacon mentioned the "kind and compassionate lady" Florence had been during the time he knew her, and the "strong faith she had in living a spiritual life by opening up her heart to Jesus." Tears came to Annie, not for Grandma Florence, but for her father. When she looked over at Uncle Skip to see if his face showed any sign of sorrow, it was obvious that her father and his older brother were similar in whatever they were feeling.

When the memorial service ended, the Carrs drove over to the little white Cape Cod on Cherry Lane for an informal reception. It had once belonged to Jake's parents, but it was Uncle Skips home now.

Annie was full of questions that would not stay put. "Dad, when was the last time you saw your entire family at one time? Was I with you?"

Jake didn't desire to supply information about anything he thought was better left unsaid. "I think your cousins from Virginia will be interested in your college plans. Kathy's oldest son is a sophomore at William and Mary...it's a terrific school."

"Dad, you're doing it again. You drive me crazy with your maneuvering around a question."

For whatever reason, Sandy scolded her daughter on Jake's behalf. "Annie, that's enough!!! Leave your father alone. I can't answer that question either. Why concern yourself about Dad's family history."

"Mom, maybe J.D. doesn't care, but I do. How could six individuals, I mean brothers and sisters, not be more involved with each other? It doesn't seem right! Why can't Dad give me an explanation?"

Jake respected his daughter enough to think she deserved a straight answer. When they arrived at the house Jake opened the door for Sandy and said, "Honey, you and J.D. go ahead, we'll be joining you in a minute. I want to talk to Annie."

"All right, you asked, so here's the story. My father was the glue, the bonding agent that held our family together. During his battle with cancer, and that was twenty-five years ago, each of us took turns visiting. While we were there, we talked with each other many times.

Lots of stories were shared around my father's sick bed. There was plenty of laughter to make him feel good. Anyway, the truth is that I suppose we did it for him because it was the right thing to do. Whatever misgivings we had with one another over family issues, past or present, we let them pass.

"After his death my sister Kathy moved to Virginia. My oldest sister, Barbara, moved down to southern Jersey. She was working for the state. Sadly, my father never got to see your Uncle Joe succeed as an actor. He continued to live in the city. He worked as a waiter and took whatever acting jobs came his way. I still haven't visited there. I have no excuse considering Joe is a decent guy. Worst of all, my little brother John just got lost. I can't even begin to explain his problems.

"Look, all I can say is what I began with. My dad was one incredible human being. I respected him more than anyone I've ever known. I loved him and that's a fact. My mother had a cold side. Leave it at that. Annie, that's my story. The last time we were together was when my sister Barbara's son got married, I think it was in eighty-six. I'm sorry for not sharing this sooner."

"Dad...I promise I won't cause you any grief with what you've told me. I would've liked to meet your father. I never knew what he meant to you. You've kept it locked up inside a long time."

"Sweetheart, I love you. Thanks for caring and especially the comment about your grandfather."

Skip and Marie made quite a spread in order to accommodate the crowd of relatives that filled every available nook of the small, two-bedroom house. By noon, it had turned into a humid muggy day and most of the guests preferred the comfort of the air-conditioning, but not Jake. He took a glass of lemonade, found a lawn chair, placed it in the shade of a crab apple tree, and parked himself there to watch the proceedings unfold like he was back at the rest stop overlooking the Missouri River.

J.D. appeared to be having the most fun as he "busted balls" with his cousins. Rocky, Frank and Joey were Uncle John's sons, who were close in age and impressed with J.D.'s biking exploits. Annie busied herself with cousins Lexi and Kristen, Kathy's kids, who were a year apart at James Madison University in Virginia. Meanwhile, Sandy circulated amongst the remainder of the family and other guests, catching up on current news and projecting an air of class and dignity.

Jake waited for the crowd around the buffet to disperse before he took his turn and complimented his brother for the sumptuous spread. "Skip, your potato salad is terrific. I'll take care of you later."

Steve knew that meant Jake would be passing over a large bill to help him cover the costs. When Jake returned to his chair with a plate full of cold cuts and salads, for whatever reason, the church deacon who presided at the service sat not five feet away from him and started a conversation.

"Your mother was quite a lady...very gracious. I know she loved her big family and spoke often about her children. You're Jake, is that right? You live up in New York State and you're the counselor. She's talked about you, my goodness, many times."

Jake was curious about his statement. So he probed a little. "Is that so, Deacon? Guess you know more about me than I figured. I mean you being her confidant and spiritual advisor. This is all very intriguing. How well did you know Florence?"

If the Deacon was startled by Jake's use of his mother's name, he didn't show it. "Your mother was a member of our church family and took the sacraments regularly. We spoke after services a number of times, and I came to develop a close friendship with her over the past six years. I liked her very much. She was a real lady.

"When she began to lose her faculties, your sister Kathy took her down to Virginia to care for her. What a wonderful act of kindness. I understand that your mother was surrounded with love. She died in her sleep because I believe the Lord wanted to spare her of any pain. Surely, she was blessed. You must have many loving memories of her time with you. You were lucky."

Jake thought for a moment before answering the deacon. However, considering the sincerity of the man's reply to his question, he was hard put not to be polite. So he gave the deacon a thank you and left.

The afternoon wore on with all members of the family engaged in ongoing conversations and the cousins sharing their respective plans for the future. Jake finally found a moment alone with Skip when everyone else was passing around family pictures that Kathy had brought along for the purpose of honoring her mother's memory. Skip went into the garage for a smoke, and Jake followed him.

When he lit a cigarette Jake passed him a fifty-dollar bill telling him, "Take this to help pay for the affair."

"Thanks for the cash. So brother, what do you think about all this?"

Jake never mixed words about family issues with his older brother. "Do you remember when I converted to Judaism? You never got hung up about it or passed judgment on my soul. You never called and asked why even though you knew I followed my eastern philosophy. I'll tell you something I never told anyone. I did it for Sandy, to make her happy. Don't get me wrong. I always thought of Jesus as someone to emulate, but to worship...I don't have that kind of faith. If he was half of what the stories say he was, shit, then he was a lonely man who wanted to change the status quo. Anyway, I'll tell you this much, the Jews found their God in the desert. I always identified with that. Truth is trying to follow the Jewish traditions when they're not ingrained in you is almost fuckin' impossible. You always feel like a stranger in a strange land. Whatever, now you know."

"Hey man, you're the philosopher and the intellectual. You understand shit that I couldn't begin to comprehend. Anyway, I never thought what you did was wrong. I enjoyed going to the Bar Mitzvahs. Your kids need to believe in something. It might as well be the Jewish version. What's the difference?"

"Check this Skip. That deacon claimed he knew Florence very well. Shit, he knew her in a way that she wanted him to know her. She must of played the dignified lady role for him. I can't fault him for falling for it. She loved being that way. How come you didn't show any emotion? The service was weird, talking about a woman who was a stranger to me. You know, I always thought of her as one of the kids, not Dad's wife. Tell me, did you ever get close to her when you lived nearby for all those years?"

"I got some leftover baggage from the past same as you. And no, I didn't get connected."

"Skip, remember that time a few years ago when you told me that all those support checks I sent Florence didn't change her opinion of me? She believed I could never be saved and condemned me. Is that bullshit or what? Self-righteous bullshit…like the nuns used to use to control our brains. In a way, you're my only family…I'm distant from the rest of the clan. Wish it wasn't that way. It's me; it's the way I've always been. I know they've tried to build bridges, especially Kathy. I've got no excuse."

"Jake, that's where you and I are opposites, you choose to be distant, that's your way. As far back as I can remember you were always on your own. You like it that way. I'd rather stay connected to people."

He couldn't disagree with Skip and appreciated his brother's honesty and told him, "When we were kids I loved the ole man but…but truthfully I was never connected to Florence. Whether it was her fault…who cares? Determining fault fucks up more people than you can imagine cause where there's fault, there's blame. And we both know that everybody wants to blame somebody for their bad karma. Skip, you know the term, *endearing?* Do ya? It means feeling beloved or being held in high regard. I never felt that from Florence. Yeah, as a kid I loved her because it was a sin not to. Whoever she was to other people, she wasn't that way with me. If people want to remember her as a saint,

I don't care."

Skip nodded in agreement and shook Jake's hand firmly.

The ride back to Middletown took three hours. The kids were talked out from socializing with their cousins and kept to themselves. Sandy closed her eyes and dozed while Jake drove. He was deep in thought with concerns about the upcoming vacation. Tomorrow he was taking Sandy to Maine for a five-day vacation. He cursed himself bitterly for the hypocrisy of it all, and yet he knew that the vacation was another concession he had to make. Annie would be leaving for college in two weeks and that would drastically alter the atmosphere at home. Jake knew he couldn't fill the void Annie would leave behind.

While driving on the Garden State Parkway, Jake glanced over at Sandy and thought. *Sooner or later I have to tell her that I'm leaving. As crazy as it sounds, I don't want to hurt her. Yet in reality, whether I left her for another woman or left her because I don't love her, it will produce the same outcome. Sandy will take it very badly and fall apart. And, if it was the other way around, maybe I'd feel the same way.*

CHAPTER 50

The mini vacation at Bar Harbor, Maine, helped take the edge off the stressed relationship between Sandy and Jake. Without question, the two days went by smoothly, because after Florence's funeral they were ready for some R & R. Acadia National Park was a familiar place to both of them and retracing the trail up Cadillac Mountain brought back memories of better times.

The three days spent at St John's, New Brunswick, were not nearly as enjoyable because the weather was cool and unsettled. There were on-again, off-again blue skies, but the temperature never got higher than sixty. Other than visiting historic sites and a couple of lighthouses along the Bay of Fundy, the experience was similar to their past vacations at Newport and Burlington. However this time, neither Jake nor Sandy opened up a meaningful conversation about the state of their marriage. Like a thoroughly beaten boxer hanging on the ropes in the final round, each refused to fall and be counted out.

The final blows were struck with indifference. They landed when Sandy and Jake came back to the motel after dinner on their last night at St. Johns. Sandy rejected an offer to walk along the harbor wharf with Jake and instead, preferred to watch a rerun of *Murder She Wrote*. Alone under a dim streetlight near the end of the harbor pier, Jake sat on a park bench transfixed by the incoming fog bank. He was grieving over the death of his relationship with Sandy and waiting for his inner voice to speak to him.

Jake, you went into this trip without expectations and you weren't disappointed. Wanna tell me why you feel sad? Did you expect a miracle to happen? The real miracle is that you've stayed so long with Sandy. You took a few walks with her along the beach in Maine. You gave her a couple of sea shells and you dined on some great seafood, but most of the time you thought of Ellen. You were bored playing the role of husband. You were polite, considerate, and flexible. So was she. But where was the love and passion that once came along on every trip? Where was the laughter? Know something Jake, you're full of shit for pretending to be what you're not, a happily married man. And Sandy is just as full of shit for going through the motions and believing the excursion north would jumpstart the relationship. You've got a ten-hour ride tomorrow. Imagine, all you want is to finish this so-called vacation. Tomorrow, you'll stop for lunch and pursue inane chatter. Of course, you'll listen to her concerns about the kids and promise her more...whatever's necessary to keep time moving along. Just remember, this was an attempt at resuscitation, but it failed to revive the heart. It's not capable of coming back to life.

Within a week after returning to Walden, it was as if their vacation never happened. The kids didn't ask much about it and there were no pictures or souvenirs brought back. Jake played as much golf as possible with Kevin O'Connor, and kept busy with home maintenance projects. Annie was leaving for college within a week, and J.D. was registered for fall classes at Orange Community College. Sandy was scheduled to take night classes twice a week in the fall, so a dynamic shift in the family routine was imminent.

"Out of sight...out of mind" took a firm hold on Sandy and Jake. They went about the business of living without missing a beat. Twin careers in education programmed their lives that way.

***

They drove Annie to American University and unloaded her gear in front of Letts Hall on the last Saturday in August. Jake bought her a new HP desktop computer and assembled it while Sandy set up the dorm room. J.D. had stayed behind in Walden with Missy but gave his sister a stuffed panda as a parting gift, which Annie placed on her pillow along with her favorite "Mangy Moose."

Through it all, Jake held his emotions in check but felt the emptiness as soon as they hit the Capitol Beltway for the return trip. Sharp pangs of separation tugged at his heart, and with them the realization that Annie was gone. All along she had been the ray of sunshine that made his sacrifices worthwhile.

Jake and Sandy returned to work the following week. She began her distance learning program with three other teachers from her school and Jake dealt with the demands of work while managing things at home. He continued to squeeze in two rounds of golf a week, one on Sunday afternoons with Kevin and the other, "the imaginary one," he used as an alibi for seeing Ellen after work at her apartment.

On a Saturday morning in mid-September the phone rang while Jake was outside washing his new truck. Sandy was putting laundry away when she picked up, thinking it was Annie, "Hi Sandy. I'm glad I caught you home. How are you? It's been a while."

"Rachel, what a surprise! I guess I'm all right. Actually, I've never been so busy keeping up with my job and working on my Masters Degree with this distance learning program from Marygrove College. You know, I've got to follow a tight schedule and it's a strain. Jake

366

keeps things running smoothly and J.D. is rarely around. He's going to community college and working, and Annie is at American. Lord, I miss her! Not all the time, but I miss her hugs and companionship. How about you? How have you been?"

"Sandy, my dearest friend... I'm fine...I've been worried sick about you. I've put off this call for as long as I could, but Arnie believes it's time to share our concerns regarding Jake. Remember when the four of us went kayaking on Labor Day? We couldn't help but notice...it was like Jake wasn't there. I mean, not only with us, but with you. We're not blind; we know you have been having a rough time, even if you won't admit it, but it's pretty clear to us that Jake doesn't treat you the way he should. It's not that he's mean or anything like that...I don't know...It's like he's so distant and chooses to be that way. I mean, he treats Arnie like he always does. I'm sorry Sandy; he's not the same Jake we've known since you joined the temple fifteen years ago. I guess I'm saying that we're uncomfortable. Not only on Labor Day but a few other times, such as the Miller Bar Mitzvah last spring and the Memorial Day B.B.Q. at our home. Sandy, can I help? Is there anything I can do?"

Sandy didn't know what to think. She was confused about her friend's intentions. "Rachel, would you clarify this for me. I don't understand. Really, I don't!"

Her girlfriend had thought she was clear. Nonetheless she continued. "Sandy, we're not the only people who feel this way. Diane and Jerry think the same way. The only difference is that Jerry doesn't know Jake very well. When Diane mentioned this recently to me I told her to keep it to herself. After the day kayaking...I couldn't keep it away from you any longer."

Sandy finally began to digest Rachel's inference although she didn't like what she heard. "I appreciate your honesty. Maybe I've been fooling myself into thinking that in public it wasn't so obvious. That somehow people wouldn't take any notice of us. Anyone who knows Jake thinks he's an unusual man and not your typical Jewish middle-aged professional...like your husband or Diane's. I'll tell you this, if our marital situation bothers you and Diane, then I'm certain you're not alone in your point of view. Remember when you asked me about our trip...the one up to Maine? The truth was that Jake was completely withdrawn and in his own world. We'd try to make conversation but it was a strain on both of us. After the first couple of days I gave up, so I'm also to blame. I've contained my frustration and disappointment for too long. If he really doesn't love me anymore...I wish he'd own up to it."

"Sandy, maybe it's his job, maybe its Annie being away from home... I don't like to say this, but have you considered there's another woman in his life. Is that possible? Could he be seeing..."

Sandy broke in while Rachel was in mid-sentence. "Rachel, stop it! I've heard enough. Why would you say something like that? That comment wasn't necessary...I appreciate your concern but enough is enough. I'll be in touch. Goodbye."

Shattered by the conversation, Sandy curled up on the bed, held on to her pillow and cried. Turning toward her dresser she noticed a picture of her parents, and then her tears of embarrassment became tears of anguish. Her thoughts became a jumbled mess of conflicting emotions: embarrassment, frustration, anger, and most of all apprehension.

As she entered the kitchen she saw J.D. sprawled out on the family room couch watching TV. Hoping for some affection, she walked over to sit next to him.

Before she got near him, he blurted out, "Mom, could you make me some scrambled eggs? I've got to be at work in half an hour and I told Big Bob I'd be in early to put stock on the shelves."

Jake came back into the house determined to finish his chores before noon. Sandy ignored him. She wasn't ready to discuss Rachel's call and began to make breakfast for J.D. While sitting at the counter, he made a request that lit the short fuse on the powder keg of pent up emotions that was hidden inside of Jake's calm appearance.

"Mom, how come there's no whipped butter? Could you melt half a stick for me in the microwave? I want it soft so I can spread it on this fresh Challah."

Jake snapped like a dry twig stepped on by a hiker's boot. For a second, he stared coldly at his son but he couldn't restrain himself enough to ignore the stupid request. He screamed, "What the hell is wrong with you? You're making your mother wait on you like she was a waitress? All week she works hard, and you make a demand like that! Soft butter, that's want you must have...huh...what bullshit!!"

Jake seized the saucer in the microwave and hurled it at his son. When it hit the counter, it shattered into several pieces. And when it broke, so did Sandy's fragile state of mind.

Horrified by the act, she started to tremble and screamed, "What are you doing, Jake? Why are you interfering with me? I'm his mother! What's the difference if I melt the butter or not? Get the hell outta here and leave us alone. Damn you, Jake! You're nuts! Nothing's right with you anymore. Absolutely nothing! I've had it! I don't want to be here...with any of you. I can't stand it."

She started toward Jake and began pounding her fists against his chest, hollering, "I'm finished! I'm done with this family! I can't take it any longer! You're all selfish and I'm sick of it! I'm taking my car and crashing it into the nearest tree. Let me out of here. I'm leaving!"

Jake knew she meant it and immediately wrapped his arms around his sobbing wife trying to restrain her. She collapsed on the kitchen floor and started thrashing about. At first, J.D. didn't move. He sat frozen. He was bewildered and frightened by his mother's total loss of control, ashamed by his own stupidity. Finally, too scared to sit still in the midst of such turmoil, he came over and helped his father hold Sandy down all the time pleading her for forgiveness and holding back his tears.

"Mom...Mom I'm sorry...I'm so sorry. Please, Mom, don't do anything crazy...I'm...I'm sorry...really...please Mom. Oh my God! Dad...Dad, don't let her go out...Don't! I'm sorry. I'm sorry!"

Together, they held Sandy until her sobbing ceased. She apparently wore herself out and sat very quietly for a moment. Carefully, Jake walked her to the couch and, with his son, tried to comfort his wife. Then he whispered to his son. "J.D., get her car keys and bring 'em to me. I'll stay with your mother."

Over the next hour Jake stayed with Sandy until she regained enough composure to get up from the couch. Now more than ever he realized just how vulnerable Sandy was and how he had to maintain better self-control. When she stood by the sink getting a drink of water, Jake apologized for his behavior.

"I have no excuse for causing this trouble. I snapped. I couldn't deal with his selfish behavior. I know I'm responsible for this mess. I should've minded my own business. Sandy, I'm so sorry. Would you like to spend some time with me this afternoon?"

"No...I don't want your company. I've got some things to sort out. Just go, and do your thing like you do every Saturday. We can't have anything interfere with that. Can we? That would be unthinkable! Don't worry, I won't hurt myself or do anything crazy. I'll probably take Missy for a walk. Go away! I want some time alone."

Jake was relieved she gave him an exit, although he knew she was pissed at him. "That's a relief. I'm gonna finish the chores. I'll be around for a while longer."

Part of her wanted to slap him right across the face and tell him to "go to hell" for his meaningless act of belated kindness. She thought it would be wiser to just let him leave. However, in view of Rachel's comments, Sandy felt compelled to make a specific request in order to clear the air later on. "I'd like you to take me out for dinner. Is that all right? I want to go to a quiet place so we can talk in private. I need to clear my head and that's how I want to do it."

Jake acknowledged her request with a nod and then cleaned the kitchen. Sandy went back upstairs and passed J.D. leaving his room. She hugged him and told him she loved him regardless of what he did. A few minutes later, as the boy was ready to leave, Jake grabbed him and stared coldly in his eyes, warning him, "It's been a month since the last time I had a serious conflict with you. Listen! I'm telling you this straight. Don't you ever put your mother in another crisis! Am I clear? Now go to work."

Jake arrived at Chestnut Hill an hour late. Ellen was patiently waiting on the front steps by the parking area when he approached. Without giving her his usual kiss, he took hold of her hand and tried to explain why he was late.

"Sorry I kept you waiting. The chores took longer than I thought they would. I promised to take Sandy out shopping later and I can only stay for a couple of hours."

Ellen immediately saw that Jake wasn't acting like Jake. "Jake, what's wrong? And don't tell me some silly tale. We promised never to hold back the truth. Stop the charade and talk to me!"

Feeling pressured, he told Ellen about the morning meltdown. "There was an unfortunate incident this morning. It was over something stupid...really stupid. I lost my temper with J.D. and it set off Sandy, set her off big time. When I left...let's just say she was hurting. Something's going on with her and I'm facing a serious situation. But that's my problem. I really shouldn't have left her alone to come here. Now I'm feeling responsible and what's worse, I'm feeling anxious. Something's brewing. Shit, Ellen she broke down, she fell apart. I hate to masquerade when I'm with her and I hate sharing this insanity with you. I'm sorry, but you wanted to know the truth."

"Don't be sorry because I've been keeping some stuff from you."

"Bullshit! You mean we're both dealing with shit?"

They sat in silence, not knowing what to say next. Neither of them wanted to cross over the line that kept their other world off-limits. It was an agreement they'd stuck to. They both knew their love was true, but how enduring was it? Ellen had promised in several letters to Jake that she never wanted to hurt his family. Similarly, Jake had withheld judgment of her former spouse because Ellen had purposely left out any mention of Guy's behavior during their marriage.

"I've got to assume that Sandy will bring up the sorry state of our marriage tonight. She wants to have dinner out and then have a talk. I want to tell her I'm leaving. I really do. But my problem is timing. Timing means everything...everything in how I try to resolve problems. Annie's been away only a few weeks and I don't know what's going on inside of Sandy's head. Damn it. I wish that meltdown..."

"Listen Jake, you've always protected me from doing foolish things by forcing me to consider the consequences. If Sandy isn't emotionally equipped for you to leave, then don't do it. Believe me, based on what you've said, she's in no state of mind to handle a disappointment of such proportion. Don't hurt her like that.

"My divorce was way overdue. It was my reason for moving back to Middletown, but I never thought the boys would choose to live with him. That was their decision. I remember being crushed and hurt beyond anything I thought possible. It was as if the kids vanished after being there every moment of my life. I never believed that Guy would switch roles or that I'd be in my current situation. I accepted the fact that my life would be that of a working single mother. Now I've finally accepted the separation from the boys. Like you taught me, it was karma. Please go home. Go now and call me whenever you can."

What Ellen purposely kept from Jake was that her weekly arrangement for visitations with the boys had run into serious problems. While she was away in July, Guy's patience began to wear thin with the responsibilities of single parenting. He resented her for taking a two-week vacation without telling him. Since her return in late July, his conversations took on a decidedly critical and negative tone.

When Jake returned home he saw that Sandy was weeding the flower bed around the mailbox. After he parked the truck, he walked up the driveway to see how she was recuperating from the breakdown. As he came near she took off her gardening gloves and greeted him.

"You're back so soon. How come? I told you I'd be all right."

"I'm here and that's what counts. What would you like to do?"

"Let's walk around the development. I have some things I want to say to you. You don't need to take me to dinner. I'm going in to wash up. I'll be back in five minutes."

Jake sat on the curb and wondered what was coming. He knew that whatever was on her mind, he'd better make damn sure he took it seriously and had enough common sense not to argue, not today. Five minutes later she showed up with Missy, and they started down Treetop Terrace.

"Rachel called this morning and she turned my world upside down. You'd better listen. You're not gonna like what you hear. Apparently, some of our friends are uncomfortable spending time with us. Can you imagine that? People are talking about us. It's no secret anymore, they're aware of our marital problems. They think you don't treat me the way a Jewish woman deserves to be treated. They resent the way you're so distant and disconnected. I'm embarrassed. Do you understand? I was embarrassed beyond words after listening to her. Those people have been our friends for a long time. They've seen our kids grow up. We've shared so many events…so many memorable times. I know you haven't any idea what my social connection to them has meant to me. Even when my parents were still alive, those people were like my other family. You don't understand that notion. You can't even comprehend it. Did you hear what I said? They have been my family since my parents died. Now because of you, I'm losing my social life. That's one issue, but if you think I'll accept their loss, I won't! You're the cause of this gossip."

His instincts told him to wait and she'd have more to say. After walking another minute, she continued. Only this time she stopped and stood face to face with him.

"Jake, there's no reason for us to continue this marriage, none whatsoever. You've slowly been leaving me for the past five years. I know you're not happy although I'm completely at a loss to explain why. I know you're a good person. You've never failed to be responsible about anything concerning our family's welfare and I've never worried about a single financial thing in twenty years. You bought me this gorgeous home and let me furnish it with the things I love. My mother used to say that you were a great provider and you deserved my support. I believed her because your actions proved it. Do you remember when we went to the marriage counselor after Annie's illness? Even though we weren't getting along we agreed to stay together because the children needed us. But has anything changed since then?

"You've always told me that you were your own best resource and your own best friend. All these years have passed and that concept is still foreign to me. I don't understand what that means. Jake, I'm not like you! So much of you is hidden underneath that impenetrable wall of yours, the wall that I can't break through."

Jake turned and started to walk away but she grabbed him.

"I'm angry because I've let you stay that way. You're a mystery…you're even a mystery to your own kids. I haven't been myself lately. I suppose I let you run away from me. I was wrong to do that. I felt like I didn't have any way of changing you. We've hung on because of the kids. I appreciate that more than you could ever know. My God, if you would've left during their high school years, I would have been broken. I don't know what comes next between us, but I don't want to continue this way."

In all their time together Jake couldn't recall when she was so serious. Without sounding argumentative or hostile, Jake responded. "I understand most of what you've said. I'm not going to argue with you about it. You made your point. **Sandy, what do you want? Should I make plans to move out?**"

"Not yet. I'd like you to take some time and decide if you're capable of making a change and if you want to stay married any longer. Maybe you should consider seeing a professional. One thing is certain, if you can't love me then why should we continue? Over the next month or two you figure it out."

It seemed that neither of them knew what else to say. Jake came very close to telling Sandy his mind was already made up and that he'd leave the first of the year. However, he believed the timing still wasn't right. Sandy assertions were well thought out, and not driven by her morning hysteria. And, in spite of the powerful temptation to respond to her condemnation, he accepted her offer.

"I accept your suggestion. I'll take some time and think about what you've said. The kids don't need to know about this. Want me to do anything else in the meantime?"

"Please be considerate of my feelings. Honestly, I never thought we'd be in a situation like this. When I met you after I spent seven years in a loveless marriage, I believed you were superman, a combination of wisdom, strength, and intelligence. I really did. You were the most unusual man I'd ever met. You weren't Jewish and that really frightened me. But you were honest and noble, and in some ways you still are. I always believed you could do anything. I knew how hard your life was growing up and admired you for never giving up. Maybe that superman stuff was childish, but I didn't care cause I believed in you. We got here because of your hard work and planning. I don't know what's next? I'm already tired and the school year is only two weeks old. Honestly, I'm doing the graduate work to keep busy. Jake, you've kept your word. I guess you don't want to be married. Well, tell me. Am I right?"

Jake realized that it was the defining question but he chose not to answer. Instead, he shrugged his shoulders in uncertainty. Then he took her hand and they walked back home completely immersed in their own thoughts. They never did go out for dinner that night.

తచ్

Another couple of weeks passed without incident, it was as though all three of them knew things were different. J.D. tried to keep his compulsive behaviors in check. How he managed to subdue them didn't matter to Jake. Ever aware of his son's attitude adjustment, Jake felt compelled to speak with J.D. after he came home from work. Sandy had left a message saying she wouldn't be home for dinner. Her graduate study group changed the day to accommodate one of the participants and she wouldn't be home till ten, so Jake took J.D. out for pizza and gave his son an update of the situation.

"For the past couple of weeks, things have been calm. Why do you suppose that is?"

"I don't know Dad. I've been going to school and trying not to cause any trouble. I don't want Mom to lose it. Shit, she wanted to crash the car. That scene in the kitchen scared me."

"Look, you're almost twenty years old. You should know the truth. Things are not good between your mother and me. I'm not sure where I'll be a couple of months from now, but there's one thing I know for sure, your mother has loved you with all her heart and deserves some extra consideration. What I'm trying to say is that I know you're being cooperative and I appreciate your efforts, honestly, a couple of weeks of peace won't affect the eventual outcome. Joshua Daniel, I don't want you to believe you can fix our problem. That's not the way it works. Be a good son. That's enough."

J.D. was shaken by his father's mention of the marital problems. It was the one thing he didn't want to know about. He had tried to escape whenever he felt uncomfortable around them.

"Dad, it isn't that hard for me to keep out of trouble. I'm purposely staying out of the house. You know, going over to James' or Matt's. Mom misses Annie and she'd be a lot better if Annie wasn't away."

"You have a legit point. I mean we aren't mall shoppers. We don't go to Friday night services at the temple all the time and neither do we share any of your mother's interests. Annie's not replaceable, but she's where she belongs. The best thing for us is be sensitive to Mom and not cause her any grief."

"All right, Dad. I'll try my best. I hate seeing you so miserable."

Later that night Jake called Ellen to tell her he wouldn't be able to see her the next day. He explained the change in Sandy's schedule forced him to cancel their date. After the disappointing news, they tried to make small talk but seemed incapable of distracting each other.

After a few minutes, Jake told her he had no intention of bringing his crap to Chestnut Hill to drown her in his problems. "I love you enough to keep you out of my turmoil. All I can say is that I'm very close to giving her my decision…probably after Thanksgiving. Hopefully things would be better after we go to parent's weekend at American University in late October. Maybe after we visit Annie, some stability might return, at least for a while longer. I want to settle this thing before too long and move out by January."

Hearing his thoughts, Ellen reassured him of her support by saying, "I've told you many times. Do whatever's necessary for your family's well-being. I know this is a difficult time for you. I'll wait."

ॐ

Jake, J.D. and Sandy returned from celebrating the Jewish New

Year, Rosh Hashanah, at her uncle's home in Monticello. It had been a long day with the three-hour morning religious service and the traditional dinner, but it was a wonderful holiday celebration and Sandy was happy. Seeing her extended family plus listening to stories about her parents worked magic on her mood. After changing out of their dress clothes and relaxing for an hour, Jake invited Sandy to take a walk around the development.

As they made the final turn and headed up Treetop Terrace, Jake heard the distinct sound of a car racing its engine. At first he thought nothing of it. But a few minutes later he heard it again, this time louder. Jake stopped dead in his tracks after rounding the corner. He was paralyzed by anger as he watched his son race his yellow Chevy Chevelle down Treetop Terrace. It was near dark, and his wife didn't make the connection. She thought it was another neighborhood kid. Outwardly, Jake appeared calm and said nothing to Sandy to indicate he knew it was J.D. causing the disturbance.

Inside, he was beyond his limit of tolerance for J.D.'s blatant disregard for his mother's sensitivities. He resolved that whatever he was going to do with the boy wasn't going to be witnessed by Sandy. He was going to shield her from the battle he was ready to wage.

When they returned home Sandy commented. "Jake, I know what you're thinking and, believe me, I'm thinking the same. How could our son be so disrespectful of a religious holiday? I'm so embarrassed for us. There's something wrong with him."

"Sandy, please let me handle this. Take Missy inside and wait for me upstairs."

"What are you going to do?"

"I'm not sure. It'll depend on him, but this...this it too much. It's a careless disregard for our reputation. Our neighbors know it's a religious holiday for us. Please...please just go in the house."

Jake took a minute to walk around the property, hoping it would calm him down. No sooner had he finished when the Chevelle raced past the front of the house. With a burst of indignation, Jake sped across the front lawn and stood boldly in the middle of the street, waiting for his son to return. A few more minutes passed, and the fuse inside burned down farther. As the car approached, the headlights came closer and closer. Jake wouldn't budge. The car stopped short thirty feet away, Jake shook his fist at the driver and then the Chevelle turned into the driveway.

"Get out of that car right now, both of you."

J.D. and James did as they were told and cautiously moved toward the garage door. The overhead floodlight showed the fear on their faces.

"James, get the hell out of here! Move it!"

Without muttering a single word, James darted away like a spooked horse that stumbled upon a rattler. Jake was in a state of rage and told J.D., "don't even think you have an excuse for what you've done. You're selfish, thoughtless, and an asshole. You just don't get it, do you?"

Jake moved closer, all the while staring coldly into the eyes of the frightened boy. Shoving his fist against the boy's chest, Jake couldn't hold back as he repeatedly pushed his fist back and forth against his son.

Then he yelled, "Two weeks ago you pushed me over the edge along with your mother. You saw her break right in front of your eyes. Are you forgetting she wanted to kill herself. Do you hear me? Now you blatantly disregard her feelings again and make a mockery of the observance of Rosh Hashanah. I could break you in half. You're gonna be twenty in two months and yet you are no different than a selfish ten-year-old who plays with his toys when he's supposed to be in bed. Damn you! I got some news for you, I'm through. Do you hear me? You've pushed me once too often. I've bent over backwards for you. Now get the hell out of my sight before I let myself give you the treatment you deserve."

The shock of his father's angry words shamed the boy, and he made no attempt to block his father's pushing nor did he try to give an excuse for showing off. However, no statement of remorse left his lips. J.D. started for his car, but as he passed by Jake jerked him back, almost throwing him down on the driveway. He'd never seen his father act like this, but something inside told him not to challenge his father, not tonight.

Jake was furious and screamed, "You get in that car and I'll take a tire iron and smash that yellow Chevelle to bits! Don't even think of fighting me! J.D., get in the house!"

Downright afraid and trembling, J.D. finally realized he had crossed the line. At that moment, he felt genuinely sorry for letting his friend talk him into the stupid stunt. He also realized that he'd shamed his family and deserved the wrath of his father. He hung his head low as walked into the kitchen.

"You know J.D., it was one thing to refuse to wear a tie for services and upset your mother the first thing in the morning. I can handle that shit even if your mom can't. But what you did tonight…that was wrong. We've put up with your selfishness and stupid behavior for too long. Personally, I've run out of patience. You hear me? Just go to your room, and don't stop by and beg your mother for forgiveness."

Jake found Sandy sitting on the couch in the living room,

pretending to read a magazine. He was emotionally spent. All he wanted to do was pack some clothes and drive to a motel. Tonight was a turning point for him with regard to the consequences of leaving his family. He didn't care any longer if they forgave him or not. He didn't care anymore what the consequences would be after he left.

When Jake entered the room, she waited for him to say something. Jake noticed the forlorn expression on her face and held back his desire to run away. Instead, he decided to let her know part of the inner struggle that was going on inside of him. "Sandy, I'm worn out. I'm empty. Not because of anything you did. Even with J.D.'s latest episode I somehow managed to handle it without resorting to extremes. I'm just trying to survive. I hate living like this. I'm looking for some daylight. I don't know what's ahead for me. I just wanted you to know that I'm running on empty. So you see I can open the gates of my soul occasionally!"

He leaned down and kissed her as an expression of his sincerity. As he started to walk away, she called to him.

"Jake, do you still love me? I wanted to ask you two weeks ago, but I was over the edge. Tell me now. I want to know if you still love me."

Rather than risk another meltdown Jake took the safe way out. "Sandy, I honestly don't know what I feel anymore…about you or about us. You gave me some time to decide and I'm taking it. I'm sorry I can't be more reassuring but I've already handled enough tonight."

CHAPTER 51

After the racing incident on the Jewish holiday, an uneasy peace emerged in the Carr household. Jake was depending on J.D. to behave telling him, "If you cause us any more trouble, believe me the strained family atmosphere will implode leaving you as a casualty." The boy took the warning seriously. He went to his college classes four days a week and kept busy with his auto restoration projects. Sandy spent most evenings doing school work and graduate studies while Jake stayed down in the basement.

Sandy's closest friends called frequently to stay in touch. During those phone conversations, she became "another woman," always showcasing her competent, fully-functional self and avoiding personal matters regarding her fragile emotional state. Jake continued to make certain the house was in order, making dinners and doing the chores. He tried to show Sandy as much kindness and consideration as he could muster, notwithstanding her disconsolate mood.

Sandy was already in bed sleeping when J.D. opened the basement door and called down, "Hey, Dad! Kevin's on the phone. Come up."

Jake grabbed the Molson next to him and hustled up the stairs to take the call. J.D. passed over the phone and then he exited the room to give his father some privacy.

"Who in the hell is calling me at ten-thirty and on a school night?"

"Hey, Jake the Cowboys are getting their ass kicked. Know something? I love watching this kind of game almost as much as I loved chipping in on eighteen yesterday. That was for a tie wasn't it? Now we'll have to wait till next weekend to see who gets braggin rights."

"No good Kevin. I can't play this Sunday. I thought I told you, we're going to visit Annie."

"Come to think of it, you didn't tell me that. You've been in another world. What ever happened to the weekly report? The one we used to give each other on the practice putting green or in the parking lot?"

"Come on, who wants to talk seriously on the golf course."

"Bullshit! Something's going on in that head of yours? Stop acting like an asshole!"

For a split second, Jake wanted to do the same routine as Sandy always did with her friends. Then again, Kevin was the only person who knew about his affair with Ellen Eastman.

"Jake, you gonna make me wait all night? Am I'm gonna miss the second-half kickoff?"

Another couple of seconds elapsed; finally Jake sucked up enough courage and let it out. "Umm…honestly buddy, things are very fucked up. I'm stuck in the mire. There's not much sunshine in my life other than knowing Ellen's waiting for me somewhere in the distant future."

"Leave Ellen out of this…goddamn it, I never even met her! This conversation is about you. Tell me! You're fucked up where, with whom, at home, at work, with your kids, is it Sandy? What're you saying?"

"Sandy and I are…we're in a real strange place. We're like two zombies. The other day she told me to make up my mind…am I staying cause I love her or am I cutting out. Meaning, either redefine the relationship or make plans to leave. Truth is, I've abandoned ship and Sandy knows it. I jumped off a long time ago and now, I'm treading through icy water, numbing up and running out of breath…All I want to do is hang on a while longer but I'm drowning. Man it sucks, big time!"

"Hey look, you've been down this road before. Maybe not with this type of shit, but there've been lots of other times when you managed to get through… sometimes against all odds."

"You don't get it. The marriage is dead, only the funeral hasn't taken place. Problem is, there are some loose ends. Part of me wants to pack up and move in with Ellen this weekend. But that would be messy, very fucking messy, because I'd be leaving Sandy emotionally battered and bleeding. The kids might suffer and I don't want that. I figure there's gotta be away of leaving with the least amount of damage. What do you think? Am I nuts?"

"Yeah, you are. You're cutting this too fine, my friend. I know you don't want anyone to get hurt but Sandy's already hurting. You think it really matters one way or the other how you leave? You just wanna hide the fact that you had an affair. You think it'll spare Sandy some pain?"

Kevin's assertion was true, but Jake persisted in trying to explain. "That's not how I want to end it. I love my daughter and maybe I'll lose her if she knew the truth. Maybe she'd never forgive me for hurting her mother. Like I said, Sandy already provided me with an opening."

Kevin finally knew the reason why Jake was scared to leave.

"You may not be able to make it for that long. I don't know how Sandy's never suspected anything. You and Ellen have been so lucky! I think that realistically, it doesn't matter what the circumstances are, ending a twenty-year marriage has gotta be tough. It's a damn shame cause you really did believe you had a future with Sandy. You loved her."

Jake appreciated his friend's sentiment and yet felt like clearing it up once and for all. "No shit! I could talk for two hours and still not give you the complete picture of my fuckin' disappointment in that woman. Do you really think I would've ever cheated on her if our love was solid and enduring, if we respected and cherished one another? I've argued with myself a thousand times about it. Remember that you were the one who encouraged me to go for happiness because you knew all along about my anger concerning that woman. Shit, I'm just glad that your second marriage worked."

Maybe for the first time since Jake told him about Ellen, Kevin knew his buddy had a pile of crap to get out of his head. If he could, he wanted to help Jake make it through the crisis. "Listen Jake, I have something I want to say. All that inheritance money ever did was cause you a lot of pain and I know you've never forgiven Sandy. She kept control of that money and it hurt you. All these years I've seen you take care of everything. It was all one-sided, and you let it eat up your insides. You're partly to blame and you know it. Joanie and I put everything in one pot. It's the only way."

Kevin was right on the mark and Jake couldn't skirt the truth. "Strike one. You hit the bullseye. I know I should have made some demands from her. Here it is. I'll give you another full blast of icy truth. I became Jewish for the sake of the kids and to make Sandy happy. I figured if I did that, there's no way our relationship would ever falter. I'm no religious ideologue so I did it for her. Imagine that? Go ahead. What else?"

"Jake, don't pull that shit on me. I've always respected you enough not to invade your privacy. You're the same way with me. Christ, it took five fuckin' years for me to tell you about my depression. You sat dumbfounded on that ride home from the golf course like I told you I had AIDS...ah fuck it!"

Jake bit on his thumbnail in an attempt to keep his temper cool. Then he said, "I suppose at the very core of it all is that I'm so fucking mad at Sandy and yet I'm the one having the affair. You know, when her parents died she carried on for so long...that was the beginning of it all going sour. I resented her big time for that. Then there was Annie's eating disorder. How the fuck did that happen? Kevin, I'm the one who's leaving and I'm angry as hell because I swear to you...I tried. I tried to make the marriage work...goddamn her and the pile of horseshit her parents put in her head. It has spoiled everything."

Kevin knew his friend was hurting. Maybe it was guilt, but he thought that Jake was empty from years of disappointment. It was a long time to invest in a marriage. "Listen Jake, you've given me your reasons, the inheritance, the Jewish thing, her old man, the grieving shit, and your own stubborn streak. But all that shit is water over the damn. Let it go."

"Kevin...I can't have Sandy falling apart. The kids would hate me."

"You've got no control over that. But I'm glad she doesn't know about Ellen. Talk about a mind-fucking of the highest order. That's what would happen. You know damn well, Sandy is as beaten up as you are. My best advice for you is to lay low with regard to Ellen. At least until you move out. And whatever you do, you better not leave Treetop and move in with her. That would really fuck things up with the kids. Don't do it! I'm sorry you're living a nightmare, but at least you can look forward to better days. Jake, go get another beer and chill out. I'll be around if you need me. You got my word on that."

"Thanks you crazy Irishman...I know my problem is that there's way too much anger in me. After tonight I'm gonna try and extinguish the fire and somehow try to pass the time quietly."

"Jake, take one day at a time. And listen lover boy, please be careful with Ellen. Why don't you tell her about all this shit? If she's the woman you say she is, she'll hang in there and help get you through it. One other thing, don't let this affect your job, that's something you can't let happen."

❧❧

Ellen was only somewhat aware of Jake's current troubles at home. Similarly, she was embroiled in her own ongoing dilemma with Guy. Since her return from the summer road trip, he had dramatically changed his attitude towards her by becoming increasingly more confrontational during her visits.

Danny had passed up an afternoon of miniature golf and pizza, but Joey went. Ellen was about to drive away when Guy came over to the jeep. Judging by his expression she braced herself for trouble.

"When are you going to do your share? When can you take the boys for a weekend so I can get away and have a life of my own? You owe me that much. You ran off for two weeks in the summer and left me without a hint of your whereabouts. That was pretty damn selfish and you didn't think anything of it. When are you taking them?"

Although Jake had warned her that sooner or later this would come up, her mind went blank. It was as if she returned to her former timid self.   "Umm...I, I don't know. I'm not sure when I'll be able to do that."

"That's not good enough. What do you mean, you're not sure?"

"I've got commitments...I can't give you an answer at this time."

"Damn you Ellen. I've done my part. You gotta take them!"

Maybe it was the tone of his voice that snapped her out of a trance, but whatever it was she realized he was bullying her again regardless of whether he was right or not.

"Guy, did they ask me to take them? Answer me…well? No, they didn't. This is all your idea and not theirs. When they make the request and ask for a sleepover, I'll deal with it."

With that blunt response, Ellen left Guy shell-shocked by her total lack of consideration for his needs. It seemed their roles were now completely reversed and he hated it.

After the face-off with Guy, Ellen began to suspect that Lucy Capone might be involved with her ex-husband. Lucy was at the Westgate home on more than a few Sundays, and Ellen figured there was more to it than just coincidence. The more she thought about it, the more she realized how foolish she was for asking Lucy to pick her up at the airport when she returned from the summer road trip. Ellen remembered the surprised look on Lucy's face when she answered an inquiry about her travel companion by stating, "I was with someone from work. We met in Denver and traveled together. It was purely platonic."

Whether Lucy believed her story was irrelevant at the time, but now it seemed she probably told Guy. Then, Ellen recalled another incident involving Lucy. One that occurred last year when Lucy asked her to go shopping on a Saturday and she declined. Ellen remembered she may have mentioned an invitation to go hiking with a friend from work. Lucy wanted to know the particulars. Ellen realized she might have dropped Jake's name thinking mentioning his name wouldn't mean a thing to her friend.

After she thought more about it, a very troubling thought crossed her mind. *Lucy might know I'm seeing Jake. I think I mentioned his name as the friend who took me on that hike. It's possible.*

When Jake came over on Wednesday their dinner conversation was lighthearted as usual, dealing with activities at work and their future plans. The fall colors were coming out and Jake wanted to return to the Delaware Water Gap. After serving him coffee, Ellen couldn't put off the bad news any longer.

"Jake, I've got to tell you something and I know you're not going to like it."

"Did you lose your job? I'm only kidding. Considering all the shit that's happened lately, I'll take my chances. Besides, the blueberry pie was terrific. Go ahead and fire away!"

"I think someone I knew when I lived on Westgate may know that I'm seeing you. Last fall, she nagged me about who I was hiking with instead of shopping with her.…I think I may have inadvertently mentioned your name. It's all foggy. I just think you should know. I'm sorry."

"So what? That was a year ago. Am I missing something?"

"Well, when she picked me up at the airport. I don't think she believed my story about traveling with a friend from work. Now I think she's seeing my ex-husband. It's all confusing."

Judging by his expression, Ellen realized that Jake still didn't appreciate the ramifications and told him so. "Jake, my ex-husband is a jealous and vindictive man. He's been asking me about my personal life ever since I refused to give up my vacation time to take the boys so he could have a break."

"Why would he care what you did on vacation or who you're seeing? What business is it of his? You're divorced! What the hell's his problem? Do you care who he dates or carries on with?"

"You don't understand. He's been angry with me for not spending more time with the boys. He thinks I should take them for a weekend. I don't even know if they want to do that and I told him so."

"Why didn't you tell me? You should've considered his request."

"Consider his request...why? What would they do over here? There's barely enough room to store my stuff. Come on?"

"Ellen, that's not his problem. What if he's had no break from single parenting? I can tell you right now. That would piss him off. Some things are not about money. The man wants some time off!"

"What you don't understand is that he's a spiteful man. If he thought I was involved with a married man, I don't know what he might do, or how it would affect the boys. He might even hurt you."

"Hurt me how? I thought you told me he was an overweight wimp. How's he gonna hurt me? What's he gonna do? Threaten to blackmail me? That shit's only on TV. In real life that doesn't happen. Nobody cares about stuff like that. Remember Clinton's troubles? Fifty percent of the population cared and the other fifty percent didn't. I'm nobody special."

"Once again, you still don't understand. It's not about you. If he thought he could hurt me by hurting you, he'd do it. He figures he's in the right. I wish I were wrong, but with him anything is possible. He's unpredictable and downright mean. I know. I lived in fear of him."

Dealing with Ellen's fears, whether credible or not was the least of Jake's concerns. His plate was already full and spilling over. Not knowing much about Guy, he couldn't take him seriously.   "Ok, now I get it. You can't change anything so let it go."

CHAPTER 52

Dr. Augustine Moore, Principal of Middletown High, stood alone in his oak paneled office looking out the oversized picture window that had a full view of the playing fields across Ridge Road. "Gus," as the seasoned faculty referred to him, thought he'd experienced the full spectrum of parental complaints until fifteen minutes ago when he received an unexpected visit from Guy Eastman.

As principal, Moore was a veteran of board politics, tight budgets, teacher union grievances, parent conflicts, morale problems, political interference, and the various whimsical school reforms that came from the legislature in Albany. He was an honors graduate of Seton Hall University and held a doctorate from Fordham. Gus was two parts past mathematics teacher, and one part principal plus philosopher. He was one hundred percent Jesuit trained, and a man who spoke with an intellectual frame of reference on any topic. He was gregarious by nature and an outstanding principal who was responsible for the education of 1,200 students and a staff of over a hundred.

As he stared at the fall foliage on the maple trees that lined the parking area, he was uncertain about the course of action he would take regarding a counselor he respected for his work ethic, professional skill, and staunch advocacy for students. Eastman claimed that Carr should be investigated for what Eastman termed, "unprofessional conduct." When Moore specifically inquired as to the nature of the conduct and if it involved any students, Eastman chose his words very carefully. "I believe Mr. Carr is having an illicit affair with my former wife. I view that behavior as unprofessional and unacceptable. A married high school counselor should not act like that. It's scandalous and I'd like you to investigate."

Turning his attention away from the outside environment, he walked over to a walnut conference table, took out a writing tablet, and considered the best course of action. He was aware that Eastman was sending him on a "fishing expedition," but what was he fishing for? Was Jake supposed to reveal something about his personal life to him? What rights did Jake have to his privacy?

Moore didn't appreciate making an intrusion into an employee's private life unless he was invited. Experience had taught him that most complaints surfaced whenever a parent "had it out" for a faculty member or a coach. However, in this particular case, Eastman's complaint was obviously meant to embarrass a well-respected member of his staff. He recalled that during the last year alone, he had to protect teachers from unjustified "witch hunts" several times. The varsity soccer coach came under fire for not giving sufficient playing time to a politician's kid. There were complaints about teachers who refused to change grades, or back off charges of plagiarism. There was also a charge of unprofessional conduct against the drama teacher for screaming at a senior girl and bringing her to tears in front of the class. And of course, dealing with the PTA activists who claimed a few teachers didn't teach and should be fired forthwith. In short, any disgruntled parent had the potential to harm the reputation of a member of the Middletown High School staff. Some of them did their dirty work through the "cocktail circuit," while others did their misanthropic deeds over the phone. Apparently it was Eastman's strategy to get his complaint on the record, therefore Gus was obligated to meet with Jake and report the complaint to the superintendent if he deemed it to be school-related.

Twenty minutes later, Gus appeared at Jake's door. Jake was on the phone at the time, so he opened the door, sat down and waited for the call to end. Jake knew something was up, so he ended the conversation.

Gus Moore started out casually, seemingly without any pretense for the visit. "Jake, how're you doing? The SATs are this weekend, isn't that right?"

"What's up, Dr. Moore? We both know you're not here to discuss the SAT test this Saturday."

"Jake, you've got a problem. I've got to ask you a personal question that I'd rather not."

"Hey look, you're doing your job. I can appreciate that and we're both veterans of parent wars. Like I tell my students, just lay it out honestly...pure and simple."

Jake sat back in his office chair with his arms crossed and waited.

"A parent came in and accused you of unprofessional conduct."

"What did I do to incur their wrath? Go to a topless bar in the city, forget to list some student activity on a transcript, or did I use an expletive during a conference...Huh?"

Moore knew that whatever direction he took was going to be a losing proposition. Jake was way the hell too knowledgeable and well versed on parent-based back stabbing. Nevertheless, he had no choice but to disclose the nature of the complaint. "Mr. Eastman claims you're having an affair with his ex-wife. He's charging you with unprofessional conduct because you're a married man. That's what he presented me with this morning."

Jake couldn't hide his utter disbelief and amusement at the audacity of Eastman. He decided to play along in spite of wanting to shut off the dialogue with an, "I don't care to comment on that" statement.

"Gus, give me a second to digest what you just said. It sounds like a rather strange complaint. Let me understand...is this the new millennium? I mean, I'm not trying to be a smart ass with you but something's not right...you said Eastman's ex-wife."

Moore appeared to be waiting for more. Scratching behind his ear to give the appearance of being in deep thought, Jake continued. "So then this complaint has nothing to do with my performance on the job. You know, like what I'm doing here from seven to three. How does he know anything about me or about my personal life? Did he hire a private eye to tail me? Does he follow me around and videotape me? Hey Gus, what am I to him? With all due respect, I don't appreciate what's going on here."

Moore was stuck. Apparently, Jake wasn't going to volunteer anything if it wasn't relevant to his job. Gus wondered why he should've thought anything different. Carr seemed unfazed by the complaint.

"I see your point. Unless you did something that warrants tenure charges...and we both know you didn't, I don't know what else to discuss with you concerning the matter."

Jake thought very carefully before he proceeded. He leaned across the desk, rested his chin on his fist and in a confident manner announced, "Think of it this way. I don't ask you what you do after work. Whether you gamble on ponies or go to the topless bars. I mean...look at it from my perspective. You know damn well it's none of his business what I do outside of school. What did Eastman do? Appoint himself morality sheriff of Orange County. So you tell me. Will he succeed in getting his way? Besides, everyone knows that legally, there is no relationship between ex-wives and their former husbands. There're supposed to respect each other's privacy when they're divorced. Anyway, I'm off on a tangent."

"Jake, I got your point. One thing's for sure, the Board of Education people are used to getting complaint letters from parents, but to my knowledge, not usually about an employee's personal life when it doesn't interfere with students. They're not in the business of abetting some individual's need for spreading scandal. At least, I'd like to think they're not in that business."

"Whoa...Dr. Moore, what do you mean by scandal? As I told you, my personal life is my business. Who I associate with or where I go after I leave my job...hey that's out of line. It's nobody's concern."

Gus shook his head from side to side before continuing. He knew the motivation behind the complaint was to embarrass Jake. Usually the general public couldn't care less what a teacher did after hours as long as they were law-abiding and discreet.

"Jake, as long as you've done nothing wrong in relation to your job, that's all that really matters to me. If the central office wants to know anything else, that's their problem. I'm sorry I had to hassle you."

"As I said before, I've done nothing wrong in my capacity as a counselor at Middletown High. The union people wouldn't like this kind of harassment by the administration. What do you think?"

"All right Jake. I've told you what's going on. If I need any more information I'll let you know. Of course, this was of a confidential talk. I don't know what's going on in your personal life. If you need a person to confide in, I suggest you see Hank today. I've got an appointment in five minutes. Thanks for your honesty, but then again, why would I think I'd hear anything else. That's your reputation."

When Moore left, Jake called Loretta and told her he needed thirty minutes to handle a crisis and to reschedule the next appointment. He also asked her to apologize to the student on his behalf.

Hank Kulley had been the Vice Principal at Middletown for over twenty-five years. Jake respected him and liked him for having similar interest in outdoor activities. Together, they'd shared many stories about their former lives when they used to climb mountains. Jake decided to run his situation by Hank, as Moore suggested. When Jake walked in Hank was standing by a filing cabinet putting stuff away.

"Hey, Jake how goes it? What brings you down at lunchtime? Do you want to make a referral on one of your wise guys? Or are we going to discuss our mutual desire to visit Alaska before we die?"

"Hank, I came for some advice. Can we sit and talk for a while?"

"I can do that. Give me another minute to finish what I'm doing. Been over the Gap lately?"

"A couple of weeks back, the colors have turned and it's beautiful."

"I got a bunch of grapes in the fridge. How about we share some?"

Jake realized that Hank thought he was here on a student's behalf. "No thanks. Can we get down to business? I'm not here for a student."

"I got the picture. I'm making my way over to the desk...what's happening, Jake?"

Somewhat similar to an upper classman who got caught playing hooky and wanted to give the bare minimum to explain things, Jake told him, "It seems Dr. Moore got a complaint from a parent saying I'm guilty of unprofessional conduct. What do you think about that? Ever happen to you?"

"Jake, cut the bullshit and just give me the facts. What's the so-called unprofessional conduct Moore's referring to? You and I both know that if it was job related or was a serious breach of the public trust or you withheld information regarding a child's welfare, shit, you'd be out of here in a New York minute. Remember that sixth grade teacher who pushed that wise ass Special Ed kid against the blackboard a couple of years ago because the boy said 'fuck you' to him. Apparently, the teacher had a momentary lapse of reason and snapped. He should have called for help or walked away. He forgot where he was and how he should have acted. Anyway, he was axed within twenty-four hours. I have no idea what ever happened to him. Come on Jake, what's the story?"

"You're really something Hank. Christ, talk about busting my balls, you're using a sledgehammer. All right…so you want to know about the unprofessional conduct. Here it is. The parent making the complaint is the ex-husband of a woman I have a close relationship with. He's claiming I'm unprofessional for…"

"What! What did you say? Ex-husband…how very interesting. So tell me. Did you have an affair with the woman? Did ya?"

Jake was getting angry and he let his body language and voice reflect what he felt. "Yeah, Hank, I helped the woman out of a mess and like I said, I have a relationship with her. I'm not going to lie about it, not to you or anyone else for that matter. I came here for advice and not a fucking interrogation. Why are you doing this to me?"

Hank got up from his chair and broke out in a hearty laugh. Inside, he was dying to know the rest of the story. He'd always liked Jake for his individuality and counseling skill, but his confession was as defiant as a kid busted for smoking pot. Amused, he walked around and sat on top of his desk in front of Jake.

"Will you please chill out? There's no way I'd ever pass judgment on you. I've seen too much on this job. I'm not a minister…so please calm down. I know you're pissed off at this intrusion into your private life, but this…what should I call him? Obviously this ex-husband has a hard on for you. In that respect, you should be expecting some shit to hit the fan. As far as your job goes, believe me, they've got to be very careful about stuff like this and they know it. Whatever employees do in their personal lives is protected by their civil rights, same as everybody else. This fool must think you live in the former Soviet Union. Shit, they couldn't even get Clinton on it…and"

"Goddamn it Hank! I can't believe you said that!"

Hank paused and then sat down at his desk. His mood changed and he wanted Jake's attention. "Jake, let me tell you something. It doesn't matter if teachers are closet homosexuals, ex-alcoholics, gamblers, or look at porn every night on the internet, as long as it stays in their private life. You know, this is lunacy...total lunacy. Knowing you, you must wanna drive over to this man's house and step on him. Forget I said that. You gotta stay loose and don't do anything that could be construed as threatening to this man. An asshole like this would file charges if you ever got in his face and bullied him."

"Now I know why Gus sent me over here. You're right. Goddamn it you're right. Eastman's baiting me with the complaint. I didn't see it at first. You're a wise man telling me to behave. I'm just friggin' mad at this weasel for causing me grief. I didn't tell Moore anything. You suppose he's..."

"Jake, believe me, he doesn't want to know. One thing's certain. Eastman must think the public schools are still operating under the moral codes of the last century. If that's where he's coming from, it's going nowhere. Once you start digging up dirt, everybody needs a shower. How do we know he's so lily white? Maybe he's got shit in his closet better left there. The best advice I can give you is to be concerned with what might happen if he shares his viewpoint with others. What if it eventually got to your wife? Nothing's going to happen. The board of education protects the privacy of its employees. They can't get involved with crap like this. No wonder you got involved with the woman. If she was ever stuck with Eastman then I feel sorry for her. Knowing you, she probably needed saving and that's what you did."

"Thanks for the perspective. You really think he'd crash into my personal life?"

By raising the question, Hank knew Jake wanted some advice and whatever he said was critical. "Listen and listen real good. You need to think hard on this. You've got a family and you don't want them finding out about this situation second hand. I think if I were in your spot...as difficult as this might be, the best thing for you to do is tell your wife the truth. Don't wait for Eastman to act. Don't do that."

"You're serious, aren't you? I hadn't planned on doing that. I mean...not today. Goddamn it, it infuriates me to no end that this turd has stepped into my life without an invitation."

"I've never been more serious. Right now, I'm trading places with you and considering what Jake Carr would tell me. You once said something like, 'it's never easy to admit your sins.' I know you and your strong and unwavering advocacy for students. Maybe this woman was like a hurt kid and you had to rescue her. You got involved, didn't you? That's what happened. And in doing so, you discovered there was more to her than you thought. Maybe you found something missing in your life...Shit, I'm sorry Jake. I'm talking too much. You're in a pivotal position. You really are. It will go down whatever way you choose. But don't do it because of the complaint or because I said so. You should do it because the time has come, like it or not. I've known you a long time and having someone make trouble for you, Jesus that must piss you off. Let it go and stay away from Eastman. I wish you the best. You're a good man!"

"Wow, talk about a role reversal. You cut through me like a knife. Thanks for the time, Hank."

"Oh, one more thing, this ex-wife of Eastman must be some kind of woman for you to get this involved. I'm sure she's worth it or you wouldn't be in this position. You got a lot to consider."

Jake left Hank's office reasonably calm. One nagging thought overshadowed everything else, *Should I keep my relationship with Ellen a secret any longer? Whatever was coming with regard to the "so-called" complaint was manageable given the protection of my tenure. But Hank was right, and like it or not, I've got to accept that there are forces beyond my control that have come into play.*

Driving home without the company of his music, Jake realized that this was a long time in coming. He'd left it on the back burner because of his concern about how Annie would take it. All along, he wanted to end his marriage with the least amount of collateral damage. Whether he should have bailed out a week ago, a month ago, or after their road trip, was irrelevant. Now there was no honorable way to leave because the opportunity was lost. And just like the fateful night when he first made love to Ellen on her birthday, he had to make another choice, one that would permanently change his life.

CHAPTER 53

Jake parked his truck in the driveway, but he didn't bother to get the mail, nor did he disturb Missy when he came through the kitchen door. Feeling beleaguered, be poured a glass of OJ and swallowed a couple of aspirins. Then he stepped out on the back deck to let the afternoon sun calm him after a restless drive home. His mind was on overload from the stressful events of the day.

Letting his eyes close to gather his thoughts and block out anything visual, he heard Hank Kulley's message reverberate in his head over and over. Instinctively, he knew it was time, time to be forthright and let Sandy know the truth. Regardless of the circumstances that set things in motion, he realized there was no further reason to carry on the charade, even for another day. Pounding his right fist into the palm of his other hand he thought, *I didn't want to end it like this...not like this. I wanted to walk away without hurting Sandy anymore than need be. She'd given me a month to decide. Now that option may not be possible. Can't I just announce I'm leaving home the first of the year and leave it at that? Would that really be so much of a surprise? I think not. But like Hank said, Sandy may learn about Ellen from a source other than me. Shit, there's no way I can let that happen. Right this moment, she's on her way home. Perhaps she's thinking I'll turn, turn and come back. Strange...so strange...karma has its own force and timetable. When I disclosure the affair, it will end my marriage and it'll be messy. I wasn't raised on promises...but Sandy was. She'll be broken and I won't be able to fix it.*

When Jake returned to the kitchen, he felt a shortness of breath and his heart pounding. A heightened level of anxiety was dominating his body. Like a tourist visiting a historical landmark, he walked by each of the kid's bedrooms and paused by the doorway. He wanted to mentally photograph everything he saw. First he visited Annie's beautifully decorated, picture perfect private domain. A pair of pink ballet slippers hung with a dried bouquet of roses on the wall over her bed. Her stuffed animals stood motionless on the bedspread, undisturbed since she left for college. The polished oak furniture looked as if it had just been delivered from the showroom. On the nightstand was a mother-daughter snapshot taken with the Black Hills of South Dakota in the background. It was in the summer of '97, when Annie finally regained her health. There was an enchanting look on Annie's face.

Choking back tears and biting his fist, Jake murmured, "Annie, as much as I miss you, I'm glad you're on your own. Last weekend I noticed how much you changed. I hope someday you'll understand. That you'll believe me when I tell you that I stayed as long as could...that I saved and sacrificed for you to have your dream."

Then he walked over to J.D.'s bedroom. A "No Trespassing" sign hung on the door. Inside was a mess of clutter. His desk was piled high with racing magazines, auto catalogues, and a bunch of CDs. An assortment of loose change, odd keys, and notes were scattered over the desk pad. Three different signature posters of Jeremy McGrath, soaring over moguls and sand pits, decorated the walls. It appeared that nothing was in its proper place, dirty clothes were piled high on the chair and clean tee shirts and socks were stacked on the dresser. His blue and white striped bedspread was crumpled on the floor, covering a boom box, and one of the closet's sliding doors was off the track. On J.D.'s nightstand was a picture of him sitting proudly atop a John Deere tractor. It was taken during the first spring when they moved to Walden. He was nine years old and cutting the lawn for the first time. Another picture was beside it; it was of J.D. proudly holding Missy in his lap when she was only a puppy.

Jake was overwhelmed with emotion from the memories; remembrances of days long past when Tonka dumpsters and Lego creations were everywhere in the house, when colored pictures of monster trucks adorned the fridge and when he sat in the rocker and read Dr. Suess and Disney adventure stories. He remembered how much the boy loved living on Sourland Mountain, and how J.D. played in the adjoining woods every day, discovering the magic of creeks, climbing trees, and using his imagination to tell tall tales of black wolves with red eyes. Jake conjured up a mental image of that first house and thought, *It may have been a small ranch on a gravel road in rural Blairstown, far away from town, but I believed it was the best of times...I loved starting a family there and living close to the forest.*

He remembered the tree house, the tire swing, the monkey bars, and J.D.'s enormous sandpit. He remembered Annie putting her stuffed animals in the "Radio Flyer" wagon and taking them for a ride on the gravel road, of setting up the sprinkler to cool the kids off on hot summer days, and of taking them for a walk every night after supper to visit a horse named, Daffodil Candy. He thought of tucking them in at night and the hugs they gave him before he left. He thought of his intense desire to be a model father and felt thankful for having spent the time with them when they were young.

In the upstairs hallway there were four framed collages with photos from family road trips during the eighties. Jake stopped and looked at each one of them. All the evidence was right in front of him. Sandy and the kids were once the joy of his life and the reason for the personal sacrifices he made. He remembered those times and realized he liked the person he was and the life he led. Sandy looked happy and healthy in the photos, holding hands with Annie on an Oregon beach, posing in front of Disney's Cinderella castle, eating ice cream cones on the boardwalk in Belmar, New Jersey, and watching the kids blow out candles on their birthday cakes.

When he stood in the doorway of the master bedroom, he had a premonition that he'd never be making love or sleeping with Sandy ever again. Disheartened, he turned away with a sense of resignation and went into the study. It was now almost 5 o'clock, and Sandy would be home in half an hour. Jake sat in front of the computer screen and tried to put his thoughts down. How does a man begin to explain when his wife screams out, "Why did you do this to me?" Of course there was no way to soften the blow of his indiscretion or dull the cutting edge of truth. Sandy was going to be a victim. The news would smash into her and cut her deeply.

Jake was a realist about how much Sandy could handle and decided to confess his infidelity without giving her either an excuse or an explanation. He believed that her initial reaction would overshadow anything he'd say. In other words, he would accept the consequences and let Sandy tell him off without hiding behind some stupid rationalization. There wasn't any excuse worth mentioning, and he knew it. He thought Sandy was entitled to say or do whatever she felt like and he'd have to take it.

After twenty minutes in front of the computer, only a single sentence was there. *I've been involved in a relationship with another woman.*

Jake finally changed out of his school clothes, washed up, and distracted himself as best as he could by checking over his accounting. Then he noticed a yellow post-it near the phone on Sandy's nightstand. All it said was "call Rachel tonight." Jake decided that he'd make that call and tell Sandy's closest friend what he was about to do and ask her to check in with Sandy later.

"Rachel, this is Jake. Do you have a few minutes? There's something I must tell you."

"Sure. I've been worried about Sandy. How is she?"

"After you hear what I'm going tell you, I think you'll be more worried. When Sandy comes home from work I'm going to tell her about a relationship I'm having with another woman. I've put it off too long and it's time. Even though our marriage has been crumbling, it's still going to crush her. Only last week after visiting Annie, I thought I'd tell her I was leaving because I'm unhappy and I've had enough. Now I can't wait any longer. I've come to realize it would be a terrible tragedy if she learned about it from some other source. Anyway, I thought it may help if you called her later."

Rachel held back her anger and remained calm instead of telling Jake off. "Jake, I didn't know about any of this. You must understand, Sandy is much too proud to share something like that...even with me. But I'll tell you this, Arnie and I knew things were going bad as far back as Annie's illness. We thought the marriage counseling had helped. I'm so sorry, sorry for both of you. In fact, I told her after the Labor Day weekend, that from our perspective, it was getting to be too much of strain on us to spend time with you. We've shared so much since our kids were young going to Sunday school...remember that? Tell me Jake, do you want to end the marriage? Are you willing to give up the other woman and ask for forgiveness? If the tables were turned and she had the affair, would you want to try and get through it? Would you forgive her and keep the marriage going?"

Rachel's questions caught Jake off guard. There was no running away. He was the one who had called her, she deserved some answers, but he couldn't give her any. After a few seconds, she continued.

"Listen Jake, some couples can survive a crisis like this. Personally, I know a few who did. But, it means learning how to forgive and there's nothing harder for a woman to do. She may say yes I forgive you and really mean it at the time, but with a woman like Sandy, honestly, I don't know. One thing you need to expect is that she's going to be very angry and say horrible things. Most of them you'll deserve. I'm sorry that the two of you lost your way. I know that Arnie and I have had issues regarding loyalty and commitment, but we survived. There's no doubt your lives changed dramatically after you left Blairstown. Was that your idea? I'm sorry. I'll call Sandy later. Good luck Jake."

Rachel's insightful comments turned his mood from somber to a state of agitation. He realized, more than ever that it was Sandy who forced the move away from Blairstown. He had wanted to move halfway and continue to stay connected to their circle of friends and the temple they attended.

It was almost impossible for Jake to get his balance back. In less than six hours he'd been through a series of emotional ups and downs that he'd never experienced before. It began with Dr. Moore's disclosure about the complaint. Then after lunch, Jake listened to Hank's advice. The photographs hit him hard with the remembrance of the kid's childhood, and, a few minutes ago, Rachel reminded him of what it was like before they moved away from Blairstown. It was an emotional roller coaster ride, and strained Jake to the limit. Sandy would be home in a matter of minutes. So Jake took a seat at the counter and tried to gather his thoughts for the confrontation he was about to have.

He heard her car pull up and he felt his heart pounding once again. Sandy opened the kitchen door and saw Jake sitting at the counter. Nothing was cooking on the stove and the table wasn't set.

"Sandy, I haven't made dinner yet. J.D.'s not here... After you change I'd like to talk with you. It's very important. I'll wait here. Ok?"

Sandy sensed that something was coming, something unexpected and tragic. "Whatever's on your mind better come out right this minute...cause you look pretty tense. Let me put my stuff down and use the bathroom. I'll be right back."

A few minutes later, Sandy sat at the end of the counter diagonally across from Jake, he had a cup of orange tea ready for her.

"Sandy, there's no easy way for me to tell you. I think I should just get it out, right now."

She took a few sips from the mug of hot tea, waiting for him to continue. After a few moments of cold silence, Jake, biting his clenched fist, finally uttered his confession.

"A year ago I met someone and became involved with her. I've been seeing her ever since. I've been unfaithful to you. I have been with another woman. I know that you gave me time to decide about my commitment to you. Right now I think it's time for me to tell you the truth. I had an affair. I don't want to wait until you hear about it from somebody else. That wouldn't be fair to you. I'm sorry things have turned out like this."

Sandy didn't immediately respond. She took another sip of tea and sat very still. Relieved, Jake got up and stood near the sliding door waiting for her to respond.

"Where did you meet this woman?"

"I met her at the parenting seminar in the spring of '99."

"Was the woman married at the time."

"She was married at that time. Now she's divorced."

"So you're telling me that you had an affair with a married woman? I...I can't believe that you would be that...that reckless. Why? You're not like that. It's a terrible thing you did...that you both did...It's absolutely shameless. So I assume she has children if she went to your seminar. What about them? What about her husband?"

"They live with their father in Middletown. She lives alone in an apartment."

Sandy couldn't hold back her shock any longer. She turned her head away from Jake and fought the urge to scream out in a fit of rage. Instead, she walked over to the opposite side of the kitchen, took some tissues out of a box and blew her nose. Standing opposite him on the other side of the counter and looking straight at him she asked, "Jake, did you have sex with this sleazy woman?"

"I did."

"How many times did you have sex with her? Well?"

This was not where Jake wanted to go. So he answered her back, declaring, "Sandy, what the hell difference does it make? It happened... numbers have nothing to do with it. I've been unfaithful! What else can I tell you? I'm admitting my affair."

Jake cupped his hands over his face. He was feeling very uncomfortable.

"Tell me... Jake, have you been so unhappy with me that this woman could tempt you that easily. What a bitch! She's wicked! She took you away from me after twenty-one years...Why Jake? Was she also that unhappy? You had to rescue her, huh? Is that it? You had to do it! Damn you, for caring more about saving her than saving us."

"Sandy, you're going over the edge. I expected it...I'm sorry but I'm not going to get into an argument over the whys and wherefores! I'm clearing the air because its time. I'm not looking for understanding and I'm not begging for your forgiveness."

There wasn't anything more for Jake to say, so he remained quiet. Sandy was totally distraught and went upstairs. After about five minutes, he walked to the foot of the stairs and listened. Everything was quiet, so he waited outside the bedroom door and listened again. He heard the muffled sound of a whimper and then sobbing. As he was about to leave, the floor creaked.

Sandy heard it and screamed out with a strident voice, "Don't you dare think I want to hear anymore of what you have to say about your behavior? Stay away from me. You no-good son of a bitch, you made your choice. You bastard! You've thrown away your life! You tossed it aside like it was nothing worth holding on to. You're a phony and a liar. You made up stories to spend time with that whore. Damn you a thousand times and damn her for interfering in our lives. Leave me alone...Leave me alone!"

Jake didn't answer. He went downstairs and fed Missy. Then he made a cup of coffee and took it to his desk. He was inclined to get in the truck and leave but thought it wiser to stay and pass the time before the next battle took place. He took out his monthly mortgage statement and wrote out the November payment. All he wanted to do was leave, but that would be an act of cowardice. After he finished the coffee he decided to take Missy for a walk and was making his way up the driveway when J.D. pulled up. Jake waved to him and J.D. parked the truck.

"Hey Dad, what did you make for dinner? Sorry I'm late, but I was in East Middletown looking at a used four wheeler. The frame was cracked and the dude thought I wouldn't notice. I made him a ridiculous offer for it. Whatever...I'm hungry!"

Jake faced his son and, with Missy pulling on her leash, spoke in a way unfamiliar to his son. "Your mother is upstairs. I guess you know we haven't been getting along for a long time. Things are bad, real bad, and I'm probably going to be moving out soon. I'm not sure when...maybe it'll be tomorrow or maybe in a couple of months. But, it's time for me to leave. I've disappointed your mom. I'm sorry to have to tell you like this. Believe me, there's no easy way to tell a son his parents are splitting up. Please be kind to your mom. I'll talk to you more about this, but not now. I promise. Try to understand, things are upside down. Make yourself something to eat and then..."

"Ok Dad, you've made it very clear to me. Holy shit, I didn't ever expect that this would happen to me... I guess I'm still a kid and I believed in miracles. Tonight's pretty fucked up...right? I'll grab something out of the fridge and go over to Matt's. I wish this didn't have to happen and I..."

"In view of what's going on, that would be the right move."

Jake returned to the house an hour later. Sandy was in the kitchen waiting for him. When he entered the room, she confronted him like an angry prosecutor in court. "Did you tell your son? Did you tell him what you did to me? Tell him you had an affair and that you betrayed me, dishonored me, and threw me away. Did you use that smooth counselor talk to make it all better for yourself? Well...did you?"

Jake knew the next few minutes would be nothing short of a total bashing and accepted what fate had in store for him. Even so, he began with an apology. "Sandy, I'm sorry. I've got no excuse for being unfaithful because there isn't any. I'm involved with another woman and I'm not going to make any excuses. I have to much respect for you."

With a voice full of venom and with the harshest tone she'd ever used on her husband, Sandy backed Jake up against the wall and yelled in his face. "Bullshit, bullshit, Jake. You're not sorry about anything you did to me. **You left me behind**! You think I don't know how easy it must've been for you to go down this road. Who seduced who? Do you want to tell me that? You really think I've forgotten the past five years?

You kept your promise and took care of us. So this is the payment you want in exchange for that? You bastard! You kept your word and didn't leave me with the kids. **What about me?** You gave up on me long ago…long ago! Then what did we have left? Yeah Jake, you **were** noble. You took care of everything around here. You paid the bills, cleaned the house, and whatever you wanted, but when was the last time you cared about me? You can't even remember. I think it was easy for you to start this fling, I should say, this extra marital affair. **Don't you ever tell me you're sorry about what you've done**! I know you're not. Now tell me what you're going to do next with this raunchy woman. Tell me that, you bastard. How dare you mention respect to me. You're full of shit! What do you have to say for yourself?"

Then she screamed again, this time with the full force of the righteous indignation she felt. "No, shut up. I don't want to hear a word out of you! Don't shame yourself any worse than you've already done. You're not sorry about anything you did and tonight you don't know what you're going to do. Do you? You've shamed me. I bet you won't tell the children about this…Will you?"

"Sandy, there's no reason to tell you what I'm doing tomorrow. So whatever else you want to say or ask, do it now, but I don't have the answers you demand."

"Was she that beautiful, cause I know how important that is to you. Well, does she love you?"

"What's the hell's the difference? Why does any of that matter? Why do you care?"

"Because I want to know if you're going to see her again…**You tell me right now**. Are you?"

Jake had confessed his sin, now Sandy wanted a definitive answer as to what would happen tomorrow. At the moment, with the crisis boiling over, he shouted back the only answer he had. **"At this precise moment, I don't know! I can't give you an answer. I don't know!"**

"That's not good enough. How am I supposed to get up tomorrow and carry on my life when you've turned my whole world into shit? Give me some advice. Come on! You always have advice. Well?"

"The same way I've always done for the past twenty years. You get up and go to work and do the responsible thing. Then you try and figure out what's in your best interest and you run with it. That's your answer. I'm not going to discuss this any more tonight. I think you'd be better off alone. I confessed what I've done. I accept the fact that you've got every right to think the worst. It's been a long day and a fucked-up evening. **I'm to blame and not you**! I'm going down in the basement."

"You and your timing…I'll never understand how something like this happened."

"Like I said, there's no need to figure it out, not tonight. I told you the truth."

"Maybe for you, Jake, you're the man who's always so sure, so damn certain of your next move. I'm not made out of the same stuff. We're different people and we have always been different. I don't think like you, nor would I want to. I'm a Jewish wife and mother. Once I believed in you. I married you for love and adventure. **That's what I wanted and what you promised.** Now I realize that you've stopped giving me the very things that brought us together in the first place. You've replaced me and given yourself to someone else. You stand there and you tell me there's no need to figure it out. You're dead wrong. The answers are obvious to me. You're a disgrace... as a husband, a father, and a man."

CHAPTER 54

Jake felt a stiff push against his shoulder, then another. He rolled over, barely awake, and rubbed the sleep from his eyes. Sandy was standing over him by the edge of the bed.

"I want you out of this bedroom. You understand what I'm telling you? I took a sleeping pill last night and didn't hear you come in. You've got a lot of nerve! You had no business sleeping with me. What the hell were you thinking? From now on use Annie's room or sleep in your basement. Am I clear about this? One other thing, move your stuff out of here. I don't want to see a thing of yours around me."

As fuzzy as his brain was, Jake knew Sandy was right in her demands. His only problem was that her condemnation came while he was still half asleep. Sandy glared at him waiting for an answer. "I heard you. I heard you. You're crystal clear. It won't happen again. I'll move all my stuff out."

"You're a jerk! What possessed you to think you could...oh, forget it. You're thoughtless when it comes to me. I'm using the bathroom now. Don't walk in on me!"

Sandy turned and went into the bathroom and Jake felt dumb for sleeping in the bedroom. Too much vodka had numbed his brain and he foolishly figured, *What's one more night?*

Later on, when Sandy came into the kitchen Jake had just finished feeding Missy and was making lunch. Feeling guilty for what he did, and trying to avoid any further confrontation, he offered to make Sandy lunch. Holding up the pot of coffee, he made a peace gesture.

"The coffee's ready. Would you like a cup? There's smoked turkey if you want me to make you a sandwich. Anything special you would like for dinner tonight?"

After he spoke, he realized how stupid he sounded, as if last night never occurred.

"That won't be necessary. I'll take care of myself from now on. You may not be here much longer. I won't be home for supper. I have my study group tonight and believe me, I'm glad I'll be out."

Jake shrugged his shoulders and went about his business. Twenty minutes later, as Sandy was about to leave, she stood face to face with him and said sarcastically, "Hey, maybe you'll get a chance to see your other woman and have some sex. Think about it, Jake. Now you won't have to be sneaky. Oh yes, and don't forget to tell her how you confessed to me...and how you fell on your knees, repented and asked for my forgiveness. Anyway, I won't be home till ten. You better think about what you plan to do in the future. Don't worry about me...you didn't yesterday and for however long you've been screwing around. When I think how foolish I was for believing you were playing golf all those times. You've got a lot of soul searching to do. If you even have a soul. Check on J.D. Unlike you, he'll be staying here."

She slammed the garage door hard enough to knock a picture off the wall in the hallway. Alone now, Jake drank his coffee in silence and skipped the English muffin. Last night after Sandy got in her last blast, she retreated to the master bedroom. Whether she was doing school work, talking to Rachel, watching TV, or reading, it was obvious that she didn't want to be disturbed. So Jake had left a note on the kitchen counter for J.D. to read if he came back to spend the night.

Dear Son,
PLEASE DON'T BOTHER MOM FOR ANY REASON. Things are bad! If you want to talk I'll be in the basement. Sorry for kicking you out...I had no other choice.
Thanks,
Dad

After posting the note, Jake had made a fifty-fifty screwdriver in a twelve once tumbler and retreated to the basement. He came up for another drink at ten, but J.D. still wasn't home. He had tried several distractions, from cable news to the Discovery channel, all of which failed. Much later on, sometime after midnight, he went upstairs and found Sandy sound asleep. Without thinking, and feeling the effects of the alcohol, he foolishly fell out beside her.

Jake's head was awash with conflicting emotions, along with a slight hangover, when he arrived at the high school. Many of his concerns had more to do with the children than with Sandy. He knew it was over between them. Only the details of his imminent departure remained; when would he be leaving and where would he be moving? Realistically, he knew that Sandy didn't expect him to pack up and leave the next day or even the next week. Her pride was hurt, but she knew Jake wouldn't be bullied into letting her "throw him out on the street." Sandy knew he paid all the bills and he figured that she wouldn't be that self-destructive about her own security. Nevertheless, he had to consider a timetable.

Jake knew it would take all his will power to make it through the day without messing up. His supervisor, Bob Washburn, greeted him as though he was unaware of Eastman's complaint. "Morning, Jake. We have a department meeting scheduled for first period tomorrow. If there's something you want on the agenda, please let Loretta know."

"Nothing I can think of at this time. Maybe something will pop in my head later. I've got a couple of kids who may want to be walk-ons for the SAT next week. I'll let you know."

Jake figured that Moore probably told Washburn about the complaint. But Bob was the consummate diplomat in any work-related controversy and most likely remained silent for that reason. It was an admirable quality but one that Jake didn't possess. He didn't make any small talk with the secretaries when he picked up his schedule. Then he went about his business as usual.

When Logan Peterson showed up for the first interview of the day, it was a godsend, as far as Jake was concerned. Logan was in Jake's exclusive "inner circle." That meant, like Leslie Warren who had graduated last June, this seventeen year-old junior had a counselor/student relationship that transcended all the normal boundaries. There was a tight bond between Jake the mentor and Logan the pupil. It centered on trust, loyalty, and the truth. That was the agreement for entrance into Jake's circle. Putting aside his personal issues, Jake shook the student's hand with a firm grip and a warm smile.

"Hey Logan, hope things are tranquil with you. How's that girlfriend of yours? Katie's a terrific kid. I wish she was one of my counselees. She'd make a great peer development leader. She oughta sign up for that program. Today's one of those days that I'd like to switch places with you."

"Mr. Carr, I'm never sitting on the other side of this desk. You're the wizard, not me. Here's the news. The marking period is over in another week. Anyway, I messed up big time. Right now, I'm barely passing English. You're going to be real pissed at me and I deserve it. That's why I came to see you. I'm feeling guilty. You tried to steer me towards reality and responsibility and I didn't listen. I wanted you to hear the news from me and not from Mrs. Lewis. I didn't follow your advice and I'm sorry. You told me to begin the year on the right track and to always consider the consequences. I blew it...blew it big time."

"Logan, you're a piece of work. I told you last June and again during the first week of classes that if you didn't do the summer reading you'd fail the first marking period. You knew this was going to happen. Here we go again...life's always about consequences and choices. **I've already taught you that...I taught you from personal experience**. Remember when I said, *To go wrong and not alter one's course can truly be defined as going wrong.* Good God, there's no way you could fool Mrs. Lewis with *Cliff Notes* or internet summaries. So now what?

You're gonna get the D you deserve, or even worse."

"Mr. Carr, I've been dealing with a lot of crap lately."

"So you say. Consider this. No matter what you get for a grade in that course...your life will still go on. Logan, let me put some perspective on this calamity."

"That's why I'm here. You once told me, that being honest with yourself takes great courage."

"I'm glad you remembered that. When you hurt your back last spring and lost the county track title in the 100 meters, you were heartbroken, but you held together. I told you to wait for another day. You also believed me when I said your back would eventually heal and you'd be able to race again. At the time, you were angry and disappointed. I also told you that your self-discipline and determination would triumph in the end, regardless of whatever setbacks you suffered along the way. You placed second in the counties. You know what to do. So why in the hell don't you push that brain of yours? Give it a workout!"

Logan hung his head in shame. But Jake wasn't through with his assessment.

"The mental workouts you currently put yourself through aren't worthy of the intellectual promise you possess. My point is that you were in control of your destiny, but you let your indifference and lack of planning take over your better judgment. Logan, whether it's you or me, we're at our worst, and we're gonna suffer, when we let things get out of control and disrupt our lives. Are you following me?"

"More than you know. Last night, I felt ashamed because I had promised Katie I'd be a better student. I lied. I lied about reading the summer assignment to keep the peace with her. You know what? She didn't tell me off. Instead, she let me off but that only made me feel worse. Honestly, I didn't want her to forgive me. I wanted her to tell me off because she'd be justified in doing it."

"Hey Logan, that's love. But I want to teach you something I hope you'll always remember. I've come to believe that love only comes after there's understanding. You'll never feel alone or defeated when you feel someone really understands you. And honestly, there's no better feeling of comfort in the whole universe. It's the ultimate gift we can offer another person. Sounds unbelievable, doesn't it?"

"I've never heard it put like that before."

"I'm sorry if I sound like I'm preaching... I hate doing that. Look, I'm glad you feel guilty enough to tell me the truth. I really am. Without that self awareness, you're stone inside."

"Mr. Carr, every time I think the worst, you make me feel like there's hope. Somehow you get me to stop being down on myself and make me realize I can turn things around."

Jake and Logan continued their conversation till period one ended with the bell. The irony of Logan's visit was that after he left, Jake realized he could have been talking to himself. Most of his words could have been directed back to him. He thought, *Christ, I should have recorded that dialogue and played it back for me. He knew the consequences of his actions and so did I. Strange...real strange what comes out of my head. I've always been my best resource throughout my life. Nothing has changed. There's gonna be another day all right, but that day is today.*

At 9:30 he called Ellen. The receptionist at Horizon Financial directed his call to Spano's office.

"Good Morning. This is Ellen Douglas. May I help you?"

"This is Jake. I'm sorry for calling you at work, but I need to see you. A whole lot's going on."

"Are you all right? Is anything wrong?"

"Let me put it this way, I'm better now than I was twelve hours ago. I can't come over tonight. Do you think you could meet me in the Horizon parking lot around 4:30? Isn't that when you get out?"

"If that's what you want. I can skip lunch and be outside around four o'clock."

"That's perfect! I really need to get home by six. I'll explain later. I promise."

"Can you tell me anything now?"

"I can tell you that I love you and I've got to get back to work. So do you. Love ya. Bye."

At least a few times during the day, Jake considered revisiting Hank Kulley. The fact that Gus Moore hadn't paid him another visit meant the complaint was under control. He trusted Moore, and firmly believed that at the very worst, it might surface in the community. But at this point in his long career, Jake couldn't care less about a backlash from a few sanctimonious parents in Middletown.

When the students were dismissed at the end of the day, he closed the door of his office and told Loretta not to disturb him. Taking out a legal pad, he began writing a letter to Ellen.

My Dearest Skye,

Last night I told Sandy about my affair. When I didn't ask for any forgiveness or indicate that I'd end our affair, she took it very badly. It was a tough night. My head has been in a frenzy ever since. Even so, I want to open up heart and tell you about the woman I'm looking for in my new life. I know beyond a doubt that you are the person I'm describing.

I want a relationship with a woman who is caring, trusting, and generous. Someone with a philosophy of life founded on freedom of expression and a love of Mother Nature. A woman who is not afraid to be herself, yet who still wants to grow as an individual. A woman who loves the outdoors and appreciates the awe and splendor of nature. Someone who loves quiet and periods of isolation to reflect on the mystery of life. A woman who enjoys the simple pleasures in life such as a walk on the trail, watching a lightening storm, or viewing a blizzard from under a porch. A physically fit individual who takes a measure of pride in her looks and glows with confidence when she dances with me. Who stays in shape in order to play hard. Someone who knows how to appreciate a delicious meal like prime rib or can taste ice cream on a hot summer day and smile like a kid after the first bite. A woman who doesn't need to be critical or mean-spirited because she knows that negative words won't produce anything positive with a man like me.

I want a companion who is more thoughtful than intellectual. Someone who has learned about life by making mistakes and then making the necessary adjustments. A woman capable of changing her mind when she learns that her course of action was wrong. I want a woman who can laugh at herself when she does dumb things. I need a woman who respects herself more than anyone else in the world, who believes in her own self-worth and has a positive attitude that reflects her inner peace and harmony. I need a woman who can relax, reflect, read, think, or walk quietly to search for an answer. I want a woman who isn't afraid to cry when sorrow overcomes her and teaches me how to do the same without feeling like less of a man. That would be an extraordinary occurrence.

I want a woman who smiles when I'm being foolish and isn't afraid to tease me when the moment is right. I want a soulmate who believes I'm worthy of her trust and love. I want a woman who doesn't worship me for my talents, resources, or life skills. I don't need to be thought of that way. I'd rather be respected. I need a companion that loves the mystery of the mountains, feels the presence of the redwoods, and listens to symphonies of the roaring rivers, hard rain and summer thunder. I want her to share my dreams of places I have yet to discover. I need a woman who loves planning road adventures with me and enjoys passing time in the truck listening to the sounds of rock music while moving her hands and feet to the beat.

Finally, I want a woman who likes being sexy. Who can laugh while we're making love and encourages me to please her. Who dresses the role of a lover and cherishes our times of intimacy. Who loves to fall out on my chest listening to my heartbeat slow after we finish making love. Who never takes me for granted and who daydreams about making love long before it may take place.

I believe you are the woman...Are you? I love you!

Jake

CHAPTER 55

Jake parked his truck in an area near the back entrance of the Horizon office building and waited. Checking his watch, he knew Ellen would be walking out any minute. The worn-out leaves, blown by the wind gusts of fall, were scattered around the pavement and reminded Jake that a gray November was coming. Where would he be a year from now? Sandy had asked the definitive question. Would he continue seeing the other woman? At that moment, he chose uncertainty as an answer. He had lied to stop Sandy's emotional aneurysm from exploding. He knew it, and cursed himself for not being honest.

When Jake saw Ellen coming through the exit door he left the truck and trotted across the lot to meet her. Disregarding the presence of onlookers, they embraced.

"Hello Skye, I parked the truck over by the dumpster. As much as I'd like to take a walk, it's too chilly and dismal right now. Could we talk in my truck?"

"That would be fine with me. I've been worried about you ever since you called. It was a hectic day. Spano's trying to land a ten million dollar insurance policy and he's crazy when he's close."

They sat in the truck neither one saying a word. She waited for him. Then Jake put his arm around Ellen. He needed the reassurance of having her near him. After a long embrace, he leaned far back in the seat and stared out the side window. Indeed, it was the moment of truth.

"Sandy knows about us. Yesterday, after she came home from work, I told her. I couldn't wait any longer. Things got out of hand. Not physically. I mean she didn't throw a plate at me. She was very much the righteous woman. I hated it. It's not something you can prepare for because you don't know what to expect. Breaking someone's heart and smashing their world by confessing your sins is bad news."

Jake began rubbing his forehead like he suddenly lost his place. He paused for a moment before continuing. Meanwhile, Ellen sat patiently waiting to hear the rest of the story.

"You can't begin to imagine the way it went. It was tough, tough for both of us. I was on the receiving end of her anger and she had every right to be that way. There's a price to pay when you tell the truth to someone who's not prepared to hear it. Maybe that happened with you and Guy. You never told me. I don't think she ever thought I was cheating on her. She has too much pride to believe another woman could be more desirable than her. I suppose I'd feel the exact same way. Know what I mean?"

Ellen's initial shock was beginning to ware off and she was curious about the timing of his confession, since she thought he was going to wait a while longer. "Jake, why did you do it last night? I mean, it's not for me to know what was in your head, but I thought you might have warned me. Am I'm wrong? So why last night? Did something happen?"

"It was Eastman. I suppose he set things in motion by showing up at my principal's office to make a complaint against me. I know it sounds crazy but he did it. No shit."

Ellen didn't understand, at least not right away, and wanted more of an explanation. "A complaint about what? He doesn't even know you."

Jake didn't hesitate and laid it out clearly. "For unprofessional conduct, I guess he thinks public schools are like the military or ran like a religious order. Anyway, he told Dr. Moore I'm guilty of "conduct unbecoming" for being a married man and being involved with his ex-wife. How or why he did...I have no clue. Right now I'm not interest in him, regardless of what he did. Let's leave him out of the conversation."

Obviously, Jake wasn't in any frame of mind to unravel the mystery of Eastman's actions.

"Seriously Ellen, I don't give a damn about the complaint. I came here because I needed to see you. Last night, Sandy asked me if I will see you again. She demanded an answer. I told her I didn't know. That was an outright lie. Now I'm asking you to forgive me. I knew she was hurting and frankly I didn't see the necessity of giving her anymore pain. Maybe I was wrong. I hope you'll understand and accept me, even with all my shortcomings. All you need to know is that I love you and regardless of what comes next, it won't change the truth. Two hours ago I wrote you a letter. Take it off the visor above you and read it. Read it like it's the most important letter you'll ever receive. I'll come back in ten minutes."

He kissed Ellen on the forehead, left the truck, and disappeared around a corner. Ellen opened the sealed envelope and focused all her attention on every word she read.

As Jake leaned against the brick wall of the Horizon building, he thought of how fast the time had passed since he first met Ellen. It frightened him to think he was fifty years old, and regardless of the shape he was in, that two-thirds of his life was over. Now he was a few of minutes away from another turn in the road if Ellen believed that she was the right woman.

Slowly, he walked back to the parked truck. As soon as Ellen took sight of him, she swung the truck door open and ran across the parking lot. There were tears in her eyes. When they met, they held on to each other without saying a word. Then Jake held her at arms length spoke from his heart.

"Ellen, I will never let you go! We've always been good together. Long ago, I made a choice to follow this path regardless of the risks involved. Maybe for the first time ever, I trusted my heart more than my head. The result is that somehow, in the midst of so much turbulence in our lives, we managed to stay together. I don't know how or why this happened. But I believe it was our destiny. "

Ellen reached out and took hold him. She buried her head on his chest and a faint sob came out before she managed to say, "Jake, I will love you forever. Words cannot begin to express what I'm feeling after reading your letter. **I am the woman you described and the one you desire!** I've become that woman. I've gained the confidence and strength to deal with my life regardless of the obstacles. I also believe it was our destiny to find each other. I was hoping for a miracle and you came along."

She kissed him with an intensity that filled him with joy. Their hearts were intertwined, and they felt connected in spirit and in soul.

Then Ellen admitted. "I fell in love with you so fast. You've convinced me that our love was our destiny...and it was about karma. I have lots of memories...memories of every time you rescued me from my fears. I could try the rest of my life to give you back what you've given me, but I could never repay you for helping me. You helped me get back my life and my youth, and for that, I'm eternally grateful. Best of all, you replaced my bitterness with hope. I'm not sorry for Sandy. Maybe that sounds harsh but she forgot who you are. I think she got lost in the pursuit of other things. What's more important at this moment is that I love you the most and I'm glad you believed I was the woman you described in your letter."

Jake took her hand and they walked slowly toward Main Street. Miraculously, the late afternoon sun broke through the gray clouds and doused them with warmth. Perhaps it was mere coincidence or one of those "signs" that people search for in the midst of turmoil.

They strolled to a bus stop and sat on a bench, completely indifferent to the strangers who passed by them. They sat quietly and let the rays of the sun comfort them like a security blanket does for a child.

"You know, Skye. I've been asked more than a few times if you were worth it. That question doesn't deserve an answer because my choices speak for themselves. Anyone can try to make the claim that if they were in my situation they'd do the righteous thing. They'd ask for forgiveness and go back home even if it meant living a lie. But what does that prove? In my mind, nothing at all, except that they surrendered to the forces that might judge them harshly. I'm not going to answer to anyone about why I did what I did. I was always conscious of the consequences involved. That's the way I am. I'll never forget the first time we kissed. Shit, I felt like my universe had changed its orbit. I knew what I did."

"Jake, you don't have to convince me about your sincerity or your motivation."

"Skye, what I'm getting at is this...I'm not sorry for anything I did nor am I ashamed. I don't give a damn what others think! My marriage was dying for a long time and yours was dead from the beginning according to what you told me. You and I connected in ways that most middle-aged people think is impossible. Yet, we are here together because we believed. I'm leaving Sandy, and my kids will have to decide for themselves about my behavior. They're old enough to make up their own mind. The same is true for your boys. You might hate Guy but he did the right thing by taking those boys. He has the resources and you don't. Frankly, I think it surprised you that he actually relished the role as their father once he was given the opportunity. He may have initially taken them for selfish reasons, but a man grows into parenthood. I know that must have happened to him because it happened to me. It's a stabilizing force in a man's life. We'll have to wait and see how it plays out. There's no reason to worry."

Ellen marveled at the clarity of his thinking and the strength of his convictions. "Jake, I'm sure you speak from experience. I know I'll have to wait and see what develops with the boys. I accept that. When will I be able to see you again? What comes next? What about Sandy?"

"I'll call you every day. I promise. Right now we'll let things settle down. We may know our way, but Sandy doesn't. A crisis like this requires time... time to return to some sense of balance. You will note, I didn't say normalcy. Realistically, I expect the blame game to continue for both of us. Sandy will demand to have answers. So will your ex-husband. Contrary to what she wants, I'm offering her no explanation that would change anything. Neither should you have to explain anything to Guy. You're divorced so what would it matter. I don't expect her to understand why I did what I did? The same is true for Guy. In their opinion, they're the righteous ones and we broke the rules. They won't ever forgive us!"

"Jake, you really seem to understand the human condition. Even so, in some ways I can identify with Sandy. I know one thing. She has to blame you as much as Guy has to blame me. During my marriage I wasn't allowed to argue with him. He was always right! Like you, all I ever did was try to keep the peace. From the start, he was the one who controlled me. That's how I lost my self-confidence."

Jake was impressed with Ellen's perspective, but had more to say. "I can't find fault with the way things turned out because in the end, we're together. I had hoped to hide the truth to protect Sandy. I guess that wasn't very realistic. To me, people may think the worst for the choices we made. Maybe even our kids. But regardless of who wants to pass judgment, in the final analysis, it doesn't matter. Our destiny brought us together."

Ellen nodded in agreement but she was still curious about the problem Eastman created for Jake. "What about school? Are you going to be all right? What about the complaint?"

Fully aware that Ellen was naive concerning Guy's actions, he explained, "I'm sure he's got his reasons. You divorced him with the intention of carrying on your life free from his domination. You said, he told you he'd do the better job of parenting. So he made the choice to be the full-time father, and I give him credit for undertaking such a challenge. I'd probably do the same. He probably figured that you'd eventually give up and return. None of that matters anymore. I've known people like Guy Eastman all my life. He can say whatever he wants about me without knowing all the facts. You'll see, he'll try to come off as the model citizen regardless of his own past indiscretions. In the end...it's all bullshit because nobody really cares."

"Jake, when I think how stupid I was to have ever surrendered my life to him. There were countless times I cried and thought I'd be stuck forever without any escape. Then you came along and rescued me."

"Ellen stop right there! All of us do foolish things when we're young. Twenty years ago, Guy knew you were naïve and he seized the opportunity to have you all to himself. You keep wondering...why did you stick with him for so long? The answer lies in your character. Knowing you, you simply wouldn't believe the obvious. You thought you could change him and...and he thought he could change you. Sandy and I went through the same thing. In the final analysis, social class, a person's background, and for sure their religion really do mean a lot. Like so many other women, I think you knew that after the kids came along...well, that's when the prison door slammed shut. But all that's past history. It doesn't matter now."

When they returned to the parking lot, he opened the door of her Jeep, put his arms around her and said, "When I began putting my thoughts together for the letter, the words of an old Don Henley song called *A New York Minute* came in my head. There have been lots of times when I'm waiting for that inner voice of mine to clear things up and out of the blue some song always seems to enter. Been falling asleep or daydreaming that way since I was in high school. I suppose that's why I let my feelings come out so clearly in what I wrote. Same was true when I wrote you that poem about my childhood. The dam inside me was ready to break. Anyway, this is the line from the song."

He held her close to him and spoke softly, as if he was saying a prayer, *"What the head makes cloudy...the heart makes very clear."*

She understood the meaning completely. Then Jake smiled and told her, "That line says it all, doesn't it? I know without any doubt that I made the right choice. Our love has held us together and fear hasn't weakened it. Just think, it would've been so much easier for us to settle for less...settle for the security of the status quo. You'd still be trapped and I still be shipwrecked. But that would've meant abandoning our destiny and I never would have let that happen."

Ellen touched his face, then she brought his lips to hers and kissed him passionately. When the kiss was over, Jake saw that Ellen smiled the pleasing smile of a heart filled with love, and he smiled back at her.

ACKNOWLEDGEMENTS

First and foremost to my wife Elleen, because without her love, enthusiastic support, and assistance I wouldn't have completed the novel. To my literary mentor, Diane Ochiltree, who labored countless hours reviewing my manuscript during the past two years and who guided me through a maze of uncertainty. To Jessica Paladini, who spent a summer editing the manuscript to insure that the story was tight and flowing. To my older brothers and sister, who encouraged me to "go for it." And finally, to the women who gave me their honest appraisal along the way. Thanks: Angela D., Mary M., Cathy G., Paula F., Lucille G., Sharon C., Jo E., and especially Suze Hewitt.